Chaos of War

Based on Historical Events

David Lee Corley

DEDICATION

Dedicated to all the men and women that fought and
sacrificed for their country.

Table of Contents

"Older men declare war. But it is the youth that must fight and die."

— Herbert Hoover

Operation Taylor Common

An Hoa Basin, Quang Nam Province, South Vietnam

At the end of 1968, U.S. military intelligence detected a large buildup of North Vietnamese Army regulars and Viet Cong guerillas in the central highlands of Vietnam. Battalion reconnaissance reported increased troop movements along the Ho Chi Minh trail network as well as construction of new supply caches and bunker complexes throughout the region.

In response, MACV headquarters approved a large sweep operation code-named Taylor Common to engage and destroy the amassing enemy forces. As part of Task Force Yankee, 3rd Battalion 3rd Marines, 3rd Marine Division was selected to spearhead the operation in the target area located near the Cambodian border.

The lead battalions of 3rd Marines were airlifted by helicopter into landing zones surrounding the suspected NVA base areas and staging points. Their mission was to conduct an aggressive search and destroy campaign, engaging the enemy on contact. Intelligence estimated up to three NVA divisions were concentrated in the area, making it potentially the largest encounter of the entire war.

The olive drab Huey descended into the remote LZ, rotors kicking up a maelstrom as Lt. Walsh jumped off into the stifling jungle heat, fatigues already soaked in sweat.

"Good Lord Almighty, hotter than a whorehouse on nickel night!" chuckled Cpl. Rogers, as the men around him laughed wearily.

"Stow it, Rogers. Save the comedy routine for another time," Walsh replied. "Intel reports an entire NVA division out here. Stay focused."

For hours the thirty-two men moved tactically, searching along Phase Line Blue. Taking the lead, Lance Cpl. Rhodes hacked through dense jungle with his machete.

Streams of sweat rolled down grime-streaked faces in the heavy air. The lead squad approached a clearing with sunlight streaming down. Walsh halted the platoon and sent Rhodes to scan for ambush.

Without warning, bursts of AK-47 cracked from bunkers. An RPG exploded a few feet in front of Rhodes, already on the ground returning fire.

"Contact front! RPGs incoming!" Walsh grabbed his radioman, Mills, as the platoon returned blistering fire. "Howe, Bressler - pin those bunkers! O'Malley, hit their flank!"

Closing in, an NVA .51 cal raked them from across the field. The Marines hunkered down in the long grass, knowing what a large caliber bullet if hit. "We're pinned down. Get me fast movers, danger close," said Walsh to Mills as bullets slapped mud around them.

Hit in the gut and bleeding heavily, Private Kaufman lay crumpled, trying to reach cover.

Within minutes Phantoms screamed in, unloading napalm and 500 pounders. The ground shuddered from jet wash until bombs detonated directly on target.

"Fry those gook bastards," Rogers whooped as explosions decimated the bunkers.

"First Platoon, push forward!" Walsh led them through smoke toward the tree line. But emerging from the jungle, an entire NVA battalion charged forward.

Relentless assaults slammed Charlie Company from three sides. Angry bugles and whistles sounded over dizzying volleys of AK-47s and thudding M60s. RPGs arced overhead, their blasts churning up mud geysers. Grenades sent shrapnel whizzing by.

"Keep firing! Cut 'em down!" Sgt. Howe screamed until AK fire ripped into his shoulder, spinning him down.

For over six nightmarish hours, Charlie Company battled for survival, ammo running dangerously low. The NVA kept coming, absorbing inhuman punishment. It deteriorated into close combat, rifle butts and fists.

"Fall back! Dig in and hold this line!" Walsh bellowed, firing his .45 until empty. He watched helplessly as Pvt. Gonzalez was swarmed and hacked to pieces by two VC. Out of ammunition, Walsh couldn't reach him and was forced to leave him in the clearing.

By dusk the NVA attack finally broke, leaving the clearing littered with mangled bodies. Charlie Company had held, but barely. Caked in filth, the survivors of Welsh's platoon staggered into jungle carrying the moaning wounded. Walsh ordered Gonzalez's body retrieved.

Trudging through black vegetation, Walsh led them to a ravine to regroup. They formed a tight perimeter. Rainclouds darkened the sky as Cpl. Crawford patched up injuries. The smell of mud and bodily fluids saturated the hollow.

"Can't stay still long. NVA will pick up our trail soon," Walsh told his men. "Get some sleep if you can."

Just before sun up, he pushed his men onward despite their wounds.

Late afternoon a monsoon struck just as 1st Squad entered a gully. AKs suddenly cracked from spider holes. "Ambush! Return fire!" Walsh shot back blindly into the sheets of rain. "Bressler, light 'em up with the pig!" Bressler fired his M60 burning through a belt. An ad hoc fire team flanked the NVA. They broke, fading into jungle once again.

Reaching Charlie company, Cpt. Hill stood unsurprised by the pitiful sight. "Got four NVA companies incoming. You leave any tripwires back there?"

"Ain't had time or the men to do shit," said Walsh clenching his jaw as his men dug foxholes silently.

"Yeah, well, ready or not they're coming. Once your boys finish digging in, you best redistribute your ammo and make sure everyone gets something to eat."

"Will do, Skipper," said Walsh gripping his M16 as he stared into endless rain, awaiting the next deadly round.

The relentless monsoon rain beat down on the ragged firebase, turning the already swampy earth into a muddy quagmire. Lieutenant Walsh stood grim-faced at the edge of the perimeter, watching as the last tattered survivors of Alpha Company came stumbling into the makeshift encampment. Many were wounded, bandaged with filthy strips of uniform, their faces gaunt with shell shock and defeat.

With the remnants of Alpha joining the few dozen able-bodied Marines of Charlie and Bravo Companies dug in here, they were up to about eighty-five men now, Walsh estimated. Hardly a force to take on what was coming their way.

Captain Hill approached, hollering over the rain to be heard. His trademark cigar was soggy but still clenched tightly between his teeth. "Battalion just radioed that regimental intel confirms an entire NVA regiment is converging on this position."

Walsh felt his gut tighten, but kept his composure. "What about those reinforcements and air support you requested, sir?"

"They assured me it's already scrambling, but we're pretty deep in the shit here. It's gonna be hours before they can get birds or ammo to us. We're the tip of the spear - and it's up to us to hold the line until the CAV can break through."

Walsh scanned the dark tree line uneasily. Out there, thousands of NVA troops were likely getting into position, preparing for an overwhelming frontal assault. Hill was right – if command said reinforcements were coming, then their duty was clear.

"We'll hold this line or die trying, sir," Walsh replied sharply.

Hill let out a chuckle, despite everything. "Oorah, Marine. Now get your boys ready, because Charlie's coming to dinner real soon. And he's real hungry."

The sun was rapidly fading when Walsh gathered the able-bodied men of his depleted platoon together in a sheltered hollow. Most were just teenagers, their youthful features darkened with fatigue, fear, and mud beneath oversized helmets. Some shivered uncontrollably, whether from cold rain or frayed nerves, Walsh couldn't tell. He addressed them with resolute authority. "Listen up, Marines. I won't lie to you - the situation is fucking messy. We got an entire NVA regiment surrounding us, just waiting for nightfall to come probing our lines in human wave attacks."

Some of the younger privates glanced around in evident terror at the news, but most continued looking directly at Walsh, waiting for his leadership despite their dread.

"Now I know you boys are exhausted and probably wishing you were anywhere but here right now. I'd be worried if you weren't," Walsh continued. "But the fact is, we're here. And there's nowhere to go but through what's coming at us."

He paced before them, making eye contact with each Marine. "We all know Charlie likes to throw his men at us like cannon fodder until our ammo runs dry. But we're gonna show those communist sons of bitches what true warriors can do when their backs are against the wall!"

Yorham, a grizzled sergeant, spoke up. "Damned right, skipper! We'll stack their bodies so high the NVA'll be climbing their own dead to get at us!"

A few weary smiles creased the mud-streaked faces. Walsh gave Yorham an affirming nod.

"Here's the situation, Marines. We've got zero chance of breaking through their encirclement - but Brigade says our reinforcement column is battling its way here, ETA 0700 hours. We just have to hold until sunrise. I know that seems far away right now, but take it one hour, one minute at a time. Focus on your sector of fire and do your job. Your buddies will be doing theirs. We protect each other. Remember your training and remember that every sorry SOB you kill is one less he can throw at our brothers coming up behind us."

He drew his KA-BAR knife and held it before them. "Fix bayonets, Marines. They want a bloodbath, we'll give em' a slaughterhouse!"

"Oorah!" the Marines bellowed back at him in unison. Their eyes hardened with resolution and Walsh knew he had them. He had given them purpose, and they would make these NVA fanatics pay twenty-fold in blood for every inch of soil. They would defend this infernal muddy patch of earth until their last breath.

As darkness fell over the jungle, the Marines took up positions in their flooded, muddied foxholes and bunkers along the eastern perimeter - the direction intelligence anticipated the main assault would come from. A light rain continued to fall, as one by one they performed their pre-battle rituals - saying silent prayers, pulling family photos from inside their helmets, sharing sips of whiskey from a flask to take the edge off.

Young PFC Grigsby sat staring at a picture of his high school sweetheart, tears mingling with rain on his cheeks until Walsh gentle squeezed his shoulder. "Stay strong for her, Marine. You'll make it through this hell and see her again - focus on that."

Grigsby wiped his eyes and managed a nod, sliding the photo back under his poncho. Walsh knew some of these boys would never see home again after tonight, but he needed them sharp and steady.

A ghostly bugle call echoed across the dark valley from the tree line several hundred yards opposite them. Walsh tensed. "Stand to! Here they come!" He slid down into the firing position, flipping his rifle to full auto. All along the line, the Marines aimed weapons over the flooded parapets, waiting for the assault to begin.

As if on que, long wavering lines of NVA troops emerged from the jungle, marching in double-time across the corpse-strewn clearing toward the American positions. Some were just boys, absently fingering the triggers of their AK-47s as if in a trance.

"Steady..." Walsh cautioned as itchy trigger fingers longed to unleash death into the apparitions. "On my command..."

He watched the human wave continue its remorseless advance. The enemy officers held their whistles ready to signal the headlong charge. Two hundred yards now and closing fast. His Marines were getting jittery, fingers tremoring near their triggers. "Wait for it..." Walsh said evenly. One hundred yards. "Wait..."

The first shrill whistle cut the night air and the communists broke into a dead run toward the Marine's perimeter.

"Fire!" Walsh bellowed.

The night erupted into a blinding chaos of tracer rounds, muzzle flashes and screams as the Marines emptied their magazines into the headlong human waves. Walsh added his M16 to the torrent of fire pouring from the line. Dozens of charging attackers were cutdown before they managed to get even halfway across the open killing field.

Unlike ambushes in the jungle, there was no escape from the Marines' scything fire with the NVA caught exposed in the clearing. Within minutes, piles of crumpled bodies and torn extremities lay heaped before the American lines. Dying young NVA soldiers cried plaintively for their mothers as tracer rounds ricocheted wildly into the darkness.

"Reloading!" Walsh ejected the empty magazine from his smoking rifle and slapped a fresh one home. "Hold the line!" Along the perimeter the Marines did the same, their weapons burning through ammo at a frantic rate. Spent brass casings clinked against each other in the mud surrounding their boots.

Before the last terrified NVA survivor could crawl back into the ghostly tree line, more demonic whistles pierced the night. Another wave was already emerging from the jungle to stampede directly over their shredded comrades. Walsh almost pitied these fanatics.

"Here they come again! Same targets, fire at will!"

The Marines resumed their blistering volleys, refusing to be overrun by the frenzied human tide. M60 machine guns chattered nonstop, filling the air with tracer rounds and full metal jacket shells. Mortar teams dropped rounds directly into the seething mobs. Recoilless rifle fire obliterated dozens at a time in eruptions of greasy flame but did nothing to slow the headlong momentum of the attack.

Wave after relentless wave came on, immune to their horrific casualties. Some made it shockingly close to the Marine lines before being mowed down. Walsh was everywhere along the line, directing fire, rallying his men. "Pour it into em! Stay sharp on ammo and watch your flanks!"

He knew from experience the NVA wanted nothing more than to overrun a section of the perimeter and gain a deadly foothold in their trenches. But his Marines held firm, ceaselessly slaughtering the endless suicidal attacks. Hot shell casings and links piled up beside them. Steam rose from the mud.

By 0300 hours, the frenzied communist assaults finally began to slow. Though individually fearless, the decimated NVA regiment could no longer sustain their all-out offensive momentum. Their fanatical courage was not enough to overwhelm the tight perimeter of skilled marksmen.

As the din of battle subsided, Walsh slumped back into the mud of his command hollow, completely drained. He gazed over the sight before them. The clearing was no longer visible, blanketed by mounds of NVA dead and carpeted with discarded weapons. Wounded enemy soldiers cried and moaned forlornly amid the piles of corpses.

"Get the 81's on 'em," Walsh ordered. Satisfying thuds announced volleys of white phosphorous rounds lobbed directly into the enemy wounded to silence their misery. There would be few prisoners.

Morning was still hours away, but the worst seemed behind them. Walsh allowed himself and his Marines a moment's respite. "Out-fucking-standing job, Marines," he told his exhausted men as they gulped tepid water from their canteens and wolfed down C-rations.

"I ever tell you boys my old grandpappy was with the 26th North Carolina? Held the flank at Gettysburg even when the rest retreated. Crowded in a trench, ammo gone, plugging Yanks with their bayonets as they came. You made 'em proud tonight, lads."

The Marines managed tired smiles. Longstreet's words came back to Walsh from that far-off age of cannon and valor: "We must win this battle or die trying."

Walsh gazed out at the sea of enemy bodies before him. It has cost them dearly, but the Marines had won this battle. A brief moment of victory and pride as
the war went on.

Nixon and Kissinger

January 2, 1969 - Nixon's Home - San Clemente, California, USA

Nixon ushered Kissinger through the grand arched doorway into the living room of his Spanish-style villa overlooking the Pacific in San Clemente. Floor-to-ceiling windows provided panoramic ocean views and bright California sunlight streamed in. "Thank you for coming, Dr. Kissinger," said Nixon, as Pat politely took his coat. "I value your perspective and expertise enormously. Please have a seat."

As Pat went to fetch refreshments, the two men sat across from each other on plush white sofas. Nixon studied the professor and foreign policy veteran closely. "As you know, I've asked you here to discuss Vietnam," Nixon began. "I'd like an honest briefing on where things stand and your thoughts on the best path forward."

Kissinger nodded gravely. "Of course, Mr. President-elect. The situation is deeply complex, as I'm sure you're aware. The war has been mismanaged by the Johnson administration at great cost, both in lives and America's global standing. Bold yet prudent action will be required."

"Perhaps you could outline specifically where things stand with the war effort currently as you see them," Nixon requested.

"Certainly. Currently we have over 500,000 U.S. troops deployed in Vietnam, along with hundreds of thousands of ARVN soldiers. However, the Viet Cong continue waging effective guerrilla warfare across the region. In recent years, North Vietnam has also sent its formal army, the NVA, to infiltrate Laos and South Vietnam. The NVA had primarily focused their efforts on securing the Ho Chi Minh trail and border regions, providing logistical support and pathways for infiltrating the South. With the exception of a few northern provinces along the border, the NVA enabled and supplied the Viet Cong guerrillas to bear the brunt of directly engaging U.S. and ARVN troops."

Pat brought in coffee and finger sandwiches. Nixon and Kissinger stopped their conversation while she was in the room and engaged in pleasantries.

When Pat left, Kissinger continued, "In the wake of the Tet Offensive and the two follow on General Offensives in 1968, the Viet Cong ranks were left severely depleted. Recognizing this vulnerability, North Vietnamese troops began maneuvering deeper into South Vietnam to take over frontline fighting while the VC regrouped. This influx of highly trained NVA battalions engaging in direct combat has presented an escalated threat to U.S. forces. They have proven remarkably resilient despite mounting casualties of their own."

Nixon nodded along, absorbing the implications of Kissinger's analysis. "I see, so the North has adapted and stepped up their formal army's role."

Kissinger continued, "Exactly, Mr. President-Elect. The Tet Offensive exposed grave weaknesses in our strategy despite heavy losses for the communists. Their will remains firm. Meanwhile our troop morale is declining, draft-dodging is rising, and protests engulf America's streets."

Nixon listened intently, frequently interjecting thoughtful questions which Kissinger addressed in detail, clearly impressed by Nixon's engagement. After an hour of candid back-and-forth, Nixon leaned back pensively. "In your view, what factors should most shape our approach moving forward?"

Kissinger paused to gather his thoughts. "In my assessment, our chief considerations should be: extricating ourselves from this quagmire with our dignity intact, preventing Communist hegemony in Southeast Asia, and restoring America's strained global prestige and influence."

Nixon nodded along studiously as Kissinger elaborated on each factor. "I'd also like your thoughts on China and the Soviet Union's roles in this situation. How does Vietnam fit into the bigger geopolitical picture?" said Nixon.

"A crucial question, Mr. President-elect," Kissinger replied eagerly. "China and the USSR are both engaged in their own complex power struggle within the Communist bloc. Historically, Moscow provided arms and aid to support North Vietnam against Western-backed South since the 1950s. They vie for wider

Communist bloc influence against China. When America expanded involvement in the 60s, Moscow ramped up missiles and funding to bog us down, draining resources from Europe."

Kissinger went on, "Beijing also armed Hanoi to undermine Soviet control of the Communist movement. Despite tensions, both continue bolstering North Vietnam to erode U.S. power. However, growing rifts in Sino-Soviet relations present opportunities America can leverage through nuanced diplomacy."

"Let's dive deeper on China and the Soviets - elaborate on the power shifts you mentioned within the Communist sphere," said Nixon.

"Of course," replied Kissinger. "Tensions have been escalating between Beijing and Moscow vying for leadership of the Communist world. Under Mao, China resents the Soviets dominating the movement. There are territorial disputes along their shared border. Moscow also cut technological aid when China's nuclear program advanced."

Kissinger expounded, "Strategically, the U.S. could drive a wedge between them. For example, by opening China trade, Moscow would fear losing sole influence over Beijing. Likewise, from Beijing's view, America counterbalances Soviet military power in Asia. This presents openings to play their rivalry to Washington's benefit."

He mused on potential repercussions, before concluding, "The larger point is this - through nuanced diplomacy, we could prevent monolithic Communist bloc opposition on Vietnam. If either Moscow or Beijing sees potential gains from cooperation with the U.S., we gain leverage over Hanoi to push toward resolution. Their solidarity weakens."

He elaborated for several more minutes on power shifts within the Communist sphere before returning to Vietnam. "In essence, skillful engagement with either Moscow or Beijing could reshape the playing field advantageously for the U.S. A renewed détente with the Soviets, or even a historic opening toward China, could isolate North Vietnam and expedite peace."

Throughout, Nixon listened captivated as Kissinger demonstrated a nuanced mastery of each facet of the multi-dimensional conflict. His keen intellect and strategic perspective left Nixon deeply impressed. Clearly, Kissinger grasped the complexities and stakes in a way few others could. Nixon was determined to utilize this brilliant mind in his administration. "Walk me through the military situation on the ground - don't hold back on the realities we face," said Nixon.

"Of course. To be frank, the Viet Cong's guerrilla tactics have unsettled our conventional forces," Kissinger explained. "They blend into villages and employ traps, ambushes, and lightning strikes before vanishing. This has neutralized advantages in firepower and technology."

He elaborated, "Morale is collapsing among our troops facing this invisible enemy and ambiguous mission. Drug usage is rampant - marijuana, heroin, psychedelics that erode discipline. With morale shattered, instances of fragging officers or refusing orders have increased sharply."

Kissinger pressed on, "Desertions and combat refusals are also rising as disillusionment spreads. The human toll keeps climbing with over 30,000 Americans already killed and many more gravely wounded - both physical and psychological trauma. Meanwhile the financial costs are ballooning toward $30 billion annually at the current force level."

Pausing to gather his thoughts, Kissinger continued, "Domestically, the scale of social upheaval and opposition to the war should not be underestimated. Campus protests now number in the tens of thousands. They are joined in the streets by a cross-section of mainstream America - clergy, physicians, even your 'silent majority.' Respected journalists and politicians voice criticism. Influential figures like Senators Fulbright and McGovern are leading calls to curtail the president's authority over war policy. Next year could see efforts in Congress to prohibit further troop deployments without legislative approval."

Kissinger adjusted his glasses. "But the diplomatic challenges may be most intractable. Our credibility worldwide has faltered in the quagmire of Vietnam. Allies question our judgment and reliability. The South Vietnamese government remains hobbled by incompetence and corruption, unable to stand on its own."

He sighed before concluding, "Most critically, Hanoi refuses any negotiations without unconditional U.S. withdrawal. They doubt our will to stay the course. We have few direct diplomatic channels to alter that calculus. In short, the situation could hardly be more complex on all fronts."

Nixon leaned back, absorbing Kissinger's sobering assessment. "You've outlined the harsh realities we face. A formidable situation. In your strategic view, what approach serves our interests best moving forward?"

Kissinger pondered the question seriously before responding. "In my assessment, our priorities should be: first, finding an honorable way to extricate ourselves from Vietnam without abandoning the South to conquest. Second, containing the spread of Communism through Southeast Asia by securing the frontiers of pro-Western nations. And third, reestablishing America's global leadership and prestige."

He elaborated, "A negotiated solution is the only viable path, but we must use judicious force and diplomacy to shape the circumstances toward an acceptable settlement. 'Peace with honor' must be the goal."

Nixon stroked his chin. "And you believe you could map out such a strategy? Apply the right combination of carrots and sticks to bring Hanoi to the table?"

"Yes, given the intricacies involved, and knowing the psychology of the men in the Politburo," Kissinger replied with conviction. "It will require both firmness and creativity, along with intricate timing. But I believe a successful end can be forged, if we avoid rigid thinking."

Nixon nodded, deep in thought. This was the visionary strategist he needed at his side to radically transform American foreign policy. Theirs would be a historic partnership.

A Sanctimonious Hack

Saigon, South Vietnam

Saigon glittered like a jewel box. Strings of red lanterns wove between buildings, mirrored in the dark Saigon River. Palm trees rustled in the breeze carrying scents of pho and incense. High above, the Continental Hotel's rooftop lounge floated over the restless city. Granite railings hemmed the edge, holding back the view - tin roofs sweeping to the horizon, dotted with plumes of cookfire smoke that rose and faded into humid darkness. Americans and foreign businessmen in loose guayaberas drank alongside stunning Vietnamese women in elegant ao dai. Chopper blades echoed in the distance mixed with an occasional gunshot. That was Saigon, unpredictable, treacherous, and beautiful.

Peter Arnett, the legendary AP war correspondent, nursed a gin and tonic at the bar with a good view of the entrance. He was waiting like a spider for a fly.

Halfway through his third drink and two bowls of peanuts, Arnett watched as Lucien Conein appeared in the doorway, flanked by two Corsican mobsters, his bodyguards. A master of dirty tricks with questionable scruples, the ex-CIA and MACV operative became a legend in his own right after he orchestrated the coup that overthrew South Vietnamese President Diem. His white suit pressed, his fedora immaculate.

The host immediately sat Conein and his Corsicans at a reserved table at the back of the lounge. It gave Conein a clear view of everyone and everything. He hated surprises. The waiter brought Conein's usual drink – a bourdon on the rocks along with the rest of the bottle and a small bucket of ice so he didn't need to wait between drinks. It was not Conein's first stop or his first drink of the night. His face was red with blotches and his eye lids heavy, a sure sign that he was well-oiled.

Arnett studied Conein for several minutes as he finished his drink, wondering if the rumors he had heard about him was true. Conein was known for being unpleasant when he drank and sometimes violent. With the ice clinking against the glass, Arnett took his last swallow of courage, paid his bill, and stood up.

Moving through the crowd, he approached Conein's table. The pair of Corsicans rose from their seats and formed an imposing human wall preventing Arnett from getting closer to the table. Conein looked through the narrow space between his bodyguards and said, "You're Arnett, right?"

"I am. Do you have a few moments for some questions, Mr. Conein?" said Arnett.

"Call me Lou and pull up a chair. You like bourbon?"

The Corsican wall parted.

"If it's the same to you, I prefer gin and tonic," said Arnett as he sat.

"It's not the same to me, but you can have whatever you want when you drink with me."

"I appreciate it."

"Aussie?"

"Kiwi."

Conein nodded with understanding, then waved over the waiter and ordered Arnett a drink. "So, is this gonna be a nice conversation or an inquisition?"

"More the later."

"All right. At least you're honest. That's more than I can say of most reporters. Ask away."

"My sources tell me that you are buying stolen American weapons and equipment on the black market."

"Your sources?"

"They're reliable."

"I'm sure. But they got it wrong. I am doing no such thing."

"You're lying."

Conein was a taken aback by Arnett's directness and said, "That was rude."

"Rumors are that you like straightforward conversations."

"I do. The rumors got it right for once. But I don't like being called a liar. It just rubs me the wrong way."

"Understandable. Look, I already have enough creditable sources to publish my story, but I believe the accused should have their say. Tell me I'm wrong and I will consider not publishing it."

"Now, who's lying?"

"The piece I am missing is who's buying the

weapons and equipment from you?"

"Maybe I'm a collector."

"I doubt it. I was thinking the Khmer Rouge, Pathet Lao, or even the Viet Cong… less shipping costs with the VC."

Conein swirled the ice in his glass taking a moment to push down his anger. "You've got some balls, Arnett. An accusation like that could get a man killed."

"Which man?"

Suddenly, Conein grabbed Arnett's shirt, veins bulging. With surprising strength, he hoisted Arnett up and over the rooftop's edge. Arnett dangled in the air, the streets of Saigon waiting four stories below. Potentially not lethal, but definitely a leg breaker.

The lounge's bouncer moved toward Conein. The Corsicans stepped in his way towering over him. Out muscled, the bouncer turned around. Arnett was on his own.

Arnett kept his eyes locked on Conein's. "Go on then. Show them who you really are."

Conein looked around and saw all eyes in the lounge focused on him and Arnett. Witnesses. Conein leaned in close, voice low but carrying. "You have no idea the forces you're meddling with. There are secrets buried here that could topple governments."

Arnett held firm. "My duty is to the public, not corrupt governments."

With a snarl, Conein pulled him back and slammed him down in his chair. Not a word was spoken by any of the patrons or staff.

"Deny it or my story runs as is. The people deserve the truth," said Arnett straightening his shirt.

"You sanctimonious hack," Conein sneered. "Who are you to decide what truth needs telling?"

"I'm Peter Arnett. Maybe you're heard of me... Lou."

Conein's jaw clenched. "Write your puny story and see where it gets you," he spat. Then he turned and strode away, guards clearing a path through the silent crowd.

The waiter brought over Arnett's gin and tonic setting it in front of him. Arnett finished it in three gulps. He had made a powerful enemy that night, but he had learned from experience... the angrier a person became at a question, the more likely he was onto something.

The thick humid air enveloped Saigon as Arnett perched on his motorcycle extinguishing the last of a cigarette and tossing it on the pile of butts beside his foot. He was staking out Conein's villa, the high stone walls capped with barbed wire and broken glass. The dark pre-dawn street was still, only a lone dog pawing through trash in the alley.

After another five cigarette butts added to the pile, the fortress gates cracked open. Conein emerged with his two Corsican bodyguards, their shoes crunching loudly in the silence. Arnett sunk lower as they piled into a waiting sedan. The engine roared to life and they pulled away into the waking city.

Staying at a distance, Arnett tailed them through the chaotic streets coming alive with vendors. The sedan wound its way to a small cramped cafe tucked deep in a narrow alley.

Arnett killed the motorcycle engine and slipped inside, the air thick with smoke and sizzling oil. He took a corner table near Conein, who was seated with an Asian man known for trafficking intelligence. Their conversation was too hushed to make out over the clatter of dishes.

Noticing an air vent on the wall nearby, Arnett made an excuse to the waiter and headed downstairs. In the dim basement he felt along the rough stone wall until he found the connecting vent. Crouching down, he could just make out the muffled conversation.

"There's a shipment coming by barge to Can Tho's floating market," said the trafficker. "Four, five days from now I'd guess. The seller is French, very picky."

"I want first chance to buy from him," came Conein's clipped reply. "Before any auction."

"That's up to him," said the trafficker. "Like I told you, he's known to be very particular."

Arnett committed the details to memory then slipped back upstairs just as the men were leaving. This story was getting bigger by the hour. He had to convince Quigley to let him pursue it.

Arnett sped directly to the AP bureau office, nearly skidding off the road in his haste. He found Quigley scowling behind a mountain of paperwork.

"There's a major arms shipment heading for Can Tho," Arnett said breathlessly. "I need to follow this lead down there."

Quigley rubbed his temples, sighing. "Peter, that region is extremely dangerous right now. And you know the risks of getting on the wrong side of a CIA operative."

"Ex-CIA operative and I'm aware of the risks," Arnett pressed, "but this is a solid lead. My source has never been wrong before."

Quigley's frown deepened with doubt. "Are you certain your source can be fully trusted? This smells like it could be a setup."

Arnett hesitated. "I'll admit that possibility has crossed my mind. But my reporter's instinct says this information is genuine."

Quigley leaned back heavily. "Instinct can cloud judgment, especially with stakes this high. Is this story truly worth risking your life over?"

Arnett's jaw tightened with stubborn resolve. "It's worth it if it exposes truth and corruption. I have a duty to chase this, regardless of the risks."

Quigley dragged a hand down his weathered face. He clearly wanted to forbid this reckless pursuit. But he knew Arnett would likely just go rogue and do it anyway.

"Peter, so help me, if you get yourself killed down there..." Quigley trailed off with a pained expression. He met Arnett's eye. "Get the story if you must. But at the first sign of real trouble, promise me you'll get out of there immediately."

"I promise," Arnett said solemnly.

Quigley waved him off, looking entirely unconvinced of his safety.

Arnett raced home only long enough to throw essentials in a bag and leave some piastres for his housekeeper. Then he rushed to grab the last overnight bus heading south into the winding backroads of the Mekong Delta.

The bus was cramped and stale, rattling loudly over the rough rural roads. Darkness descended quickly outside. Occasionally they passed a remote village, faint voices and cooking fires flickering in the blackness.

Arnett dozed fitfully, starting awake whenever they hit a particularly jarring pothole. Predawn light was just breaking through the misty rice fields when the bus finally groaned to a stop in Can Tho.

Stepping off into the swirling humidity, Arnett made his way on foot through the awakening streets to a small hotel on the waterway. The ancient ceiling fan did little to cut through the already oppressive heat. After a poor attempt at sleep, Arnett set out to explore the sprawling floating market as it stirred to life — hundreds of sampans tied to each other lined the shores and congregated in detached lumps in the middle of the river. Some shoppers arrived in boats while other walked along the shoreline browsing at the selection of goods and the food being cooked in giant woks or roasted over hot coals. The smell was a sharp mix of chilis, fresh herbs, and fish sauce.

The next few days Arnett wandered the chaotic market from open to close, blending into the hordes of locals. He kept an eye out for Conein or the French arms dealer, but neither had appeared yet. Occasionally he picked up whispers of an arms shipment coming, but no specifics.

Each night he returned to his mildewed hotel room grasping at rumors but with nothing solid. He knew Conein would arrive at some point, but the waiting wore on his nerves.

Finally on the third morning, his vigil paid off. A black sedan cruised into the market area. Arnett's pulse quickened - it was Conein.

He trailed carefully as two Corsican guards emerged from the car. They opened the back door for Conein, who stepped out adjusting a crisp suit jacket and fedora. His eyes were hidden behind dark glasses.

Arnett shadowed their path through the bustling market to an old warehouse built on pilings over the waterway. He watched from nearby as Conein, flanked by the Corsicans, knocked at a side door which was opened by a powerfully built Vietnamese man. A quick introduction and the guard told them to wait while he closed the door and went inside to confer with someone. When the door opened again, Conein and his bodyguards were ushered through the doorway.

As they disappeared inside, Arnett crept up to the side of the warehouse and found a broken slate in the structure's weathered wooden exterior. Pressing his ear to the gap, he could just make out the muffled conversation within. They spoke in French. Arnett's understanding of French was mediocre at best. He listened to the cadence of the conversation and pieced together the words he understood deriving the gist of what was being said.

Inside, the burly guard led Conein and his Corsicans to a cluttered office with windowed walls where Marcel Dubois sat smoking a cigar and sipping Absinthe. His eyes narrowing when he saw Conein. Conein was shocked to see that the seller was Dubois, an old comrade in arms from WWII.

"Well I'll be damned... Lou," Dubois said sardonically. "I'd heard you turned up in Vietnam but never expected our paths to cross."

Conein shifted uneasily. "Dubois. When I heard you had been captured by the Nazis and assumed the worst. I thought you were dead."

"Almost. The SS that interrogated me were not kind, I assure you."

"Believe me, I regret having left you that day."

Dubois's eyes flashed. "Regret changes nothing. You saved yourself at the cost of your honor." He sipped the green liquid. "But the past is done. What brings the infamous Lucien Conein all the way to Can

Tho?"

Conein shifted uncomfortably before adopting a businesslike tone." Let's speak plainly Dubois. I know you have a large weapons cache arriving tonight. I'm interested in acquiring it."

Dubois fixed him with a cold stare. "You seem misinformed. That merchandise is already promised elsewhere."

Frustration flashed across Conein's face. "At least tell me the name of the buyer," Conein insisted. "I have a right to know."

"You have no rights here, Lou. But I will tell you anyway. In fact, I think you know him… Pham Vinh An."

"Yeah, I know him. He's a Viet Cong collaborator. For fuck's sake, Dubois, if you sell to him the weapons will go directly to the rebels."

"That is not my concern. He offered a fair price and I accepted. The deal is done. Unlike some, I am a man of my word."

Conein slammed his fist down angrily and said, "I can't let that happen."

"It's not up to you, Lou."

"Are you sure about that, Dubois?" said Conein as his Corsicans stepped forward pulling out their hidden weapons.

"Quite sure, Lou," said Dubois as six heavily-armed Vietnamese henchmen stepped from the shadows around the warehouse.

"It seems you have overplayed your hand, mon ami," Dubois said softly. "I believe our reunion has come to end. Leave now or face the consequences."

"You're making a serious mistake," said Conein as he motioned his Corsicans to back down.

"My first mistake was putting my trust in you, Lou."

Conein and the Corsicans backed out of the warehouse while keeping their eyes locked on Dubois and his henchmen.

As Conein and his bodyguards withdrew from the warehouse into the twisting alleyways of Can Tho, Arnett followed at a distance.

Conein was boiling over with anger. He was not a man that accepted defeat well. After returning to the square where his sedan was parked, Conein found the closest bar next to the river and went inside along with the Corsicans.

Not wanting to be seen, Arnett moved around the bar discreetly looking through the windows until he spotted Conein sitting on the back patio overlooking the river. Arnett entered the restaurant next to the bar and asked for a seat by a window overlooking the bar's patio. Through the window, Arnett watched Conein drinking glass after glass of bourbon with ice. Arnette wondered how Conein was still conscious or even alive after consuming so much alcohol. Deep in thought, Conein watched the boats heading upriver, his mind conjuring Machiavellian plots. Occasionally, he would turn to one of the Corsicans and say something. Arnett was too far away to hear what was being said, but he dared not moving closer.

As the sun set, Conein continued to watch the passing boats on the river. Arnett ordered a bowl of Pho and continued watching Conein.

In the distance a barge going upriver approached. Conein studied it, especially the armed guards riding with the cargo. It was Dubois's barge, he was sure of it.

Tossing several bills on the table to pay his tab,

Conein rose and caught a glimpse of Arnett, looking down at his supper in the restaurant next door. Conein whispered something to his Corsicans, then moved off to find the toilet.

When Arnett looked up and saw Conein and the Corsicans gone from the patio, he panicked. He paid his bill and left without finishing his meal.

As he exited the restaurant, he surveyed the square. Conein and his Corsicans were nowhere in sight, but Conein's sedan was still there. He moved into an alley leading back to the area where the warehouse was located. Dim lanterns revealed the path. As he rounded a corner, a fist hit him in the nose with a loud crack. He fell onto his back, hitting his head on the concrete walkway. He was dazed. Backlit by an overhanging lantern, two silhouettes appeared over him. One reached down and pulled him up to his feet. He saw their faces clearly now – the Corsicans.

Three hard punches to the face in rapid succession and Arnett fell unconscious, the only thing holding him up was a Corsican's massive hand. The Corsicans discussed Arnett's fate. One wanted to gut him right then and there in the alley. The other feared pissing off Conein if they killed the journalist without Conein's express permission. Arnett groaned, coming around. The Corsican dropped him like a bag of potatoes. He hit the ground hard. Kicks to the gut and fists to the face flew. Arnett, normally sturdy, was in no shape to fight back. He took the beating until they finally stopped and vanished, leaving him in the alley.

Upriver, Conein watched as the barge docked next to the warehouse. The night sky darkened as the clouds overhead boiled. A monsoon was coming.

Dubois appeared. He used a walking cane to support himself, his leg permanently damaged from his old wounds. Dubois greeted the captain of the barge and handed him an envelope filled with US dollars. He nodded, satisfied. Dubois's henchmen took over for the barge guards as they moved off to get paid from the envelope of money. Once they had their pay, they disappeared into the alleyways looking for the closest whorehouse and opium parlor.

As Dubois went below to inspect his weapon cache, Conein studied the henchmen's positions on and around the barge. He made a crude drawing on a notebook he carried in his pocket along with a pencil. Satisfied that he had the layout of the guards, he walked back toward the square where his car was parked.

A flea-bitten dog licking the blood on his face, Arnett groaned as he woke in the alley. His whole body screaming in pain, he managed to stagger back to his hotel room. He cleaned and dressed his many wounds as best he could. He looked in the mirror. His face was swollen, both his eyes encircled by rings of purple, his nose broken in two places, his lip and eyebrow cut and in need of stitches. He considered finding a doctor. That would have been the smart move. Instead, he picked up his camera bag, slung it over his bruised shoulder, wincing, then left the hotel in search of Conein and Dubois.

When Conein arrived in the square, the Corsicans were waiting by the sedan. He asked them about Arnett and they explained what they had done and that they had left him alive... barely. Conein was pleased. He showed his bodyguards the drawing of the henchmen's positions and explained their next move which was to kill the henchmen and steal the barge holding the weapons.

He opened the sedan's trunk revealing a stack of weapons and three armored vests. Each Corsican put on an armored vest, then chose their weapons – M60s with extra belts of ammunition that they wore bandelier-style. Slipping on his own armored vest, Conein pulled out a newly developed China Lake pump-action grenade launcher. He loaded three in the tube and one in the chamber. He grabbed a bandolier filled with a mix of high-explosive, phosphorus, and smoke grenades. He slung the China Lake and the bandolier over his shoulders, then pulled out a Heckler & Koch MP5 submachine gun with extra magazines in an over-the-shoulder satchel. Just three, but experienced killers. And well-armed.

Conein turned to his men, voice low. "We hit hard and fast. Knives first, then weapons free. Priority is securing the weapons cache."

The Corsicans nodded.

Conein and his Corsicans moved stealthily along the shore of Can Tho's crowded floating market. The air hung thick with the scents of fish and engine oil. Makeshift vessels jammed the waterway - sampans, skiffs, rickety houseboats doubling as shops. Merchants hawked bright-colored fruits, vegetables, flopping fish, and live chickens in woven cages. Merchants loudly hawking their wares.

Arnett emerged from an alley. Finding his way back to Dubois warehouse beside the river, he spotted the six henchmen standing guard at the barge. He snapped photos from a hidden vantage - evidence for his story.

Dark clouds were gathered over the delta. The wind picked up and the first fat drops of rain began to fall pelting the surface of the river. Vendors pulled plastic tarps over the heads and merchandise.

Nearby, Conein and Corsicans stayed hidden as they observed the barge with its guards. On Conein's nod, the Corsicans drew their knives and faded into the shadows like wraths. Conein moved to create a diversion. He stepped onto a pilotless sampan, cut the fuel line, and snapped open his lighter. The blaze was hot and furious. Jumping back on shore, he shoved the boat towards a cluster of boats huddled together.

Seeing the approaching inferno, the wide-eyed vendors jumped into the muddy river, some unable to swim but preferring to drown than burn. The burning sampan crashed into the cluster and set several more boats ablaze. Far more than a distraction, the conflagration spread swiftly through the market.

Mesmerized by the fire and screams, Conein watched the mayhem he had created, thinking maybe he went a little overboard.

On shore, Arnett photographed the tragedy. Panning his camera, he spotted Conein on the shore and snapped the shutter. His dirty tricks a secret no more.

With all eyes on the river, the Corsicans moved up behind three of the henchmen individually. A swift slice of their knives and the grisly job was done. The odds were now even. They rejoined Conein and retrieved their heavy weapons. They watched as Dubois, holding a case, and the VC collaborator emerged for the hull of the barge to witness the chaos.

Seeing the weapons cache in danger, the VC collaborator pulled back the case holding the money from Dubois's hand. Dubois ordered his three remaining henchmen to keep the burning sampans away from the barge.

It was at that moment, Conein stepped out of the shadows with the China Lake in hand. He made sure Dubois saw him before firing three 40mm, phosphorus grenades in rapid succession into the warehouse. The white-hot explosions set the wooden building ablaze.

Dubois, seeing his livelihood being consumed by flames before his eyes, ordered his henchmen to return to fire on Conein and the Corsicans. Grabbing their submachines guns, they did so.

The Corsicans responded with their M60s. Tracer rounds crisscrossed the floating market. Conein fired his last grenade at the barge. He missed Dubois but hit the VC collaborator square in the chest with a high-explosive round. The stupefied buyer disappeared in a cloud of red.

"Problem solved," said Conein to himself.

Dubois looked over at the blood spot that was once the buyer and sneered as he flipped Conein off. Conein laughed and shouted, "I warned you."

Arnett kept snapping photos as fast as possible, reloading the camera several times with fresh film, tucking the exposed cartridges into his camera satchel.

With flames growing in every direction, the back of the barge caught fire.

Conein saw the fire and stopped smiling. The weapons were on the barge. He waved to get Dubois's attention, then shouted and pointed, "Your ass is on fire."

Dubois turned and saw the flames. He hobbled

across the deck grabbing a mop and bucket. He used a gaffing pole to lower the bucket into the river, filling it with water. He pulled it up and drenched the mop with river water, then attacked the flames with all the vigor he could muster. It wasn't enough. The flames spread down the greasy barge.

While taking photos as fast as possible, Arnett saw a woman drowning in the river as the storm raged. He set his camera down and jumped in to save her. Having watched Arnett jump in the river, a young boy sees the camera sitting unwatched and steals it along with the camera satchel full of film.

A kerosene lamp in the pilothouse of the barge fluttered in the wind, then tipped over smashing the glass. The kerosene leaked out and caught fire when it touched the white-hot wick still burning. The fiery liquid flowed across the deck and down through an open hatch into the cargo hold. Moments later, a crate of mortar rounds cooked off. The multiple explosions punched a large hole in the ship's side. The river flooded in.

The Corsicans finished off the last of the henchmen strafing him with bullets. "Secure the weapons," barked Conein.

The Corsicans jumped onto the barge and opened the hatchway to the hold. Below they saw the water rising, already covering most of the ammunition and weapon crates. They exchanged a look, neither wanted to tell Conein.

But Conein didn't need to be told as he watched the barge list to one side and said, "Oh, shit."

Unstable on a good day, Dubois lost his footing and

fell, sliding across the deck. The ropes securing the crates on the deck snapped tight. The fire grew as Dubois attempted to get up. The ropes caught fire and quickly broke freeing the crates. The heavy crates slid across the deck toward Dubois and crashed into both his legs, pinning him. He screamed in pain.

Conein watched from the shore. He had heard the scream of pain thirty years before, when Dubois was wounded from Nazis bullets. It all came back in a flash – Dubois pleading for help, the Nazis advancing, and Conein running away to save his own life over his friend's.

Staring at the rising flames, Conein knew this was his shot at redemption. But did he care? Dubois would not do the same... not for him. He watched at the bow of the ship dipped below the water line. It was sinking. Dubois would be dead soon and the screams would stop. Conein could go on with his life. Why risk it?

Conein's eyes shifted as he saw the Corsicans leaping off the barge into the water and swimming for shore. "Where the hell are you going?" Conein shouted.

One of the Corsicans stopped swimming, looked at Conein, shook his head, and gave him the slit throat sign signaling that it was hopeless. Conein was angry but couldn't blame the Corsicans. He knew he could only push them so far before they turned on him like starving hounds. They climbed up the muddy bank and collapsed trying to catch their breath.

"Fucking clown circus," said Conein to no one in particular.

He turned his attention back to Dubois still pinned against the heavy cases. The water level was rising faster as more of the barge sank below the water line.

"Don't do it, Lou," he said to himself. He didn't listen.

The barge slipped under the water taking Dubois with it. "See. There's nothing you can do. It's over," he lied.

"Goddammit!" he said as he pulled off his shoes and jacket, then dove into the river swimming toward the barge. He shouted, "Idiot!" before disappearing below the surface.

Beneath the surface he saw the barge sinking toward the muddy bottom. He couldn't see Dubois and wondered if he was even still alive. It would be easy to turn back. But he didn't.

Swimming further he saw Dubois on the stern still pinned as the barge sank deeper. Bubbles rose up as Dubois expended his last breath. Conein swam over to him. Dubois was already unconscious. Conein put his back against the crates and his feet on a deck cleat. He pushed with everything he had and nothing happened. He was out of air. He swam to the surface, took a big breath, and dove back down. He tried again with his back against the crates and his feet on the cleat. He pushed. This time the crates moved freeing Dubois who began slowly floating upward. Conein wasted no time, grabbing Dubois, and pulling him to the surface.

Conein pulled Dubois onto the muddy shore and breathed life back into his lungs. Conscious again, Dubois was surprised by Conein's actions and, to be honest, Conein was surprised too. Hearing a loud noise above the storm, Conein and Dubois looked over at the river as a huge bubble appeared on the river's surface, the last gasp of the barge released before hitting the muddy bottom of the river. The weapon cache was gone.

"That was very noble of you, Lou," said Dubois.

"I figured, I owed you one," said Conein.

"You are still a prick for setting my warehouse on fire but thank you."

"Don't mention it."

Dubois looked back at his warehouse. A fire crew had almost extinguished the flames. "I've got a bottle of Napoleon Brandy in my desk if it didn't burn up. Thirty years old, I think," said Dubois.

"Guess there's only one way to find out," said Conein rising to his feet, then helping Dubois up. They walked together toward the warehouse. "So, did you ever get married?" asked Dubois.

"I did," said Conein.

"Poor girl."

"Yep."

Arnette pulled the drowning woman to the shore upriver. She coughed up half the river but would survive. He walked back to where he left his camera and satchel. They were gone, along with his evidence backing his story. "This has not been a good day," he said to himself as he started back to his hotel.

Hammered & Honed

January 20, 1969 - Washington DC, USA

Richard Milhous Nixon placed his left hand on a Bible and solemnly swore to preserve, protect and defend the Constitution of the United States. With those words, he became the 37th President of the United States.

Nixon had secured a narrow victory over Democrat Hubert Humphrey in the 1968 election after a tumultuous year marked by bitter division and unrest. Now he stood on the steps of the U.S. Capitol speaking to a nation hungry for the restoration of stability and confidence in the presidency.

In his inaugural address, Nixon acknowledged the turmoil and uncertainty facing the country. "We find ourselves rich in goods but ragged in spirit; reaching with magnificent precision for the moon, but falling into raucous discord on earth," he lamented.

Yet the new president expressed faith that through shared sacrifice and determination, America could overcome its challenges. He called upon the "great silent majority" of lawful citizens to unite behind his leadership.

Most significantly, Nixon used his speech to signal a shift in strategy for the increasingly unpopular Vietnam War, which had so bitterly split the nation. "The greatest honor history can bestow is the title of peacemaker," Nixon declared to the 200,000 people gathered before him on the National Mall.

He rejected calls for immediate withdrawal, yet also vowed to actively pursue a just and lasting peace. Nixon spoke of scaling back America's involvement through a policy that would soon become known as Vietnamization. The South Vietnamese military would gradually take on greater responsibility for the war effort as U.S. troops withdrew.

This policy aimed to achieve "peace with honor," as Nixon famously put it. America would exit the conflict without the shame and demoralization of what critics called a direct defeat.

To North Vietnam's leaders, he addressed a pointed warning: "We cannot expect that you will negotiate in good faith until you are convinced that we will not be defeated." Nixon made it clear he was willing to continue fighting while also seeking avenues for peace.

For the American public, weary after years of bloody stalemate in Southeast Asia, the speech struck a note of cautious optimism. Perhaps this new president could steer the nation off its destructive course.

But having campaigned as the law-and-order candidate who represented the "silent majority," Nixon also ignited fear among anti-war activists that he would aggressively pursue military victory rather than compromise.

True to his word, Nixon expanded bombing campaigns in Vietnam while also opening secret peace talks in Paris through his National Security Advisor Henry Kissinger. He sought to pressure North Vietnam's leaders while building support among Americans for a face-saving exit.

This "Madman Theory," as some called it, presented Nixon as willing to take extreme action to defend South Vietnam. His unpredictable image complicated Hanoi's calculations.

Yet the divisions plaguing America could not be resolved through rhetoric alone. Despite Nixon's calls for unity, campus protests continued to roil across the nation. The country remained deeply split over the course of the war.

For the troops on the ground in Vietnam, the speech offered both hope and skepticism. Nixon's withdrawal strategy suggested an endpoint to the interminable deployments. But his willingness to continue fighting tempered premature optimism.

Some in the Pentagon and defense establishment bristled at the notion of turning over combat responsibilities to South Vietnamese forces before total victory was achieved. Others saw virtue in cutting America's losses.

In Saigon, South Vietnamese president Nguyen Van Thieu anxiously monitored Nixon's speech for signals about his nation's future and sovereignty. Thieu opposed unilateral withdrawal timetables, relying on continued U.S. backing.

And in Hanoi, North Vietnam's leadership took note of Nixon's muscular tone but saw opportunity in his openness to negotiations. They remained confident

America's will would break before their own.

Both at home and abroad, Richard Nixon's inauguration marked the beginning of a new unpredictable chapter in the long nightmare of Vietnam. The incoming president faced tremendous obstacles and conflicts as he sought to steer the ship of state away from its present disastrous course.

For the exhausted American public, it kindled a flicker of optimism that new leadership could bring order, peace and reconciliation after years of turmoil. But many challenges lay ahead on the road to ending the war Nixon inherited on that cold January morning.

Phoenix Training Camp – Central Highlands, South Vietnam

Thick humid air clung like wet gauze over the covert CIA base nestled deep in vine-choked jungle. Granier stood rigid, arms crossed, as Green Berets bellowed at raw Viet Cong prisoners doing punitive exercises in the bare dirt courtyard under the unrelenting midday sun. Rope burns on their wrists, eyes hollow yet still smoldering with impotent rage. Granier knew such fury, like mercy, exacted its own price when unleashed or restrained.

A dozen fuzzy-cheeked American and South Vietnamese boys awaited him now represented the best and brightest recruits culled through exhaustive screening for induction into the elite Phoenix Program. Some still chinless beneath cap visors, buzzcuts fresh and pristine. Their crisp fatigues and upright stances not yet worn down by the realities to come. Though elite selections, they were still unblooded youths. Granier's vital job was to cultivate the cunning, the killer instinct, and the mental armor needed to survive this shadow war. Or to bury what bodies could eventually be recovered when luck and time ran out. Most likely the latter.

"Ten Hut!" Granier's drill sergeant bellowed in his freshly ironed fatigues. The boys snapped to attention under the unblinking jungle sun, eyes forward, sweat dripping down youthful necks.

For the next grueling hour the sergeant ran them into the ground with punishing sets of exercises timed to the ticking of his wristwatch. Granier watched, looking for weakness. Jumping jacks. Flutter kicks. Iron Mikes - knees skyward while balancing on forearms. The boys drenched their uniforms in sweat, retched stinking fluid into the mud when muscles could take no more. Then peeled themselves up time and again when ordered to continue the brutal conditioning. All except one.

Dao Minh moved with wiry grace and precision, completing each demanding drill without evident strain or stumble. Twenty-five perfect chin-ups in smooth motion. Fifty scissor-kick sit-ups barely breaking a sweat. Seventy-five pushups with backpack loaded, breath steady as a metronome. A man with wolves in his blood beset by puppies. Granier made quiet note of this outstanding recruit. Raw material here to be hammered and honed.

By week's end, Dao had outclassed all other recruits in firearms assembly and tactical medical skill evaluations. As the jeepney rumbled into Saigon for their first R&R, the boys jostled and bantered loudly, impressing local girls suddenly dominating thoughts that had focused solely on survival just days prior. But Dao sat silent and apart, keenly scanning alleys and rooftops as they rolled through the teeming city, primed for threats.

One night in the humid mess hall reeking of boiled cabbage and twelve unwashed young men, Granier approached Dao eating alone by flickering candlelight casting shifting shadows over his smooth taut features. Nineteen - maybe twenty - yet possessing eyes that had already seen too much. Granier settled onto the rough bench across from him with the casual manner of a friendly uncle.

"Where you from, Dao?" he asked. Making conversation, tone mild.

"A village in the Central Highlands," Dao answered without looking up from his plate of gristly mystery meat and gelatinous gravy. Scraping every last morsel cleanly. Good discipline, no waste.

Granier nodded, waiting in silence. He could play the quiet game too when needed. Waiting until Dao was close to finishing his meal, Granier asked, "Who taught you to shoot?"

After swallowing the last bite, Dao spoke again to his empty plate. "My uncle. Hunting first. Then for the army. He fought for ARVN."

"He taught you well."

Dao nodded once, face revealing nothing. That would be the full extent of personal intel Granier could coax from him in this first informal attempt. But the grizzled instructor recognized the casually modulated danger coiled just beneath the surface of Dao's disciplined reserve. Hidden currents ran deep behind those opaque eyes.

The ensuing weeks brought intensified training designed to forge lethal instincts and eradicate any trace of hesitation. Ten-mile timed humps through

sucking mud while laden down by sixty-pound
rucksacks. Surviving days alone in harsh terrain
equipped only with random equipment and native
cunning to trap wild boar and elusive monkeys for
sustenance. While other recruits hacked desperately at
thick jungle vines forcing passage with bulky machetes,
Dao learned to slip through natural shadows
soundlessly with preternatural bush awareness.
Keeping mental track of every contour. Granier
decided the promising recruit was ready for live
reconnaissance.

Now hunkered low together in the damp skeletal
remains of a long-abandoned village with just rifles and
one shared canteen, seasoned instructor and prized
student held vigil under corroded tin roofing. They
took turns napping and watching through a spider-
webbed aperture onto the adjacent tree line as hard
rains swept by in gray sheets. Monsoon winds keened
through glassless windows like mournful souls. Dao
scanned the swaying wall of vegetation intently,
tracking phantom shapes only his sixth sense could
detect. Every sense primed for trouble. Poised for
controlled violence upon Granier's word.

Just as the sun sank behind the jagged mountains to
the west, backlighting the jungle canopy in flame, a
column of eighteen VC foot soldiers skirted the edge
of the village, jungle carbines slung low. Clearly moving
with purpose toward some hidden base beyond their
sight. Dao's eyes sparked with banked hunger at their
presence. Fingertip curling reflexively on his rifle's
smooth stock. Granier firmly gripped the recruit's wrist
and shook his head once in warning. Their duty was
only to observe and report from hiding, not engage
regular forces ten times their size. Dao's muscles

untensed marginally in compliance. His razor focus remained unwavering. He was a hunter that could be trained with patience.

For three rain-soaked days and nights they held their covert position, rotating brief catnaps to maintain alertness, reporting details of VC movements using coded double click radio bursts. Dao never wavered or lost discipline. Hardship only honed his edge. Then finally came the recruit's trial by fire.

Part of a six-man night patrol was halfway through a tight ravine carved by a muddy creek when all hell burst around them in flashing fire and thunder. Raking AK-47 volleys shredded leaves above their heads. Dao instantly fell prone into the rocky creek bed just as grenades detonated in geysers of dirt and shrapnel behind them. Red tracers from Soviet belt-fed machine guns crisscrossed the darkened jungle as the VC ambush enveloped them.

From a natural channel carved out by the water's flow, Dao snapped off four precise shots from his M-16 into the blackness. Four muffled cries confirmed his rounds had found their marks, neutralizing VC machine gunners trying to pin them down. Granier watching. The boy moved and reacted like he had been born to the task, without hesitation.

"Stay low! Cover the left approach. Fifty meters!" Granier shouted over the maelstrom of automatic rifle fire at the wide-eyed recruits hunkered frozen nearby. He bellied up beside Dao in the ravine overhung with tangled tree roots as hostile rounds cracked and popped through the darkness. A meticulously executed ambush, but the VC had made one miscalculation - the lethality of this untested recruit when cornered.

As the overcast monsoon sky unleashed pent up

rains in a hissing downpour, visibility dropped further and Granier weighed their limited options. Dao hugged the muddy bank unflinching, his rifle barrel instinctively tracking left and right for more threats even as AK-47 rounds split the rotten logs and eroding earth inches above his head in bursts of spray. Intermittent muzzle flashes marked VC shooters in the darkness, answered by Dao's disciplined return fire. Along with the fainter screams when his bullets inevitably found human flesh and shattered bone.

Dao alone became the front line keeping the enemy pinned down while Granier led the survivors on a flanking maneuver. The deluge masked their own sloshing approach through the creek. Moving by sound and touch more than sight. They managed to encircle and neutralize the VC crew served weapon bunker with hurling grenades and point-blank rifle shots accompanied by shrieks and curses in foreign tongues. The few VC still mobile withdrew in panicked retreat, leaving only their dead behind.

In the smoke-shrouded aftermath, Granier firmly clasped Dao's shoulder and just nodded, no need for words between professionals. Though just a boy still, Dao had coolly reacted with the instincts of a natural born killer. He had saved their vulnerable lives. And in doing so earned undying loyalty. Granier felt unease at the bestial instincts clearly being awakened in his prized protege. For some doors once opened can never again be fully closed.

In the drying blood-caked day that followed, Granier observed Dao gazing oblivious into crackling campfires long after the others had collapsed exhausted in their makeshift hammocks. The faraway thousand-yard stare in those brooding eyes was all too familiar. Memories of lives snatched away and spilled blood still fresh mingled with survivor's guilt. Granier knew intimately the psychic tolls this shadowy business exacted. The stains never fully washed clean.

Whatever black trauma and smothered demons truly drove him, Dao did not waver from fulfilling his duties with tireless perfection. So, in response Granier resolved to take the promising recruit fully under his wing. To patiently mold Dao through these critical months into the elite operative the Phoenix Program desperately required. To hone his formidable skills further, tighten his reflexes to a coiled spring, and compartmentalize any qualms in the lockbox of professional necessity.

For in this bright young man whose eyes had already glimpsed too much, Granier believed he had discovered a chance to increase his own value to his country. A worthy apprentice to receive the lessons which experience so painfully provided, so the next generation avoided needless loss. The gifted loner possessed raw courage and hunger. Granier would carefully shape his potential heir into a fearsomely effective, clear-thinking scalpel in the dead of night.

A day later, the helicopter's thumping rotors stirred the humid jungle air as it touched down at the secluded Phoenix Program outpost. A man in uniform without insignias jumped out of the doorway as somber-faced recruits hauled out two body bags containing their fallen comrades, the latest casualties in the shadowy war.

Granier observed the new arrival crouching away from the chopper's blades in scuffed jungle boots. He moved with crisp focus, scanning the camp with sharp eyes. The man approached and extended his hand in greeting. "Rene Granier. Alex Harmon." His grip was firm. "Blowtorch Bob ordered me to conduct an investigation on the ambush."

Granier bristled slightly at the implication of mistrust but understood the need to investigate any mission where recruits were killed. He simply nodded. "This way."

All eyes watched as Granier led Harmon to the bunker serving as their operations center. Within the windowless sandbag walls, an overhead kerosene lamp cast gloomy shadows. Both men took seats at the battered table.

"Do you have any questions before we begin?" said Harmon.

"No," said Granier.

"Okay. Let's get right to it," Harmon instructed, removing a tape recorder from a satchel and pressing record. "Recount the mission details from the beginning."

Harmon's nondescript appearance and direct manner revealed little about him. Granier studied this unknown investigator carefully as he recounted the ambush events.

Harmon asked probing questions, pushing for specifics on their route, arms, casualties. Granier answered precisely but without elaborating. At the end, he asked to separately interview each individual involved in the mission. Granier nodded agreement. He walked toward the entrance, then turned back and said, "It's a war. Shit happens."

"I am aware… and when it happens we investigate just to make sure it's not something else. I'm sure you understand," said Harmon.

Granier grunted and left.

Harmon interviewed each recruit, taping their conversation. Their weary voices echoed faintly through the door as Granier paced outside. He trusted these hand-picked men.

When at last Harmon called him back inside, Granier sat down expectantly. He was ready to conclude the fruitless inquiry. But Harmon's grave expression surprised him.

"I believe your unit has been compromised," the investigator stated.

"A mole?" Granier recoiled. "I selected these men myself. Their loyalties are unimpeachable."

"With respect, the enemy's ambush was perfectly positioned. They knew your plans down to the exact detail," Harmon countered. "Only one with inside knowledge could inflict such damage."

"An accusation like this can destroy a unit's morale."

"We don't need to tell them what we suspect."

"What you suspect. And they're not idiots. They are going to know something is up."

"Granted. But it can't be helped. We need to be thorough."

Granier wrestled down his defensive instinct. He knew Harmon had sound reasoning for his suspicion. But the thought of a traitor among his tight-knit recruits cut deep.

Sensing Granier's turmoil, Harmon adopted a more reasoning tone. "I know this isn't easy. They're your men. But whoever the mole is, we need to uncover them before more lives are lost. I need your cooperation despite any personal loyalties."

Granier hesitated, then gave a solemn nod. The

gravity of this threat to the Program outweighed all else. If there was a traitor, together they would shed light on his betrayal, no matter the outcome.

Operation Dewey Canyon

February 22nd, 1969 – A Shau Valley, South Vietnam

The A Shau Valley was a rugged expanse of treacherous topography that stretched along the border of Laos and South Vietnam. Framed by jagged mountain ranges, its floor was a labyrinth of dense jungles, tangled underbrush, and narrow waterways. The valley served as a vital section of the Ho Chi Minh Trail as the communist supplies and weapons entered South Vietnam, making it a hive of North Vietnamese activity.

Bisected by a meandering river, the landscape appeared from the sky like a gnarled, green hand, its many fingers reaching into hidden recesses and dark corridors of foliage. Its remoteness made it an ideal conduit for clandestine operations. The thick canopies of trees concealed troop movements, supply caches, and fortified positions. It was a place where the earth itself seemed in collusion with those who knew its hidden trails and shadowed alcoves. Clouds often hung low, creating a natural veil that obscured aerial reconnaissance and complicated navigation. Rainfall was frequent, turning the soil into a muddy quagmire that swallowed boots and vehicles alike.

The valley's strategic importance was not lost on the American commanders. To control the A Shau was to hold a chokepoint on the Ho Chi Minh Trail, to sever a critical artery in the enemy's vascular system of war. For these reasons, the valley became the target for Operation Dewey Canyon.

Led by General Raymond Davis, U.S. Marines sought to achieve multiple objectives. First, they aimed to capture key hills and fire support bases, like Cunningham, Razor, and Russell. These high points would provide artillery and observational advantages, aiding in the interdiction of enemy movement and supply routes. Second, they planned to locate and destroy North Vietnamese weapons caches and fortified positions, further impairing the enemy's capability for sustained operations. Lastly, Dewey Canyon intended to create a scenario too perilous for the North Vietnamese to ignore, pulling enemy troops away from other key fronts, forcing them to engage and reveal their positions.

The strategy for the Communist forces was built around the defense of the Ho Chi Minh Trail. Recognizing its significance to the larger war effort, they undertook the mission to protect, counter, and disrupt American advancements. The North Vietnamese Army aimed to inflict enough casualties to make any American gains costly and, therefore, temporary. They hoped to prolong the conflict, undermining American resolve through the attrition of resources and morale.

Before dawn's first light bled over the craggy mountains, Gunnery Sergeant Buck Kovacs stood alone smoking a cigarette down by the airfield, the rest of his platoon still racked out back at the firebase. Twenty-three and already feeling like an old man. He scanned the dark rustling treeline uneasily. Another day, another deep-country mission no sane man would volunteer for. Just his goddamned luck.

The monsoon gusts had finally died down overnight, leaving a heavy mist hanging over the tarmac that muffled sound and reduced visibility to twenty yards. Hunched figures in fatigues materialized out of the fog, assault packs over their shoulders. 1st Recon Battalion was being airlifted out ahead of the main force to scout and mark landing zones along the North Vietnamese Army supply line near the Laotian border. A hundred miles west as the crow flew - much further on the map of boot leather.

In Buck's experience, thinking too much about what Charlie may or may not do was a quick path to disaster. And he aimed to arrive breathing, collect his paycheck, and keep all limbs attached. At least until his tour ended, knock on wood.

The first chopper roared out of the soupy darkness, skids nearly brushing the tarmac. It kicked up tornadoes of wet gravel that sandblasted skin and gear alike. Kovacs flicked his spent butt away and shouldered his pack. Just another glorious day in paradise.

They crammed into the shuddering metal birds, Lucky Strikes and soggy porn mags tucked in their sleeves. Nobody said much. New guys nervously checked weapons again and again. The old salts leaned back and closed their eyes, conserving strength. Sleep never came easy out in the bush. Kovacs dry swallowed a couple black beauties, then passed the bottle around. The rush would keep him sharp till nightfall. Couldn't slip even once in country this unforgiving.

As the choppers banked northwest, orange sunrise glowed on the horizon. Towering ridgelines materialized from the mist, tree cover impossibly thick between sharp ravines and cliffs. Lush canopy stretched unbroken as far as the eye could see. Finding one tiny clearing in this wilderness would be like picking out a single blade of grass back home in Kansas. Needle, meet haystack. If NVA really were scarce up here, perhaps they'd luck out. Regardless, Kovacs knew today was gonna be a long hard bastard. And tomorrow would be worse.

The lead chopper descended into a clearing no larger than a tennis court carved out of the jungle. Wheels crushing ferns as it touched down. The squad deployed in textbook fashion. Lieutenant Bressman and two point men plunged into the wall of vegetation first while Kovacs and the BAR gunner provided cover. The triple canopy swallowed them immediately. No sound or sight of enemy fire, just pulsing jungle all around. Maybe Allied intel had been right for once.

They slashed a path through the brush just wide enough for single file. Sweat bees swarmed faces slick with perspiration. The point men worked machetes nonstop to keep the trail open. Steam from their sopping fatigues attracted mosquitoes that sounded like lawnmowers in their ears. Every sense strained for tripwires or snipers among screeching birds and chittering monkeys. This terrain was ideal for ambushes. Eyes peeled all day, they encountered nothing but more vegetation.

At 20:00 hours, Bressman gave the hand signal to pull off the trail and form a tight perimeter. They'd covered only eight klicks by Kovacs's reckoning. Felt like thirty. Exhausted men gulped canteens dry then broke out C-rats as darkness descended fast beneath the dense canopy. Eating meatloaf and stale crackers beat the hell out of freeze-dried veggies, their bodies starving for protein. Smoke drifted up from two small fires as they burned leeches off soaked boots and socks.

The LT tapped Kovacs for first watch. He leaned against a fallen log, scanning the night jungle and listening close. No wildlife sounds now. That was the giveaway. Something had them spooked. After endless silent minutes standing sentry, Kovacs squeezed off two quick shots from his grease gun into the brush. Frantic rustling followed.

The gunshots roused Bressman the platoon as VC scouts slipped away into the night having marked their position. Everyone understood wordlessly. Sleep would be scarce until they reached higher and more open ground.

Dawn came slowly between the ancient tree trunks. Mist turned clothing clammy. They chomped cold beans from the can and saddled up. Lizards skittered across the narrow trail and faded into the ferns like ghosts. Strange primeval calls echoed through the dripping forest.

By midday the terrain began sloping upward noticeably. They climbed east into rougher country, all ravines and tangled brush. Jagged limestone peered through the thinning forest canopy. The day inched by without contact. Once they surprised a family of pongos at a stream, the silverbacked primates scattering shrieking into the treetops.

Near nightfall the point element hand signaled a halt after glimpsing stone structures through the trees. The Lost City, ancient ruins blanketed in moss. Tree roots had cracked walls timelessly apart in slow motion. They hunkered down to wait for dusk, senses on high alert. The ghostly relic meant they must be nearing the Laotian frontier by now. Just two klicks south, supposedly. Close enough for Kovacs.

Darkness fell, heavy with anticipation. A light rain pattered on broad leaves. They chewed more stale rations, sipped the last tepid canteen drops. Clean socks were only a distant memory. Bressman decided to advance a few klicks deeper under cover of darkness before digging in for the night. Kovacs shook his head but didn't object. Officers never listened anyhow.

They moved silently between crumbling temples and monuments, weapons tight to shoulders. A mile on, Bressman froze and raised a clenched fist. Voices ahead. Kovacs listened closely, skin prickling. Was that...singing?

The LT signaled them forward into a thicket overlooking a torch-lit camp. Forty or fifty NVA regulars sat chatting and cleaning gear around cooking fires. Some laughing together over rice wine. Then distant whistles pierced the night, answered by rallying cries from the camp. The singing cut off abruptly as men scrambled to form ranks. Bootsteps faded into the rainforest. Charlie was on the move en masse just as Allied Command predicted.

The Americans were preparing to slip away quietly when an explosion of gunfire ripped through the night.

"Ambush!" someone screamed over the melee of AK-47s and pinging ricochets. Kovacs glimpsed muzzle flashes high on the ridge where the NVA company had been headed. Clever bastards had doubled back and circled their small patrol under cover of darkness.

"Get down!" Bressman yelled. "Set up fire sectors!" Kovacs belly crawled behind a collapsed statue, blinking blood from his eyes that wasn't his own. Through crumbling stone feet he glimpsed NVA fighters maneuvering with precision across the muddy slope, trying to encircle them. He let off bursts from his grease gun that sent two sprawling. No time to check whether they stayed down.

Grenades whistled in, blasting trees to splinters that needled exposed skin. From behind the carved head of a forgotten king, Kovacs sighted down his weapon and slowly squeezed. An NVA officer leading the charge staggered but kept advancing. Muzzle flashes revealed blood spreading down his uniform. Zipperheads were like ants - kill one and two more turned up angry.

Over the screams and clatter Kovacs heard Bressman calling in air support on the radio in clipped jargon. Napalm would purge this whole accursed jungle - friendly and foe alike. Their only slim hope. Kovacs dropped two more charging shapes, then his grease gun just clicked empty. As he fumbled to reload, an NVA fighter emerged from the darkness and swung an AK barrel at his head. Kovacs rolled right, drawing his trench knife in time to parry the next blow. They grappled chest to chest, boots grinding wet earth.

Kovacs drove his blade to the hilt into the man's ribs, twisting hard. Hot blood spurted over his fist and sliced arm. As the NVA soldier sagged, deadweight Kovacs heaved the limp body into the next wave charging upslope. Screams and crashing bodies bought a few critical seconds to slam home a fresh magazine.

He flipped prone again just as brilliant orange flame blossomed on the ridge like sunrise. Fighters on both sides halted, mesmerized by the blossoming inferno. The question in the minds of friend and foe – where was the napalm headed? The napalm strike swept downward, swallowing the foliage and crude shelters. Men lost cohesion and fled screaming before the angry dragon's breath. Kovacs shielded his face from the searing heat, coughing in the acrid smoke.

After untold eons the fiery gusts died down to glowing coals. Smoldering branches cracked and popped as they cooled. The ambush had broken with a dozen NVA bodies left blackened and contorted around the camp. But Kovacs spied three still forms in charred fatigues - his guys now - gone forever.

He staggered over to Bressman slumped against a blasted tree, somehow still breathing. Blood bubbled on his lips as he tried to speak. Kovacs told him to save his strength. They'd be evac'ing soon as cleanup crews arrived. Both knew that was a lie meant as comfort. Some fates couldn't be cheated.

Kovacs stayed kneeling with Bressman until the end, not leaving him to die alone. He owed the LT that much. He mumbled a few remembered lines of half-forgotten prayer then simply sat numb as dawn broke red over the smoldering ruins. The Corps had nine fresh graves to dig. And he had carried this war's dirty secrets in his marrow for another day. That was victory of a sort.

The chopper barely cleared the trees when it arrived two hours later. Kovacs turned his face away from the downdraft's stinging force. He drifted somewhere outside his battered frame as they lifted up and over the endless green. Watched the jungle canopy blur into welcome nothingness.

He'd survived to fight again another hellish day. But no more delusions of glory remained. There was only duty now...and death. Always death.

Kovacs stood stiffly at parade rest, staring past the sweat-ringed armpit of the bellowing sergeant inches from his face. Morning formation on the firebase after Dewey Canyon felt perversely mundane. The brazen sergeant ranted about lapsed standards and discipline within the company. A familiar tune Kovacs drowned out while sifting through memories as gritty as sand.

The dull thud of mortar rounds leaving tubes provided background rhythm to the haranguing. Giant black bags were being loaded onto a cargo helicopter - the most tangible remnants of those left behind. Kovacs's thousand-yard stare remained locked over the sergeant's shoulder. Just one in a long line of gravediggers in this place, sowing a fresh crop of corpses.

The nebulous jungle op was already dissolving into the roiling mists of Kovacs's mind. He compulsively checked his compass and map several times an hour now, craving certainty. But the coordinates of their scattered souls could never be fixed again.

Chow was powdered eggs recongealed and black coffee. Kovacs chain-smoked through the mess, forcing down what flavors he could coax from the rations. Never knew which meal might be your last. Better to face death on a full stomach.

By mid-day, 1st Recon Platoon was choppered back out toward the Cambodian frontier. Different jungle, same dire odds if things went sideways. Kovacs leaned forward this time, peering down through the open door as tree canopies blurred by beneath them. He cradled his grease gun tight across his lap like a loyal hound that had saved his hide repeatedly against the odds.

Without orders, Kovacs's eyes scanned ahead seeking signs of trouble in the restless vegetation. Instincts honed to razor sharpness by weeks surviving the bush. He knew better than to depend on rank or protocol now. When ambushed, only quick action decided who walked away.

They touched down in a sun-speckled glade, rotorwash flattening the chest-high ferns. Kovacs inhaled deeply, savoring the rich scents. Brief seconds of stillness the brain captured for unknown purpose. The engines wound down to urgent shouts and bootsteps receding into emerald shadows. Back into the maw.

They advanced abreast hacking through snarled vines beneath the triple canopy, alert for any human traces. The point man nearly stumbled over the first body lying face down on the game trail. An NVA scout with throat slit, shriveled by days in the sun. Sabotage or warning? Impossible to know. They pressed on; weapons ready.

An hour later the lead squad nearly walked into a tripwire trap strung across the path. Kovacs traced the near invisible strands to clusters of nailed-together 105mm shells hidden under palm fronds. Crude but lethally effective. He swallowed bile at the near miss, imagining being vaporized into pink mist. Fortune's hand touched them gently today. Thus far.

Approaching dusk, Kovacs shot a monkey

scrabbling through the high branches that would become their dinner. Iron-rich meat for tired blood. They dug in on a low rise surrounded by elephant grass, camouflaging the position. A three-man watch was set. Then they listened to the rhythm of the jungle as the velvet night descended.

Kovacs chewed tough charred meat, mind wandering to home. To familiar creaking halls and Kathy's long strawberry hair curled on the faded floral pillowcases. Her sleep-warm body tucked against his own, so impossibly far away now. He swigged tepid canteen water to force down the sudden lump in his throat. Wrong time for Kathy. Stay focused or die.

Second watch came and went uneventfully, the smoking ember at watch's end passed from hand to hand. Kovacs rolled himself tighter in his dew-soaked sleeping bag, yearning for even an hour of true rest. His subconscious knew better, denying the relief. Too vulnerable. So, he lay breathing shallow beneath the black canopy, surrounded by men but utterly alone.

The ghosts woke him instead. Shrill whistles split the darkness. Cries in foreign tongues as booted feet trampled through the elephant grass. Kovacs was up firing on instinct before his eyes fully opened, the grease gun bucking hot in his hands. Muzzle flashes revealed NVA regulars meters away storming through the grass toward their position. The jungle erupted again in chaos.

Grenades burst blinding and deafening, shredding knotty roots and pulping flesh. Kovacs scrambled low, changing position every few seconds. Muzzle flare guided his full-auto barrage cutting down charging shapes that toppled and twisted before dissolving into the dark. No time to confirm kills - only survive the swarm.

"Air support, now!" came the screams over the din. "POSREP follows!" The radioman read off coordinates between bursts of rifle fire from the perimeter.

The Forward Air Controller circling high above guided the jets to blanket the area of heaviest resistance. Within minutes the first jet wailed overhead, dropping lower. Tracers arced up from the tree line, chasing the roaring phantom. Then brilliant orange flame blossomed between the trees as napalm splashed and spread.

The aircraft kept up their deadly vigil, circling back again and again to strike targets marked by radio from the ground team. After endless sweat-soaked minutes, the chaos subsided to sporadic shouting from the dark then silence. Smoking shapes lay like ghastly logs around the perimeter.

Kovacs did a quick ammo and casualty check. Miraculously their whole unit had survived this time, with only minor wounds. He moved among the men still wired, clasping shoulders and seeing the animal fear receding from wide pupils. Nobody slept again that night, instead watching the orange coals slowly expire into darkness.

At first light Kovacs gazed at the blackened, contorted bodies while smoke still curled from seared clothing. Exactly like Dewey Canyon days prior. The same stinking primal fury unleashed again beneath these ancient boughs. He turned away numb and moved to gather gear. There was nothing left to learn here.

Operation Dewey Canyon became a concentrated

microcosm of the larger strategies employed by both sides throughout the war. While the operation did yield short-term tactical gains for the United States, the Ho Chi Minh Trail remained largely intact, and the North Vietnamese Army proved adaptably robust. The questions raised by the operation continue to linger: What is the cost of temporary disruption, and how do short-term victories and losses measure against the backdrop of a protracted, complex war? Dewey Canyon remains an enduring example of the challenges faced in Vietnam—a blend of military strategy and harsh terrain, immediate objectives and long-term goals, each side trying to dictate the terms of a conflict that defied easy solutions.

Hidden Truths

White House, Washington DC, USA

The Oval Office late in the evening. Five men sat under the pale yellow lamps, their faces etched with shadows. Cigar smoke drifting up to the ceiling. President Nixon sat behind the big desk, Chief of Staff General Wheeler, Secretary of Defense Laird, Air Force Chief of Staff General Ryan, and Chief of Naval Operations Admiral Moorer across from him in the sofas and chairs. No one spoke at first.

Finally, Nixon broke the silence. He asked for potential targets. Plain and direct. General Wheeler opened a folder, slid out a map. He pointed to the red circles marking targets along the border in Cambodia. Wheeler spoke about stopping the flow. Of supplies. Of troops. The North Vietnamese were using bases in Cambodia to stage attacks across the border into South Vietnam. Laos too. Hitting villages. Convoy ambushes on the highways. Rockets and mortars raining down on

Saigon. They had to cut the communists safe havens.

Secretary Laird nodded along. Admiral Moorer just watched, his face unreadable.

Nixon asked about consequences. Public perception. Widening the war. General Wheeler pushed back. He called it an operation. Limited strikes. A way to force negotiations. Secretary Laird echoed the point. He emphasized the word peace. Still Nixon hesitated. His fingers drummed the leather desktop. His eyes were distant in thought.

Admiral Moorer finally spoke. His voice was low. Calm. He said casualties from the cross-border attacks were already high. The bombing must continue. Momentum must not be lost. It was the only way forward. The room stilled. All eyes went to Nixon behind the desk. His face clouded with an inner struggle. He took a breath. Looked from man to man. Then Nixon gave a slight nod. It was decided.

They began to file out in silence. Nixon stopped Wheeler at the door. He spoke in a near whisper. This stays between us. No paper trail. And for God's sake, no media. Total secrecy. Wheeler nodded. They exchanged a long look. An understanding.

"No ground forces though, correct?" Nixon asked.

The general hesitated. "We'll reassess as needed," Wheeler replied carefully.

Nixon's jaw tightened, but he gave a curt nod. Then Wheeler too was gone. The room was empty and still. Nixon sat alone again under the pale lamps, their light refracting in his glasses. His fingers returned to their quiet drumming on the leather desktop. The only sound in the room.

March 18, 1969 - Cambodian Border

The Vietnam War had bogged down by 1969. North Vietnamese troops and Viet Cong guerillas continued to infiltrate South Vietnam from bases and sanctuaries in neighboring Cambodia and Laos. The Cambodian government, under Prince Norodom Sihanouk, tried to maintain neutrality but did little to stop communist forces from operating along their border.

President Nixon hoped to put pressure on North Vietnam and the Viet Cong by cutting off their supply lines and disrupting their staging areas in Cambodia. This became known as Operation Menu - a massive, sustained aerial bombing campaign conducted in absolute secrecy.

For security reasons, only a small circle knew of Operation Menu - Nixon, National Security Advisor Kissinger, Secretary of Defense Laird, the Joint Chiefs, and a few senior commanders. Nixon did not inform Congress or the American public, as he knew the operation violated Cambodia's neutrality and feared a backlash for widening the war.

B-52 Stratofortress bombers flying at 30,000 feet dropped hundreds of thousands of tons of ordnance on suspected communist bases and supply corridors along the Vietnam-Cambodia border. Targets included troop concentrations, storage depots, truck parks, and jungle hideouts. The bombing was relentless, with multiple strikes per day, and continuous for fourteen months.

The Buffs as they were called flew from bases in Thailand and Guam. They were supported by F-4 Phantom fighter-bombers providing tactical reconnaissance. A wide array of munitions was used, including high-explosive bombs, cluster bomb units, daisy cutters, and napalm.

The White House hoped Operation Menu would destroy enemy sanctuaries, buy time for Vietnamization, force concessions at the Paris peace talks, and serve as a display of Nixon's willingness to take tough measures for peace. But the true effects remained uncertain.

The bombings of Cambodia during the Vietnam War remain deeply controversial from an ethical standpoint. While the strategic motives behind Operation Menu are subject to debate, the human costs inevitably raise moral questions.

The sustained B-52 bombardment of rural Cambodia inflicted terrible suffering on civilians living beneath the bombs. Villages decimated. Lives and livelihoods destroyed. The elderly, women and children killed indiscriminately. Those surviving left impoverished and traumatized.

While the full civilian toll may never be known, estimates range from 50,000 to over 150,000 deaths, with some suggesting the higher figure is more credible. The bombing deeply destabilized Cambodian society, damaging infrastructure, displacing hundreds of thousands, and helping to radicalize segments of the population.

The secrecy around Operation Menu meant little effort was made to avoid civilian casualties or calculate the extensive damage. What was certain is that for Cambodians, the devastation proved incalculable, leaving scars felt for generations.

Caravelle Hotel - Saigon, South Vietnam

The lobby lounge at the Caravelle Hotel was filled to

capacity as usual, a refuge awash in amber light and old stories. Journalists adrift from home shores find their anchor there. Karen Dickson, an AP photojournalist, sat in the middle of a booth squished between two large journalists oblivious to girth and their flying elbows. Beers and half-empty cocktails tipped over with regularity. Smoke from too many cigarettes hung like a thunderhead above the table. "Central Park in autumn, man. Miss it?" said the first journalist.

"Miss it? I'm still trying to forget the stench of the subway in August," said the second journalist.

"You've never had a Texas barbecue summer, have you?" said a third journalist.

"Barbecue? We're talking sweat and grime, and you bring up food?" said the first journalist.

Laughter. The war kept at bay. Glasses clink. "So, have you guys heard the rumors?" said Karen, changing the subject to more serious matters.

Mirth evaporates. Faces grow long.

"They say it's the knockout punch. Seal the Ho Chi Minh Trail, and boom, they'll have to talk peace," said the second journalist.

"Ah, peace through escalated war. That's a fresh take," said the third journalist.

"Not for the people under the bombs," said Karen.

"Look, if this gets our guys out, why not?" said the second journalist.

"So, you'd trade their civilians for our soldiers?" said Karen.

"Damned right I would. It's their war, not ours."

"They're Cambodians. They're not part of the war."

"Not yet. 'Sides, they're letting the NVA and VC set up camp on their side of the border."

"It's easy to talk ethics from a barstool in Saigon.

Our guys are in the mud and the blood," said the first journalist.

"And dropping those bombs puts blood on our hands, too," said the third journalist.

"Blood's already there. Can't wash it off," said Karen.

"A quick end. That's what they're saying. Isn't that worth something?" said second journalist.

"Quick for whom? A kid who loses his whole family, what's quick about his suffering?" said Karen.

"No one said it's ideal. It's ugly. But war is ugly," said the second journalist. "But could this be the thing, the last ugly thing that needs doing?"

"Or the ugly that begets more ugly. Where does it end?" said Karen.

"War ends when one side crumbles. Isn't it time?" said the second journalist.

They look at each other. Each face a mirror of doubt, of questioning. Glasses empty. Refills delayed. In that room, they share a pause, heavy with the things they can't articulate. The night stretches out, the war grinds on. No answers. Just questions that hang in the smoky air.

AP Bureau - Saigon, South Vietnam

His office door was ajar, Quigley sat behind a desk stacked with dispatches, photographs, the detritus of war stories. Karen stepped in. Her camera, a silent witness slung over her shoulder. "Quigley, we need to talk," she said.

"Do we? I'm swamped," said Quigley keeping his eyes focused on his work.

"Cambodia. I need to go."

Quigley looks up. Eyes meet. "Cambodia is off-limits. You know that."

"I know it's dangerous. But listen—"

"No, you listen. It's not just dangerous. It's unauthorized, off the record, political dynamite."

"So is Arnett's work. He goes places he isn't supposed to. Gets the stories no one else can."

Quigley leaned back, running fingers through greying hair. "Arnett is Arnett. A star gets certain liberties."

"Ah, liberties. So that's what we're calling it now."

"Don't twist my words. It's not about gender."

"If it quacks like a duck…"

"That's not fair and you know it."

"Then what is it about? If we're here to bear witness, let's bear witness where it matters most."

"It's not that simple."

"It never is. We make the choice, don't we? To go or not to go."

Quigley leaned forward, folded his hands on the cluttered desk. "And if you go and something happens? What then?"

"That's a risk I'm willing to take."

"It's not a risk I'm willing to permit."

Karen's eyes lock onto his, a tempest of unspoken thoughts swirling between them.

"This isn't about permission. It's about responsibility. If we don't document this, who will?"

"It's a responsibility I can't afford right now. Not with the stakes this high, not with the eyes of the world turning toward this conflict. The answer is no, Karen. It's final."

Karen nodded. No yielding in her stance, but acceptance of the wall before her. "Final is a word seldom true in times like these."

She leaves. Door closes behind her with a soft click. Quigley looks at the door, then at the piles of unending war on his desk. Sighs. Returns to his reading. Outside, Karen stood, thinking, camera in hand, but not shooting. Not yet.

Karen's Apartment – Saigon, South Vietnam

Karen's apartment felt like a monochrome world, walls dressed in framed black and white photos. Some captured the grim intensity of battlefields in Vietnam, faces contorted in a mosaic of fear and courage. Others showed Vietnamese children, barefoot, eyes gleaming with innocence and bewilderment. A different kind of warfare hung beside them: protests in American streets, faces full of defiance, signs screaming for peace. Her previous beat.

The room bore minimalism like a badge. No soft furnishings, just the stark contrast of her work, her visual chronicle. She looked at each frame as if trying to draw some resolve, as she wrestled with a decision that felt like a stone in her gut.

Rucksack sprawled open on the floor, she deliberated over its contents. Her fingers grazed rolls of film, each a potential chapter of truth. She had to make room. Reluctantly, she removed dry socks, spare underwear. She traded comfort for the weight of extra lenses.

Her pistol sat apart on a wooden table, cold and aloof. It was an illusion of safety, feeble against the kind of firepower she could encounter. She left it behind, convincing herself that being unarmed would underscore her intent—she was a gatherer of truths, not a soldier.

Money, American bills crisply folded, went into various hiding places—tucked into the lining of her worn jacket, inside a money belt that had seen better days, under the insole of her shoes, even in the inner rim of her hat. Enough stashes to recover from the inevitable robbery, enough to buy her way back to some semblance of safety, to the promise of a hot bath and temporary oblivion.

Her gaze wandered back to a frame capturing an anti-war protest back in Washington D.C. She wasn't Peter Arnett, she didn't have the luxury of indisposable presence. She was disobeying her boss, Quigley. Would she have a job when she returned? Would they even notice if she were gone? Her absence, just another hole in a narrative already riddled with them.

The rucksack felt heavier as she hoisted it onto her back, as if absorbing her trepidation. She grabbed her camera satchel, her constant companion, and approached the door. Her hand hesitated on the knob, a brief moment teetering on the edge of choices and their echoing consequences. She opened the door, took that irrevocable step into a night that swallowed her whole. Somewhere in that abyss lay Cambodia, hidden truths, and an uncertain destiny. Her footsteps grew faint, but inside her apartment, the wall of photos stood unchanged, silent keepers of the world she left behind.

On the street below, a taxi waited. Unwilling to let them out of her sight even for a moment, she placed her rucksack and camera satchel on the backseat next to her. She handed the driver a note with directions written in Vietnamese. He nodded and drove. No words necessary. The driver looked in the rearview mirror at the rucksack wondering about its contents.

Why did she keep it so close? Was it valuable? She was just a woman and could easily be overpowered. It was still dark. Seeing the driver's eyes wandering, Karen snapped her fingers as if angry. The drive scowled and turned his attention back to the road. Riding through the streets without traffic of Saigon, dawn broke, the night diluted by the dim light.

An hour later, the taxi rolled to a stop next to an old French airfield with battered asphalt hemmed by reluctant green. A pilot leaned against a battered Cessna, eyes weighed down by lines and years, ash of a cigarette dancing with the breeze. Karen stepped from the vehicle removing her rucksack and satchel before paying the driver the agreed upon price. No tip. He sped off, the rear door closing itself.

The pilot, a foreigner with an unknown accent, walked over to help Karen with her bags. She shook her head carrying everything herself despite the weight. They climbed into the aircraft. Doors shut.

The twin engines roared, metal bird lifting into a sky undecided between night and day. Flight low, skimming the quilt of green and brown beneath, avoiding both the eyes of men and the reach of bullets. They were entering VC territory.

Two hours later, the pilot pointed to an airfield in the jungle, a scar in Earth's hide. Grass runway hemmed in by walls of viridian. The landing was bumpy but uneventful. The Cessna braked to a stop, then turned around at the end of the runway. Karen paid the pilot. He nodded his thanks. She climbed out with her rucksack and satchel. No one in sight. The pilot took off. She was alone in the jungle. Not a good thing.

A few minutes of waiting and a jeep appeared.

Karen eyed the driver as he approached. Why was he late? A stop for a quick Vietnamese coffee, or something else? The driver, a Vietnamese, stopped and got out. Again, she shook her head when he reached for her bags. She placed them behind the passenger seat and climbed in. There was an inch of rusty water sloshing around on the floor. No top. "Money?" he said.

She pulled out the agreed upon amount, held it up, and said, "When we arrive."

He nodded his acceptance and drove to a crude road into the jungle. He was careful not to break an axle as he hit pothole after pothole. Karen hung on. It was going to be a long drive.

Four hours of being treated like a human milkshake, the driver motioned to the road up ahead and said, "ARVN."

It was a roadblock. Karen reached into her jacket and pulled out a wad of bills wrapped with a rubberband. She handed it to the driver. No words. No need. He understood. The jeep pulled to a stop as the soldiers approached. A quick conversation, an exchange of money, and the jeep was waved on. The soldiers eyed Karen as she passed. A savory cut of American meat. Karen had been in the jungle plenty of times, but she was always surrounded by her colleagues and American soldiers. The rules seemed different now that she was alone, lines were more willing to be crossed.

Another hour and the jeep came to a stop in a village. The road ended. Karen pulled out the driver's money and handed it to him along with a small tip. He nodded his thanks. Karen stepped out hoisting the rucksack and grabbing her satchel. It was getting late.

The jeep left.

Karen loathed being in the jungle at night. Using one American dollar, she made a deal with an old woman to stay the night in her hooch. The accommodations came with a meal of boiled meat and wild herbs. Karen didn't recognize the grayish meat, but ate it anyway. Gamey. She secured her gear in the hut, then laid down on a grass mat and fell asleep within a minute.

The next morning, she checked her map and compass after a breakfast of root porridge and smashed mango. She set out on a trail leading to Cambodia, still many miles away.

Dappled light on skin, the double canopy above. Hot and humid. She knew not to drink too much water or she would cramp up. She was alone, unafraid, in the moment. The stillness was broken by hushed voices in the distance. Familiar voices with an Americana twang. A US patrol. She folded into the undergrowth disappearing into the palette of shades.

She watched as the soldiers passed. A part of her wanted to call out. They meant safety. But she knew she was on a different path and remained silent as they disappeared down the trail dissolving into the jungle.

She was about to step back onto the trail, when an inkling warned her. She looked around studying the forest around her, then down at her boots – a tripwire. She had no idea what it was attached to, but she didn't need to know. It was death. That was enough. She moved her boot carefully away from the wire. She focused her boots and the foliage they were stepping on as she moved back onto the trail. She needed to be more careful. This was Charlie's jungle.

She continued her journey toward Cambodia. The

trail forked. She studied her map and compass to determine which path to take. The direction was not clear. A coin flip. She stepped onto the right path, walked ten paces. Bad feeling. She had learned to trust her intuition. She returned to the fork and took the left path.

The sky darkened as the sun descended below the mountain peaks. Night had arrived and she still wasn't in Cambodia. She hated the idea of sleeping in the jungle alone without a fire. She had slept in the jungle before, but always surrounded by a unit of Marines. Now, she was alone. She decided not to stop. She pulled out her flashlight and continued down the trail keeping the light's beam focused on the ground. The spiders and bugs near the border were enormous and many were poisonous. If she kept moving, they couldn't crawl into her sleeping bag. Moving meant safety. The mosquitos were another story. They seemed to fly in squadrons blocking the trail at times. Exposed skin bathed in mosquito repellant, she soldiered through.

Another mile down the trail, she heard voices in the distance. She stopped and studied her map. There was no village nearby. Another patrol? Too many voices for a patrol. There was laughter too. It was directly in front of her. She looked at the jungle abyss considering a detour around the voices. Walking at night in the bush? Not a good idea. Not without Marines to protect her. Going back seemed just as dangerous as going forward and it took her no closer to her goal – the truth. She turned off her flashlight and moved toward the voices, cautiously.

The moon ascended over the indigo sky, bathing the ARVN camp in a glow. The soldiers moved among tents, fuel barrels, crates, and trucks. A supply depot. Lanterns flickered as they passed, scattering dappled light that mingled with night shadows. On the camp's periphery, Karen felt like an intruder in a secret world.

With a brittle snap, a twig broke under her boot. Heads turned her way; handheld radios crackled with indistinct chatter. Her heart pounded in a rhythm of both fear and urgency. But no one approached her, no one stopped her.

After a few moments, she moved into the thick jungle undergrowth. The gravitational pull of the camp waned as she distanced herself, passing through the initial line of sentries, sinking deeper into the vegetation beyond. She fought her way through thickets of thorny brush, her pant legs snagging, her progress a series of quiet rips and muttered curses. The air was a humid curtain, filled with the scent of damp earth and the intermittent calls of unseen animals.

She emerged on a narrow road, its surface compacted by the tires of countless military vehicles. Engine noise approached; her heart climbed to her throat. She bolted into the foliage on the road's edge, her form disappearing into a realm of shadow and leaf. A truck surged past, a military canvas top flapping. The ARVN soldiers within were but brief silhouettes in the cab and truck bed. Their faces were impassive, locked in postures that could be boredom or tension or both.

Karen waited, listening to the fading rumble of the truck. Solitude reclaimed her, and she stepped back onto the road. Not far ahead, an expansive field stretched into the distance. She paused, watching as the natural order of the world was violated anew: from the distant mountains in Cambodia came flashes of light accompanied by the distant thud of bombs or artillery.

Each detonation was a vibration in the land, felt through the soles of her boots, traveling up her spine, an outrage registered in both dirt and flesh. She took out her camera, attached her zoom lens, and snapped a few photos of the flashes. It wasn't much in the way of evidence, but it was a start. She checked her map and compass, then resumed her trek down the road.

Finally, she reached a bridge—a modest span of wood and rusting metal, a geographic pause that marked the border she was to cross. Money exchanged hands with a pair of sentries, their indifference a product of routine and corruption. Her footsteps sounded hollow as she moved across, each plank echoing a note of finality. Once on the other side, she took a deep breath. Her camera was ready, her eyes keen. As the sky lightened from the approaching dawn, she snapped a photo of the bridge, proof she had crossed the border. She moved into the Cambodian landscape, a scene of uncertainties and hidden realities, each step a descent into an unfolding story.

Karen walked in a void of the palpable and the seen. Jungle all around, a haze of verdant life untouched by what she sought. Sweat ran in rivulets down her face, salt in her eyes, stinging. The smell of body odor, her smell, mixed with decomposing vegetation, an assault on the nostrils. Every click of the shutter yielded nothing but foliage, mud, and the gnarled roots of ancient trees. Her boots sank into the earth, each step an ordeal, pulling her down as if the jungle itself resisted her quest. Insects danced around her, humming in her ears, biting through the thin fabric of her shirt.

Her camera swung from her neck like a useless talisman. Its lens saw nothing of what she'd risked, its film unburdened by the weight of revelation. The unexposed film cannisters in her bag anxious for truths not found.

Her muscles ached, each step compounded misery upon misery—heat, humidity, biting flies. The tedium was punctuated by the occasional thorn snagging her sleeve or her boots tripping on hidden roots that seemed to mock her futility. She wiped the sweat from her brow, questioning, doubting. Each mile traversed seemed a jest, the jungle a labyrinthine maze indifferent to her purpose. She began to feel unwelcome, as if she were disturbing spirits that would rather remain undisturbed.

Then a glint of sunlight broke through the canopy. She approached a clearing. The camera readied in her hands. Her heartbeat quickened. Onward she pressed, into the revelation that awaited.

Emerging from the jungle's tangled dark, Karen stepped into the clearing washed in the harsh sunlight. A boundary between life and death. Her irises bounced, trying to adjust from dark to light. She squinted, senses shifting to make sense of the image she was seeing. What stretched before her was not mere destruction; it was obliteration. The village had known time, maybe days, and the air still carried a haunting cocktail of smells: charred wood, decomposing matter, the caustic aroma of burnt metal.

Underfoot, the earth crunched with the charred remnants of a life once lived here. Each step kicked up little plumes of blackened soot as she moved further into the ruins. Shattered bamboo, burnt palm thatch, walls reduced to skeletal outlines. Her camera came up instinctively. The click of the shutter froze the terrible moment. Another click, another.

A faded Viet Cong insignia, scorched but still discernible on a remnant of cloth, snagged her attention. Lens focused; she snapped the shot. Her heart drummed within her chest. Where had they fled? Did anyone survive this hell?

Eyes scanning, she took in the scene more wholly. Here were the emblems of normal life thrown into chaos: pots and pans scattered beside fire pits now cold and gray, a singed family photograph curled at the edges resting near a child's burnt straw doll, its black seed eyes pleading in a grotesque stare. Click. Click.

Then she reached the edge of a bomb crater—so deep it could not be from anything but the aerial bombardment of a 1,000 pounder. American B-52s. The earth here was ruptured, gouged, torn asunder in a way that mocked natural law. Her stomach tightened at the sight of the crater's contents. Tattered garments, shards of what had once been everyday utensils, and bleached fragments of human bone intermixed with the blackened soil. The camera came up, its weight heavy in her hands, a tool of truth in a world gone mad. She focused and clicked.

Securing the exposed film canisters in her bag, the full gravity of her mission settled over her like a shroud. A rustle snapped through the eerie quietude—animal or human, she couldn't tell, but she knew she had overstayed her time in this place of death. A last sweep of the viewfinder captured the village in its gruesome entirety. Click.

Slinging her bag over her shoulder, she stepped back into the obscurity of the jungle, leaving behind a wasteland that would now be documented, its story told.

Khmer Shangri La

Cambodian Border

The sun dipped low, casting long, dark shadows across another abandoned village. Each empty hooch seemed to catch the fading light, holding it for a moment before surrendering it to the encroaching darkness. Karen's camera clicked, capturing the desolation. Her fingers marked her map, the ink blending with her sweat. Time had scarred this land; each burnt wall stood as a silent, damning accusation.

Her hands shook as she reloaded her camera. A fire kindled within her. The patriot in her soul confronted the cost of a war defined by shadows and ash. Each frame a still from a reel of sorrow and madness.

Leaves whispered in the distance, carrying murmurs she couldn't ignore. She sank into a thicket, disappearing in the green. Breath held, camera poised, she waited. A procession of Viet Cong emerged from a tree line across the river making the border, wounded carried on makeshift stretchers. A ford was marked with a stack of rocks. The VC crossed the river, a natural line dividing one horror from another. Faces etched with pain and fatigue, they moved with purpose, their retreat into Cambodia almost solemn. Another angle of her story.

As they passed, silence returned, and she eased out of her hiding spot. The jungle whispered secrets she followed—bootprints in the mud, discarded wraps of rice. Hints leading her deeper into a world she had only glimpsed from afar. The trees parted like an opening curtain, revealing a hidden outpost camouflaged with nets beneath the jungle canopy.

Karen surveyed the encampment from a hidden vantage point, its details written in the lines of tired faces and hastily erected bamboo shelters. A makeshift hospital rose from the chaos, nurses rushing about, men lying on cots, doctors marked with blood. This was a sanctuary for the wounded, a waystation before the Viet Cong would strike again across the border. She edged closer, her camera at her eye, framing each shot to reveal the hidden layers of this war.

A group of soldiers lifted a wounded comrade from a stretcher, his face twisted in a grimace of pain. It was a moment that captured the complex tapestry of war—suffering and solidarity, vulnerability within the shell of militancy. She was close, perhaps too close. Her finger hesitated over the shutter. She took the shot.

Her finger pressed down, and the shutter clicked. Heads snapped in her direction. She vanished into the foliage, heart pounding as she wrapped her camera in a poncho to protect it from the drizzle. Her ears caught the sound of hurried, hushed conversations approaching her position. Then another noise—a wild boar broke through the undergrowth, grunting and tearing up the earth, its arrival like an omen or a savior. Viet Cong voices converged on the boar, the creature's sweet meat a brief reprieve from a diet of stale rice and tinned fish.

She waited, her heart still pounding. When the VC retreated, she emerged from her sanctuary. Silence returned, each step taking her further from the immediacy of danger but closer to a larger, more complex peril. She found a spot to rest, her back against a tree, contemplating the weight of the moments captured in her camera's lens.

As she moved, the jungle closed in again. Each shadow stretched into a lurking menace, each rustle a potential threat. She picked her way carefully, vigilant until she reached the rendezvous where she had hidden her rucksack.

The sky broke, releasing a torrential downpour. She fumbled to wrap her camera and film in her plastic poncho as the heavens unleashed their fury. A nearby stream, a benign companion earlier, suddenly swelled into a monstrous force. The flash flood surged, unyielding and merciless. Fast water flowed everywhere. The saturated soil beneath her boots collapsed. Karen clung to a sturdy tree as the water raged by, taking with it any remnants of the world she'd just traversed. As quickly as it came, the flood ebbed, leaving her soaked, shaken, but still alive.

Karen's boots caught on vines, her every step an intrusion. Breath heavy with the tang of wet earth. Her compass seemed lost as she, pointing nowhere. Heat like a shroud, sweat a torrent. Jungle thick as a wall, suffocating her in chlorophyll and despair. Repellant empty. Mosquitoes feasted, red welts on pale skin. Spirits cracked, patience strained. She cursed softly, doubting. The path she walked, the choices made. Then doubt gave way to anger—fury at her country, the faceless makers of these invisible borders, these killing fields.

Ahead, a break in the foliage. Light filtered through, tantalizing, as if a different world beckoned. What lay beyond? Another scene of devastation? More lost souls?

She stepped out of the jungle into a Khmer Shangri La untouched by time or war. A clearing. In it, life. Thatch-roofed huts arranged in a semicircle around a towering Bodhi tree, its leaves like hands in prayer. Children playing in the grass. An old man sitting alone, contemplative. All eyes turned to her, a foreign apparition. The children approached first. Their curiosity casting aside caution. They touched her fair skin, her thick hair, laughter bubbling like a forgotten melody. In the midst of it all, a young girl—Apsara— eyes like captured twilight. Their eyes met. A simple bond formed.

A young man, Chhay, approached. "You speak English?" he asked, words tinged with a local accent.

"Yes," she replied, feeling as if she had landed in a different dimension.

"You are American?"

Karen was more cautious in her reply, holding back, then, "Yes. American. Photographer."

She held up her camera as evidence. Chhay smiled and said, "Take my photograph?"

"Oh, sure."

He stood, back straight, head level, serious expression. She focused. Click. The children moved in, each wanting their own photo. She didn't have the film to spare. She herded them into a group shot. Huge grins and laughter. The silliness of children. Click. More villagers approached. More photos. Click, click, click.

Karen entered an untainted world, a momentary escape from the war that bled the land.

Chhay spoke to an elder, Sovann, and his wife Malai. Sovann's eyes, pools of wisdom, assessed her. "You stay," he said through Chhay's broken translation.

Apsara tagged along, daughter to Sovann, grabbing Karen's hand. Apsara looked at Karen as one would a strange, beautiful bird. Her curiosity was a balm, soothing Karen's war-weary soul.

Camera in hand, Karen paced through the village. Each click of the shutter captured laughter, kinship, simplicity. Her unexposed film counted down, each frame a decision. But here was a story untouched by the cruelty she had seen. A counterpoint.

Days folded into one another, a tapestry of momentary peace. Karen and Apsara, bridging language through gestures and smiles. Sharing meals, stories in the air. A respite. Time stretched like the shadows over the village. Karen—now called "Srey"— moved to the rhythms of communal life.

It was a sunny afternoon when Karen gathered her eager pupils for their English lesson. She led them to the edge of the village clearing and pointed at a tall plant. "Tree," she enunciated clearly.

The students smiled and repeated "Tree!" Karen picked up a round stone. "Rock," she said, tossing it gently up and down. "Rock," the villagers imitated.

Entering the jungle trail, Karen made a fluttering

motion with her hands and tweeted. "Bird," she said, pointing skyward. She held up a fallen feather and they passed it around, fascinated.

Further along, she scratched under her arms and knuckled the ground while vocalizing. The children laughed, mimicking her monkey gestures.

At a mossy log, Karen balanced across carefully, arms extended. "Log," she declared. Little Apsara held her hand tightly, tentative but beaming when she made it all the way across.

Karen kept new words simple, letting the objects and actions speak for themselves. The village pupils could not get enough, begging for more impromptu lessons. Their joy in learning brought Karen a pride no classroom could ever match.

Carrying her mud-caked clothes in a basket, Karen followed Malai down to stream and learned how to wash with a rock. Malai carried the clothes away to lay them out in the sun. Karen was alone again but felt no fear. She moved down the stream until she came up a shallow pool of backwater. Stripped bare, she climbed in. The water felt unbelievable good, relaxing. Then she felt something strange. She reached down and touched a lump on her side. She rose from the water and saw a leech clinging to her skin. It wasn't the only one. Eyes wide. A scream. Malia returned. Carefully pulled the parasites off, one by one, ensuring that the head wasn't left in the wound. Karen was terrified. Malia laughed. No big deal. Nature to be avoided. That's all. Realizing she was being foolish, Karen laughed. In the last few weeks, she had seen true horror. Malia was right... no big deal.

After a moment, Karen noticed Malia staring at her body, the white skin, no hair under her arms, her toenails trimmed. Smooth. Pure. Karen said nothing letting her stare as long as she wanted. A mystery revealed.

Evening fell, fires kindled. Sovann, through Chhay's tongue, spoke carefully. "You happy. We happy. Family?"

His words danced around the air. Karen felt the weight of it. Here, a world unscarred by the brutality she had witnessed. Could she? Should she?

"No," she said softly, her gaze meeting Sovann's, then Malia's. "I can't. I've got to go back."

Chhay translated. Nods. Resigned understanding.

Morning dawned on her last day. Karen packed her things, her camera gear. Apsara came to her, holding a trinket made of twine and beads. "For you," she said in almost perfect English.

"Thank you," Karen said, tears brimming but unchecked.

Villagers gathered for her departure. She took one final photo, a tapestry of faces she'd carry wherever her path led. She stepped away, back into a world torn asunder, carrying a slice of one that wasn't.

Karen's boots sank into the soft mud as she walked, the leaves whispering their secrets. Air thick. Heart heavier. A mile from the haven she'd found, something shifted. A sensation, a ghost in the air. Karen felt it before she heard it—the prickling on the nape of her neck, a charge in the air. Something amiss. The jungle paused. Her eyes darted upwards, tracking the thin contrails snaking across the sky from distant B-52 bombers. A moment held its breath. Then the whistle of air being split by falling iron. The earth roared, shuddering beneath her boots as if in agony. She felt it in her bones, a resonance with the wounded land. "Oh,

God. No," she prayed.

She flung her rucksack into a thicket of ferns, kept the camera satchel over her shoulder, and turned, heart pounding, running for whence she came. Branches whipped her face, each stride a desperate plea to undo time. Her boots slammed into the ground, kicking up mud and rotting foliage. She burst into the clearing, her soul crushed by the sight. Where homes once stood, huge bomb craters gaped like open wounds in the earth. A haze of acrid smoke filled the air, stinging her eyes and biting into her nostrils. Columns of fire clawed at the sky, claiming homes and lives.

Pushing herself forward, fearful of what she would discover, she found villagers in states of raw desperation. They were digging frantically at the piles of earth flung from the craters, lifting fallen trees, searching for loved ones now part of the scorched and cratered landscape.

Amidst the chaos, she found Apsara, knees in the dirt, staring at the twisted forms that were once her parents. Sovann, unseeing eyes reflecting a sky he could no longer behold. Malia, her delicate form crumpled and broken. Karen tried to pull Apsara away, to shield her from this apocalypse rendered in fire and blood, but the girl resisted. A sound erupted from her, half-scream, half-wail, a vocalization of pure loss. Her small hands dug into the earth as if she could pull her vanished world back from below.

Unable to lift Apsara from her sorrow, Karen shifted focus. She moved, stumbling, half-blind, tripping over debris and dodging the fingers of flame that reached out to claim her. She helped where she could, throwing handfuls of earth on the smaller fires, comforting a crying child, her camera forgotten in the maelstrom of grief and urgency.

Finally, the villagers congregated. Elderly men and women in a circle, their weathered faces like ancient parchments upon which sorrow had written a tale too long and too cruel. No time for proper graves; the unknown loomed heavy. Viet Cong, Americans, ARVN, or even the Khmer Rouge—no one knew who might come next to claim their sanctuary turned inferno.

Bodies were moved—too few left to move—and wrapped in palm leaves. They were placed upon hastily made pyres of damp wood that smoked resentfully before reluctantly accepting its grim duty. Flames flickered upwards, seeking heaven. Souls on a journey.

Karen's camera hung heavily at her side. She raised it, looked through the viewfinder, focused—and then lowered it. Her hands shook. It wasn't right; some truths were too raw to be captured, too sacred to be relayed.

As the night encroached, the survivors whispered of a deeper jungle, a place where even the war might fear to tread. A place to mend their shattered lives. Apsara, her face vacant, clung to Karen, her fingers gripping the fabric of Karen's shirt as if it were a talisman. Neither spoke; there were no words left.

Rain began to fall, droplets like tiny mourners from the heavens, soaking the ashen ground, streaking faces clean of grime but not of sorrow. Monsoon tears, an indifferent universe weeping for a broken world. Karen closed her eyes briefly, feeling the rain against her skin, tasting its fresh bitterness on her lips. When she opened them, her gaze fell upon the lingering plumes of smoke ascending from the pyres. They climbed slowly, indifferently, dissolving into the darkening sky—a final farewell, a grim punctuation to the day's tragic prose.

Silence enveloped them all as they moved away from the grave site. There was no time to waste. No time to mourn. The elders led, deciding silently to march deeper into Cambodia, toward territories whispered to be even less kind than their lost home.

Karen stood at the fringe of the gathering; camera heavy at her side. Karen met the eyes of the elder who seemed to speak for the group. No words. Just a nod. The old man returned it, his face a relief map of hardships endured and yet to come. She was no longer an outsider with a camera; she was one of them, a witness to their grief.

Her gaze met Apsara's, the girl clutching a tattered doll. Behind her, the jungle whispered of unmarked trails, possible escapes. In her bag, rolls of film ached for the light of day, for eyes to witness the truths they held.

Could those truths wait?

The refugees began their march into the jungle's murk. Apsara tugged her arm, a wordless question in her eyes. Karen felt the gravity of the choice. Each frame of film in her bag was a plea for justice, yet here was another plea before her, immediate and raw. She zipped the rucksack shut, leaving its contents to the dark as she swung the load onto her back.

As the sky wept overhead, Karen took a last lingering glance at the pyres, their embers struggling to survive in the rain, a testament to resilience, to the indomitable spirit that had brought her here and would now lead her deeper into the labyrinth of human sorrow. She felt Apsara's hand slip into hers, and as they turned away from the only home the girl had ever known, Karen knew that her quest for truth hadn't been abandoned—it had evolved. Duty to world set aside for duty to one.

Together, they joined the line of refugees, their faces marked by the same tapestry of emotion, each carrying their own hidden worlds of sorrow and minute hope. And so, they moved, a solemn procession swallowed by the enveloping green, leading into the unknown.

The Cajun

A Shau Valley, South Vietnam

Under an evening sky, the A Shau Valley spread out before the NCOs and officers of 3rd Brigade, 101st Airborne. The landscape unfolded in gentle waves, hills rolling under a sky soon to be striped with the streaks of conflict, a quiet reminder of the balance between brutality and beauty that defined this land.

Colonel Ryan Bennett stood before the assembly, a seasoned shepherd ready to guide his flock into the labyrinth that wove its way through the valley. With the lanterns casting long shadows, the officers and NCOs gathered, poised to absorb the strategy that would navigate them to the enemy strongholds they would be tasked to destroy.

"The valley before us is more than a stretch of land, gentlemen. It's the heartbeat of the enemy, their refuge and their vantage point. We are here to sever the ties that feed their resistance, to claim this territory as our own and cut off their lifeline. This operation is called Apache Snow," Bennett stated, his words resounding with a solemn gravity.

A large map stood before them, a charted dance of potential clashes and decisive maneuvers, pathways winding through the terrain like the tracks of ancient rivers. As Bennett traced the routes with his finger, a narrative began to unfold, a strategy woven with threads of courage.

Listening, Sergeant Nathaniel Black, a man molded by the bayous of Baton Rouge where he grew up. His presence was a grounding force amidst the swirling energies of anticipation and resolve that stirred amongst the men under his command.

When the briefing finished, Colonel Bennett found Nathaniel in the dispersing crowd and said, "How's your lieutenant, Nate?"

"Too young like all lieutenants. But a good man that's learning," said Nathaniel.

"You let him lead, but you keep him alive. We need all the experienced junior officers we can get."

"You can count on it, Colonel."

As night gave way to the approaching dawn, Nathaniel stood amidst his soldiers, witnessing the interplay of nerves and camaraderie that colored the moments before an operation.

"Listen up, ya'll," he began, "When you're out there, you stay focused and keep your intervals. Don't bunch up and make you and your buddies a target."

The men nodded, the weight of his words settling upon them, grounding them in the harsh reality of the battlefield. In that moment, they were not just soldiers, but brothers, bound by a shared purpose and the understanding that survival lay in unity.

"Keep your emotions in check and don't do anything stupid. Stupid gets you killed. And above all, remember your training, but trust your instincts. God gave 'em to ya to keep you alive."

"Ya reckon we'll see any action, Sarge?" a wiry soldier from Brooklyn inquired, his tone carrying a note of eager, yet naive courage.

Nathaniel glanced at him, his eyes bearing the tranquil depths of the bayou at night, "Cher, we'll see action, alright. But remember, it ain't no child's play, this. Stay sharp, stay alive."

"Sarge, I just...I mean, we're ready. We won't let you down."

"Son, it ain't about lettin' me down. We're a team, bound tighter than family. We watch out for each other, cover each other's backs. That's how we've always done it, and that's how we'll do it today. We're Airborne. Remember, it ain't about proving who we are. It's about getting every single one of us back home."

"Oorah!" They responded in unison.

As the first whispers of dawn began to stir, the distant throb of helicopter blades hummed a prelude to the unfolding narrative of battle. Faces turned skyward, marked by the subtle hues of the emerging day, young men standing at the brink of the unknown.

The helicopters descended, their powerful blades whipping up a whirlwind of dust and debris. The behemoths opened wide to engulf the troops, the echo of whirring engines enveloping them in a cocoon of noise and trepidation.

Nathaniel settled across from Lieutenant Daniel

Reed, a conscious choice to offer unspoken support to the young man shouldering newly minted responsibilities. A simple nod bridged the gap between them, a promise of solidarity amidst the unknown dangers that awaited.

Outside, the sky held its breath, caught in the delicate transition from night to morning. Inside, the soldiers absorbed the murmur of conversations and the muted sounds filtering through the small windows, their faces reflecting a gamut of emotions from raw anticipation to restrained fear.

The helicopters lifted off, abandoning the familiarity of solid ground to embrace the open sky. They became transient beings in the vastness, swaying in tune with the whims of the guiding winds. Hands gripped onto cold, unyielding metal, physical evidence of the growing tension within.

Below, the A Shau Valley unfurled with vivid greens and ancient secrets. The chatter among the soldiers gained momentum, personal tales weaving seamlessly with tactical discussions, a brief and fragile semblance of normalcy in an otherwise surreal setting.

As the helicopters neared the landing zone, a once lush terrain appeared, now scarred and battered with artillery and bomb craters. Pilots expertly navigated through, the helicopters dancing gracefully.

The soldiers tensed as ground approached, a shared breath of readiness that echoed through the confined space. Stern faces and tightened grips heralded the impending descent, a silent preparation for the clash that lay ahead.

The descent was quick, the rapid drop stirring gasps and quickened heartbeats. As they touched ground, a rush of movements spilled the men into the valley's awaiting arms. In this hurried transition, Nathaniel and Lieutenant Reed met eyes once again, sharing a moment of understanding before stepping into the narrative that awaited them, a chapter marked by unity, courage, and an unyielding spirit to survive.

The elite soldiers disembarked hastily, forming a protective ring around the landing site. As the helicopters ascended and headed back to base, the air, filled with the distinct earthy scent of the valley, bore a heavy silence, a quietude that seemed almost surreal after the clamorous journey through the sky.

Nathaniel moved with an ease honed by years in the field, his bayou upbringing infusing his movements with a feral grace. His Cajun accent broke the stillness, "Remember, we bunch up, we become easy targets. Don't give them that."

Lieutenant Reed stood a little apart, the uncertainty in his eyes giving way to a steely resolve. The young officer squared his shoulders, stepping beside Nathaniel. The subtle transformation didn't escape Nathaniel's seasoned eye, a flicker of pride warming him against the morning chill.

The valley seemed to be waking up with them, the first rays of sun filtering through the canopy, casting long shadows that seemed to beckon them further into its depths. Birdsong began to fill the air, contrasting sharply with the grim undertone of their mission.

With stealth and discipline, they moved, their footsteps a soft percussion mixed with the morning sounds.

As the scouts moved ahead, Nathaniel led his unit with an innate understanding of the terrain, his senses finely tuned to the subtle shifts in the environment. The men followed, a living, breathing entity moving as one.

The soldiers trudged through the A Shau Valley, surrounded by the quiet whispers of leaves and the soft gurgling of distant streams. It would have been beautiful and serene if it weren't for the impending promise of conflict. The path was narrow and flanked by thorns that snagged at their uniforms unkindly. Fabric and flesh torn with indifference. A few curses filled the air, misery all around, yet they moved onward. No enemy contact - a two-edged sword. Were they watching? Were they waiting?

As day gave way to night, the group settled into a temporary haven, the darkness providing a false blanket of security. The weight of steel pressed against their bodies, a constant reminder of the ever-present danger. Conversations hushed to whispers, stories exchanged in low tones, a bonding that happened in the shadow of conflict.

Throughout, Nathaniel watched over them, a guardian figure. He listened to their tales, their fears, and their dreams, a solid rock against the flowing currents of youthful energy.

With the morning came new challenges, an unexpected encounter with a local village that brought with it a wave of tension. The villagers eyed the Americans with a mix of curiosity and fear, their lives a constant tug of war between conflicting sides.

And as Nathaniel and his men left, figures emerged from the shadows, the enemy taking shape, solidifying from whispered fears to tangible threats. At a distance, a lone figure separated from the rest, his focus sharp, a deadly intent clear in his movements. Nguyen, a VC sniper, had found his prey, and the hunt had begun.

In the undulating shade of the A Shau valley, a ghost

materialized from the underbrush; Nguyen followed the Americans at a stealthy distance, blending seamlessly with the whispering leaves and dappled sunlight. The world narrowed to the sight of his rifle, honing on the enemy with predatory precision.

In a clearing where sunlight seeped through the canopy, the Americans paused, their shoulders slumping ever so slightly as they embraced a moment of respite. Nature hummed around them - a chorus of insects, the rustle of leaves underfoot, the distant chatter of birds, all forming a harmonious backdrop. The soldiers exchanged weary smiles, their camaraderie evident in the teasing jabs and shared laughter that momentarily lightened the heavy burden they carried.

"Man, I never thought I'd miss the bayou, but this place makes it look like paradise," Nathaniel mused, his lilting accent bringing a sense of familiarity among the alien surroundings.

Private Jackson, a younger soldier with a spark of playfulness still preserved in his youthful features, chimed in, attempting to mimic Nathaniel's accent, "Ah'm tellin' ya, once we get out of this mess, first thing I'm gonna do is get myself a big, juicy gator burger, ya know?" The others chuckled, even as they exchanged knowing glances at Nathaniel.

The tranquility of the moment was rent apart by a sharp, singular crack that echoed ominously through the trees - the unmistakable report of a sniper's rifle. Time seemed to stretch, the moments elongated as every soldier froze, their faces morphing from ease to alarm. The laugh lines smoothed out, replaced by taut expressions of fear.

"Sniper! Everyone get down!" Nathaniel's command sliced through the air, instilling a semblance of order in the frantic moments that followed. The men scrambled, diving behind the scant cover the undergrowth provided, their trained eyes scanning the foliage as their hands worked to ready their rifles.

And there among the turmoil was Jackson, standing still for a second that seemed to last forever, his hand reaching up to grasp his throat, a vivid stream of blood flowing between his fingers, staining the vibrant green leaves beneath him with splashes of cruel red. His eyes filled with a terrible understanding, an artery hit, the life force rapidly ebbing from him. And then, with an eeriness that juxtaposed the surrounding chaos, he slowly fell over, his body hitting the ground with a thud that echoed like a final note in a tragic symphony.

The forest was alive now with a different kind of melody, one laden with hearts pumping in high gear, the chorus of men shouting, directing, and gasps of breath drawn in fear and exertion. There was a rustle, a quickening in the undergrowth as soldiers darted with practiced agility, seeking cover, their movements calculated from hours, days, months of training now called upon in the severest of tests.

Nathaniel, his eyes momentarily lingering on Jackson's fallen form, the medic trying to pump life back into him. Nathaniel clenched his teeth, pushing down the surge of anger and grief threatening to engulf him. This was not the time for mourning. "Williams, Garner, take the left flank. Watch for a muzzle flash, and for God's sake, stay low," he barked, his accent thickening with the gravity of the situation, as he relayed quick instructions, his mind analyzing, strategizing, working overtime to salvage what he could from the sudden assault.

Lieutenant Reed, his face a canvas of raw, youthful

fear and responsibility, turned towards Nathaniel, his voice slightly shaky but determined. "Sergeant, I think we should..." he began, but Nathaniel interrupted, his voice a potent blend of command and assurance.

"Not now, Lieutenant. Stay focused. Protect the men," Nathaniel said, his eyes flickering with an untold understanding.

Reed nodded, swallowing hard, a visible effort to steady himself, to rise to the occasion that demanded more than what his young shoulders seemed prepared to bear.

With a swift, silent gesture, Nathaniel beckoned to Hanson, the seasoned scout who had seen more battles than most in the group. Without a word, the two men split from the unit, delving deeper into the forest, the lush foliage swallowing them whole as they became shadows hunting a ghost.

Back in the clearing, Reed rallied his men, his voice gaining strength and certainty as he directed them, the initial indecisiveness giving way to a burgeoning leadership. "Martinez, O'Brien, circle round, make sure we aren't getting flanked. Johnson, with me. We need to secure Jackson. The rest of you stay low, stay focused. Find that bastard and kill 'em," his orders flew, a beacon of structure amidst the chaotic tendrils of battle.

In the deeper reaches of the forest, Nathaniel and Hanson moved with a predator's grace, their senses heightened, attuned to the subtle shifts in the surroundings. A flicker of movement, a leaf fluttering unnaturally, a distant echo of a twig snapping underfoot - all potential signs of the sniper's presence, Nguyen, the invisible foe who held death in his fingers stayed motionless, watching as they drew closer to his position. There was still time to run, but he chose to stay.

The forest around them transformed into a living entity, where the lines blurred, where the hunter could swiftly become the hunted. It was a test of skill, of patience, of resilience, as the two experienced soldiers tracked their quarry, and their quarry spied them. The scent of danger heavy in the humid air.

Unseen, Nguyen waited until they passed, then followed at a distance. The hunters and the hunted switched places time and time again as they tried to outmaneuver one another.

The chase stretched on, minutes morphing into hours, the sky slowly darkening as evening approached, casting long, eerie shadows that played tricks on the eyes, transforming into potential threats at every blink. Yet, amidst the swirling fears and palpable tension, there was a silent respect, an understanding of the skill and courage it took to be a hunter in this deadly game.

As Hanson and Nathaniel closed in, the forest seemed to hold its breath, the weight of the impending confrontation hanging like a question unanswered. It was Hanson who broke the silence, his voice a low warning, "He's close."

Nathaniel nodded, his senses tuned to the silent language of the forest, every whispering leaf and rustle a message to decipher. Each passing moment a tightening coil of anticipation and dread.

At last, in a small glen where rays of the setting sun pierced the canopy, creating patterns of light and shadow on the forest floor, Nathaniel spotted a figure, partially concealed in the undergrowth. A distant silhouette, a ghost finally materializing in the waning light. The heart of the hunter raced, a quiet whisper of triumph and dread mingling in his veins. He whispered orders to Hanson who gave no visible sign of agreement, short of blinking twice. That was enough. The contract was made. Hanson peeled off to the right.

The ensuing confrontation was swift, a whirlwind of movement and gunfire, a ballet of death choreographed in the dying light of day. Hanson, the bait, pinned down by precise shots from Nguyen, found himself in a perilous position, while Nathaniel maneuvered with quiet agility, a shadow stalking a shadow.

In the end, as darkness embraced the forest in its nightly grasp, Nathaniel emerged victorious, the invisible foe finally visible, the ghost turned mortal in the harsh reality of war. A bullet through his left cheek and the back of his skull shattered, Nguyen lay still, his sniper's journey ended in a final confrontation that bore witness to the cycle of violence, the cost of conflict, the relentless march of soldiers caught in the currents of history's ruthless tide.

Nathaniel and Hanson returned to the unit, their silhouettes appearing like phantoms from the shadows, their gaze bearing the weight of actions taken, lives lost, and a relentless pursuit seen to its bitter end.

Back at the clearing, Reed stood amongst his men, his posture no longer that of the inexperienced officer but of a leader who had faced the crucible of battle and emerged forged anew. The exchange between him and Nathaniel was silent, an understanding glance that spoke volumes, a quiet acknowledgment of growth, of duty carried, of the relentless cycle of war that demanded sacrifices and forged leaders in the vessel of fear and courage. The night seemed to hold its breath, respecting the gravity of their moment, its stillness a balm to the turmoil that stirred within them.

Under the gaze of the moon, the clearing transformed into a makeshift camp. Reed organized the men with newfound authority, his voice no longer quivering but asserting, a steady beacon in the dark. The men responded, their movements synchronous, a living organism adapting and surviving in a hostile environment.

Around the dwindling embers of a small fire, Nathaniel found a moment of respite. The firelight cast flickering shadows across his face, flames reflecting in his eyes that held stories too vast for the young night to comprehend. His hands, stained with the grim realities of war, moved with a refinement that belied their deadly proficiency, as he cleaned his rifle with quiet reverence.

Far from the huddled group of men, the forest unfolded in deep shadows, its boundaries blurred in the moonlight, an enigmatic entity that held secrets and memories. It had seen countless suns rise and set, had witnessed the fleeting lives that danced upon its stage, ever-changing, ever-repeating in a cycle of creation and destruction.

In the distance, the murmurs of water whispered tales of time, echoing through the valley like a timeless concerto that serenaded the moon and stars. This was the backdrop of their lives, a canvas of surreal beauty and brutal realities, intertwined in an intricate ballet that spanned the ages.

Back in the camp, Lieutenant Reed approached Nathaniel, his silhouette framed by the glowing embers, a young warrior coming into his own under the watchful eyes of the older, seasoned soldier. Reed's voice broke the stillness, a ripple in the tranquil night as he sought counsel, sought understanding in the complex web of duty and morality that bound them.

"Sergeant, how do you...how do you reconcile it? The loss, the killing?" Reed asked, his voice tinged with the weight of command, with the burden of lives held in the balance.

Nathaniel looked up, his gaze finding Reed's, a well of experiences reflected in his depths. He paused, allowing the gravity of the question to settle, to resonate in the silent night that enveloped them. Then, with a quiet sigh that held the echoes of countless battles, of friendships forged and lost in the furnace of war, he spoke, his voice carrying the resonance of a man who had traversed the dark corridors of humanity, yet found light in the midst of darkness.

"It ain't easy, Lieutenant. It never is. But we carry it, we bear the weight because that's our duty, our responsibility to the men, to the people we're sworn to protect," Nathaniel said, his words passed down through generations of warriors who stood guard over the fragile sanctity of life.

Reed nodded, absorbing the truth in Nathaniel's words.

In the moonlit clearing, under the silent canopy of ancient trees, the men gathered around the fire, their faces illuminated by the flickering flames of primal energy. Stories flowed, laughter echoed, a semblance of normalcy, an ability to find joy, to connect, to heal.

The morning sun lazily pushed its rays through the thick canopy as the men advance through the valley, the burden of their journey evident in their stoic faces and muddied uniforms. The brush gave way to a clearing where the remnants of a once bustling village lay, a grim testimony to the ravages of war. Reed hesitated, his gaze scanning the desolate landscape before him. No sign of life. Nothing.

Nathaniel stepped beside him, his seasoned eyes studying the young lieutenant. "We can't linger here, LT," he urged softly, his voice carrying a weight that seemed to anchor Reed back into the present. With a resolute nod, Reed signaled the men to move forward.

As they navigated the decimated path leading through the village, the silence seemed almost tangible. The soldiers moved with a quiet reverence, their weapons held ready as they carefully stepped over debris and the ruins of lives once lived. Soon, the forest would reclaim its territory, trees and foliage intertwining with the remnants of civilization in a harsh yet oddly poetic embrace. Reed and Nathaniel led the formation, their senses heightened as they traversed the narrow trail that wound like a serpent through the undulating landscape.

A burst of gunfire shattered the silence, bullets whizzing past with malevolent intent. Everyone hit the dirt. Reed found himself pinned down as an enemy machine gun chipped away at the fallen log in front of him. He glanced at Nathaniel, who returned his look with a steadying gaze, his body language conveying a calm that seemed almost surreal amidst the madness.

The ragged edges of the sun sliced through the looming foliage in stark contrast to the escalating battle. Reed's chest heaved mirroring the frenetic rhythm of gunfire and frantic shouts. Nathaniel remained a sturdy figure beside him, his experienced eyes darting through the forest, his hand effortlessly communicating with the men.

The enemy swelled like a tide, advancing at a run toward the Americans, yelling their battle cry.

Airborne laid out a wall of bullets cutting the enemy down as it closed on their lines.

Watching the enemy approach, Reed swallowed, gripping the radio tight in his hand, the metal a cold reminder of the responsibility bestowed upon him. "Sierra Three, this is Bravo Six," he breathed heavily into the receiver, his voice a touch shaky yet resolute. "Requesting fire support at grid..." he rattled off their coordinates, pausing to steel his resolve.

A voice crackled in acknowledgment, punctuated by distant of artillery guns aligning, ready to rain hellfire upon the advancing enemy.

Nathaniel moved swiftly, his voice carrying through the commotion. "Mason, flank to the left! Hanson, I need your team to secure our six!" Orders were barked with precision, Nathaniel's commands weaving through the noise. His decisiveness a calming force, guiding the men.

The heavens split open and the ground shook violently as the artillery unleashed its fury. Trees splintered, smoke and debris clouded the vision, a maelstrom of nature and man-made violence intertwining.

Reed stood tall, his voice finding strength against the mayhem. "Hold the line, men! Hold the line!" he shouted, anchoring the men with newfound authority.

"Get down, Lieutenant," said Nathaniel. "Before you get your head blown off."

Reed lowered to one knee and said, "I just wanted to set a good example."

"You're doing just fine," said Nathaniel with a reassuring nod. "No shame is laying on the ground."

The men responded, a living entity that moved with a singular purpose. Shouts of acknowledgment resounded through the ranks, their unified front a bulwark against the relentless assault. Minutes felt like hours, the air thick with the scent of gunpowder and damp earth.

Slowly, the furious onslaught of the enemy ebbed, the forest ringing with the retreating footsteps, leaving an eerie silence in its wake.

The soldiers remained poised, eyes darting, weapons at the ready, as Reed and Nathaniel surveyed the forest, their faces etched with grime and determination. Nathaniel gave a curt nod, his eyes meeting Reed's in a silent exchange of mutual respect.

Reed finally allowed his shoulders to slump, the weight of leadership momentarily eased. He caught Nathaniel's eye, the older man offering a tired yet proud smile. "Together," Nathaniel murmured, his voice tinged with a Cajun lilt.

Reed nodded, his chest swelling with a mix of pride. "Together," he repeated, his gaze sweeping over the men who stood with them, united in purpose, ready to face the challenges that lay ahead in the unforgiving depths of the A Shau Valley.

Under the scant moonlight, Nathaniel and his troops advanced, weaving through the narrow trails of the valley. Reed, once hesitant, now moved with purpose, issuing commands that were both firm and considerate. The darkness seemed to amplify his resolve, shaping him into a leader attuned to the pulse of his men. "Secure our flanks. Keep it tight and quiet," Reed instructed, his eyes scanning the shadowy periphery where secrets might lurk.

Reed had found his tempo, striking a balance between authority and empathy, harmony that resonated with the men under his lead.

The moon unveiled a village nestled in the valley, a place seemingly untouched by time, where past melded with the present. Candlelight in windows and doorways verified there was life. The people too frightened to show themselves.

A sudden rustle nearby jolted them, snapping the soldiers into a formation that mirrored the readiness of a coiled spring. Nathaniel gestured, and two soldiers moved towards the sound, their steps barely disturbing the carpet of leaves underfoot. The world held its breath, nerves stretched taut in anticipation.

The tension dissolved as a dog, more shadow than flesh, emerged from the underbrush. A light ripple of laughter passed through the unit, easing the tension that had clung to them moments before.

Nathaniel leaned towards Reed, the murmur of his words breaking the night's silence, "Seems we got a scout on our side, Lieutenant."

Reed's smile broke through, a brief flash in the moonlit darkness. Together, they pressed on, the moon guiding their path as they ventured deeper into the A Shau valley.

The morning was a fickle mistress, gracing the grizzled men with rays that cut through the canopy, casting elongated shadows that mingled with the slithering mist. Nathaniel walked, his eyes always probing his surroundings, the air tasting of impending metal and fire. Next to him, Reed, too close to the front, pushing himself to lead his men by example.

With the subtlety of a shadow passing over the sun-dappled jungle floor, the NVA scout nestled deep in the foliage, unblinking eyes riveted on the approaching American platoon. He issued the warning on his handheld radio, a succinct triple click.

On the other end of the radio, the NVA commander, an older man with a hundred battles in his past, listened to the clicks. In hushed tones he issued his orders for his soldiers to man their positions and ready for the impending ambush.

Positioned between two towering hills and the end of a long slope, the stronghold hidden in the trees and foliage had taken weeks of hard labor to build. Machine gun and recoilless rifle teams manned their posts in the blockhouses fortified with thick logs and sandbags, their fingers a hairbreadth away from unleashing a torrent of lead. RPG gunners and riflemen nestled in spider holes, eyes flickering with a predator's anticipation. High above in the trees overlooking the slope, snipers settled within their bamboo nests, their rifles cool and expectant against their palms. The flanks were formidable, armored with sandbags and light machine guns, an unyielding barricade against the impending onslaught. It was a well-built trap waiting to be sprung on the unsuspecting Americans.

Nathaniel, with skin etched by the braille of war, surveyed the encompassing terrain, the unease knotting tighter within him. He leaned in close to Lieutenant Reed, his voice tinged with an urgent sotto, "Lieutenant, the terrain ahead... it's a damned kill box. We oughta skirt around those hills."

Reed's face was a canvas of youthful defiance, a brazen trust in invincibility overshadowing caution. "We're late hooking up with battalion as it is. We go forward, Nate. No second-guessing."

Nathaniel pulled back, allowing Reed to lead, yet his instincts blared warnings, prompting him to gesture frantically to his men to widen their intervals, their senses stretched taut as bowstrings.

Within the canopy, the NVA commander observed the advance, his hand hovering in a brief, weighted silence before slashing downwards in a decisive stroke. The jungle erupted in a frenetic salvo of death, bullets storming from all corners, a deluge that sought flesh.

Near the head of the platoon, Reed's form crumpled abruptly, a puppet severed from its strings, his youthful visage marred by the cruel kisses of a machine gun's bullets.

Seeing the lieutenant fall, Nathaniel lunged forward with bullets zipping around him. Sliding to a stop beside Reed, his hands sought to quell the red rivers that surged from the lieutenant's neck and arm. "Doc," he shouted, then turned to lock eyes with the frightened lieutenant.

"You gonna be just fine, cher

. You hang in there. Doc'll fix you up good," Nathaniel said, lying. He knew the neck wound was hopeless. Too much blood spurting from a severed artery. Reed's face bone white, speckled with blood.

Doc crawled over and saw the pool of crimson already on the ground. He tried to save the lieutenant anyway. His eyes met Nathaniel's. They both knew what came next. "Tired," gurgled Reed.

"It's okay. I got this. LT. You rest," said Nathaniel, his eyes moist.

Reed jerked twice, the last of his energy, then his head fell back, his eyes frozen. Dead. The Doc continuing to try to save him, knowing he was too late. Nathaniel put his hand on Doc's, "Let 'em rest, Doc.

See to the others."

Doc nodded and moved off. The battle raged as Nathaniel took one more moment to gather himself, then sprinted to his radioman, grabbing the handset. His voice boomed against the maelstrom, a desperate cry that reverberated through the radio, "Eagle Nest, this is Bravo Six, we need air support! Coordinates 25.30, 40.60. Danger close, I repeat, danger close!"

Minutes later as the battle thundered, the sky roared in fury, the Grumman A-6 Intruders tearing through the clouds, their bellies pregnant with retribution. The earth shook as fire kissed sky, a cataclysmic union that bore down on the stronghold. Unforgiving. Flames sprouted monstrous limbs, reaching hungrily to consume wood and flesh, a fiery leviathan.

"Bravo team, left flank! Alpha, on me!" Nathaniel shouted, his figure a silhouette against the inferno. The soldiers responded, a phalanx of grit, their war cries mingling with their gunfire.

Through smoke and fire, they charged, their spirits ignited. Bullets sung their serenade of death and survival. The air was thick with the iron tang of blood and charred flesh, the grim smell of war.

Among the remnants of the shattered fortress, smoke spiraled into the sky, remnants of napalm mingled with burnt flesh and timber. Nathaniel moved forward, his demeanor more storm than man, vengeance fueling each deliberate step. The enemy, once fierce, now seemed almost pitiful, their eyes mirroring the horror of their fiery demise. Nathaniel's rifle barked sharply, followed by the thuds of bodies hitting the earth. Around him, his men advanced, sweeping through the smoking ruin, leaving no quarter, remembering their fallen friends.

In the ashy haze, Nathaniel encountered the enemy commander, a figure more char than man, his uniform still aflame, skin bubbling and peeling away in gruesome sheets. The commander's eyes met Nathaniel's, a desperate plea flickering within. There was a brief, terrible moment where time seemed to fracture, leaving only the two of them. The commander's mouth moved, a raspy whisper of an appeal for death escaping from blackened lips. Nathaniel's gaze remained unmoved, a rock against the pitiable cries before him. He moved on, leaving the commander to his fiery fate, a monument to the hell that engulfed them all.

As the stronghold yielded, its defenses crumbling under the relentless onslaught of the platoon, Nathaniel stood, his face a canvas of grief and resolve. With heavy steps, he returned to Reed's lifeless form.

He knelt. Tears mingled with the ash and sweat that marked his face, a bitter stream that bore the weight of promises unkept. Colonel Bennett's words ringing in his mind, "You let him lead, Nate, but you keep him safe." The mission won; he had failed. He whispered, his voice ragged, "I'm sorry, cher."

The Sanctuary

The Jungle - Cambodia

The lush Cambodian jungle closed in around the weary group of villagers as they continued their arduous journey seeking refuge. Six long days had passed since American bombs ravaged their homes. Now far from any established paths, they navigated by instinct and shouts when the tangled greenery became too thick.

At the rear, Karen helped support an elderly man named Som whose leg was badly wounded by shrapnel. Each faltering step shot agony up his weathered face, but he refused to be left behind.

"We must endure this trial together," he would say whenever Karen suggested resting. "Our fates are bound as one now."

Up ahead, Karen could hear the pained moans of other wounded being hauled on makeshift stretchers of fraying rope and bamboo. The lack of medical supplies haunted her. Their healer had perished in the bombing, taking her wisdom of jungle cures.

By day, Karen maintained a strong face, sharing encouraging words and smiles with the refugee children clinging to her side. But inwardly she grappled with feeling responsible for these civilians while trying to maintain journalistic distance. Each small kindness and comfort offered eroded her ideals of neutrality.

At night, frightened whispers circulated about those likely to perish by morning from festering shrapnel wounds or infection's fevered delirium. Karen lay awake racking her brain for any wilderness treatments learned from years reporting on war. But the death toll mounted daily.

Ominous flashes lit the night sky as bombs fell miles away. Karen imagined other villages meeting the same fiery end. The survivors were deeply shaken, flinching at any unexpected sound.

Young Apsara pressed a few precious cashews into Karen's hand one evening. Karen's facade nearly cracked at this selfless act. She hugged the orphan girl wordlessly, their fates intertwining tighter.

Soon the rains came, making the winding jungle paths slick and treacherous. Rivers swelled rapidly, cutting off crossings. Soaked and shivering, the group took shelter in a cramped cave. But even nature's wrath could not break their spirit. Each new trial fueled Karen's determination to be the guardian they deserved.

The downpour continued relentlessly, cascading through the jungle canopy in sheets. Karen and the other able-bodied took turns holding tarps and leaves above the elderly and children. But they were still soaked and shivering, morale rapidly sinking.

Without warning, a distant roaring swelled above the rain's din. "Mud comes!" someone cried in Khmer. Panic flashed across faces.

Thick, muddy torrents crashed through the underbrush toward them. Villagers scrambled for higher ground, but the surge came too fast. Many were swept away. Karen pushed Apsara and two other children up into the crouch of a nearby tree. The mudflow surrounded Karen and the children still on the ground. It was too late to save more. She gripped the children tightly as the violent sludge swept their legs out from under them. Apsara clung to the other children in the tree with iron resolve, eyes wide with terror as Karen disappeared below the surface.

Chaos reigned as villagers collided into debris and trees. Poking her head out of the slurry, Karen fought to keep the kids' heads above the churning mudflow. "Hold on tight!" she shouted over the roaring brown waves.

Nearby, a grandmother lost her grip on a root and was pulled under by the angry current. Her wails faded chillingly downstream. Others joined hands, forming a human chain to withstand the brutal battering.

After agonizing minutes, the deluge began draining away. Caked head to toe in mud, the survivors regrouped, shuddering and weeping with relief. Only then did they realize one child was missing - a boy named Thy.

Frantic, Karen led the search downstream through tangled thickets. They discovered the boy lodged against boulders, frighteningly still. Karen's heart dropped, but she detected a faint breath. "He's alive!"

They bore the small battered body back to the cave on an improvised stretcher. Though weakened, young

Thy had survived miraculously. The group rejoiced, praising Karen's level head and courage.

She brushed off their gratitude with a tired smile. "We must have faith in one another. Our bonds give us strength." But inwardly, her reporter's objectivity now seemed a lifetime away.

After days of more grueling jungle treks, the group finally emerged into a sunlit clearing, grass and wildflowers swaying gently. Spirits lifted at this serene patch of nature's reprieve.

Young Thy spotted a nest of warbler fledglings chirping hungrily. "Good omen!" he declared. Karen smiled as she bandaged elders' feet blistered raw. For a brief interlude, their trials seemed held at bay.

As the jungle's shadows began encroaching, a decision was made to camp in the clearing that night. A small fire was lit, cooking the last of the rice. In the flames' glow, Karen told stories of her Chicago youth, using her hands to describe majestic skyscrapers that left the children wide-eyed.

Later, she wrote by firelight in her worn journal, documenting the people who had come to mean so much in just days. Objectivity had given way to intimate bonds. Each entry now was not just prose but a witness to carry on if she did not survive this trial.

Karen was jarred from her writings by tiny arms encircling her waist. Little Apsara had crawled into her lap and now slumbered peacefully. Gazing at the innocent face pressed against her heart, Karen knew she would walk through fire itself to protect this makeshift family.

The next morning as the villagers continued the journey deeper into Cambodia, scouts returned breathless with news - an abandoned village nestled in the hills ahead. The elders were understandably timid about the unknown village. Undaunted, Karen joined the scouts to assess this potential refuge. Approaching cautiously, they found households emptied in haste - belongings strewn, meals half-eaten. What had panicked the inhabitants?

Despite the eerie atmosphere, Karen's spirits soared. After the exposed jungle, the solid structures and belongings left behind were luxuries beyond imagination. This could become their sanctuary.

She beckoned the others, who overcame trepidation and reverently explored each vacated hut. Personalities of the vanished owners sprang to life through forgotten keepsakes. When medicine was uncovered, cheers rang out, swallowed quickly by the empty dwellings.

Karen allowed herself to daydream about this becoming the villagers' new home. A haven to blossom into prosperity. She imagined Apsara attending a village school, learning free from fear.

But what unfathomable forces still lurked in this war-torn land? Ominous questions lingered. For now, Karen tucked away doubts. Tonight, bellies would be full on huge baskets rice left by the previous occupants. Their bodies would be sheltered while they slept. That was enough cause for joy.

She drifted off reflecting on soon traveling safely to Saigon with their remarkable story. Surely this tragedy would spur world aid and hope. Tomorrow their new lives would begin...

Karen was jolted awake before dawn by Apsara's urgent shaking. "Soldiers!" she whispered. Peering out, Karen glimpsed armed men at the village edge - the dreaded red scarves of the Khmer Rouge. Karen's blood turned to ice. She had heard the rumors of their brutal treatment of prisoners. The villagers' haven had become a trap.

She grabbed her camera, bag, and Apsara's hand. "Run!" They fled into the jungle as screams arose behind them. Several soldiers saw her and gave chase.

Karen and Apsara crashed through dense jungle, feet tearing across knotted roots and sharp rocks. Karen's lungs burned but terror drowned all pain. Behind them, angry soldiers plunged heedlessly through the undergrowth.

Low-hanging vines lashed their faces as they tore blindly ahead. Karen felt warm blood trickling down her cheeks from cuts but didn't dare slow. She gripped Apsara's hand tightly, half-dragging the stumbling girl along.

They fell into a fetid bog, stagnant water swallowing them to Karen's waist. Karen gasped from the crushing cold but knew stopping brought death. She lifted Apsara up to keep her head above the filth. They thrashed onward through the slime until reaching firm ground again.

The putrid smell of the swamp still flooded Karen's nose. Or was that smoke? Ahead, the trees were strangely aglow. Soldiers must have circled around and set the jungle alight. Smoke from the damp foliage would force them into the open.

Karen veered sharply left, ignoring Apsara's exhausted whimpers. As they crossed a stream, the current nearly swept the girl away before Karen seized her collar. She hoisted Apsara onto her back, feeling the small body shivering uncontrollably.

"Be brave, I've got you!" Karen panted, though her

own legs were jelly. She fixed her eyes on the jungle ahead, silently repeating her vow - no one else dies today. We are getting out of this alive!

The sounds of pursuit were fading, but Karen didn't dare stop. She tuned out all pain and fatigue, focusing only on each next step carrying them closer to safety...and farther from the hell engulfing their refuge.

Onward through dense wilderness they pushed, the vines and brambles oblivious to their desperation. But while breath remained, Karen's determination could not falter. Salvation lay ahead somewhere. She would find it or die trying.

Exhaustion finally overwhelmed Karen. She stumbled to her knees, legs caving beneath her. Little Apsara tried tugging her onward, but Karen could not summon another step. Moments later, soldiers emerged from the foliage, weapons raised triumphantly.

"Please, she's just a child!" Karen pleaded as they wrenched Apsara away. But the soldiers dragged Karen forcibly to her feet, binding her wrists. They had run straight into the trap.

Back at the village, more soldiers awaited with the terrified group. Karen scanned the villagers' faces desperately until she spotted Apsara tucked behind a mother and her children. Their eyes met briefly in farewell before a soldier pulled Karen away.

She was shoved to her knees before the rebel commander, who studied her intently. He barked questions in Khmer and then French, growing frustrated. Finally, he noticed her AP press badge.

"You...journalist? American?" His eyes narrowed. Turning, he instructed his men in Khmer, "Take her to the district base. Our leader will know what to do with this spy."

Karen wanted to beg the commander to have mercy on the villagers, but knew it was futile. As she was dragged away, she said a silent prayer over her shoulder. Apsara was safe with a caring family, she had seen it. Now Karen prayed for the courage to withstand what was to come.

The Khmer Rouge's presence so far east in Cambodia was ominous. With the Cambodian military having abandoned the border zones to avoid conflict between North Vietnamese and South Vietnamese forces, the communist insurgents were exploiting the power vacuum. Entire villages were being overrun as they expanded their ruthless vision inland. Now they had added Karen to the enemies in their grasp.

For three days she was dragged through dense jungle, given barely food or water. Her hands remained bound, skin chafing raw against the ropes. Mosquitos assaulted her each night, too exhausted to even swat them away.

She knew the Khmer Rouge's reputation for cruelty. But she would not break, whatever they did to her. She would survive this ordeal, escape someday, and expose their atrocities. Light always overcomes darkness...she clung fiercely to this truth as the base loomed ahead.

Finally, the soldiers brought her to a makeshift camp carved out from the living jungle. Karen was thrown in a cramped bamboo cage, left for hours in the blazing sun. Throat parched, she dreamed of the mountain springs of her youth.

When eventually fetched, Karen was hauled weakly before the commander. He casually ate roast pork and drank wine, regarding her with amusement. "The great American journalist, reduced to this. I offer you only what you tried denying my countrymen."

Warily she accepted morsels of food and sips of wine, nearly weeping in relief. But she remained silent, sensing his intent. After eating ravenously, she met his gaze. "I only wished to show the innocents' suffering."

The commander leaned back. "Ah, so the mute speaks! And in an American accent..." He smiled coldly. "Your people continue bombing my country claiming self-defense. Yet you attack civilians like cowards."

Karen bit her tongue, knowing indignance could mean death.

"My superiors will contact America soon," he continued. "Your life depends on their retreat. Be grateful you may serve the revolution in some small way before the end."

Karen suppressed a shudder at his veiled threat. She would endure this with courage, find some way to smuggle the truth out. Apsara's smiling face flashed in her mind, renewing Karen's fortitude. She would live to see the girl again. If she was to survive, she had to cling to that hope.

The Mole

Phoenix Training Outpost - South Vietnam

The training outpost was situated in a small clearing within the dense jungle, ringed by towering trees draped in vines. A perimeter of sandbags and concentina wire encircled the modest camp, which consisted of about a dozen green military tents clustered together. Several concrete bunkers were also dug into the ground around the perimeter, providing reinforced shelter and firing positions during attacks.

The tents housed sleeping quarters, a mess area, an armory, and a few basic offices for strategizing and intelligence work. At the center of the outpost stood a weathered wooden platform used for training the recruits. The red earth was packed hard by the bootsteps of soldiers over many years of this site's use.

Just short of the wire perimeter, foxholes and machine gun nests were strategically placed within the camp, ready to repel any enemy assault. The air was always heavy with humidity, the songbirds and insect chatter providing a constant jungle soundtrack. Supply helicopters periodically landed on a cleared patch to deliver food, weapons, and ammunition.

The men tried to make the rugged outpost as livable as possible, but the underlying atmosphere of danger never fully lifted. They were deep in the jungle, isolated and vulnerable. Constant vigilance was key to survival.

In the operations bunker, Granier wiped away the sheen of sweat beading on his brow and leaned closer to scrutinize the stack of personnel files on his desk, searching for any clues that could help expose the mole Harmon suspected was lurking amongst the new recruits.

Too many good men had lost their lives over the last few weeks, and the leaked intelligence pointed to someone on the inside. Granier knew he needed to uncover the source before the body count rose any higher. His instincts, honed from countless battles and years navigating the shadowy world of espionage, were on high alert.

Granier's piercing gaze settled on the sparse file of Nguyen Dao, one of his most experienced recruits. After a moment's consideration, he slid the folder from the stack and flicked it open, fingers sifting through the handful of documents inside. Date of birth, place of origin - nothing overtly suspicious jumped out at him. But Granier's gut said to dig deeper. In his experience, enemies often hid behind unassuming facades.

The oppressive humidity had his olive drab cotton shirt clinging uncomfortably to his skin, dark half-moons blooming under the arms. Granier barely noticed the physical discomfort, too consumed with studying each document intently, searching for any wisp of a clue. Men's lives hung precariously in the balance, all dependent on him finding the thread that could unravel the web of deception.

Taking in all he had read, Granier moved to the aging field radio set up on a folding table in the corner. The faint hiss and pop of the open mic provided ideal cover as he established a secure connection. Even here, far from the forward operating bases, one could never be too cautious about keeping transmissions under wraps. Careless words carried consequences out in the bush.

Granier dialed in a frequency rarely used. "Harpy, this is Cobra, do you copy, over," Granier spoke into the handset, his baritone voice made gruffer by the day's exertions. A few seconds of static hiss followed before a voice replied.

"Cobra, this is Harpy, over."

On the other end of the tenuous connection sat Dinh Hoai Thieu, a comrade in arms from the early days of the Vietnam War who now worked counterintelligence back at headquarters in Saigon. Granier could practically see Thieu sitting there in his cramped, smoke-filled office, surrounded by mounds of reports and maps marked up with the latest incident locations. A bowl of hard candy always within reach.

They exchanged coded pleasantries, performing the requisite ritual to confirm identities before any sensitive intel could be shared openly. Granier didn't have patience for excessive cloak and dagger pretense, but he understood the need for certain precautions.

After the greetings were finally dispensed with, Granier got down to business. "I need anything you can dig up on a new recruit by the name of Minh Van Dao, originally out of Hue. The father's deceased, details unknown." He listened to the popping static for a few moments while awaiting a response.

"I'll shake the bushes and see what crawls out," came Thieu's eventual reply, his voice somewhat garbled by intermittent interference. "Anything particular you're looking for in this recruit's history?"

Granier's eyes narrowed, his gaze focused into the middle distance. "Anything off-color. Family trouble, associations with undesirables. The more light you can shine on his past, the better."

There were sounds of scribbling and the flick of a lighter on the other end of the line. "Consider it done," Thieu assured him around the cigarette now dangling from his lips. "Ten packs of Lucky Strikes."

"It was only six last time."

"Times are tough. I smoke more."

"Ten packs then."

"I'll radio back when I've got something."

Satisfied by his colleague's confidence, Granier gave a gruff word of thanks before terminating the connection. Now came the part he hated most - the waiting game. He hoped Thieu's report would provide the leads he needed to expose the mole and stop the bleeding. In the meantime, he could only grind his teeth and continue running down what meager leads he had.

The next morning, Granier entered the intelligence bunker an hour before dawn, hoping to intercept any early check-ins from Saigon. He had slept poorly, his dreams haunted by visions of shadowy figures passing coded missives and whispered orders for ambushes. The enemy within was proving difficult to smoke out, but Granier wasn't about to let up the pressure. Too much depended on uncovering the truth.

As the first hints of orange sunrise lightened the sky outside, the radio set suddenly crackled to life. Granier lunged to retrieve the handset. "Go ahead, Harpy."

Through a wash of static came Thieu's voice, surprisingly clear at this early hour. "Got that intel you requested on your man Dao. Born in Hue, 1938. Father's name was Nguyen Quang Dao, served in some administrative paper-pushing position for the French forces during the Indochina War."

Thieu paused for effect before continuing. "Now this is where it gets interesting. Back in '49, the elder Dao was accused of passing information to the Viet Minh resistance. Got himself arrested and tossed in a detention center for questioning."

Granier's grip on the handset tightened, his knuckles going white. This was far from the benign history he had expected from his protege.

Oblivious to his friend's reaction, Thieu pressed on. "Old man Dao never admitted to the charges, of course. Kept proclaiming his innocence right up until his death during interrogation in French custody. Left behind the wife and a young son, maybe around eight years old at the time."

"How exactly did he die?" Granier interjected sharply, his mind racing.

"It was conveniently classified as death by suicide," came Thieu's sober reply. "But those French garrison boys had ways of...hurrying the questioning process along, if you catch my meaning. The official records say it was hanging, but there are some who reported he was worked over pretty good in the hours prior."

Granier's jaw tightened, the muscles pulsing as he processed this. The sins of the father now painted the son in a far different light. A man who grew up with that kind of legacy, under the shadow of dishonor and betrayal, could easily harbor deep resentments that festered over time. It was the perfect breeding ground for deceit and treachery to take root. Try as he might to see the best in recruits like Dao, Granier's instincts told him that the past could rarely be outrun or forgotten.

"Anything else come up in your digging that could prove useful?" Granier asked after a pause, daring to hope for more puzzle pieces he could fit together.

"Afraid not," Thieu replied apologetically, the line crackling as he exhaled a drag from his cigarette. "Once the French pulled out and we took over operations, records get spotty. Could've tried tracking down the mother or other relatives, but that would've taken more time than you've got. This is all I could piece together for now."

Disappointment and frustration warred within Granier. But he realized Thieu was likely right - more elaborate avenues of investigation would take time they didn't have. "I understand," he acknowledged gruffly. "You've given me context. I'll take things from here."

After signing off, Granier slowly set down the handset and leaned back in his well-worn chair. The groaning wooden frame protested his considerable bulk. Granier sat brooding. This changed everything. Granier didn't know how exactly, but he knew the truth about the young recruit Dao was more complicated and dangerous than any had realized.

Rising decisively from his chair, Granier strode for the doorway. There was one man on this base who might hold additional keys to unlocking Dao's past. And it was high time they had a very serious talk.

Harmon looked up from the action reports he was reviewing outside the mess tent, sensing a change in the mood before he even saw the source. Soldiers milling about shifted their gazes warily as Granier came marching across the compound, making a beeline straight for Harmon.

"We need to talk now... in private," Granier growled without preamble.

"Sure," said Harmon getting up and following Granier to the closest bunker.

Entering, Granier ordered those inside to leave without explanation. They did so. Granier turned to Harmon and said, "You knew."

Deciding not to play games, Harmon responded, "I suspected."

"Two of my men died. Your information could have prevented that."

"No. We can't go around accusing recruits of treason until we are absolutely sure. I wasn't sure. I'm still not."

Granier eyed Harmon knowing he was right. "So, what do you know?"

Harmon considered how much to reveal before responding, "Dao's father was accused by a Vietnamese colonel. Some say he was corrupt and Dao's father stuck his nose where he shouldn't. The rest was easy. Subjects die all the time in interrogation, especially if they don't give the answer their inquisitors want. I'm sure the official story is...incomplete, shall we say. Many who served the French regime met dark fates when their power faded."

Granier considered for a moment, then said, "I still believe we must judge young Dao by his own merits, not outdated accusations against his father."

"Outdated?" Harmon exploded, his face flushing angrily. "Dao was barely eight years old! You think a son simply forgets a thing like that? Or maybe you just don't care, so long as he fills one more slot in your ranks. Never mind where he came from or what he might really be after, eh? Just make those recruitment numbers at any cost!"

The unfair accusations struck a nerve, as Harmon had intended. Granier straightened, feeling his own anger spark. "You go too far, Harmon," he replied icily. "I understand you're under strain, but your insubordination toes the line."

"My duty is to the integrity of our military," Harmon shot back venomously. His hands had curled into tight fists at his sides. "But by all means, let's continue coddling this viper I've brought to your attention, rather than taking prudent precautions. And by the way, I don't need your permission. Like you, my orders come directly from Director Komer."

The two men stared each other down as the tension in the small room reached a dangerous boiling point. Granier considered his next words carefully. Losing his own temper would only exacerbate the issue at hand.

"This is getting us nowhere. I say we question Dao," said Granier.

"If I question him, he'll know we're on to him. I'm not sure that's wise at this point," said Harmon calming down.

"Dao has a right to respond to these accusations. It's only fair."

"We're not in the fair business. But alright. Maybe we can smoke him out and get a confession."

"I wouldn't be so sure of that."

"I'm not sure of anything. But I follow my gut and my gut says the kid's a traitor."

"I want to be part of the interview."

"No."

"Why not?"

"You're the kid's commander. He's going to act different with you there."

"How will I know you're being fair?"

"It's not your call. It's my call. 'Sides, I'm not a heartless idiot. I know what it means if I accuse your man of being a traitor."

"They'll hang him."

"Maybe. At the very least, he'll be court-martialed and spend the rest of the war in the brig."

"Alright. You question him alone."

"Again, my call, not yours."

With obvious reluctance, Granier offered a rigid nod. The matter was settled for the moment, though the mood remained strained. Watching Granier leave the bunker, Harmon sank down heavily into his chair. He removed his glasses, rubbing at the headache building behind his eyes. Something told him this issue was far from put to rest. But he could only deal with one firestorm at a time in this endless goddamned jungle.

As humid dusk settled over the compound that evening, there was a tentative knock at the door of Harmon's bunker. "Come," he beckoned, setting aside the intelligence reports he'd been reviewing.

Dao entered through the doorway and stood at stiff attention, his youthful features set in a mask of stoic calm. But Harmon could detect a subtle unease in the faint sheen of sweat on Dao's smooth brow, the tightness around his dark eyes. Being summoned here alone at end of day could not be a good omen.

"At ease," Harmon invited gently, attempting to set the young man more at his comfort. "Have a seat." He gestured to the simple wooden chair across from his desk. Dao hesitated briefly before acquiescing, folding himself down into the offered seat. He sat with his back ramrod straight, not leaning against the hard slats. Harmon studied him for a long moment, considering his words carefully. He needed to get to the heart of matters, but with tact.

"I'll get right to the point, son. It was recently brought to my attention that there are some...gaps regarding your father's history and service." Harmon watched Dao closely for any reaction as he continued. "The details remain unclear, but sources indicate there may have been some accusations of unauthorized ties with the Viet Minh resistance prior to his death."

Harmon let that sink in before pressing gently. "I know this is difficult subject matter, but I must ask if you have any personal knowledge about those events. We need to fully understand the context."

Dao stared down at the rough-hewn wood surface of the desk, his shoulders tense. When he responded, his voice was strained but steady. "Very little, I'm afraid. I was quite young when my father passed away. And my mother refused to speak of him afterwards."

He raised his eyes to meet Harmon's, his gaze unwavering. "I cannot speak authoritatively about whatever circumstances or accusations may have surrounded his death. There was...much confusion, during those times of transition."

Studying his face, Harmon saw no obvious deceit, just a reserved grief welling beneath the surface. Sons were not always privy to the deeds and secrets of fathers. He was inclined to take the boy at his word, but needed definitive proof of guilt or innocence. There was much at stake. The interrogation continued as Harmon leaned forward intently. "So, you have no inkling of his dealings with the Viet Minh or the nature of his death?"

Looking up, Dao held his piercing gaze. "As I said, my mother refused to speak of him afterwards. The past was too painful for her."

"And yet these recent events have created questions of loyalty and reopened old wounds," Harmon pressed. "Wounds that fester can poison even the most honorable men."

Harmon could see Dao's jaw clench. "I serve only my country. My father's legacy does not sway that duty."

Harmon stood abruptly and leaned in to Dao. "Doesn't it? Can we ever truly escape the shadows of our past? What was done to your father demands justice, does it not?"

Dao paled, but his voice was steady. "Justice is not mine to mete out. I seek only to serve with honor."

"Even if it means serving those complicit in crimes against your family?" Harmon slammed his hands down on the desk. "Where does your honor lie then?"

Dao recoiled, distress cracking through his calm facade. "I..." For a moment he wrestled inwardly before collecting himself. "The past holds much we wish we could change," he said slowly. "But we must look ahead. Or risk being blindsided by fresh dangers."

His dark eyes spoke volumes in the heavy silence. Harmon eased back, considering the unspoken plea. Perhaps he had pushed hard enough for today. What mattered now was ensuring those sentiments aligned with deeds, past and future.

"I admire your fortitude in the face of difficult memories," Harmon said finally, gently. "A man's heart is his own. But do what's right, son. For yourself, and for your country."

Dao's relief was palpable as Harmon dismissed him. But rattling cages often had consequences, intended or not. A minute later, Granier entered. "Well?" he demanded without preamble. "What did Dao say?"

"Only what I expected - that his memories of that time are vague at best. I can hardly blame the boy for his family's silences. But still, there is something about him…"

"What the hell does that mean?"

"That we keep digging until we're sure, one way or the other."

"That could take too long. I need to take these men into the field. It's the only sure way they will learn and the program needs them."

"Then do so. But keep an eye on Dao."

An unspoken tension permeated the compound. Rumors of what was said during the interrogation had spread through the camp like wildfire, skewed and adjusted with each telling until a dozen conflicting stories circulated as supposed fact. Soldiers darted quick, assessing glances at Dao when they thought he wasn't looking, the only evidence of his guilt an interview with Harmon and Granier more grumpy than usual.

Dao himself behaved impeccably, speaking when spoken to and attending to his duties with stoic discipline, as though no shadow now marred his service.

Granier suspected the young man could feel the weight of suspicion and mistrust settling upon him like some unseen burden bowed between his shoulders. The hounds now had the scent though, and Granier knew they would not rest until the whole matter was settled one way or another. Granier knew they needed drastic action to determine the recruit's true loyalties.

He found Harmon reviewing reconnaissance photos in his tent. The air was thick with humidity, the canvas walls damp to the touch. "I have a plan to expose whether Dao can be trusted," Granier said without preamble.

"Yeah. What's that?" said Harmon.

"I'll take him into the field, use myself as bait to gauge his reactions."

Harmon shook his head firmly, brows knitted together. "Too dangerous. I cannot sanction such a high-risk operation."

"It's the only way to know if he'll break under pressure. I'm going, with or without your approval."

Swearing under his breath, Harmon scrubbed a hand over his unshaven face. Dark circles ringed his eyes from too many sleepless nights. "Dammit, Granier. You're bullheaded. At least take Lt. Baird as backup."

"No. Any whiff of a set up and Dao will bolt." Granier checked his sidearm's magazine with a satisfying click. "This needs settling once and for all."

At dusk, the air still clung with moist heat. Granier and Dao carrying packs and sniper rifles slipped past the camp sentries, boots sinking into the muddy earth. "When are you gonna brief me on what we're doing?" said Dao.

"Right about now," said Granier as they entered the jungle. "I have orders from Saigon to eliminate a Viet Cong collaborator in a nearby village."

"Why wasn't I briefed before we left camp?"

"Couldn't risk any leaks with a possible mole about," Granier replied gruffly, swatting at the whining mosquitos.

"So, why isn't the whole group going?" Dao asked.

"Your fellow recruits need an attitude adjustment. This is my way of slapping them upside the head. 'Sides, this is a two-man job. I want to move fast."

They pushed deeper into the tangled vegetation, leaves and vines clawing at their uniforms. Their breaths came hard in the soupy air. After forty tense minutes, Dao broke the silence. "How will we recognize this collaborator?"

Granier withdrew a crumpled photo from his pocket, the image bleached by humidity and sunlight. "That's him. Phan Van Toan. Runs black market goods and intelligence for Charlie."

Dao studied the grainy image. "And you're certain he's in this village we're headed to?"

Granier nodded tersely. "Solid intel. We'll surveil first to confirm his location. If you get a clean shot, take it. No heroics necessary."

"This seems rushed. I don't like it."

"No one asked you. Sometimes it's best just to keep your mouth shut and obey orders. This is one of those times."

They continued their hazardous trek into the night. In the long intervals of tense silence, Granier spoke in a low voice about growing up in France with his grandfather. Dao wasn't fooled and said, "If you have a question about my childhood, just ask it."

"Alright. Were you close to your father?"

"I suppose. When he was around. He worked long hours."

"Pushing paper?"

"Collecting intel. He was in counterintelligence."

"That's not what his record says."

"Personnel profiles don't always tell the whole story, especially for a spy."

"Fair enough. How come you never mentioned it in our interview?"

"Do you trust spies?"

"I am a spy and so are you."

"You make my point."

"Settle down there, Bucko. I'm still your boss."

"I don't mean any disrespect. We're trained to lie. It's an art."

"Okay. But we don't lie to each other."

"Now who's being naïve?"

"Did you lie to Harmon?"

"No. But I only told him what I needed to tell him."

"Deceit?"

"Convenient silence."

"Spoken like a true spy."

"Don't get me wrong. I'm a patriot. But even a patriot knows when to keep silent. There are things that some people will never understand. Those things don't make me a bad guy. All I ask is to be judged by my deeds, not suspicions and rumors."

"I agree with that. But just know, if you hold yourself to such a high standard and you misstep the hammer comes down. Fair?"

"Fair."

They hiked on in silence. Granier wasn't done probing. The truth would protect or condemn Dao.

They each had enough to chew on for the moment.

Reaching the outskirts of the village at midnight, they took up positions overlooking what was believed to be the collaborator's headquarters - a sprawling brick dwelling, its perimeter guarded by silent VC sentries. Dao shifted nervously atop the soggy carpet of decaying leaves. "Never killed a man in cold blood before," Dao admitted with a whisper. "It's always been in battle and they were shooting back."

Granier kept scanning the compound through his rifle's scope, alert for any activity. "In war, lines blur between right and wrong. You just do your duty and leave the decisions and consequences to others more informed."

Sighting their target through a well-lit window, Granier pointed to the collaborator and whispered, "He's your kill."

Dao nodded, shored up his rifle, and aimed. Dao hesitated for a long moment... "Is there a problem?" whispered Granier.

"There's no honor in executing a man like this," Dao whispered back.

"Do your duty, recruit," said Granier firmly.

Before Dao could respond, VC exploded from camouflaged spider holes around them. Granier grappled with a wiry insurgent whose black pajamas blended with the night. A rifle stock crashed against his temple, plunging him into darkness. Through the pain and blood hazing his vision, he glimpsed Dao slip away untouched into the darkness. A bitter realization crystallized in his fading thoughts - it had all been an elaborate trap.

Before Dao could respond, VC erupted from camouflaged holes surrounding them. In the chaos,

Granier grappled with a wiry insurgent. As they wrestled for the rifle, another insurgent clubbed Granier from behind.

Vision swimming, Granier saw several VC wrestling a ferociously fighting Dao. The recruit drove an elbow into one man's throat then smashed the butt of his rifle into another's face, breaking free for a moment.

"Run!" Granier choked out before a boot stamped the air from his lungs. Dao swept his rifle butt at another man rushing him, then turned and sprinted into the dark foliage.

Relief flooded Granier as Dao escaped. Then his world went dark.

Granier emerged from unconsciousness sometime later, head throbbing. He found himself bound to a chair inside a dingy hut, the air thick with mold and sweat. The collaborator from the photo stood before him, his silk shirt sharply creased.

"You Yankees are so predictable. You think you control everything. I assure you, you do not," Toan chuckled. "Your secrets are ours."

"You're a traitor and you're gonna die," said Granier.

Granier grunted as a rifle butt smashed into his jaw. Toan grabbed a handful of Granier's sweat-slicked hair, wrenching his head back. "Bravery means nothing when you're already dead."

"Get on with it. I'd rather die than hear you drone on."

Another blow to the head with a rifle butt and darkness claimed Granier again.

Granier drifted in and out of consciousness. Suddenly, bursts of automatic rifle fire and screams jarred him alert. Through the battered hut wall, he glimpsed shadowy struggles. A guard was hurled violently against the wooden door, collapsing it inwards.

Silhouetted in the doorway stood Dao, chest heaving and uniform torn, an AK-47 gripped tightly in his hands. "Stay quiet, I'm getting you out," Dao said, stepping over the guard's motionless body, cutting Granier's bonds with his knife.

"Can you walk?" Dao asked urgently, pulling Granier to his feet. Granier stumbled, his legs like jelly, his vision fogged.

Supporting his weight, Dao guided them outside. In the dirt, two more guards lay unmoving, bullet holes marring their black pajamas. The compound beyond was strangely deserted.

"I figure we have a couple of minutes head start before reinforcements arrive. We've got to make the most of it," Dao explained between ragged breaths as they limped across the open ground. "Hang in there. You can rest once we get deeper into the jungle."

"Don't worry about me. Just keep moving," said Granier groggy.

The compound was eerily still and empty, scattered grass mats flapping in the breeze. Reaching a gap in the perimeter fence, Dao hoisted Granier's weight across his shoulders and plunged into the jungle.

Behind them, outraged shouts in Vietnamese signaled their escape's detection. Gunfire tore through the canopy as they scrambled desperately through the dark tangle of vines and leaves.

A platoon of VC was crashing recklessly after them. Dao's young face was locked in resolve as he half-dragged Granier onward. Granier clung to consciousness purely through force of will.

Up ahead, the muddy river's shoreline beckoned tantalizingly. But suddenly Granier was ripped away from Dao's arm, a brawny VC soldier tackling him down. Granier thrashed violently as his captor leveled a pistol. Dao was busy firing at the other soldiers approaching. Granier knew he was on his own, his mind still unclear. His instincts took over. Granier kicked as hard as he was able, connecting with the VC's knee, breaking bone, bending it backward. The soldier screamed in pain, dropping his pistol. Granier grabbed it and fired, his target a blur. The soldier went limp. Dao grabbed Granier lifting him once again, "We got to move."

Granier did his best to help him, supporting his own weight as they ran deeper into the jungle. but couldn't focus his eyes, the jungle a green and black gauze. Dao firing at the enemy chasing them, his rifle clicking empty. He threw it away, lightening his load. Granier fumbled the pistol taken from the fallen VC soldier and pressed it into Dao's hand. "Few rounds left," he slurred through the blood pounding in his skull.

Dao took the pistol with a grim nod. "I'll make them count."

They staggered on through the tangled undergrowth. Dao helped Granier over a gully, just as two VC soldiers crashed through the bushes ahead, rifles leveled. Dao fired twice, dropping them both before they could shoot.

"Nice...shooting..." Granier gasped as they clambered over the fresh bodies. They both grabbed the fallen soldiers' weapons. Granier could tell Dao was tiring from half-carrying his weight, but the young man's eyes remained hard with fortitude.

The jungle thinned ahead and Granier smelled water - the river. Sanctuary lay just across the muddy bank. With the last of his strength, he shoved Dao forward just as bullets ripped through the space they'd just occupied.

"Go...I'll draw them off..." Granier rasped, fumbling for his weapon. He knew he wouldn't make it far, but maybe could buy Dao precious time to escape back to their lines.

Dao grabbed his arm fiercely. "We cross together or not at all!" Before Granier could argue, Dao was dragging him towards the swirling dark river looming ahead. Shouts sounded behind them, almost upon them.

A rifle scope crosshairs targeted Dao, then switched to Granier as they approached the river. The unseen sniper was in front of them, not behind. The gun slowly squeezed the trigger.

Granier stumbled, falling to his knees just as rifle shot sound from across the river. A bullet whizzed past where he was just was, missing his head by inches. "Sniper," said Granier pushing Dao to the ground near a pile of river rocks. Dao scrambled behind the rocks. Granier found cover behind a fallen log a few feet away. Another sniper's bullet tore into the wood above Granier splintering it.

Dao turned back toward the enemy following them, now appearing fifty feet back through the jungle. He fired driving them to cover. Granier peeked above the log for a brief moment, then back down as another shot splintered the log.

"Did you see anything?" said Dao.

"No," said Granier. "You?"

"Nothing. Not a good situation."

"No. Not good. I'll going to roll out from cover. When he fires, you kill him."

"That's a lousy plan."

"It's the only one I got. Ready?"

"Hang on," said Dao firing down the trail to keep their pursuers' heads down. "Ready."

The sniper glassed Granier as he rolled from behind the log into the open. The sniper's crosshairs centered on Granier's face. It was an easy shot. A shot fired. The Sniper's face grimaced. He was hit… in the back. He slumped, dead.

"Nice shot," said Granier, grateful to still be alive.

"It wasn't me," said Dao bewildered.

Across the river, Harmon, holding his own sniper rifle rose from his hidden spot and ejected a cartridge from the rifle's chamber. He trotted over to check on the dead sniper and rolled him over to reveal Sgt. Tam, the training camps radio operator. After a brief moment, Harmon raised his rifle and fired at the communists chasing Granier and Dao.

Seeing their opportunity, Granier and Dao headed down the slope and entered the river. The water was moving fast making the trek across treacherous.

Reaching the other side, Dao looked down at Sgt. Tam's corpse and said, "I don't understand."

"The mole," said Granier.

Harmon fired another shot forcing the emboldened enemy down once more. "We need to move."

"I'll take point," said Dao starting down the trail back to their camp.

"I'll keep 'em busy," said Granier leveling his rifle behind.

"Not this time. Go," said Harmon. "Head for our camp."

Granier was going to argue, but then thought better of it, his eyesight still not completely recovered, his head still spinning. He followed Dao. Harmon fired two more shots then followed Granier. Running through the trees and underbrush, they made good time closing on the training camp.

The VC chased after them, stopping every few hundred feet to fire their weapons at the fleeing trio.

Granier and Dao entered a clearing, Harmon followed a few moments later. They headed across, no cover in sight.

The VC came to the edge of the clearing and fired.

Harmon was hit in the leg and crashed to the ground. Dao and Granier turned back, picked him up, and carried Harmon placing his arms around their shoulders.

The VC closed on them quickly, firing as they crossed the clearing.

The trio reached the opposite side. The treeline erupted in a barrage of shots from sniper rifles. VC dropped like rocks.

Entering the jungle on the opposite side of the clearing, Granier saw his other recruits each firing their sniper rifles, taking down the VC. A minute later, it was over. The VC had grabbed their wounded and dead, then retreated the way they came. The recruits were glad to see their instructor still alive.

In the newfound silence, Granier and his team exchanged resolute nods, their bond solidified in battle. Without grand words or sweeping gestures, they moved together as one, vanishing into the jungle's embrace.

Khmer Rouge Jungle Camp, Cambodia

Karen awoke to the familiar ache of hollow hunger. How long had passed in this lightless cage? Days blurred together marked only by cruelty. Karen's body was withered, spirit wavering. Each passing hour felt heavier knowing her adopted kin likely suffered similar fates, or worse. She yearned to hold Apsara close again.

Stubborn as always, Karen refused to let hope flicker out. She passed long empty hours picturing the peaceful village revived, children playing freely. She etched each beloved face in memory, drawing strength. Giving up now would betray them, she repeated doggedly to herself.

Early one morning, Karen was jolted awake to explosions rattling her cage violently. Distant rumbles had swiftly crescendoed into a barrage rocking the camp as American B52s flew overhead at 30,000 feet dropping their payloads.

Bombs unleashed their lethal cargo in fiery arcs, huts and trees erupting into swirling flame and smoke. Tents blown into pieces, hurling shreds of burning canvas. Flaming trails streaked through the jungle canopy, the world coming apart around her. Karen braced herself as shockwaves buffeted the cage. She could feel the heat singeing her skin even from dozens of yards away.

She wondered if a bomb would snuff out her life in a brief moment of pain and if that was better than the cruel death the Khmer Rouge would give her now that the Americans had killed more of their comrades.

Through the bamboo bars, Karen could see soldiers desperately firing rifles skyward, but their pathetic resistance seemed to only enrage the metal beasts further as more bombs exploded. Karen glimpsed the commander's headquarters explode in a direct hit, the force nearly lifting her own cage from the ground. As the smoke and dust cleared, only a crater and scattered body parts remained. She hoped the commander was somewhere in the gore. Scared out of her wits and crazed from starvation, Karen laughed at the Khmer Rouge receiving their just rewards.

In the fiery maelstrom Karen knew her life hung by a thread. She stopped laughing and curled into a ball, praying as wooden shards and dirt pelted her. A direct hit nearby hurled her cage through the air like a discarded rag doll. Karen cried out as she slammed back to earth, the wind knocked from her lungs.

She was surprised when no guards came to check on her. They were too busy saving their own skins to worry about the duplicitous American. The acrid smoke burned Karen's lungs as she warily uncurled from her shattered cage. The bombs had granted her salvation, if she dared seize it. She climbed out cautiously and slowly walked away from her prison, her legs unsure.

Through the haze she witnessed bombed out huts - papers and furniture ablaze. Bodies lay strewn about in pieces, a hand there, a leg still wearing a boot dozens of yards away. Karen suppressed a gag, creeping haltingly through the hellscape.

Reaching the edge of camp she spotted a dead soldier, guts spilled out. With apologies she took the man's rifle, then slipped into the surrounding jungle. Behind her shouts of pain and confusion, but Karen pushed herself forward vanishing into the green maze.

Heart hammering, she expected any moment to hear her name or a rifle crack. Gasping, Karen struggled forward until the sounds faded behind her.

When she finally collapsed in darkness, phantom explosions still thundered in her mind. Though scorched, hope yet survived. Weak and exhausted, she could no longer keep her eyes open and fell asleep.

At dawn, Karen woke and surveyed the surrounding jungle. Somewhere hidden lay the evidence - her film, record of this tragedy. She set off toward the vacant village, driven by duty not yet fulfilled.

Karen moved swiftly under nightfall's cloak, pausing only for dirty pools of rainwater to quench her parched throat.

As pale dawn crept over the horizon, Karen risked stopping to forage for edible plants and herbs. The meager morsels barely dulled her hunger pangs but provided scarce sustenance.

Landmarks began appearing familiar—the strangler fig tree, crooked bamboo stalks. She was close now. Karen steeled herself for the empty echoes that would resound through homes once alive with laughter and friendship.

When smoke plumes appeared above the trees, Karen halted, her heart pounding with anticipation. Had villagers returned and resettled? Was Apsara with them? Moving closer cautiously, she saw not refuge but a chilling scene.

Khmer Rouge soldiers wandered the dirt paths like ghosts, emerging from dwellings with scavenged goods. Karen's fury overflowed at these intruders pillaging her cherished village. She froze, knuckles white on her rifle. These monsters had no right to befoul her village with their presence. How easy it would be to end them with the rifle she still carried, granting herself some small vengeance amidst the smoldering ruins of her old life.

The Karen who first came to this haven would never have fixated on dealing death. But the jungle had infected her with its savage chaos. No rules or mercy, only vicious survival. If she betrayed all she once stood for, Karen might save a few of the innocent from the Khmer soldiers but would lose herself forever.

This place of refuge called her back from the brink, like an old friend whispering gentle reminders. Karen forced her rigid fingers to relax their grip on the rifle. She would not become another predator haunting the helpless.

Slipping silently past the occupied dwellings, Karen reached the trail she had stumbled down with Apsara in another lifetime. If her compass yet remained here, she could find her way again.

Karen slipped into the thick vegetation bordering the village, retracing hurried steps from what felt another lifetime ago. She was certain she had hidden her camera bag in a crooked tree near the trail.

Scanning the jungle surroundings, a tree up ahead caught her eye. Karen rushed over expectantly and stepping on its gnarled roots to reach its lowest branches. But she found nothing.

Growing uneasy, Karen inspected several nearby trees, plunging her hands into leaf piles and hollows. Still no bag or camera emerged. She forced down panic, trying to focus. Could the Khmer soldiers have found her camera and bag? She knew that there was still enough savage in her that she would kill to recover the film and reveal the truth if necessary.

Karen returned to the original twisted tree, running her hands over its mossy bark. Then down in the leaves piled at its base, her fingers closed around soft leather.

Karen exhaled in dizzying relief as she pulled the camera bag free. Hands trembling, she opened it and there lay her camera and film canisters tucked inside.

She clutched it all to her chest, overjoyed and grief-stricken at once. Here was her lone proof this village existed, that people lived and laughed here. A lone voice to speak from the darkness after all else perished.

Karen thought of the undeveloped film inside, lessons and smiles peering back at her. She kissed the camera through joyful tears.

Her body and spirit drained, Karen sat a long-time bonding silently with the camera that had witnessed what others might too easily forget. When she again moved, Karen felt part of herself left behind - the scarred, feral residue of nightmare jungle and cages. If future light could be kindled somewhere, it began here.

Karen trudged onward through the dense jungle, muscles aching and skin slick with sweat. For days she had navigated by instinct and memory alone, driven by her goal of reaching South Vietnam. The sounds of gunfire and artillery echoing through the hills told her she was nearing the border. With her camera ready, she approached cautiously.

Peering through the brush, Karen saw North Vietnamese troops bombarding Khmer Rouge trenches ahead with mortars and recoilless rifles. Once allies, they now clashed over disputed territory.

She snapped photos of shells exploding around desperate soldiers. The Khmer Rouge returned fire with machine guns and RPGs against the North's infantry charges. Karen's lens captured the faces of young men in combat, displaying both fear and determination. Death was caught in mid-stride, as the fatally wounded fell to the earth.

American F-4 Phantoms screamed overhead, dropping payloads of napalm canisters that skipped and tumbled across the jungle canopy then erupted in great mushroom clouds of flame. Fire spread through the jungle, igniting trees and soldiers alike. The air filled with screams and the sickly-sweet smell of scorched flesh. Karen's eyes watered, but her gaze never wavered through the camera lens.

As she changed positions, Karen had to step over mutilated corpses left steaming in the sun. She paused only to reload her camera, whirring through roll after roll of film.

From the direction of the Cambodian border, advancing US ground troops appeared. Karen was stunned - US forces weren't supposed to be here. Chaos ensued as all three sides exchanged fire, the Americans clearly seeking to smash both opponents in one secretive thrust across the border. She snapped photos winding the film as fast as possible.

After endless days and weeks of searching, Karen could hardly believe she had found it - the untold story she had risked everything for. Adrenaline pumped through her exhausted body as she documented the secret US campaign in Cambodia. This was the photographic proof she needed.

North Vietnamese PT-76 amphibious tanks returned fire alongside infantry armed with AK-47s and RPGs. The air was choked with smoke and the stench of scorched earth and charred bodies.

US helicopters strafed trucks, tanks, and troops with machine guns and rockets. American snipers picked off exposed Khmer Rouge from the tree lines. The North Vietnamese dragged their wounded comrades into banana groves, leaving bloody trails in the dirt.

In a lull, the smell of spent gunpowder hung over scattered corpses left in the aftermath. Karen changed angles, lenses, determined to document the losses on all sides of this hidden conflict. She knew these images would shock the world and illuminate the unvarnished truth of war's cost.

Moving forward in the long grass, Karen risked shots of overwhelmed American medics frantically treating injured soldiers. Spotting Karen, a North Vietnamese soldier took aim and fired, just missing her. She took cover in an irrigation ditch, camera still held steady, documenting the battle.

She snapped shot after shot, following the arc of American bombs as they exploded in plumes of dirt and shrapnel amid North Vietnamese troops. Soldiers' bodies were shredded and flung through the air, their last moments captured in gruesome detail.

Karen's hands trembled, but her focus was razor sharp, peering through the viewfinder to capture every moment. She felt the same passion that had driven her into war journalism now reaching its apex. No one could deny this evidence of overreach and hypocrisy from an American government publicly denying this incursion.

After hours of explosions and gunshots, she saw the targets were demolished, the communist armies in retreat. Under the cover of lingering smoke, Karen escaped east into South Vietnam, collapsing into the arms of stunned ARVN patrol soldiers. She had made it back.

Exhausted and still in her torn and sweat-stained clothes, Karen entered her apartment and smiled. It felt so good. She gazed proudly at the black and white photos on the walls that she loved - images from an accomplished career. Soon she would add more.

She moved into the bathroom, shed her filthy jungle clothing, and turned on the shower water. Nothing. She had not paid the water bill. All she could do was laugh. After a moment, she walked naked into her tiny kitchen and retrieved a large drink water bottle. She took a long pull, then walked back into the bathroom and stepped into the shower. She poured the water over her rinsing away the mud and grime. She soaped up a washcloth and scrubbed. It would take three soapy passes with the washcloth before she felt clean. When she stepped out of the shower, she looked in the mirror. Her face, arms, and legs were covered in mosquito bites, cuts, and more bruises than a two-week-old banana. She didn't care.

Finally clean, she collapsed into bed. Eighteen hours of deep sleep later, she awoke.

Dressed neatly, Karen headed to the AP office.

She entered Quigley's office with the hard-earned contact sheets, ready for her redemption.

Journalists sitting at their decks did a double take as she entered and walked toward the darkroom. The lab technician was waiting for her with contact sheets in his hand. "Has he seen them?" she asked.

"No. And I haven't said a word," said the technician.

"Thanks."

He handed her the contact sheets and said, "They're really amazing."

"I just hope they're in focus."

"They are… mostly."

Karen walked into Quigley's office, his nose deep in

a reporter's story, his red pen marking it up like a football play. "Got a minute?" said Karen.

He looked up and stared slack-jawed, "My God, you're alive."

"Yep."

"Look. I'm glad your safe, but you're fired."

"I know. I just came to get your opinion. It would mean a lot if you'd look at my contact sheets."

Quigley hesitated, then took out his magnifying loupe, "Let me have 'em."

Karen handed him the sheets and he began to examine them. "You know I will still give you a good recommendation. You're an excellent photographer." At first, he seemed unimpressed, then his expression changed to astonishment. "Oh, my God." He moved the glass from photo to photo, each better than the last. "Oh, MY GOD!"

"Wait. Is this a thumb?" He squinted. "Whose thumb is covering the lens?"

"That would be my thumb," Karen replied sheepishly. "Photography isn't easy when you're running from gunfire."

"Right. Of course."

He went on to the next photo, then the next, and so on. "How did you do this without a military escort?"

"I think it was because I didn't have a military escort that I was able to get so far."

"How far did you get?"

"I don't know exactly. I was taken captive by the Khmer Rouge."

"What?!" said Quigley going back over the contact sheets looking for the Khmer Rouge.

"You won't find them. I had to hide my film and camera before they took me. I didn't want them confiscated."

"Jesus. What did you do?"

"I suffered… a lot."

"But you're here."

"Yeah. I escaped during a bombing raid. I made it back to where I hid my camera and film. I got lucky. They were still there."

"Holy shit," said Quigley, then leaned out the doorway and said, "Dolores, get me Arnett. Tell 'em he's got a story to write. Front page tomorrow."

Quigley turned back to Karen and said, "Unless you want to write it yourself?"

"Me write? No, thank you. I'm sure Peter will do a better job."

"Well, he's got a knack for this sort of thing."

"So, am I still fired?"

"Yes. I can't have my journalists disobeying me. But I am rehiring you as a freelancer effective immediately."

"That's gonna cost you."

"It's okay. You're due a raise. Well done, Karen."

Tears welled up in Karen's eyes. Quigley walked over and hugged her. "It's okay. You're home. You're safe."

She wept uncontrollably as Quigley held her tight.

Vietnamization

White House – Washington DC, USA

Nixon stood scowling out the Oval Office windows, watching a throng of rowdy anti-war protestors beyond the White House gates. Their incessant chanting and sign waving had given him a throbbing headache and soured his mood. "How am I supposed to get anything done with these blasted agitators caterwauling right outside?" Nixon fumed as Secretary of Defense Melvin Laird, briefing book in hand, entered for their morning meeting.

"My apologies for the disruption, Mr. President," Laird offered sympathetically as he took his usual seat on the yellow brocade sofa. "But I believe I may have a solution that takes some wind out of their sails."

Intrigued, Nixon turned from the window and settled on the sofa across from Laird, forgetting his cooling coffee on his desk. "I'm all ears, Mel. What do you have?"

Laird opened his briefcase on the coffee table between them. "I wanted to outline a new strategic concept for facilitating the withdrawal of US forces from Vietnam."

Nixon leaned forward over his desk intently. "Let's hear it."

"Essentially we would shift the burden of combat operations to South Vietnam's military over the next few years through comprehensive training programs and augmented equipment provisions," Laird explained.

"Interesting... What are you calling the program?"

"We're calling it 'Vietnamization' for now, but that's just temporary. I'm sure our boys will find something better as we develop—"

Nixon held up a hand. "No, I like it. Vietnamization....very concise, easy to grasp." He nodded firmly. "That's what we'll call it. The American people can understand Vietnamization."

Laird looked mildly surprised but quickly covered it with a nod. "Yes, Mr. President. Vietnamization it is."

"Go on, Mel. I want to hear everything."

Laird continued explaining, "As South Vietnamese forces gain strength and experience through Vietnamization, they can take over defending their nation's territory while America's direct fighting role decreases."

Nixon stood and began pacing pensively behind the sofa, the presidential seal tracking his movement. "A gradual hand-off strategy...intriguing."

He turned back to Laird. "What timeframe are you proposing for the initial troop withdrawals?"

"If we supply robust support, the first 25,000 could

likely be redeployed within a year or two. Then we'd accelerate—"

Nixon cut him off with an impatient wave. "Not quick enough. The doves and the silent majority demand dramatic action now, not prolonged timetables."

He resumed his seat across from Laird, his expression intense. "I want the first contingent home within months, not years. Ramp up whatever is needed to make that happen."

Laird's eyes widened slightly. "Months is extremely ambitious, Mr. President. There are complex factors in—"

"Then be more ambitious," Nixon insisted, pounding his fist on the back of the sofa for emphasis. Outside, the protestor's chants continued unabated.

Nixon pinned Laird with his gaze. "You know the pressure I'm under here, Mel. It's time to regain control of the narrative. You've got the right strategy. Now make it happen."

Laird drew a deep breath. "Of course, Mr. President. We will accelerate the Vietnamization program as rapidly as possible."

Nixon smiled tightly and extended his hand. "Good. That's what I need to hear."

After Laird's departure, Nixon watched the waving protest signs outside the White House gates. Their theatrics had provoked him into action. But soon, he would steal the thunder on ending this conflict. Careful execution of Laird's Vietnamization approach could pacify the critics and fulfill his own desire to go down in history as the president who extracted America from Vietnam's quagmire.

June 8, 1969 - Midway Island, US Territory

Midway Island was a remote coral atoll in the vast Pacific. As Nixon's helicopter descended toward the naval base, he gazed out at the two sprawling runways that had helped cement Midway's place in WWII history. Now it served as a strategic outpost for America's military presence in Asia.

Nixon needed to talk with the South Vietnamese president, but he didn't want to bring him to the United States where protestors were sure to make a scene and the media would gobble it up like everything sordid that they loved so much. Nixon couldn't afford for Thieu to be distracted by angry mobs of college kids. The protests were a sideshow that garnered far too much attention. The matter they needed to discuss was important and yet Nixon wasn't sure how the president would take it. Midway Island was as remote a location that he could find. And best of all, he could control the media's access to the island.

Upon landing, Nixon was ushered into a nondescript cement building serving as the operational headquarters. Inside, a gloomy conference room had been hastily prepared, the smell of fresh paint lingering in the tropical humidity. Cheap wooden chairs surrounded a rectangular table topped with a plastic cloth. A clattering fan overhead did little to alleviate the stifling heat. Not an ideal ambience for diplomacy, but time was short.

Nixon rose from his peeling chair to greet South Vietnam's President Thieu. Their formal attire looked distinctly out of place in these bleak surroundings. As aides brought lukewarm cups of tea, the gravity of their discussion became palpable.

"Let me be candid," Thieu began solemnly, beads of sweat pooling at his brow. "My people worry any American troop withdrawal signifies abandonment, leaving us vulnerable. We were assured by your predecessor, President Johnson, America would stay committed until the war was won the communists were vanquished."

Nixon nodded thoughtfully. "I understand your concerns, Mr. President. But this phased transition is only possible because of the immense progress training your forces to defend South Vietnam independently."

Thieu still appeared unconvinced. Nixon adopted a reassuring tone. "You'll soon command the strongest military in Southeast Asia, with ongoing American advisory support and accelerated provision of weapons and aid. We are committed to fortifying your self-sufficiency."

"Yet the Viet Cong once again gain ground daily," Thieu countered with an edge of bitterness. "How can we succeed alone?"

Nixon held up a placating hand. "You won't be alone. But after paying an extraordinary price, America longs for a reprieve from combat operations. I know you understand such burdens. This marks a transition to empowering South Vietnam to shape its future stability and prosperity. With all the support we have given you and will continue to give you, you are more than up to this challenge."

Thieu considered before nodding cautiously. "I hope your faith is well-placed. We will shoulder more responsibility but need ongoing partnership. While I am sure the United States does not want to appear to the rest of the free world as abandoning their most important ally, our alliance remains vital to the survival of democracy in Southeast Asia."

"Absolutely, Mr. President. You have my full commitment," Nixon reassured. The first phase was secured.

As Nixon bid his ally farewell, he felt the promise and peril of this remote waypoint shaping history. The course was charted - now steady leadership must follow through on its designs. An alliance hung in the balance, while outside, war machinery roared onward toward ambiguous horizons.

July 20, 1969 – The World and the Moon

It was a hot July evening. A sense of anxious anticipation gripped the nation and the world. Across America, families gathered in living rooms lit only by the glow of their television screens, faces upturned expectantly.

In Houston, engineers held their breath as Neil Armstrong and Buzz Aldrin guided the Lunar Module Eagle toward history.

In a planning room deep below NASA's bustling Houston complex, engineers from around the world took a collective breath as the module touched down intact. "We did it," an Indian programmer whispered reverently.

His Ghanaian colleague clasped his shoulder, "We bent the horizon."

Cheers roared throughout the world. Humanity was united, almost…

Deep in the jungles, Viet Cong comrades huddled in damp hideouts, listening intently to crackling radio dispatches describing humanity's first steps on an alien world. Emotions mixed. Was this a victory for all mankind or just the Americans? What would this mean to the communists' glorious crusade to unify Vietnam and expel the foreign invaders?

In crowded Hanoi buildings, North Vietnamese government officials stared stone-faced at staticky TVs. "This changes things," one general muttered darkly. "The Americans now possess technology beyond imagining."

His companion nodded. "We must redouble efforts to galvanize our people against their imperialist ambitions."

Yet doubts gnawed beneath their stoic communist facade. This staggering show of technological force would reshape global hierarchies in ways still unfathomable.

As the ghostly image of Armstrong climbing down the ladder to the moon's surface flashed globally, rapt viewers from Brooklyn to Bombay felt time itself suspended.

At a joyous Houston house party, a diverse crowd cheered each footfall, reveling in this transcendent human achievement.

In a quiet Ohio suburb, a boy wearing homemade astronaut wings gazed awestruck at his family's new color TV, dreams igniting.

As the crackling broadcast captured Armstrong's first footsteps on powdery lunar soil, he sensed the many eyes tracking this eternal moment. "A giant leap for mankind," he intoned. This achievement transcended borders and politics, binding humanity to shared possibility and vulnerability. All inhaled the ripe potential while gazing back at the orb of life suspended fragile in blackness.

In the Oval Office, President Nixon watched

tensely with his advisors and Pat Nixon. This crowning feat of American innovation and grit vindicated years of national investment and sacrifice. Nixon met the triumphant mood with resolve. "Let the Soviets deal with the stars and stripes on the moon. A victory for American grit and innovation."

Outside the White House, protesters fell into awed silence as they listened on a portable radio, some lowering angry signs. A young woman whispered, "I forgot how much I love this crazy country." For this fleeting moment, anger softened into pride.

Elsewhere, skepticism tempered awe. In Moscow, KGB officers muttered about fabricated Yankee theatrics. "The Americans may be the first, but the Soviets will be the last," said an officer. "We'll take the moon like we take everything else… with strength and force."

In African villages, citizens felt stirrings of inspiration but also unease knowing this expanding technological might would reshape global hierarchies. Would the African people be forgotten?

In a bar in Cheyenne, a group of locals watched the broadcast with skepticism. "It's all staged for the cameras on some Hollywood sound stage," one man muttered derisively. "Just some damned made-up publicity stunt." His friends nodded, taking swigs of beer. "Now they're even faking the moon. More tax dollars wasted."

Inside the Pentagon viewing lounge, top generals and advisors watched the broadcast intently. "Outstanding, we've claimed this ground first," remarked one general. "We need to secure and fortify our lunar assets."

His colleague nodded gravely. "Agreed.

Establishing bases and defensive systems on the moon needs to be a top priority before foreign powers attempt to encroach."

A NASA advisor interjected nervously, "With respect, sirs, space should remain free and peaceful exploration for all nations. Weaponization could provoke instability."

The generals exchanged skeptical looks. "Come now. We'll defend our interests off-world just as at home. We know the Soviets are already plotting to militarize space."

The advisor fell silent, realizing Cold War mentalities already viewed the moon's grey expanse as the next field of conflict. Idealism faltered against harsh political realities.

For a brief moment, most of humanity felt united by both wonder and disquiet. Technology's forward march, visible from every shore, would be neither smooth nor equitable but inexorable.

In Beijing, Chinese leaders watched stone-faced as the stars and stripes staked its claim overhead. "The Americans flaunt their technological arrogance," spat one official. "Planting their flag where no man stood before."

An elder general shook his head. "Do not underestimate their prowess. In time, we too must reach for the heavens."

They sat pensively weighing opportunity and threat. Would space bring humanity together or sow division's seeds upon another barren world? Time would tell if this achievement awakened mankind's best or worst instincts.

In a dugout bunker near Da Nang, a group of battle-weary American soldiers gathered around a crackling field radio, faces tilted upward as it broadcast the moon landing thousands of miles away.

"Hard to imagine all that fancy technology and sterile environments when we're out here eating with the rats and dodging bullets," one man remarked with a hollow laugh, swatting at the humid air.

"Yeah, I'd take a spacesuit over this hellhole any day," another grunted, wiping sweat from his brow.

A third gazed thoughtfully up at the narrow strip of night sky visible through the bunker opening. "Still, must be something to see old Glory planted up there first. At least we got that going for us in this mess."

His comrades nodded, a fleeting sense of wonder penetrating their cynicism. For a brief moment, the miracle unfolding far above Vietnam's blood-soaked jungles helped them forget the trenches and reconnect with hope for the future.

One soldier raised his canteen in a mock toast. "To Armstrong and Aldrin up there living the dream. And to us poor bastards down here slugging it out in the muck." A hint of pride entered his tired voice. "Maybe we'll all make it home soon."

As one flag was planted in the soil, all sensed a threshold crossed, realities shifting under their feet though the vast expanse between Earth and her gray companion remained unbreachable.

September 2, 1969 - Hanoi, North Vietnam

The end came quietly for the iconic leader known to his people as Uncle Ho. In his simple stilt house in Hanoi, the whispers of attending doctors and nurses fell silent as Ho's chest stilled its rise and fall for the final time. A long revolutionary life, devoted with single-minded zeal to the goal of Vietnamese independence and unity, reached its close.

In a dimly lit room inside the Party headquarters, Le Duan received the fateful call informing him of Ho Chi Minh's passing. Replacing the handset slowly, Le stood in solemn silence for a long moment.

Ho had been both mentor and adversary over Le's long rise in the party ranks. Though Le chafed under the legendary elder's moderating influence at times, a grudging respect endured. "So, the old man finally rests," Le murmured. "He was a stubborn counterweight, but also a unifying symbol for the cause."

Le's ambitious instincts sensed opportunity arising from this absence. But privately, he grieved the loss of connection to revolutionary glory days past.

Turning to his assistant, Le said briskly, "Notify all provinces that Uncle Ho has departed this world. Call emergency Party meetings at every level. We must ensure unity and discipline are maintained."

The assistant hesitated. "And... your role, comrade? Will you at last assume your rightful place leading the Party?"

Le waved a hand dismissively. "All in due time. We must observe proper mourning for now." But behind his impassive expression, political calculations churned busily. An era had ended, clearing space for new eras to begin.

News of Ho's passing rippled rapidly through the crowded Hanoi streets. "Our beloved Uncle has left us!" sobbed an elderly woman, comforted by her neighbor. "But his vision must live on in our hearts!"

At a steel factory, laborers wept openly as the superintendent announced the tragic news. "We have lost our father and liberator!" cried one man. "But we shall continue his legacy of defiance!" roared another through angry tears.

In lush jungle hideouts, Viet Cong fighters gathered around crackling radios, their cheering and chanting for evening battle plans transforming into stunned silence. A commander urged firmly, "Dry your eyes and prepare your souls! Tonight we honor Uncle Ho's spirit by striking down his enemies with double fury!"

In the Presidential Palace, North Vietnamese leaders stood somberly before a portrait of the now immortalized revolutionary martyr. "We must amplify his exalted status to spark greater unity and zeal across the people," remarked one official pragmatically. His elder colleague added gravely, "And closely guard his preserve his Marxist vision against dangerous perversions."

Across South Vietnam, under cover of darkness, citizens whispered excitedly of the news drifting down from the North. "The Father of our Nation is gone, but his dream of a unified Vietnam lives on!" an old shopkeeper told his grandsons, all Viet Cong collaborators. "We shall honor him by keeping up the struggle."

In America, President Nixon received confirmation of Ho's death from National Security Advisor Henry Kissinger. "Our most stalwart adversary in Vietnam has exited the stage," Kissinger remarked. "Perhaps this shakes their resolve." But Nixon shook his head grimly, "They will only intensify their efforts to fulfill Ho's vision. We should anticipate increased violence ahead."

The next day's newspapers proclaimed the death of the mysterious Vietnamese leader. Some anti-war protestors fell silent in sober reflection, remembering Ho's long battle against foreign domination. But most Americans felt only relief that this elusive symbol of communist insurgency was finally gone from the stage. A thorn removed, yet the painful conflict lingered on.

The body of the venerable Uncle lay embalmed for all to honor as fighting raged on. Both sides invoking his spirit in the struggle to shape Vietnam's future, bound by the words Ho had spoken as bombs rained down: "Nothing is more precious than freedom and independence."

October 15, 1969 - Boston, Massachusetts, USA

The crisp fall air was electric with defiant energy as thousands of protesters streamed toward Boston Common. Students, professors, clergy, nurses - marchers from all walks of life chanted and brandished signs reading "End the War in Vietnam Now!"

On the Commons, a young man handed pamphlets to new arrivals. "It's time to make our voices heard and our numbers seen!" he shouted passionately. "This unjust war is tearing our country apart!"

Nearby, a college student strummed an acoustic guitar, leading the crowd in songs of peace and unity. An older woman with a weathered face waved a flag with a peace sign, crying out, "I lost a son in Vietnam. Not one more life!"

In other cities across the nation, similar scenes unfolded. In Washington D.C., thousands surrounded the White House waving candles amid solemn choruses of "Give Peace a Chance." In San Francisco, Vietnam veterans in ragged fatigues marched side-by-side with businessmen in wool suits. In Chicago, protesters tussled angrily with helmet-clad police as orders to disperse were ignored.

The defiant masses chanted as one, diverse voices blending together - "No more war! Bring our boys home!" They marched for those already lost, and those whose fates still hung in the balance. For a brief moment, deep divisions were set aside to demand change from a nation their elders had entrusted them to transform for the better.

As evening fell, the impromptu communities dispersed back into their separate lives. But the calls for peace rang out long into the night. Those shining moments would fuel righteous momentum as the movement gained power from its growing numbers. The national conscience was stirring.

November 3, 1969 - White House, Washington DC, USA

A hush fell over the crowded Oval Office as President Nixon prepared to address the nation. Technicians made final adjustments to the hot lights and camera angles, conveying the gravity of this primetime appeal to an anxious populace.

At precisely 9pm, the cameras blinked on, transmitting Nixon's face into millions of homes. He exuded resolve tempered with sincerity. This was a fight for the heart of America itself.

"Good Evening," Nixon began grimly. "I want to talk to you tonight about peace. No issue is more important, or commands greater urgency."

Nixon described wanting nothing more than to end the conflict and bring every soldier home. But a rushed exit would abandon allies to annihilation, tarnish

America's word, and cement a Communist foothold endangering freedom across Asia.

"The more divided we are here at home, the less likely the enemy is to negotiate," Nixon implored. He understood many opposed the war on principle. But undermining vital leverage betrayed both troops abroad and families longing for normalcy.

Then Nixon spoke directly to the Silent Majority he knew supported steadfastness with honor. He heard their unvoiced anguish and determination. Though drowned out by zealous protestors, their spirit would reclaim America's self-confidence.

"To you who believe America should quit this war overnight, I urge you to reconsider your views," Nixon implored. "To simply walk away would demean our Nation and dishonor the sacrifices of too many American soldiers and their families." There was no easy path, but abdicating now would haunt America's conscience for generations.

Nixon's voice took on a tone of grave urgency as he implored, "The more support that you give to the enemy today, the more casualties that you are going to have tomorrow. Let us understand: North Vietnam cannot defeat us. Only Americans can do that."

Speaking directly to the silent majority, Nixon lit a torch to guide the weary nation. "I am sure that you, the great silent majority of Americans, are not going to let that happen. The time has come to take a stand and let that voice of the great silent majority be heard."

He spoke of weighing life against life, considering the hundreds of thousands threatened by abandonment. There was no easy or painless solution after years mired in distant conflict. But America must emerge on the side of humanity and its own ideals.

To the great silent majority torn between principle and patriotism, Nixon offered a battle cry. "Take your stand, make your voice heard. You can sway the future of this nation."

He touched the nerve of a group who felt forgotten between radicals and elites. Nixon called them into action as stewards of the national course. Millions suddenly felt seen, their unspoken anguish given voice on the largest stage.

Some felt further divided between "real Americans" in Nixon's silent ranks versus "radical fringe" of protesters. Many activists recoiled at being marginalized and discounted. Cries for immediate withdrawal intensified in fury over this polarization.

"The time has come for Americans who really care about peace to take a stand, and say America will never surrender," Nixon declared with fiery conviction. "Together, we shall forge a just and lasting peace!"

As the cameras switched off, the heavy silence lifted from Nixon's shoulders. He had given voice to the voiceless, lighting a torch to guide the weary nation he was duty-bound to lead. Now came the hard work of resuscitating America's greatness. But failure was not an option when so much hung in the fragile balance.

The address generated thousands of grateful letters and calls. Troops abroad took heart knowing those at home appreciated their painful sacrifices. For a brief moment, the fractured country glimpsed unity's distant shore again. The long, hard journey back began with a single plea into the camera's void.

December 1, 1969 – All Across America

The morning of December 1st dawned crisp and

ominous. Across America, young men gathered anxiously around televisions as news anchors prepared to broadcast the very first draft lottery since World War II. The stakes could not have been higher. With Vietnam casualties mounting, the lottery would call eligible men to service randomly.

At Selective Service headquarters, uniformed officials solemnly loaded blue capsules containing every possible birth date - from January 1st to December 31st - into a large glass jar. The jar held 365 capsules total, representing each day of the year.

The draft lottery would pull these birth dates at random to assign them a number between one and 365. Men born on dates that were selected early would get low numbers, making them most vulnerable to being drafted within the next year. High numbers offered the hope of avoiding the dreaded draft notice in the mail.

Only men born between 1944 and 1950 were eligible for this 1969 draft lottery. Other factors like medical fitness and student deferments could still protect some, but one's birth date would now be the biggest determinant of who got called up.

"The lottery is necessary to restore fairness and order," stated an Army general gruffly. "But make no mistake, anyone trying to evade their duty will face consequences."

In homes nationwide, eligible young men watched in anguish or relief as the randomized numbers sealed fates. Now more than ever, chance and luck dictated who would shoulder the burden of combat in Vietnam. The lottery crystallized the scars the divisive war was carving across the nation.

Critics decried the lottery as disproportionately burdening the underprivileged unable to afford college deferments. Chants of "Hell no, we won't go!" erupted from crowds of protestors at college campuses and public squares. They denounced the draft as an instrument to prop up an immoral war. Flags and draft cards went up in flames as rage mounted.

Many Americans viewed the lottery as the most even-handed path forward. Previous deferments had protected the elite while the poor fought and died. Everyone's birthdate now went into the pool, subject to the fates.

In a humble Brooklyn apartment, a family embraced their son in tearful relief as his number came up 305. He was likely spared from the jungles of Vietnam. But in small towns and suburbs across America, uncertain boys wondered if their futures were now sealed within a numbered blue capsule.

The lottery added fresh fuel to a fiery national debate over rights, privilege and duty. In a democracy's grand experiment, the people themselves must determine what burdens they are called to shoulder together. As old orders vanished, new ones struggled violently to be born.

January 18, 1970 - Saigon, South Vietnam

Hidden in thick jungle near the Thu Duc Military Academy, Viet Cong cell leader Tan studied the compound through binoculars. The South's future officers studied there - removing them would sap morale from the military.

He turned to his top saboteur, Bao. "The academy must be torn from within. You and your team will sneak in the compound tonight and plant explosives in the main barracks."

Bao nodded.

Bao met with the two other VC saboteurs to review their plan one last time.

"Remember, use the pliers to expose just enough wire for the junction box," he said, demonstrating the junction box setup. "Keep your movements low and slow to avoid notice."

Under moonless cover, Bao and his two comrades scaled the perimeter fence stealthily. They slunk along walls until reaching the barracks. Pulling out bundles of dynamite, his two saboteurs swiftly set charges under the building.

Slipping through an open window, Bao entered the barrack's bathroom, carefully concealed two more bundles of dynamite in the wall cavity, then threaded the firing wire out a small hole, burying it under tile grout. He moved to the doorway and peered in the barracks where fifty cadets slept. He moved back to the open window and slipped out unnoticed.

Once outside, Bao placed a junction box at the base of a wooden support and threaded the firing wires leading to the explosives into the box. He combined the stripped ends of the wires into one wire and closed the box. He led the wire out through the perimeter as the other two saboteurs covered the wire with dirt.

Once outside the perimeter, Bao attached the ends of the wire to a plunge detonator and waited while his comrades holding their submachine guns kept watch.

The next morning, the cadets rose at first light for muster. Bao watched from afar as they lined up innocently - minutes from oblivion. He gripped the detonator anxiously.

At 6:15 AM, as the cadets returned to their bunks

to prepare for classes, Bao twisted the plunger. The barracks erupted in massive explosions, collapsing the building in plumes of smoke and screams. Chaos gripped the academy as the dead and wounded lay strewn about the ruins.

Bao smiled coldly at the devastation. "The imperialist students have received their lesson." He and his two comrades melted back into the jungle, leaving smoldering carnage behind. The final tally was eighteen dead and thirty-three wounded of South Vietnam's brightest future leaders.

Only Fools Rush In

January 20, 1970 - Mu Gia Pass, North Vietnam

The morning calm over the mountains of North Vietnam was shattered by the roar of US Air Force jets. Two F-105 Thunderchief fighter-bombers swooped low through the river valley, racing toward their target – North Vietnamese SA-2 missile sites protecting the Mu Gia Pass.

In the lead F-105, Major Tom Carlson and his navigator, Captain Mike Murphy, scanned the sky as puffs of smoke appeared from enemy anti-aircraft batteries. "We've got incoming at two o'clock!" Murphy shouted over the engine noise.

Carlson banked hard right but couldn't evade the cannon fire that tore into the aircraft, causing it to lurch violently. "Dammit, we're hit!" Carlson yelled. "Controls are all messed up. We are losing our hydraulics. We gotta punch out!"

Training took over as Murphy initiated the ejection

sequence and the cockpit canopy blew off. Their seats rocketed out as the crippled jet spun down toward the jungle.

From the remaining F-105, the pilot called out in dismay as the wounded jet crashed into the side of the mountain and the two parachutes drifted down into the dense jungle. "Goddammit, Lead just punched out!"

The navigator watched helplessly as the chutes carried the airmen into the mountains. "I don't know how the Jolly Green is gonna reach them before Charlie gets them."

He radioed frantically, "All players, Lead is down at the Mu Gia Pass, two airmen on the ground needing immediate extract!"

The navigator kept scanning the rugged terrain. "It's dense jungle, they have no way to signal their position."

"Come on, come on," the pilot muttered, desperate for a response.

Finally, the radio crackled, "Copy, we are scrambling rescue bird to that location, ETA forty mikes..."

"Shit. They'll be long gone by then," the navigator said.

The pilot closed his eyes briefly, anguished. "Hang tight, guys, we're getting you help."

He reluctantly turned the jet toward home, sick about abandoning his comrades.

Within the hour, an Air Force rescue helicopter named Jolly Green 71 arrived, desperate to find the downed airmen before enemy forces. "Keep scanning, they gotta be close," the pilot told his crew as they searched.

Out of nowhere, a missile struck the helicopter's

fuselage, causing it to erupt into a fireball before crashing, killing all on board.

At the Pleiku Air Base just across the southern border, veteran pilot Tom Coyle heard the news of the tragic crash of the rescue helicopter and the deaths of the six crewmen. It was a bad day for the US Air Force. He wondered about the two downed airmen still in the jungle as he thought of his son flying missions over Laos.

Coyle went to the base commander's office. He pushed his way past the receptionist into the office and found the commander sitting as his desk studying a map of the crash site. "You gotta try again," said Coyle.

"Please come in," said the commander sarcastically.

"Sorry. You need to send another rescue team."

"No. I don't. I've lost enough good men today. Besides, we haven't heard any radio communications from the downed crewmen."

"There could be lots of reasons for that. Their radios could have been damaged."

"Both of them?"

"Okay. They're in the mountains. The radio signal may be too weak."

"I've considered that."

"You've got to do something."

"Like I said... no I don't. Why do you care so much?"

"I don't know. Scott, I guess."

"Scott's fine, Coyle."

"Yeah, I know. But still... those men... we can't just abandon them."

"It's a shitty job, but it's my job, not yours. I'm not sending another rescue crew. There is too much anti-aircraft in that area. They'll just get killed."

"Alright. Then send me."

The commander looked at Coyle like he was joking, "You don't fly helicopters."

"I don't need to. I can use an STOL and find someplace to land."

"In the middle of the mountains and jungle?"

"Let me worry about that."

"You're a great pilot, Coyle. But nobody's that great. The answer is still no."

"Then I guess it's a good thing that you're not my boss."

"It's my air base, not the CIA's. Don't piss me off, Coyle, or I'll have you thrown in the brig."

"Well, we don't want that."

"I'm not kidding."

"Neither am I," said Coyle leaving.

The base commander was angry, but part of him hoped that Coyle disobeyed his orders. If anyone could save the downed airmen, it was Tom Coyle.

Coyle waited until nightfall and then quietly prepped the Fairchild AU-23 Peacemaker, a rugged STOL aircraft he used to resupply SOG outposts in Laos. It was lightweight and only required 100 feet to land and takeoff. He maxed out the fuel by securing an auxiliary fuel bladder in the cargo area to extend his flying range. He knew that the extra fuel weight would prevent him from carrying the two airmen if he found them, but he also knew that it would take time to scour the area where they landed, and he would use up most of the fuel lightening the aircraft's load. If he planned it right, the airmen would be ready for pickup just as the fuel bladder emptied. If not, he could also empty the extra fuel in the ground.

He gathered flares, parachute signal capsules, first aid supplies, and survival gear in case he crashed in the jungle. It wouldn't be his first time. Coyle had the dubious honor of crashing more aircraft than any other pilot in Southeast Asia.

Slipping away unnoticed in the dark, Coyle took off from the air base and was soon approaching the border into North Vietnam. He switched off his lights making his aircraft a dark mass moving across the moonless night sky. Only the sound of the engine gave away his existence flying over the jungle. He purposely changed his course so that it would appear to the enemy that he was heading toward Hanoi.

As he crossed the border entering North Vietnam, anti-aircraft fire erupted around him. Coyle dove to treetop level and pushed the throttle to full power, twisting and turning, racing through the valley at breakneck speed to evade the anti-aircraft artillery and machine guns. He could barely see through the darkness. The plane's wheels clipped the top of the trees snapping outstretched branches, sending a tornado of leaves above the canopy.

After one minute of hell, the flak subsided. He leveled out and pulled up a few feet more from the top of the jungle canopy giving himself some breathing room. Using the experimental AN/PVS-1 Starlight scope he brought with him, he searched the horizon for any sign of enemy aircraft heading toward him. If the North Vietnamese scrambled their Migs, he was a dead man. His hope was that his aircraft was too small to bother the limited number of jets and instead they would let the anti-aircraft batteries knock him out of the sky like a pesky mosquito. Nothing in the air above the horizon was visible through the bulky scope. A good sign. He switched off the scope to save its battery, then waited another three minutes before correcting his course toward the area where the F-105 had gone down. The ink-black canopy stretched unbroken in all directions, concealing the crash site somewhere within its tangled depths. The only indication of the crash site was the coordinates from the radio report given by the aircraft's wingmen.

Coyle's eyes darted between the instruments and the void outside, watching for any sign of enemy aircraft or anti-aircraft fire. He knew air-to-air missile or anti-aircraft flak from a hidden battery on the ground could tear through his plane's thin metal skin at any moment. Chasing the thought from his mind, he flew onward, deeper in North Vietnam.

Reaching the coordinates where the F-105 had gone down, Coyle cut speed and circled slowly in a wide pylon turn with the reported coordinates as the apex.

Coyle switched his radio to the downed pilots' frequency. "This is rescue bird, calling missing flight. Do you copy, over?"

Static answered him. Coyle waited a long moment before trying again. "Missing flight, this is rescue. If you can hear this transmission, give two clicks on your radio immediately."

Coyle counted the seconds in his head, straining to hear any sound over the static. Still nothing. He switched on the night scope once again and searched for any signs of the lost aircrew. Nothing. He considered dropping his aircraft's anti-missile flares but decided now was not the time. The flares would give away his position and draw anti-aircraft fire. It could also give away the position of the crash site and endanger the missing aircrew if they were still in the area. He decided to wait on using the flares until he had the location of a landing site. He sent one last radio call, "Missing flight, hang tight, brothers. I'll get you out of there. Rescue bird, out."

Switching the radio off to prevent the enemy from tracking his aircraft, Coyle blinked back his frustration and anxiety. Wherever the pilots were, they either could not hear his calls or could not respond. Coyle didn't like leaving the area, but he only had so much fuel and he was burning through it at a fast rate. Unwilling to give up hope, he pushed on deeper into the mountains.

As dawn lightened the sky, Coyle anxiously scanned the rugged mountain terrain for any sign of a possible landing spot. No luck. With fuel running low, he knew he'd soon have no choice but to abandon the rescue unless he could find someplace in the unforgiving jungle to land his plane and pick up the airmen if they were still alive. His rescue mission was becoming more of a longshot as time passed. Was this whole thing just a fool's errand?

Just then, the valley opened up revealing terraced rice fields cut horizontally across a mountainside. Coyle's pulse quickened—it could work if the soil was dry enough.

As he continued to fly deeper into North Vietnam so as not to give away his possible landing site to any enemy in the area, Coyle radioed a covert Lima site across the Laotian border requesting a weather report for the area. The last week had been hot and rain-free - promising news.

Coyle turned the plane around and passed over the rice field once again. He studied the direction and depth of the rows in the soil. Two farmers were harvesting the mature rice and covering the field with the chaff making harder to see the rows. Even so, Coyle figured it was the airmen's best shot and he was going to take it. He scanned the area and the sky above for any signs of the enemy. It was clear… for the moment. He aimed the plane back to the crash site about three miles away and he studied the terrain so he could estimate how long it would take the airmen to travel to the rice field if he could contact them. It was a lot of "ifs" …

With fuel running out, Coyle flew back to the F-105's last known location, circling while trying again to reach them by radio. "Missing flight, this is rescue bird, do you read me, over?" Only static answered.

Desperate, Coyle wrote the rice field's coordinates in the message capsules but encrypted them using recent baseball stats, hoping one was a fan. He dropped capsules across the jungle as he scanned for any sign of the airmen below.

But the canopy yielded no clues, only endless green. As the fuel bladder emptied, Coyle knew he had one chance left to signal them. He flipped the switch igniting the anti-missile flares and pushed the last parachute capsule through the opening in the side window.

As he expected, the jungle erupted with gun and cannon fire from hidden anti-aircraft batteries. Coyle threw the plane into evasive maneuvers, racing away as tracers streaked past the cockpit. Several bullets pierced his left wing, but miraculously did not damage the hydraulics and control systems. He was still flying and there was still hope in saving the airmen.

Once free of the anti-aircraft fire, Coyle corrected

his course back to the rice field. It took less than three minutes to reach the potential landing site. Circling above the quiet terraces, Coyle watched the treeline anxiously for any sign of friend or foe. He had done all he could to lead the pilots here. The only question - was it enough? He could only wait and watch for the airmen to emerge from below.

In the distance, he spotted three trucks approaching the rice fields. He suspected it was an NVA platoon searching for the airmen. The airmen's time was running out once again. He radioed again, hoping to hear from them. Nothing. His mind raced for a solution. Any chance he could give them before the enemy troops arrived, he would do not matter the risk. Then, it occurred to him...

If the NVA were chasing them, the airmen could have reached the field but were waiting for him to land before revealing their position in the surrounding jungle. Another longshot. But like everything in his life, he would risk all to save his fellow airmen. He turned and aligned his aircraft for landing. He thought about McGoon, his best friend that had died in a fiery crash at Dien Bien Phu. He wondered what get-rich scheme he would have come up with when the met again. He thought of his two children, Karen and Scott, and wished he could say goodbye one last time. Maybe he could impart some fatherly wisdom to guide them through their lives. He thought about the women he had loved and – Time was up, time to land. The farmers scattered as the metal beast descended on their livelihood. The aircraft's wheels touched down and found their way in between the rows. Coyle carefully touched the brakes, too much and the plane could flip. The plane slowed to a stop. Coyle revved the engine and turned around for takeoff. Then, he waited, keeping his eyes glued to the treeline. Nothing. Two minutes, then three. Still, nothing. He calculated how long before the three trucks with the platoon of enemy troops arrived. It wasn't much. Maybe a minute or two. He picked up the radio handset one more time and spoke, "Rescue bird to missing flight. Are you there, boys?" Nothing in response. Coyle wanted to cry. He had to leave or risk capture himself. He would wait until the last possible second before –

And then it happened, static on the radio. He listened. "Rescue bird, this is missing flight. We are coming in hot. Thirty seconds out." Coyle's eyes well up in tears. He watched the treeline. Movement. Then, Carlson and Murphy emerged from the jungle. Murphy was limping badly, Carlson helping him as they ran toward the plane. Coyle reeved up the engine and prepared to release the brake. A squad of NVA emerged from the jungle and fired at the airmen. Coyle pulled his sidearm, pushed open the side window and fired back. Something caught his eye – the first of the trucks pulled up and twelve enemy soldiers jumped out of the back. "Oh, come on, God! Give us a fucking break, will ya?" said Coyle as the enemy troops opened fire from the opposite side of the field. Several bullets pierced the aircraft's fuselage. Carlson and Murphy reached to cargo door and opened it. Carlson pushed Murphy inside. A bullet hit Carlson in the shoulder. He slumped. Murphy grabbed him by the collar and pulled him into the aircraft. Coyle didn't wait for the door to close before he started his takeoff. A bullet shattered the pilot's window, a piece of glass cut his ear. Blood flowed. Coyle stayed focused watching the speedometer and keeping the aircraft as straight as possible within the field's rows. Moments later, the wheels lifted off and they were in the air. More bullets pierced the metal skin, but nothing found its mark. Five seconds later, the gunfire faded. They were clear. They all laughed. "Wow," said Coyle.

"Who the hell are you?" said Murphy.

"Coyle."

"We owe you our lives?"

"You're damned right you do. I expect free beer when we get back and both of you will name your first born after me."

They laughed. "So, what's your first name?"

"Doesn't matter. You will name them Coyle."

"What if it's a girl?"

"Then she will get teased a lot. Coyle stands."

"You're a cruel man."

"Yep."

They all laughed as they flew back to the border.

February 12, 1970 – Son Thang, Quang Nam
Province, South Vietnam

The Marines of 3rd squad pushed through thick jungle, closing in on 2nd squad's last known position. Radio contact had gone silent three hours ago, setting the men on edge.

They entered a quiet clearing and froze. Nine mangled American bodies lay torn apart in the grass, charred uniforms and gear identifying them as the missing 2nd squad.

"Perimeter, now!" Sgt. Walker ordered. The Marines swiftly took up defensive positions scanning for any threat.

Walker rushed to the nearest man, Pfc. Scott,

staring vacantly skyward with his torso shredded by shrapnel. "Dammit." he said trying to keep his emotions in check.

Cpl. Gonzalez grimly checked each man for pulses he knew weren't there. "Bastards took their dog tags," he said bitterly.

Methodically they searched for intel and salvaged what gear could be carried. Nothing would be left for the enemy. There wasn't much. The VC had already looted the bodies. Sgt. Walker's face was stone, torn by the decision they faced.

"We gotta leave them for now," he ordered through gritted teeth. "We're too exposed to carry them all safely and maintain security."

"What? We can't abandon 'em, Sarge!" Gonzalez protested.

"I know how you feel, but we don't have a choice," Walker replied firmly. "I swear we'll be back with more men to bring them home."

One last time, the Marines said silent goodbyes to their fallen brothers. Marking the location on a map, they slipped back into the jungle, duty and training keeping their rage in check - for now.

Back at their base, the rage in the Marines' eyes said enough. Ever since finding their mutilated brothers left to rot, the Marines had gone cold and quiet. But inside, storms brewed.

During chow, the men sat staring at trays, chewing methodically. Anger simmered just below the surface, waiting to be unleashed.

In their barracks, they honed KA-BARs with long, deliberate strokes, until the blades' edges gleamed, razor sharp.

At the rifle range their shots grouped tight on targets without needing to imagine faces. Tonight, vengeance would take form. The debt would be repaid in blood.

They said nothing about what was to come. Words weren't needed for men in sync. All knew the score that must be settled.

February 20, 1970 – Son Thang, South Vietnam

Karen drove a sedan down the dusty road toward the hamlet of Son Thang, reporter Greg Howard beside her looking uneasy. In the backseat, Huan, their translator sat silently, grateful for the work. At the village entrance, two stone-faced Marines stepped forward to block their path.

"The area's off limits. Turn this vehicle around," one ordered sternly.

"No," said Karen.

"We aren't asking, lady."

"We're journalist from Associated Press. The public has a right to know what happened. Shoot us if you must, but we're going in."

Greg shifted nervously. "Hey now, let's not get dramatic..." But Karen had already taken her foot off the brake and the car crept forward.

"Relax, Greg. They're not going to do anything."

"You don't know that."

"Yes, I do."

The Marines raised their rifles warily. "Halt! Last warning!" one shouted. Karen kept crawling forward at 5 mph.

Greg cringed, holding his breath. "Are you trying to get us killed?" he hissed. The Marines glanced at each other, then reluctantly lowered their weapons.

"Fine, but this ain't a picnic spot, lady," the guard grumbled as Karen coasted by toward the ravaged village, her eyes fixed firmly ahead. She would not be deterred from revealing this tragedy.

"You're crazy, Karen," said Greg.

"Sometimes, crazy ain't so bad," said Karen with a wry smile.

Pulling to a stop at the edge of the village, Karen stepped from the sedan and froze. In the village lane lay a row of bodies covered in blood-soaked clothes, flies swarming overhead.

Greg gasped audibly seeing women, even small children by the shorter length of their bodies. "Good God..." he uttered.

Huan made the sign of the cross, murmuring what sounded like prayers in Vietnamese. Karen steeled her nerves and stepped forward, camera raised to document the atrocity from every angle.

She photographed a mother clinging to the hand of her dead infant, both brutally slain. Karen's vision blurred with angry tears, but she kept snapping photos steadily.

Greg hurriedly jotted observations, his normal detached poise crumbling. "How...how could anyone do this?" He shook his head as if to negate the harrowing scene before him.

Karen's camera did not waver, driven by a righteous obligation. As her shutter clicked on relentlessly, she fought back the tears.

Greg moved among the stunned villagers, Huan translating his questions softly. An elderly woman began recounting between sobs. She described Marines entering at dusk, dragging families from homes. Hiding in a crawlspace, she helplessly heard gunshots and screams.

Karen entered a small hut, camera raised. Dark blood-stained sleeping mats where victims fell. She fought back nausea and photographed close-ups of spent shell casings, a child's wooden doll spattered with dried blood. Karen photographed the hut's blood-spattered interior from every angle.

Stepping back outside, her boot nudged something metal - a dusty rifle shell casing in the dirt. She knelt down and examined it closely blowing off the dust. Stamped on the rim was "7.62mm M80" along with the manufacture's initials. Karen felt her stomach twist. It was Marine ammo. She took a close-up photo capturing the crisp military markings.

More examples lay scattered about, glinting coldly in the sun. Fingerprints potentially waited beneath the microscopic grooves. There was no denying the awful truth now. Tears rolled down her face.

Karen slipped the damning casing into her pocket. She found more grisly evidence. Greg crouched by the well, peering at bullet holes piercing the brickwork just above the waterline. His eyes closed as he realized the implication - execution.

Karen's camera captured everything mechanically - walls pockmarked by bullets, trails of blood leading to a ditch. Her tears had stopped, leaving only a hollow focus on exposing every detail.

Saigon, South Vietnam

The courtroom had a stark, somber feel. Karen stood before a raised wooden platform where three officers in crisp dress uniforms sat as judges, American flags behind them. The walls were unadorned white plaster and harsh fluorescent lights cast a pale glare across the dark wood benches packed with observers.

Karen felt all eyes on her as she took the stand. She wore her nicest dress, though it did little to abate her nerves. The four defendants that had been charged sat behind Karen in matching drab uniforms, their gazes aimed down at the scuffed linoleum floor. Armed with rifles, MPs with stern expressions guarded each exit.

The air was heavy and tension palpable in the windowless room as Karen gave her testimony, prosecutors referencing evidence items numbered on a table. "Please describe for the court what you saw as you entered Son Thang, Ms. Dickson, said the prosecutor, a Marine officer.

"I...I'm not sure where to begin," said Karen. "It was clear something horrific had happened. There were bodies, lined up along the road, just lying there..."

"Take your time. What condition were the deceased villagers in?"

"Most were shot, multiple times from what I could see. Nine women and eleven children had been killed. Some were just...mangled beyond recognition."

"What else did you find?"

"I found a well with bullet holes precisely aimed at the water line… like someone had been hiding inside and was executed. There was a lot of that type of thing throughout the village."

"And you took photographs that day?"

"Yes. I'm a photojournalist of Associated Press. I shot three rolls."

"I would like to submit copies of the photographs that Ms. Dickson took the day after the event as evidence."

Receiving a nod from the judges, the prosecutors placed the prints on the table for the judges to review. Even for military officers, they were shocked by what they saw.

"Ms. Dickson, just to be clear… did you stage any of the photos you took?"

"Absolutely not. That's what it looked like just as I saw it."

"Thank you, Ms. Dickson. No further questions."

With relief, she stepped down after being dismissed. She returned to her seat at the back of the courtroom. Nearby, a captain who signaled that she could take three photos in the courtroom, as previously agreed.

Karen retrieved her camera and composed the shots - one of the full tribunal, a close-up of the judges, and finally, the defendants from behind, their identities obscured.

As she pressed the shutter, Karen wondered if these images might also serve as solemn documentation of justice being carried out, even belatedly. There were always more perspectives to convey.

After her photos were taken, Karen sat numbly as the rest of the proceedings played out. The verdict saw two of the defendants acquitted, one of defendants was found guilty of premeditated murder and sentenced to life in prison with hard labor, while another defendant was found guilty of unpremeditated murder and sentenced to five years in prison.

When the final gavel fell signaling the end of the trial, a complex mix of emotions flooded through Karen. There was some sense of justice, but it could never undo the massacre or restore what was lost. Karen hoped her small role here helped honor the victims by contributing to accountability. Perhaps her stark images would remind others of war's immense cost.

February 17, 1970 – Capital Hill, Washington DC, USA

The distinguished senators of the Foreign Relations Committee shifted in their leather chairs, faces taut with skepticism. Before them sat William Colby, head of CORDS in Vietnam, his demeanor calm and posture perfect. He had been called to testify on recent allegations of an illegal targeted assassination program being run out of the Phoenix offices in South Vietnam.

Senator Church glanced at his notes then leaned into the microphone. "Mr. Colby, what can you tell this committee about an operation known as Project Phoenix?"

"Phoenix is an intelligence coordination and exploitation program," Colby replied evenly. "Its goal is to disrupt the Viet Cong infrastructure by capturing or convincing insurgent leaders to rally to the government."

"Isn't it true this disruption involves the use of systematic terror and assassination?" Church pressed.

Colby hesitated before answering. "There have been some illegal killings, which I do not condone. But assassination is not Phoenix policy."

Another senator interjected, "But isn't the neutralization of 19,534 suspected VC collaborators your stated goal for this year alone?"

"Those are for detentions, not assassinations," Colby clarified. "Our focus is on carefully dismantling the leadership, logistics, recruitment and other support networks that keep the insurgency alive. In that regard,

Phoenix has been remarkably successful."

The committee members exchanged skeptical glances. Colby maintained an outward calm, but inside his guts churned. The operation was yielding results, but not without collateral damage. Blurred lines existed between neutralization and assassination, success and abuse. Justifying such complex gray areas would prove difficult, but the truth of Phoenix lay somewhere in the murky middle - neither black nor white, but a subtle, ominous shade of gray.

February 21, 1970 - Laos

The airfield was a bog of mud from the monsoon downpour. Pathet Lao soldiers positioned in the jungle treeline awaited their moment to attack.

The strategic importance of Xiangkhouang airfield and the Plain of Jars stemmed from their location in northern Laos along the Ho Chi Minh Trail logistics route. The Plain of Jars plateau contained crucial stretches of the trail, allowing North Vietnamese forces to avoid the demilitarized zone and sustain operations in the Vietnam War. Xiangkhouang airfield provided an invaluable staging point for US bombing raids to interdict the communist supply lines and troop movements through the Plain of Jars region. Control of the airfield and plain would give North Vietnam control of this critical logistics artery while denying US air power the ability to disrupt the communist supply network.

Inside the control tower, Phoumi, the commander of the airfield, tracked the few remaining Royal Lao Army C-47s transport planes through binoculars. Most had evacuated west already, but these last aircraft were trapped on the flooded runway. He knew the communists would seize them and use them against loyalist forces if given the chance.

A rumbling grew over the rain's constant din. Phoumi looked up to see a dark shape—an American B-52 bomber—through the low clouds. The ground shook violently as its payload struck the ridge east of the airfield. Explosions ripped through the jungle, sending plumes of fire and shrapnel high into the air. Phoumi allowed himself a faint grin, thankful for the air support despite the U.S. drawdown of SOG forces.

The bomber faded into the distance. In the following calm, a high-pitched whistle pierced the air. Mortar shells arced over the treeline, crashing onto the runway in eruptions of mud. The mortar crews were careful not to damage the aircraft they hoped to capture. The jungle edge burst open as Pathet Lao infantry charged out, swarming toward the airfield.

Phoumi grabbed his rifle and ran downstairs. His men hunkered down behind sandbags, returning fire at the human wave rushing toward them. They were drastically outnumbered.

"Fall back to the tower!" Phoumi ordered over the gunfire. "We'll make our stand there."

His soldiers disengaged and retreated through the muddy chaos. A mortar blast sent shrapnel slicing past Phoumi's head as he followed. Reaching the tower entrance, he turned to see the airfield overrun with Pathet Lao forces. They had lost the ground battle. Their only hope now was to hold out for evacuation.

In the control room, Phoumi's radioman desperately called for assistance between bursts of static. Phoumi took position at the shattered tower window, manning a machine gun. Through the rain he saw the airfield swarming with enemy fighters, their battle cries rising over the storm's din. He squeezed the trigger, cutting down the first wave despite knowing he only delayed the inevitable.

The C-47s remained vulnerable on the runway below. Phoumi grabbed the radio handset from his radioman and switched frequencies. "Destroy the transports," he ordered, his heart sinking. "We cannot let them fall into enemy hands."

On the runway, loyalist soldiers doused the parked C-47s in fuel before retreating. Tracer fire lit up the tower window as Phoumi provided covering fire. Watching his troops retreating from the fuel-soaked aircraft, Phoumi redirected his fire to the C-47s. The tracer rounds ignited the fuel and fire engulfed the transports. Destroying the aircraft had been a grave sacrifice, but he could not allow them to fall into enemy hands. Explosions rocked the airfield as the aircrafts' fuel tanks blew up, their burning wreckage keeping the enemy at bay for a few moments more.

It would not be enough. The Pathet Lao closed in through the fire and smoke. Phoumi and his men would make their stand here, buying time for any other friendly forces that could still escape. He steeled himself as the communist forces breached the tower entrance below.

Flames engulfed the runway as the last C-47 erupted into a fireball. Phoumi watched from the control tower window, providing covering fire as his remaining men retreated inside the tower.

A barrage of rifle fire rang out as Pathet Lao fighters breached the tower entrance. Phoumi's men barricaded the stairwell with furniture and shot back through the gaps. "We need to get to the roof!" Phoumi yelled over the raging gunfight. "It's our only chance for evacuation."

The defenders abandoned their post and ascended the steps. Phoumi's radioman desperately called for extraction between bursts of static, then abandoned his post and headed up the ladder to the roof as the first enemy soldier fired through the furniture barricade into the control room.

Outside on the rooftop helipad, howling wind whipped through the airfield's darkness. It was a fool's hope that the Americans would come.

Suddenly, a bright searchlight blinded them. Phoumi shielded his eyes to see the dark shape of a US Air Force HH-43 helicopter emerging through the storm clouds. It hoovered above the roof amidst the gale force winds. The crew chief lowered a rope through the open doorway and waved to the soldiers on the crowded rooftop to climb.

"Go, go!" Phoumi ordered his men.

They scrambled aboard the rescue chopper under heavy enemy fire from below. Tracers zipped overhead as the last soldier climbed inside. Phoumi provided suppressive fire with his rifle out the side hatch as the HH-43 lifted off.

Looking down, he watched smoke rising from the airfield where raging flames now engulfed the control tower. Xiangkhouang was lost, but Phoumi had completed his mission - evacuating his men and denying the communists their prize. They ascended into the thunderheads, disappearing westward to fight another day.

March 11, 1970 – Phnom Penh, Cambodia

Sok stared up at the North Vietnamese embassy, a nondescript two-story building along Monivong Boulevard. This was not just any day - Prince Sihanouk was abroad and the streets belonged to the people. It was time to send a message.

Turning to the angry mob assembled behind him, Sok raised a megaphone to his lips. "Too long have these Vietnamese dogs disrespected our nation with their presence! Today we show them how Cambodians deal with unwanted guests!"

The crowd roared in agreement, brandishing sticks, stones and fury. They began advancing on the embassy behind Sok.

Inside, the staff rushed to lock gates and doors. Sok pounded the front entrance, shouting, "Your time in Cambodia is over! Get out now!"

When no response came, the mob began hurling rocks, smashing windows. They tore down the wrought iron gate and flooded the lobby. Papers were thrown into the air among wrecked furniture and shattered glass.

Sok watched with grim satisfaction. The Vietnamese had refused to leave when warned, instead fortifying their presence. Now they cowered like rats while Cambodia flexed its strength.

Leaving the ransacked embassy, the mob moved on to the Viet Cong facility. More gates were torn down. More glass smashed. More retaliation for each Cambodian life lost to the spreading Vietnam conflict.

By day's end, the embassy grounds lay in ruins. Sok knew there would be fallout, but he had no regrets. Sometimes you needed to yell to make your voice heard. That was a language the Vietnamese understood well.

March 18, 1970 – National Assembly Hall, Phnom Penh, Cambodia

The shouts and broken glass had scarcely been cleaned up when the National Assembly convened for an emergency meeting. Sok sat amongst the tense delegates, awaiting the inevitable response to the unrest.

Lon Nol stepped to the podium, his expression grave. "It is with regret that I must report Prince Sihanouk will no longer be fit to lead the nation. The damage inflicted to our Vietnamese guests while under his protection makes his position untenable."

Angry murmurs rippled through the crowd. Sok remained still, hands clenched below the desk.

"Therefore," Lon Nol continued, "I call for an immediate vote to remove Prince Sihanouk from power and install new leadership - in an acting capacity - until elections can be held."

Cries of dissent echoed against the wooden walls. *This was rash*, Sok thought. *Dangerous.*

"Order, please!" Lon Nol shouted over the din. "I too wish this were avoidable. But the dignity of Cambodia is at stake. I ask that you search your hearts and vote what is best for the nation."

When the roll call vote finished, the resolution passed unanimously. The assembly erupted into uncertain applause for their new leader, Lon Nol.

Sok kept his seat, realization sinking in. By giving voice to the people's frustrations, he had helped unleash powerful forces beyond his control or intent. The consequences would be grave indeed.

March 22, 1970 – Hoc Mon District, Saigon, South Vietnam

Just outside of Saigon, darkness shrouded the Buddhist temple complex before dawn's first light. Moving swiftly, Viet Cong guerillas scaled the back wall and dropped down into the vegetable gardens. Their satchels bulged with explosives and triggers.

The leader signaled his men to fan out. They silently placed bombs beneath the kitchens, beside the ancient stone fountain, and among the rows of cushions inside the main shrine. Trip wires were strung and timers activated.

By the time the eastern sky glowed pink, the VC had vanished back into the jungle. Moments later, monks emerged to begin their morning rituals, unaware of the deadly trap set in their midst.

The temple yard bustled with activity as villagers gathered for the Buddhist meeting. Children laughed and chased each other around the stone fountain while monks in saffron robes chatted softly amidst the sweet smell of incense.

Venerable Thich sat meditating beneath a sprawling banyan tree, the morning sun warm on his shaved head. Soon he would offer blessings to start the day's observances. Close by, a young monk named Tanh swept leaves from the temple steps.

Suddenly a deafening boom shook the ground, followed by screams. Billowing flames and rubble erupted from the main shrine where devotees had already gathered.

"No!" Tanh cried, rushing toward the blast. Thich grabbed his shoulder, holding him back.

"Stay here! Check the yard for more bombs," Thich

instructed. His young pupil reluctantly obeyed.

The shrine was engulfed in a choking cloud of dust and smoke. Bloodied bodies lay strewn amid smoldering debris. Thich joined the shocked villagers trying to pull survivors from the rubble.

Another explosion thundered, this time from the kitchens. Then another beside the fountain. The pastor's yard became an inferno of twisted wreckage.

When the chaos finally settled, Tanh found Thich kneeling beside a row of lifeless bodies - fourteen in all. Most were mutilated beyond recognition.

"Why would anyone commit such evil?" Tanh asked bitterly.

The old master shook his head. "Hatred only breeds more hatred. The Viet Cong sow suffering to reap but one sad harvest - more suffering."

His voice was steady, but inside Thich's heart grieved. The war's cruel hand had found them, even here. What more would it take before the violence ceased?

April 4, 1970 – National Mall, Washington DC, USA

Frank gripped his American flag tight as the bus approached the National Mall. All around him sat like-minded folks - veterans, parents, teachers - all rallying for victory against the communist threat. Dan Fowler, Frank's old football coach, leaned over from the seat behind. "We're not gonna let Nixon go soft on the Viet Cong, are we Frank?"

"No, sir," Frank replied. "We'll remind him why we need to be there - my brother almost died taking Hill 755. We can't just walk away now."

Stepping off the bus, Frank was amazed by the sea of supporters waving banners and signs. Chants of "Win in Vietnam!" echoed across the grass. On stage, preacher Carl McIntire, a fundamentalist radio evangelist, railed against Nixon's broken promises to fund the war effort.

Frank fell in with the crowd marching on the Capitol, his legs stiff from the long bus ride. But he'd endure far worse for his country. Walking beside him, Mrs. Andrews, the 8th grade history teacher who'd inspired Frank's fierce anti-communist views. "I hope President Nixon can hear us today," she said. "We need to defend freedom for the generations to come."

They all wanted the same thing - total victory over North Vietnam and the Viet Cong traitors. But Nixon was reducing troops and giving ground hard won by American blood. It sickened Frank to watch politicians feign support for the military while stabbing them in the back.

The march halted at the Capitol steps. Frank could see counter-protestors waving peace signs on the sidelines, mostly unwashed college kids. "Hey! Don't you know communism means no free speech?" he yelled. But his voice was lost in the crowd's roar shouting down the anti-war protestors. Frank believed in peace, but not through surrender.

As another speaker took the stage on the Capital steps, a surge of applause washed over the Mall. Frank raised his voice, straining to be heard. "Win the war!" he shouted until his words grew hoarse.

By day's end, Frank left exhausted but fulfilled. His generation knew the high price of freedom. If the Washington elite wouldn't take a stand in Vietnam, ordinary Americans like him would.

Operation Texas Star

April 1, 1970 – A Shau Valley, South Vietnam

Private Jim Ward shoved down the last mushy bites of powdered eggs in the mess tent. All around him soldiers hurriedly ate before gearing up. Word was they were finally assaulting the A Shau Valley today.

They could hear the distant artillery exploding, one-after-another, constant hellfire as they moved back to their barracks. "Never seen artillery prep like this before," said Private Wells, the new guy. "Them arti-boys ain't leaving anything standing down there."

Private Kowalski grinned. "Just be glad you're not on the receiving end."

Ward heard helicopter blades already thumping the air. He looked up to see the sky covered with black specks as the squadron of Huey's landed at the airfield.

"Saddle up, we're moving out!" Sgt. Ryan shouted as Ward and the others entered the barracks.

Men scrambled to grab rucksacks and rifles. Ward's

gut tightened with anxious excitement. This was it.

Grabbing their gear, the men bantered to cut the tension. "Whoever gets the least kills buys the beer back in Da Nang," Kowalski challenged.

"You're on," Wells replied. "Loser buys all night."

As they made their way to the airfield, a swarm of Hueys awaited, whipping dust in all directions. They would be inserting under heavy artillery bombardment of the valley. Ward took a deep breath to settle his nerves.

Packed tight in the lead chopper, Ryan gave the signal to check weapons as the Huey approached the landing zone. Ward racked back the bolt on his M-16, palm sweaty against the grip. Like the others, he kept his weapon's barrel pointed to the deck.

Across the valley, NVA Lt. Tranh watched the opening artillery barrage, massive and ceaseless. His men waited silently in their dugouts, the earth trembling with each explosion. *They were ready*, Tranh thought. *Ready to teach these Americans that the valley belonged to Vietnam.*

When the first Hueys descended through the smoke and chaos, Tranh bellowed his order: "Fire!"

Anti-air gunners unleashed a torrent of lead upward. Operation Texas Star had begun.

Sgt. Ryan braced as the Huey dropped into the smoky valley. Ward gripped his rifle, heart thumping. Just before the skids hit the ground, the chopper pitched right to avoid incoming fire. It came down with a hard thud. "Here we go!" Ryan shouted. "Go go go!"

The men poured out firing as the barrels of NVA gunners flashed from the surrounding long grass.

Ward's boots hit the muddy earth and he sprinted for cover behind a boulder.

Kowalski provided cover fire while Wells advanced. A burst of rounds ripped into Wells's shoulder, sending him spinning down. "Man down!" Kowalski yelled. Ward and Ryan rushed to drag Wells behind a boulder. Bright red stained his fatigues.

"You're gonna be alright, stay still," Ward assured him, although he knew the wounds were bad. Wells's face had gone ghostly white.

Ryan got on the radio, calling for a medevac while scanning their position. NVA resistance was stiffening as more enemy troops reinforced.

"Ward, hand off your weapon and get Wells's M60 set up on the right flank," he ordered. "We got to break through before those bunkers get manned."

Ward scrambled to set up the M60 on their right flank as ordered. Incoming fire pinged off the boulders around him. Once mounted, he let loose a barrage of suppressing fire toward the tree line.

In the NVA bunkers, Lt. Tranh monitored the American advance. Their air cavalry had secured the western ridge but were struggling to push east.

"Comrades, we must hold them there," Tranh said. "Ready the RPG teams."

NVA gunners began moving Russian RPGs up the hillside. Ward spotted the movement through his scope.

"Sarge, they're bringing RPGs up," he called to Ryan.

The sergeant got back on the radio, requesting air support. "Danger close, we need napalm on that ridgeline now!"

Moments later, Ward saw two jets scream past. A wall of flame erupted on the hillside, engulfing the bunkers. The surviving NVA fled for cover.

"Forward, let's go!" Ryan ordered.

Laying down suppressive fire, Ward and the others leapt up and began advancing toward the burning bunkers.

Ward moved cautiously through the burning hillside ruins, M60 aimed and ready. The air stank of charred flesh and scorched earth. In the distance, he could hear chopper blades and fresh small arms fire as more units inserted into the valley.

Rounding a collapsed bunker, Ward came face to face with a severely burned NVA soldier. The man raised his trembling rifle with one seared arm but lacked the strength to fire before Ward cut him down with his machine gun. Ward felt nothing. It was a mercy killing.

"Clear left!" Ward called out.

"Clear right!" answered Kowalski, emerging from the smoke.

They pressed forward, Eventually the trees thickened and the smoke dissipated. Ryan signaled a halt at the tree line.

"Alright, we're pushing into heavy jungle now," he said. "Keep sharp and watch your spacing."

Ward took a knee, gulping water from his canteen. He knew the NVA had more men and traps waiting within the dark cover of those trees. But there was no turning back.

After a brief pause to reload and regroup, the men started their advance into the foreboding jungle, weapons ready for the next contact.

Ward moved cautiously through the thick jungle

underbrush, rifle sweeping left to right. Visibility was poor, with vegetation clawing and tangling his every step. The air hung heavy and damp, devoid of birdsong or wildlife. It was strange. There was almost always some noise in the jungle.

A rifle shot cracked sharply from up ahead, followed by screams.

"Ambush!" Kowalski yelled.

Suddenly the jungle erupted with gunfire. Ward dove behind a fallen log as bullets snapped by overhead. Through the chaos, he could make out NVA troops firing from camouflaged spider holes and tree platforms.

"Return fire, return fire!" Ryan ordered.

Ward popped up and sprayed rounds back at the hidden VC. Leaves and branches shredded under the barrage. The men advanced steadily, driving the enemy back under their relentless counterattack.

A VC fell dead from a platform above, his AK clattering to the ground. Ward snatched up the weapon as he pushed forward. The familiar shape and heft felt good in his hands.

"Keep moving, stay tight!" Ryan commanded.

The men advanced steadily, driving the enemy back under their relentless counterattack. Ward fired controlled bursts into the jungle as he moved, the M60 bucking is his hands. Leaves and branches shredded under the barrage. On his left, Kowalski lobbed grenades at NVA muzzle flashes, the explosions sending plumes of pulverized vegetation into the air.

Sgt. Ryan coordinated supporting fire, calling in artillery strikes that tore apart the jungle canopy. Hot spent casings rained down as the platoon unleashed unrelenting fire. Step by step they pushed forward, boots crunching over broken branches and cracked RPG rounds.

Ward kept his eyes peeled for spider holes or any sign of movement. The NVA ambushers were well-concealed but not invincible. An AK barrel flashed from a thicket and Ward took it out with two quick bursts. The heavy rounds chopped through brush, smoke curling from the barrel.

Under the platoon's sustained counterattack the enemy fire steadily slackened. By the time the last shots faded off in the distance, the jungle lay ravaged and smoking, vegetation shredded by ordnance. The ambush had been shattered, but at a cost. More men were down, their fate unknown.

Ward loaded another belt of ammunition, chambered another round, and pressed on with the platoon. His senses keyed up. The battle was over, for now. Danger always lurked just a few feet away, shrouded by the jungle's veil.

The platoon moved upslope toward craggy limestone cliffs. Loose rocks shifted underfoot, making the terrain treacherous and exhausting.

Hidden above, an NVA observer tracked their progress through binoculars. At just the right moment, he radioed to the mortar teams dug in behind the ridgeline.

Ward was scanning the cliffs above when the world exploded in deafening, bone-jarring blasts. Mortar shells rained down on the platoon's position, explosions shredding trees and throwing shrapnel.

"Cover!" Kowalski yelled.

The men dove for whatever cover they could find - rubble, craters, thorn bushes. Shells pounded the ravine relentlessly as Ward scrambled behind a boulder and curled up in a ball to make himself as small as possible.

Sgt. Ryan was shouting into the radio, calling out grid coordinates between explosions. Moments later came the shriek of approaching jets.

"Danger close, I need ordnance on that ridgeline now!" Ryan ordered.

The hillside erupted in curtains of napalm, engulfing NVA bunkers and gun pits. Mortar crews died at their weapons under the onslaught of fire.

In the echoing silence that followed, Ward cautiously lifted his head, his ears ringing. Muzzle flashes still winked along the smoldering ridgeline. How anyone had survived he didn't know.

"Up and at 'em, go go!" Ryan commanded.

Rifles blazing, the platoon surged upslope to finish off the staggered NVA resistance. Ward put down withering machine gun bursts on the enemy positions until the last of the muzzle flashes winked out. By day's end, the valley clung to an uneasy calm - both sides bloodied, but neither broken.

Ward awoke at dawn, joints aching from a night on jagged rocks. All around him soldiers stirred, worn down by days of brutal combat. Despite seizing key terrain, the NVA still held the high ground, raining mortars on each hard-fought gain.

Nearby, the medic dressed Kowalski's shrapnel-torn arm, the bandage soaked red. Their ranks were dwindling from the endless skirmishes. Nerves were frayed thin.

Sgt. Ryan studied his map, face gaunt and unshaven. His company commander's talk of quick victory had faded. The NVA were too dug in, the jungle too harsh.

"Third battalion took heavy losses on Hill 471 last night," Ryan said. "We reinforce at 0800. Expect fierce resistance."

At sunrise, Ward forced down the tasteless contents of an MCI box, his appetite gone. The battle had become a bloody brawl in endless jungle and hills. Ending it would demand more blood. Always more blood.

Ward sat watching the valley wake up, the morning sun just cresting the eastern ridges. In the distance, artillery thumped and helicopter rotors chopped the air. Contrails crisscrossed the sky revealing jets somewhere high above.

Kowalski eased down beside him, wincing as he adjusted his bandaged arm. "How you holding up, Ward?"

"I'm alright," Ward replied. "Just thinking about home I guess. Never thought I'd miss Nebraska, but I'd give anything to see those cornfields again."

Kowalski nodded, lighting a cigarette. "Keep your head down today. It's gonna be tough, but I got a good feeling about today. Third Battalion has tried twice to take that hill. The way I see it third times a charm."

"Hope you're right," Ward said. "Feels like the NVA are everywhere out here."

Before Kowalski could respond, Sgt. Ryan approached them. "Get your gear checked and ammunition topped off. We step off for Hill 471 in five mikes."

"What's the situation looking like up there, Sarge?" Ward asked.

Ryan shook his head grimly. "A meat grinder from the sound of it. Reports of tunnels and trenches all over that hill. It'll be a nasty fight."

Ward felt his stomach tighten but kept quiet. He knew there was no sense asking about their odds today. Either they took the hill or died trying. Simple as that.

After gathering ammo and supplies, the platoon headed out, anxious but resolved. Hill 471 loomed in the distance, its slopes still wreathed in predawn mist. Ward took a deep breath and joined his comrades into battle once more.

Ward's platoon moved cautiously through the jungle towards Hill 471. The sounds of battle grew louder - small arms fire, mortars, men shouting. As they drew closer, the hill itself came into view. A smoldering wasteland of craters and fallen trees. Bodies and wreckage littered the slope.

"Steady now, watch for snipers," Sgt. Ryan said, signaling a halt at the base of the hill. He consulted briefly with the company commander.

"Alright, listen up," Ryan addressed the men. "C Company is pinned halfway up. Our job is take out the enemy's machine gun emplacements so C Company can reach the summit. Ready weapons."

Ward steeled himself and did a last ammo check. His hands trembled as he adjusted the spare belt of 7.62mm rounds digging into his neck. Kowalski gave him a grim nod before donning his helmet.

"Move out!" Ryan ordered.

They advanced through smoke, stepping over mangled enemy corpses and loose rocks. A machine gun in an NVA bunker opened up, driving them to cover. Ward returned fire, shouting to Kowalski, "Welcome to Hell!"

Kowalski grinned, priming a grenade. "Hell's got nothing on Philly in August!"

He lobbed the grenade at the bunker as Ward

covered him with the M60. Their combined assault eventually suppressed those inside the bunker. But as they leapt up to advance, a machine gun in other bunker roared to life, pinning them down once more.

Ward hunkered down as machine gun fire raked the hillside. Dirt and pulverized rock sprayed his face. To his right, a soldier in C Company tried to crawl to safety, only to be nearly cut in half by the sustained barrage.

"We gotta shut down that gun!" Ward yelled over to Kowalski.

His friend gave a thumbs up and pointed to a fallen log twenty yards ahead. It would offer cover to get within grenade range.

Ward tapped Sgt. Ryan's shoulder and gestured to the log. Ryan nodded and called out to the rest of the platoon.

"Ward and Kowalski are going for that log on my command! Give 'em covering fire. Ready...GO!"

As the platoon laid down a base of suppressive fire, Ward and Kowalski scrambled in a low run for the log. Dirt kicked up at their heels but they made it safely.

Inching forward, they could see the bunkered machine gun, sandbags stacked high. The NVA crew strained to keep the barrel from melting.

Kowalski pulled the pin and gently lobbed a grenade. "Fire in the hole!"

The blast shredded sandbags and elicited screams from inside. Ward and Kowalski leapt up, charging the nest to finish off any survivors. The machine gun fell silent at last.

With the machine gun silenced, C Company resumed their advance up the hill. Ward felt a rising sense of momentum. The NVA resistance seemed to be crumbling.

"Let's keep the pressure on!" Sgt. Ryan yelled. "Push forward!"

Ward was about to move when he noticed Kowalski still lying motionless next to the bunker. He rushed over and turned his friend's body over to find a gruesome wound where a bullet had ripped open his abdomen.

"Medic!" Ward screamed. But it was too late. Kowalski was already gone. Ward shook with rage and grief as the battle raged around him.

"I'm getting you out of here," he said through tears. Leaving his M60 on the ground, Ward hoisted Kowalski's body on his shoulder and began stumbling his way off the battlefield. He passed dazed soldiers from C Company securing the summit, barely noticing as the American flag was raised over Hill 471.

Reaching the base of the hill, Ward finally set his friend down. He couldn't contain the anguish any longer as tears welled up in his eyes. He wept.

Ward sat numbly beside Kowalski's body as darkness fell over the valley. The sounds of battle had faded, leaving only a heavy silence. He barely noticed Sgt. Ryan approaching until he spoke.

"Ward, you can't just abandon your post, even for..." Ryan's voice trailed off as he saw Kowalski lying lifeless on the ground.

"You left your M60 behind," Ryan said, holding the weapon out to Ward. "That's grounds for disciplinary action. But hell, I can't bust your rank, you're already a private."

Ward didn't respond or reach for the heavy gun. He just kept staring at his friend, hollowed out inside.

Ryan exhaled and lowered the M60. "He was a good

soldier. A good man. We'll make sure he gets home."

Placing a hand on Ward's shoulder, Ryan gazed out into the darkness. "Nothing will fill that void. But you have to carry on. That's the only way any of this means something."

Operation Texas Star continued for five more months, as brutal and bloody as the first days. When it finally ended on September 5th, over 1,700 NVA and VC had been reported killed. American casualties numbered 386 killed and nearly 1,000 wounded. The ARVN lost 370 soldiers killed.

The NVA had been ejected from the valley but not vanquished. And for those who survived, the dead were never far from memory. They had charged courageously into battle. Now came the long march home under the growing shadow of loss.

Under The Eyes of Lincoln

April 11, 1970 – Princeton, New Jersey, USA

The Gallup organization's offices were busier than usual for a Saturday. Pollsters sat in rows, donning headsets and dialing numbers across America to ask opinions on President Nixon's Vietnam policy.

"Good morning, I'm calling from Gallup. Do you have a moment for a brief survey?" pollsters recited hundreds of times that day.

In kitchens and living rooms nationwide, Americans answered the ringing phone. Some hung up immediately. Others gladly gave their views.

"Do you approve or disapprove of President Nixon's handling of the situation in Vietnam?" was the key question. The answers poured in as Gallup's team meticulously tallied each one.

By mid-afternoon, the results were complete. Gallup's analysts reviewed the data in detail to ensure accuracy before submitting their report.

The next morning, Sunday's newspapers carried the headline: "48% Approve of Nixon's Vietnam Policy."

The White House breathed a quiet sigh of relief at the findings. Just below fifty percent approval was not ideal, but far better than the thirty percent approval ratings of years prior. The polls indicated Nixon's Vietnamization strategy was working to win back public opinion, if not yet unanimous support.

For anti-war Americans, the forty-eight percent figure was dishearteningly high given the ongoing stalemate in Vietnam. But forty-one percent disapproval gave them hope that dissent was still strong. If the tide of opinion could be turned further, policy changes might follow.

Both sides scrambled to spin the poll numbers favorably in the media. But the raw data spoke for itself - the nation remained deeply divided over the war in Vietnam.

April 13, 1970 – Xom Bien, Cambodia

Father Andre knelt in prayer inside the chapel as the clock edged just past midnight in Xom Bien. For months, paranoia and suspicion had been spreading as the Vietnam War spilled into Cambodia. Rumors flew that Vietnamese-speaking Cambodians were traitorous communists allied with the Viet Cong.

When Lon Nol took power, he capitalized on these fears, accusing Vietnamese Cambodians of undermining security and ordering the ANK to eliminate them. That evening, Andre had pleaded in vain with the ANK commander to spare his villagers. But the orders from Phnom Penh were clear. All the men and boys in the village were gathered by the ANK troops and herded to the banks of the Mekong River.

The old priest's heart pounded, though he dared not leave the mission grounds where the women and children of the village had come for protection. Gunfire cracked in the distance, then silence.

At dawn, small boats floated down the blood-red Mekong, filled with the contorted, bullet-ridden bodies of over 600 innocents, carrying them back to South Vietnam. Entire families decimated, lost in a senseless act of cruelty fueled by unrestrained xenophobia and militarism.

Though the logic of violence often escapes reason, Father Andre prayed the truth of this barbarism might someday temper the fires of fear and hate that had burned so hot in those who carried it out.

April 20, 1970 – White House, Washington DC, USA

President Nixon stepped up to the podium, looking out at the gathered White House press corps. Camera shutters clicked as all awaited his anticipated remarks on Vietnam. "Good morning," Nixon began. "I am announcing today that America will begin withdrawing an additional 150,000 troops from South Vietnam over the next twelve months."

Murmurs swept through the room. Anti-war critics had demanded larger reductions, but many still viewed the decision as a dramatic shift in policy.

"As the South Vietnamese forces grow stronger, they are taking lead responsibility for defending their nation," Nixon continued. "Reducing our combat role allows America to move closer to the goal of bringing our boys home, while still protecting our hard-won gains in Vietnam."

"This withdrawal plan depends on tangible progress at the peace negotiations in Paris," Nixon emphasized. "For America to continue reducing its combat forces, North Vietnam must show reciprocal restraint and good faith."

He elaborated further, "They cannot continue demanding an immediate and total US withdrawal while refusing to compromise on their own military activities. Hanoi must be willing to moderate their demands and allow the South Vietnamese people to determine their own political future with free and fair elections."

Nixon concluded firmly, "Without North Vietnamese reciprocity and flexibility in Paris, it becomes very difficult for me to justify bringing more of our men home. The ball is in their court now to take constructive steps toward ending this war."

The president then reiterated that such progress on both sides could greatly enhance the chance for peace. However, he cautioned that nothing was guaranteed, as the path forward remained complex and tenuous.

As Nixon departed, reporters raced to file stories on his "Vietnamization" plan coming to fruition. Dovish lawmakers felt the president had finally bent to their pressure.

For now, Nixon had managed to placate all parties with a delicate policy balancing act. But as U.S. planes carried troops back home, many wondered if the reduced American presence could prevent Saigon from eventually falling to the communists. The South Vietnamese president feared being abandoned prematurely.

May 4, 1970 – Kent State University – Kent, Ohio,

USA

It was a temperate May morning when Allison arrived on the Kent State University commons, the grass still sparkling with dew. She clutched her homemade protest sign tightly, scanning the crowds already gathering. It was hard to believe just a month ago, her dreams had still been occupied with cheer squad aspirations and malt shop dates with high school sweethearts bound for the football hall of fame.

Meeting the intense graduate student Tad at freshman orientation changed everything. He caught her eye with his edgy goatee and sleeves of justice tattoos. When he invited Allison to an anti-war rally, she jumped at the intrigue of this sophisticated older activist showing interest. The injustice of this conflict raging overseas initially felt abstract to her.

At that first rally, hearing Tad's fiery words and seeing the conviction blazing from students and clergy and neighbors alike stirred something in Allison's soul. The raw agony of boys just barely older than her being ripped away to die in stifling jungle chaos suddenly felt deeply personal in a way cheer uniforms and cotillions never had.

After that rally ended, she confessed to her new roommate Emily, "I'm just so angry all the time now. It's like everything my parents' generation worked for is being thrown away in Vietnam." Emily nodded knowingly, having come from a family of peace activists.

In the following weeks, Allison's worldview expanded exponentially through late night debates clouding their dorm room with cigarette smoke. Radical graduate students like Tad paced as they lectured, igniting the crowd of students.

"Don't you see, the government rains bombs daily on innocent villages!" Tad thundered. "Nixon ruthlessly targets civilians in Hanoi against all codes of decency. Will we turn a blind eye as they murder children in our name?"

"No!" students shouted back, pounding fists. Allison felt swept up in the impassioned fury swirling around her.

When Emily timidly suggested peaceful protest may be best, angry voices drowned her out. "The time for peace is past!" an activist shouted. Chastened, Emily shrank back as Allison watched, realizing dissent was dangerous here.

She immersed herself in their mimeographed chronicles of government lies and oppressed voices. The injustices beneath the gilded American facade were now exposed in blazing color.

That fiery sense of purpose drove Allison to join the swelling crowds of protestors gathering on the commons nearly every day as tensions mounted. She let her schoolwork slide, feeling that stopping the war was far more important. She felt utterly caught up in the exhilarating sense of being part of something so much larger than her small-town Ohio upbringing. At last, the future seemed hers to mold rather than just passively inherit.

Tensions on campus had already been escalating for months amid swelling divides over the Vietnam War. News of Nixon's decision to secretly expand bombing into Cambodia ignited a firestorm. Allison felt pure outrage reading reports of the indiscriminate destruction and flagrant executive overreach. The United States military was losing its morality as well as its way in the jungles of Southeast Asia.

The campus outrage exploded into unrestrained protests that descended into violence. The administration building was vandalized, rocks hurled at police vehicles, the ROTC building torched - a symbol of the military presence students were rising up against. The wanton destruction prompted Kent's panicked mayor to call in the National Guard. To embittered students, Nixon's shocking Cambodia bombing was the final blow that escalated already volatile tensions past the breaking point into deadly chaos. The president himself had lit the fuse that would claim innocent lives across oceans and now on Ohio's green commons.

Within days of the chaotic downtown riots that prompted the mayor to call in the National Guard, Allison found herself facing down rows of armed soldiers. Many of the guardsmen were also Ohio boys just past high school, but worlds apart in circumstance. To them, these demonstrators were petulant punks whipped into lawless frenzy by professors with an extremist agenda. They had not signed up just to police provocative teens and young adults whose campus freedom they privately envied.

Knowing that a protest was scheduled for the next day, University officials try to prevent the gathering by printing and distributing 12,000 leaflets that stated that the rally had been canceled. It didn't work. The activist organizes had learned this tactic and sent word through their student grapevine that the rally would indeed take place at the appointed time.

The morning of May 4th dawned with a bite still lingering in the spring air. Despite the university's attempt to quell the rally, 2,000 students and local supporters gathered on the university commons in front of Taylor Hall and Prentice Hall. While many were just spectators on their way to classes, a core group of 300 protestors gathered around the Victory Bell, normally used to announce football victories. Tad rang the iron bell to signal the beginning of the protest.

Allison met Emily to grab a quick breakfast before joining the hundreds already chanting and singing on the commons. The gathering had swollen far beyond expected numbers as outrage intensified over the perceived overreaction of calling in actual troops simply to intimidate legitimate protest. Both carrying their homemade signs, Allison and Emily joined the core group surrounding the bell.

Bryan, a young guardsman, stood sweating in makeshift mess hall down the street, mechanically spooning runny eggs into his mouth. He had mustered out on a brutally early call-up after a long night downing beer with his buddies. Most were still snoring, but he had always been an early riser, in a hurry to make something of his young life.

Back home, his father never missed a chance to lecture Bryan for being too good to work at the radiator factory right out of school like he had. "College punks forget where their bread's buttered till the real-world hits 'em," the old man would grumble. Bryan had joined the National Guard both for the meager pay and to escape the suffocating expectations of becoming just another inhabitant of this fading industrial town.

Bryan dreamed of becoming a police officer after completing his tour of duty with the guard. Protecting the innocent and serving his community felt far nobler than mindlessly tightening bolts on an assembly line. He knew that despite the recent unrest, most of these students shared the hopes and fears of any twenty-year-olds suddenly thrust into adulthood. Their lives were not so different but for the fickle luck of circumstance.

The duty they were faced with left little room for such nuance. Guard commander, Brigadier General Robert Canterbury, had been abundantly clear on the mission - put down these disruptive protests with decisive force if needed. There could be absolutely no wavering under stress.

Bryan had faithfully attended every training drill, eager to prove his capabilities and loyalty. But silently he prayed cooler heads somehow prevailed before matters escalated beyond reason.

The screech of chairs on the mess hall floor signaled the rushed arrival of the remainder of his unit. "Get your asses in gear, we're moving out!" Sergeant Willis bellowed. "The hippies are stirred up into a hornet's nest again down on the commons."

Bryan stood to dutifully follow, smoothing his impeccably pressed uniform. But his stomach roiled with dread as they made their way down the street thronged with onlookers toward the chaotic din already audible blocks away. As he crested the hill and stared down at the seething mass of students surging against their barricades, fear quickened his pulse.

From his vantage point at the rear, the guards' hastily assembled lines looked pitifully sparse against the enraged hundreds they were tasked with containing and dispersing. A stray rock hurled from somewhere in the crowd ricocheted off a helmet near Bryan, eliciting profanity from the assaulted guardsman. More projectiles quickly followed as the chasm separating the groups erupted into open fury.

A large group of curious students moved up the back of the hill, unintentionally surrounding the outnumbered guardsmen.

Beside Bryan, Sergeant Willis ordered the tear gas barrage, his craggy face unmoved by the coughing throngs enveloped in acrid smoke. "Disperse 'em now before they get completely out of hand!" he barked at no one in particular.

Allison and Emily could not believe their eyes taking in the heavily armed lines of soldiers standing on the hillside. Allison wondered how just an hour before, their lusty chorus of "Ohio" by Crosby, Stills, Nash & Young ringing out seemed the most momentous event in her lifetime to date and now this. "They can't possibly shoot people just for yelling and holding signs on their own campus," Emily whispered in stunned disbelief. But uncertainty and dread hung palpably in the atmosphere as the guardsmen held their M1 Garand rifles in front to keep the protestors at bay.

A guardsman officer used a bullhorn borrowed from the University police and ordered the crowd of protestors to disperse.

Using his own bullhorn, Tad shouted, "Pigs off campus," then flipped off the guardsmen on the hill. He was joined by the entire crowd of 2,000 raising the hands into the air, gesturing the obscenity. The crowd ignored the repeated orders to disperse and leave the commons.

Tensions escalated as guardsmen periodically fired M79 grenade launchers loaded with tear gas cannisters toward clusters of protestors, enveloping them in choking clouds of the noxious gas. Coughing students scrambled for air, their eyes burning and noses dripping.

The guardsmen countermeasures only enraged the mob further. Assaulted from all sides by deafening threats and hurled rocks, many guardsmen like Ryan feared for their very safety as the situation rapidly deteriorated into chaotic violence. They were untested recruits - clerks, plant workers, tradesmen - utterly unprepared for confrontations with these provocative legions whipped into lawlessness.

In retaliation, a barrage of rocks and unopened soda cans rained down on the guardsmen's position. One guard dropped as an array of soda cans exploded against his face shield. The sporadic volleys of makeshift missiles and debilitating gas fueled the chaos, drawing both sides closer to the brink as projectiles filled the air between them.

After failed orders to clear the area, Sergeant Willis felt the thinning blue line of guardsmen wavering perilously. They were outnumbered ten to one, with no clear exit strategy from the green war zone unfurling below them. As a stray brick glanced off his helmet, Willis made the reluctant decision to fall back and regroup.

The mob's frenzy only escalated at the sight of the retreating guards. Willis's heart hammered, flooded with outrage and helplessness. How had things spiraled so disastrously out of control? He should never have let the men be deployed here - they were untested damned kids themselves barely older than these belligerent punks screaming epithets inches from their boyish faces.

Willis glimpsed the naked taunting fear in their eyes

as his unit retreated uneasily up the hill like whipped dogs. The humiliation was too much for his swollen pride and defective judgment to bear. His power and authority were slipping through his hands as the jeering horde pressed their momentary advantage relentlessly.

Somewhere in the discord, he thought he heard shots ringing out, though no clear order had been given. The enraged mob continued surging heedlessly forward against the wavering guards. Time crashed into slow motion as Willis's twenty years with the guard collapsed to this single agonizing moment - fight or flee. In that suspended instant, one decision would define his legacy irreparably.

The beast in Willis chose fight, consequences be damned. He would not slink away in disgrace from snot-nosed punks who would learn submission one way or another. With a primal roar, he raised his rifle and unleashed scathing fire into the distant swirling chaos until the magazine finally clicked empty. He was joined by other guardsmen, some firing in the air, others firing directly at the students. Only the ringing in his ears punctuated the nightmarish silence left in the bullets' wake.

In those fevered seconds of gross lapse and overreach, Willis had irrevocably crossed the line he once swore to defend. A part of his soul perceiving his graver sin died with the innocents bleeding out on the green grass below. He had forfeited forever the moral high ground and bright future awaiting a good man if only given a chance at redemption.

In thirteen seconds, twenty-nine of the seventy-seven guardsmen on the hillside had fired sixty-seven rounds. Bryan had chosen not to fire into the crowd or even overhead. He felt like a coward, letting down his fellow guardsmen. But he couldn't do it. It was wrong. He looked down at the bodies lying on the grass below. Tears welled up in his eyes. He shouldered his rifle still holding a full magazine. He didn't care what happened to him. He was done.

As the echoes faded, a ghastly silence fell. Emily knelt frozen, staring in mute disbelief at Allison collapsed beside her, vivid red blooming rapidly across the white dove on her shirt.

"No, no, no..." Emily moaned, crawling desperately to her friend's side. Allison's chest heaved erratically, her unfocused eyes wide with childlike confusion.

Emily pressed her hands futilely against the wound, blood seeping relentlessly between her shaking fingers. "Just hold on, help is coming!" But deep down, she knew the hope was as hollow as Allison's increasingly ragged breaths.

"Hurts. Can't breathe," Allison whimpered, face contorting with animal panic. A thin trail of blood trickled from the corner of her mouth.

"I know, I'm here," Emily choked out through sobs, cradling Allison's head gently in her lap. She softly stroked her friend's hair, tears dripping down her cheeks onto Allison's ghostly complexion.

As Allison's terrified eyes dimmed, her slight frame going limp, Emily threw back her head and howled in primal agony to the uncaring sky. Her dearest friend was gone, every hope and dream they had shared snuffed out in one senseless instant.

Nearby, Tad had just turned to flee when bullets ripped through his back, severing his spine with ruthless efficiency. He collapsed instantly, limbs splayed at unnatural angles. The ambitious young activist would spend the rest of his days paralyzed and bedridden, filled with impotent rage over all the lost futures.

In the massacre's aftermath, the commons lay silent save for Emily's anguished sobs as she clung to her murdered friend's body. A fallen placard lying on the grass nearby read, "Books not Bullets." The world had fractured irreparably for all caught in the violence's maelstrom. Nothing would ever be the same.

May 8, 1970 - The National Mall – Washington DC, USA

The humid night air was electric with anti-war chants as over a thousand protestors kept vigil at the Lincoln Memorial.

The Nixons rode in contemplative silence through the streets of DC after a press conference where he revealed that the US had been bombing Cambodia. The bombing of North Vietnamese camps and supply depots fed from the Ho Chi Minh Trail, had bought the South Vietnamese military eight months of time to implement Vietnamization. He claimed to be expanding the war to shorten the war and bring US troops home as soon as possible. The critics and journalists were harsh.

As they approached the White House, the president gazed down at the candlelit scene from the limousine with a pensive frown. "Would you look at that? Even at this hour there are protestors keeping vigil at the memorial."

Pat peered out at the flickering candlelight in the distance. "My goodness, you're right. Don't they get hoarse from shouting all day?"

"It's passion for a cause, misguided as it may be,"

Nixon replied. Turning to the driver, he ordered "Pull over up ahead."

The Secret Service agents exchanged concerned looks. Alarmed, Pat exclaimed "Dick, what are you doing?"

Nixon patted her hand reassuringly. "Don't worry yourself, Pat. I just want to observe them more closely."

Hearing the president's plan, one of the Secret Service agents said, "Sir, we strongly advise against approaching that crowd." But Nixon was already stepping out, buttoning his jacket, jaw set stubbornly.

The two Secret Service agents climbed out of the limousine, already radioing for backup. "Tom, please take Mrs. Nixon safely home. I'll see you there shortly."

"Now wait just a minute!" Pat cried as the president closed the door and the car began moving again. But her indignant shouts went unheeded. She huffed in frustration as the Lincoln Memorial's glow receded behind them.

One of the Secret Service agents called out as they scrambled to catch up to Nixon, "Mr. President, where are you going?"

"I'm going to talk to those kids," said Nixon striding toward the memorial, the Washington Monument lit up dramatically behind him.

The rowdy chants faded to stunned silence as the President of the United States marched directly into the mass of protestors without protection. Nixon's piercing eyes scanned the sea of wary young faces. He cleared his throat. "I know you think I'm an SOB. Frankly, you have reason to," Nixon began bluntly. "But I hope you'll hear me out. I want you to know that I understand your anger and frustration."

The crowd was taken aback by this candid admission. A long-haired young man finally retorted, "If you understand, then end this unjust war!" Others echoed his cry.

Nixon held up a hand. "It's not so simple. If we just up and leave Vietnam overnight, the result would be slaughter on an unbelievable scale. We have a duty to our allies and the South Vietnamese people."

The protestors shifted restlessly at this familiar rationale. But Nixon's willingness to engage surprised them.

A college girl spoke up hesitantly, "So you're saying more lives will be lost either way?"

"You say more lives will be lost either way," Nixon addressed the young woman who had spoken up. "You're not wrong. But we must weigh life against life. A bloodbath of tens, maybe even hundreds of thousands of innocent South Vietnamese will occur if we abandon our allies prematurely. We must choose the path that ultimately saves the most lives. It's a hard truth."

A voice called out, "So end the draft immediately then! Why should more Americans die for a war our allies need to fight themselves?"

Nixon paused reflectively before responding. "You pose a fair question. I wish the defense of liberty abroad didn't require such sacrifice. But freedom must be vigilantly defended everywhere, or it withers everywhere. We are bound to South Vietnam by treaty and by conscience."

"But at what point is the cost of conscience too high?" another protestor challenged. "And does defending liberty abroad mean neglecting the fight for equality and justice at home?"

Nodding thoughtfully, Nixon replied "I don't claim to know where exactly the line of too high a cost lies. I wrestle with that question myself daily. I do know America must stand for justice both within our borders and beyond."

"Four students were just murdered in cold blood at Kent State. How can you defend that slaughter?" said another protestor.

"The tragedy at Kent State was an enormous mistake, one I know we cannot take back. I ache for those families just as all Americans do. But more violence will only breed more hatred. We must find a way to heal these divisions between us," said Nixon.

As more Secret Service agents arrived, they kept their distance, giving the crowd space as long as they remained peaceful. Nixon spread his hands entreatingly. "I realize many of you have come to see this war as unjust. But surely you understand the agony of watching brave South Vietnamese who have fought by our side being slaughtered if we abandon them."

A young man with glasses shook his head forcefully. "With respect, Mr. President, the Diem regime we propped up was also responsible for slaughtering and oppressing its own people. Propping up such corruption undermines our moral authority."

This insight gave Nixon pause. After a reflective moment, he responded "I wasn't president at that time or I might have handled it differently. But hindsight is always twenty-twenty, and you may have a good point. In geopolitics there are rarely perfect options. But we cannot make perfection the enemy of the good when lives hang in the balance."

For over two hours the bizarre conversation continued under Lincoln's thoughtful gaze. The protestors were skeptical, but admired Nixon's willingness to listen. In the frank discussion, seeds of understanding took fragile root.

As Nixon finally turned to leave, the crowd spontaneously parted to let him pass. A young man called out, "I still think you're wrong about this war, but you've got guts!" Nixon just waved in weary acknowledgment before disappearing into the night.

May 15, 1970 - Jackson State University – Jackson, Mississippi, USA

While Kent State captured headlines, far less attention went to the police violence against student protestors at Jackson State soon after. On May 14th, a protest erupted over racism at the historically black college.

As the crowds grew rowdy, local police and state troopers deployed to campus, many harboring deep feelings of animosity against the activist students. Unlike Kent State, the victims were predominantly African American.

While suffering racism, black students felt emboldened by the civil rights movement to demonstrate for equality. But many white officers saw only lawless anarchy that needed suppressing by any means.

James, a normally peaceful student, clutched a protest sign as he joined the swelling crowds outside, indignant over the police encroaching on his campus. "They think they can intimidate us with guns and hoses like we're still living in the 50s," he spat. "But we won't be silent anymore!"

Outrage also brewed over the disproportionate drafts of young black men being shipped to die overseas. "How is it right they get shipped off while white boys get exemptions?" James's cousin Andre shouted. The inequality cut deep, fanning the flames of dissent.

As the crowd grew boisterous, hurling bricks and epithets, police opened fire recklessly with pistols, rifles, and shotguns firing 00 buckshot. Officers sprayed streams of shotgun pellets rather than targeting individual agitators.

James dove for cover, screams piercing the dark. Nearby, officers peppered the girls' dormitory with shotgun pellets without warning or restraint, their bias turning lethal. The victims included female students simply watching from their dorms, shot through walls and windows.

As the gunfire decreased, then stopped, James saw fellow students sprawled bloodied nearby who just hours ago had simply been laughing and talking about summer break. He fell to his knees, agony and fury coursing through him.

When it was over and the smoke had cleared, two students had been killed and twelve wounded. A total of 460 shotgun pellets had struck Alexander Hall wounding many of students in the women's dormitory. The killings illuminated the stark double standard in reactions to black versus white protestors, deadly force versus restraint. While Kent State made headlines, few outside Jackson State grasped that racism also fueled this tragedy.

Operation Jefferson Glenn

September 5, 1970 – Demilitarized Zone, Vietnam

Inside a humid command tent, American and ARVN officers gathered around a map, finalizing plans for Operation Jefferson Glenn. "Our objective is to push into the DMZ to destroy their supply bunkers and depots," explained the Marine colonel. "It will disrupt NVA operations for months."

The ARVN captain nodded eagerly, but an American advisor spoke up. "The NVA are dug in deep there. Our own casualties could be severe for limited strategic gain."

The colonel frowned. "The operation has been approved at the highest level. This is our chance to deliver a decisive blow."

"At what cost?" the advisor pushed back. "Hanoi will just rebuild eventually. We should conserve strength for more vital areas."

"We're going ahead as planned," the colonel said

firmly. "Our artillery and air support will carry the day."

The officers locked eyes, tensions simmering beneath the surface. Both knew the coming battle would exact a steep price from their men. But the orders were set. "As you say, Colonel," said the advisor.

In a stark bunker across the DMZ, Commissar Tran, the political officer assigned to the NVA 57th Battalion addressed NVA officers grimly. "The imperialists are coming to crush our supply lines - but they will drown in their own blood! We will make them pay dearly for every inch."

The major eyed Tran warily. "Our mission is clear: defend the motherland at all costs. But we must be prudent as well. Over-committing would leave our flank exposed."

Tran's eyes narrowed, sensing dissent. "There is no price too high for final victory. We will fight to the last man if needed!"

The allied officers saw a precise military objective. The communists saw an existential struggle requiring absolute sacrifice. Soon, blood would be spilled over these irreconcilable ideals.

The pale light of dawn bathed the edges of the jungle canopy in a gray glow. Hidden among the ferns and thickets, the NVA soldiers donned their gear in silence. For many, this was their first time crossing into the Demilitarized Zone that divided North and South Vietnam. They were young, frightened, but resolute.

"Stay focused. We must show the imperialists our strength," barked Commissar Tran. His job was to ensure loyalty during combat. To his left stood Private

Nhi, nervously adjusting the magazine on her AK-47. At seventeen, she had volunteered for the front lines after her brothers were killed in Hue. Though slight of build, she wanted to fight.

"Commissar, do you really think the imperialists will come today?" she asked, fingers fidgeting on her rifle. "What if...what if we fall back and regroup? We could better fortify the ridges to the west."

Tran's expression hardened. "No! We will not yield one inch of our sacred homeland! Your brothers died courageously defending the revolution. Do you doubt their sacrifice?"

Nhi looked down, chastised. "No, Commissar. I will fight without question or retreat. For my brothers, and for Vietnam."

She raised her rifle and peered out from the trench, scanning for any sign of the coming enemy. Any nerves were replaced by simmering anger for those who had torn her family and country apart. She was ready.

Several miles south, the American Marines made their own final preparations. Corpsman Mike Walters checked and rechecked his medical supplies, mentally steeling himself for the violence to come. This was his second tour, and the things he had witnessed haunted his nights. He missed his infant son back home, the innocence of the boy's eyes.

The sergeant gathered the platoon for a briefing before the operation. Walters stood with the Marines, his corpsman's helmet marked. At times, he wondered if the red cross on the helmet was meant to be a target for the NVA snipers.

"Alright, men, today we push into the DMZ to knock Charlie off his heels," the sergeant bellowed.

"Heavy artillery and air support will soften 'em up first."

The Marines nodded, stoic and determined. The sergeant concluded his briefing to the platoon. "Now gear up and prepare to move out! Oorah!"

The Marines replied in unison, "Oorah!"

As they dispersed, Walters pulled the sergeant aside. "Some of these kids are greener than grass, Sarge. This is their first time in the DMZ. I'm worried they don't fully grasp what's coming."

The sergeant nodded grimly. "I know, Doc. But that's war - we work with what we've got. Just do your best to watch out for them."

Walters sighed, feeling the weight on his shoulders. "Will do, Sarge."

He headed off to join his assigned squad, resolved to shield those young men however possible. If he could help even one make it home, it would be worth it.

The Marines checked their rifles and packs. Moments later, they were off, vanishing into the lush jungle.

As the sun rose into the grey sky, the thunder of naval artillery roared offshore. On the USS Newport News, a heavy cruiser, the gunnery officer checked coordinates before giving the order. "Commence firing!"

The ship's three enormous triple 8-inch gun turrets elevated and unleashed salvos of high explosive shells weighing up to 260 pounds each toward the coastline over twelve miles away. Gouts of flame erupted from the three barrels of each turret with earth-shaking blasts.

On the NVA positions, the first salvos impacted with devastating effect. Shells exploded in blinding flashes, cratering bunkers and trenches while shredding any soldiers caught in the open. Shrapnel scythed through tree branches as dirt fountained high into the sky.

In her muddy trench, Private Nhi huddled with arms clasped over her head as earth erupted around her. Each deafening naval blast felt like it would collapse her ribcage.

In a momentary lull, curiosity overcame fear. She slowly peeked above the trench, hoping to spot the unseen enemy ships offshore. But all that met her gaze was a horizon obscured by smoke and haze.

The elusive fleet continued pouring fire upon her. She dropped back down, resigned to enduring the relentless bombardment. A blast landed meters away, its shockwave knocking her down.

She trembled uncontrollably, mind blank with primal survival instincts. But deep inside, a flicker of hatred and defiance remained alive. She would not break, even if reduced to dust like the earth itself.

Aboard the Newport News, "Adjust azimuth two degrees starboard," called out the spotter, observing the impacts. The gun turrets incrementally shifted direction and fired.

The gun crews worked at blazing speed, hauling shells from the magazine deep below decks. This orchestrated chaos continued for forty-five minutes until the order finally came to cease fire. "Check fire! Check fire!"

The gun decks fell silent, smoke still wafting from hot barrels. Offshore, other cruisers like the USS

Galveston had joined the bombardment, firing 8-inch and 5-inch naval guns in coordinated strikes.

Ashore, the NVA positions were pulverized, huge craters making the trench line almost unidentifiable. After a moment of silence, Allied artillery and mortars took over supporting the assault again pounding the NVA trenches, then move back to the Communist reserve units and mortar emplacements behind the front line.

The jungle erupted with gunfire as the American Marines and ARVN troops launched their assault. They emerged from the underbrush like ghosts, charging across the DMZ toward the NVA trenches. American and ARVN machine guns support their advance.

Major Phan observed the chaos from his hidden observation post. His battalion had borne the brunt of the artillery onslaught, losing thirty soldiers in the opening salvo. But discipline held firm. As the foreign troops advanced, his men opened up with machine guns, recoilless rifles, and mortars, scything through the elephant grass. "Hold them back!" he ordered over the radio. "For our homeland!"

On the left flank, Private Nhi manned the machine gun emplacement that covered a barren hill. Her hands sweated on the trigger as shadowy figures came into view. She squeezed off bursts, and Marines crumpled and rolled back down the slope. To her right she saw two comrades fall to a grenade. She redoubled her fire, teeth gritted. The Americans seemed to materialize out of nowhere, supported by ARVN troops.

As the allied forces moved deeper into NVA lines, the jungle erupted into untold savagery. Men who minutes earlier had been whole were fed into the meat grinder of hot shrapnel. Corpsman Walters was in the thick of the carnage, moving from casualty to casualty, trying frantically to stop bleeding and dull agonizing pain. Morphine could only do so much - the sounds of the wounded crying out haunted him as he worked.

Major Phan observed a squad of American tanks maneuvering to support their infantry. He radioed coordinates to his heavy mortar crews, who quickly targeted the lumbering metal beasts. Shells rained down, blasting the tanks into twisted hulks. But Phan's moment of satisfaction turned to horror as jet aircraft suddenly screamed overhead, dropping strings of canisters along the tree line. Napalm splashed across the landscape, the inferno consuming all in its path. His left was decimated, platoons disappearing into curtains of fire.

Private Nhi was knocked unconscious when an artillery shell exploded meters from her position. She came to minutes later, her eardrums ringing and body peppered with dirt and debris. All around her the world was burning, green jungle turned to fields of fire. Forging ahead through the smoke and chaos, she re-manned her battered gun, knowing her comrades depended on her. She would not yield.

The allied forces were now deep behind enemy lines, but the way forward was paid for in blood. The platoon was pinned down as machine gun fire raked the hillside. Dirt erupted around the Marines flattened in the grass. Their nineteen-year-old sergeant, Evans, crawled to the lieutenant's position. "Sir, we're sitting ducks here! Request permission to take out that nest."

The young officer grimaced as rounds cracked overhead. "Go ahead, Sergeant! We'll give you covering fire."

Evans scrambled back and rallied his men. "Alright men, follow me up this hill! Stay low and move fast - we're taking those bastards out!"

He vaulted up, running crouched with rifle aimed. A squad followed. The pinned platoon laid down suppressing fire as the Marines charged up the slope. Bullets sliced through ferns around them.

Closing on the nest, Evans primed a grenade and hurled it. "Fire in the hole!" The blast disrupted the machine gun just long enough for the Marines to overrun it in savage close-quarter-combat. Evans plunged his KA-BAR knife into one defender while a private's rifle butt crushed another's temple.

In moments, the nest was taken. But only eleven out of seventeen Marines had made it to the hilltop. Evans looked back grimly at the trail of crumpled bodies marking their sacrifice. The day's bloody price was still rising.

As the long day wore on and the monsoon rains came, the forces of both sides were depleted nearly to the breaking point. Corpsman Walters had treated countless wounded - some too far gone to save, others he desperately hoped would make it home. In his mind, he tried to picture his infant son - so he would remember there was still good left in the world. But the scenes of horror surrounded him.

Major Phan surveyed the wreckage left behind as the Americans finally withdrew across the DMZ. So many promising lives lost. But tactical victory meant nothing without political victory. He took some small solace knowing they had bloodied the invaders. Commissar Tran appeared, his uniform filthy with mud and blood. "A great day for the revolution, Comrade Major. Our martyrs did not die in vain."

Phan nodded grimly. "Indeed, their sacrifice brings us closer to unity and ending this war. But at such cost."

He looked at the body-strewn quagmire that had been jungle just hours before. Was it worth it? Could any cause be worth this? Somewhere in the distance, machine gun fire still crackled through the dusk.

The sun sank low over the war-ravaged landscape, the last light fading from the blood-soaked earth. Exhausted soldiers on both sides retreated into their routines - meager rations, fitful rest, nerves frayed. They would need their strength again soon.

In a field hospital tent behind American lines, Corpsman Walters slumped over a cup of cold coffee, his uniform stained with the remnants of the day's horrors. Around him, the groans of the wounded mingled with hushed voices of doctors and nurses making their rounds. For many, these cots suspended between life and death would be their last.

Walters rubbed his eyes, willing his mind to push the visions of violence away, if only for a moment. He longed for sleep, but more for the tender embrace of his wife and the innocent laughter of his son. Just a photo of their smiling faces seemed anchored to another world altogether.

A young private two cots down was crying for his grandmother. Walters went over and gripped his hand. "It's okay, you're going to make it. Stay strong, buddy." Hollow platitudes - but what else could he offer? The private's eyes locked onto him, brimming with terror, before a dose of morphine took him under.

In a cratered command bunker across the DMZ, Political Officer Tran paced relentlessly, rage simmering just beneath his fanatical shell. The setback only strengthened his zeal. He would double down on political education, make the soldiers see the sacrifices required for victory. This was but one battle in a much larger war.

He glanced over at Major Phan studying maps, no doubt contemplating their next maneuver. Tran knew Phan's commitment to the revolution was slipping. Such doubt could spread like a cancer if not eliminated. He would need to be monitored closely. For the socialist motherland, Tran mused, no measure was too extreme.

Nearby, Private Nhi winced as a field medic wrapped bandages around the shrapnel wounds on her back and arms. She was lucky to be alive. Though just seventeen, she felt as old as the war itself. How much longer could they endure? She thought of her village - was it still standing or swallowed by bombs like so many others? Had this butchery served any purpose at all?

Nhi remembered the words of Commissar Tran, thundering that their sacrifice would unite Vietnam and deliver it from imperialism. Such conviction once inspired her. But now, gazing at the blood-soaked ground and vacant eyes of her comrades, she wondered how anyone could be so certain of anything anymore. All she knew was that come dawn, the killing would begin again.

Nhi tried to shut her mind to the horrors surrounding her. She found a relatively sheltered crater and huddled with her rifle clutched close to her chest, seeking any comfort she could find. Sleep came in fitful bursts filled with haunting images that made her jerk awake in a cold sweat.

Dawn's pale light eventually filtered through the smoke-filled sky. Nhi peered out from her crater at the remains of the battlefield—smoldering craters, mangled bodies, the rich earth soiled by blood. The sight twisted her stomach.

Footsteps approached, and she spun around raising her rifle. It was just a haggard soldier bringing tins of rice and tea to the weary defenders. His eyes were dark hollows. Neither spoke. They simply sat together, taking silent sustenance for the day of violence ahead.

When it was time, Nhi steadied her breathing and took her place at the battered machine gun nest. While checking her supply of ammunition, she thought of her brothers, remembering their smiling faces before the war took them. Gripping the gun tightly, she steeled herself once more. Let the imperialists come again. She would be ready.

Back in the command tent, the Marine colonel studied aerial reconnaissance photos that revealed the devastation along the enemy's defensive line. Bomb craters and charred trenches attested to the punishment already inflicted. "The NVA withdrew most of their forces under our barrage yesterday," the colonel said. "But pockets of resistance remain. We'll blast them before out assault, then move up to secure the area."

The morning sky flashed orange as the naval guns resumed their thunderous bombardment. In the nearby Marine encampment, the weary troops sat in groups laughing and trading banter as they ate hot breakfasts dished out by the field cooks.

"Bacon and runny eggs again? These cooks have no imagination," joked PFC Jenkins, poking at his plate.

The cook shot back, "You're welcome to come spice things up. My recipe's called 'Hand Grenade Hash.'"

"Think I'll pass!" said Jenkins, shoveling a mouthful of eggs eagerly.

Sgt Evans shook his head and grinned as he sipped black coffee. "Enjoy it while you can, men. We've got a long day ahead."

Somewhere beyond their lines, the jungle erupted in pillars of fire and shale. Explosions ripped through jungle as shells pounded the remnant NVA fortifications.

As the ship's big guns offshore resumed their thunderous roar, the Marines found respite and camaraderie over plates piled high, their spirits still intact. The storm would arrive soon enough. Let the Navy have its moment.

From her muddy hole, Nhi cradled her head and gritted her teeth. Each impact rattled through her weary bones. She tried to focus on memories of her family, but they flickered out like a fragile candle flame against this fresh onslaught.

When the naval fire finally ceased, the Marines rose from their positions to advance through the smoldering trees. They reached the enemy's front line to find it mostly abandoned except for dazed, wounded troops unable to withdraw the previous day.

Private Miller climbed over the remains of an enemy trench, peering through the swirling smoke. He noticed movement ahead - young Nhi, bleeding from a head wound, struggling to raise her rifle toward him.

Miller was momentarily mesmerized by her tenacity

even badly injured. Nhi pointed the barrel of her rifle at Miller. But before he could react, a shot rang out from his left. Nhi jerked and collapsed to the muddy ground, rifle falling from her grasp.

Private Miller turned to see Corporal Davis lowering his smoking M-16. "Damn, did you really have to do that?"

Davis shook his head. "Do you have a death wish, Private?"

"No, it's just...she reminded me of a girl back in high school is all," Miller replied somberly.

"Don't be an idiot," Davis scoffed. "This ain't the prom. Can't hesitate out here."

Miller nodded reluctantly. He took one last look at Nhi's body half-sunk in the mud, then followed David as they pressed on through the wasteland.

Corporal Davis and Private Miller regrouped with the rest of their platoon as they pushed deeper into enemy territory. There was little resistance now except for isolated snipers harassing their flanks. It seemed the bulk of the NVA forces had withdrawn during the night.

As the Marines fanned out to sweep the area, they came upon grim evidence of the bombardment's fury. Skeletal trees stood charred and splintered, the earth furrowed with craters. They discovered corpses and body parts buried in the churned soil.

Some Marines set C4 charges to destroy bunkers and tunnels too damaged to clear manually. Muffled booms echoed through the jungle as they detonated the explosives. Thick plumes of smoke drifted up through the canopy.

They reached a hill that had been an enemy command post. Now it was a pulverized moonscape of rubble and bomb casings. The Marines took up positions, establishing a perimeter while awaiting further orders.

Though they had advanced, the landscape felt hauntingly desolate. Davis wondered how much longer the NVA could endure this onslaught. But he knew each day would exact its share of blood as long as they fought on.

The Marines moved deeper into the bombarded terrain. Corpses, craters and shattered trees surrounded them. Then through the smoke, Private Miller spotted something - the crumpled tail boom of a Huey helicopter.

They approached cautiously and discovered the fuselage buried nose first into the earth. The naval bombardment must have sheared away the massive tree it crashed into over a year prior.

Sgt Evans ordered a perimeter setup while Corporal Davis checked inside. Corporal Davis cautiously approached the downed Huey, rifle ready. It was possible that the wreck had been booby-trapped by the enemy. Peering inside the fractured fuselage, the horrific wreckage came into focus. The pilot and co-pilot sat motionless, strapped into their seats, uniforms faded and bones showing through decaying fatigues. The crew chief's body was in the back on the deck. His hand was still holding the handle of the M60 in the doorway. It had been ripped from his body during the crash. Large ants still roaming the corpses for scraps had picked the flesh clean.

Despite the year that had passed, a faint but sickly sweet stench still emanated from within. Davis gagged. Composing himself, he leaned in to search for dog tags, trying not to disturb the remains.

He located a chain around each man's neck and gently lifted their dog tags over their skulls. Davis paused and offered up a silent prayer for these men who had fallen in service to their nation so long ago.

On the instrument panel, Davis noticed a faded photo. It showed a smiling pilot with a woman and two young children. Davis carefully removed it, wondering if the wife was still hoping her husband would return.

Emerging from the Huey, he handed the photo and dog tags to Sergeant Evans. "Pilot was Greenberg. Married with two kids according to the photo. We should make sure his family gets the photo."

Evans nodded, examining the faded photo and tags. "We'll get these men home. They deserve that dignity."

Carefully the Marines removed the skeletal pilots, still strapped into their seats after all this time.

The Marines carried the bodies out and bagged the remains. They marked the coordinates on a map for recovery later by Mortuary affairs. They couldn't linger. Evans signaled the collapse of the perimeter. It was time to advance. But none would forget this haunting memorial to those who had fallen before.

As the Marines prepared to advance, the roar of helicopter rotors swelled overhead. A squadron of Cobra and Huey gunships suddenly crested the smoldering treeline, racing past in pursuit of fleeing NVA forces.

The lead pilot spotted an enemy tank and armored personnel carrier exposed in the open below. "Tally ho!" he called out over the radio. The gunships wheeled around in unison, bringing their arsenals to bear. Rockets streaked downward, erupting in brilliant fireballs that engulfed the armored vehicles, leaving behind only twisted metal. Their hunt continued further north, seeking out remnants of the battered enemy.

Pushing deeper into NVA territory, the Marines entered a clearing containing the smoldering remains of an enemy supply depot covered in torn camouflage nets. A direct naval artillery strike had ignited the ammunition and fuel stores, leaving raging fires and twisted wreckage scattered about.

Circling the periphery, the Marines could make out piles of destroyed mortar tubes, crates of ammunition split open and charred black, and the melted hulks of trucks used for transport. The air reeked of scorched metal and lingering cordite. Signs indicated the NVA had already removed their dead and anything left of value before abandoning the demolished depot.

After ensuring no enemy forces lingered nearby, the Marines began gathering up slightly damaged weapons and material to evacuate. Rifles, machine guns, mortar rounds - whatever looked salvageable was carried to a central point.

A large CH-53 Sea Stallion helicopter descended into the clearing, its ramp lowered for loading. The Marines swiftly transferred armfuls of recovered NVA weapons and ammunition into its cavernous belly.

Within minutes, the chopper was fully laden. It ascended over the smoldering depot, the downwash from its rotors whipping up clouds of black smoke. The hard-won spoils were headed back to base, another small victory claimed amidst the greater devastation.

In the end, the allied forces accomplished their objective, inflicting severe damage on NVA fortifications and weapon caches in the DMZ. But the cost was sobering – seventy-eight Marines and over 100 ARVN killed, with hundreds more wounded. The NVA suffered catastrophic losses of over 2,000 dead defending their stronghold.

Neither side gained any strategic advantage. But the Marines took pride in overcoming a determined, well-entrenched adversary. As they withdrew south, this battle became one more scar in the grinding conflict that had years left to run.

Dancing Downhill

Scott piloted his Huey over the dense Vietnam jungle canopy, rotors thumping over endless shades of green. Steam rose in wisps from the shadowy undergrowth as sunlight filtered onto the treetops. It had the deceptive appearance of tranquility from above, masking the danger that lurked within.

Scott was distracted, not a good idea for a pilot flying over Viet Cong territory. His thoughts were troubled after picking up two VC collaborators from a hamlet deep in the jungle. One of the captives was a teenage girl, her eyes wide with fear when she was blindfolded by his crew chief. Standard procedure before prisoners entered the chopper. Usually, he could shut out those images, but her face stuck with him. He flew the captives to a Phoenix interrogation center. He knew she what would happen if she didn't give the interrogator what he wanted which was usually the names of other collaborators and any planned attacks she might know of. Whatever she gave him wouldn't be enough. He would want more, and the torture would start. A shiver went down his spine.

"Ten minutes out," his co-pilot Jake reported, snapping Scott back to the present.

Soon they cleared the mountains, and the airbase came into view, its runway and clusters of structures carved out of the jungle interior.

Scott landed the Huey kicking up plumes of reddish dirt. As he went through shutdown procedures, Jake asked "Hey, want to catch the USO show tonight? Redd Foxx!"

"The black guy?" said Scott.

"Yeah. I listened to one of his records. He'll say anything no matter how dirty. He's funny as hell. Plus, he'll have some singers and dancers too."

Scott powered down the chopper before answering. "Not really in the mood for a show tonight."

"Ah come on!" Jake cajoled as they climbed out. "It'll be good R&R. No pass required."

Scott walked around doing a post-flight check looking for bullet holes and any damage as they talked. "I'd rather just clean up, grab some chow, and get some rack time."

"You know, more and more you sound like my grandmother. Heading in for the early bird special?"

"Fuck off."

"That's a possibility if we can find some nurses at the show. But ya can't fuck what ya can't find." Jake followed him persistently. "When's the next chance we'll see entertainment like this out here? It'll be fun!"

Scott stopped and put a hand on the Huey. He stared off at the jungle, still picturing that girl's face. "Alright," he finally conceded. "I guess it could be a decent distraction."

Jake grinned and clapped his shoulder. "Atta boy!

Meet me at the officer's club at 1830. One quick drink and we'll head over to the show."

Scott watched him go, hoping the show might temporarily get the images of the day's mission off his mind.

The officer's club was packed with pilots drinking and playing cards. Ceiling fans stirred the humid air, rotating shadows over the dark wooden bar.

Jake sipped a Tiger beer, chatting up Mai, a petite Vietnamese waitress in an ao dai dress. She smiled politely at his mangled Vietnamese compliments.

In Vietnamese, Mai greeted her friend Suzi, another Vietnamese waitress. "That tall American is trying to flirt with me. His Vietnamese is awful. It hurts my ears," she said giggling. "You should flirt with his friend. He's a pilot too."

Suzi glanced at Scott brooding over his drink. "So serious looking," she replied.

"Yes, but very handsome."

Mai touched Scott's arm lightly to get his attention. "This my friend, Suzi," she said, gesturing to the other petite Vietnamese girl. "She think you very handsome."

Suzi grinned shyly and gave a little wave. "Hello..."

Scott nodded his greeting, trying to be polite though his mind was elsewhere.

Mai looked between Scott and Suzi expectantly, hoping they would converse more. When Scott remained silent, she shrugged and said something quickly to Suzi in Vietnamese that made her giggle behind her hand.

Jake overheard and chuckled. "Mai's trying to play matchmaker for you two," he teased Scott. "She wants you to buy Suzi a drink after the show."

Scott managed a faint smile for Suzi's benefit, though his thoughts were still flying over the dark jungle, unable to focus on the lighthearted banter around him.

Jake said to Scott, "We should invite these lovely ladies to join us at the USO show tonight."

Scott shook his head. "I'm not really feeling up to it."

"Oh come on, it'll be good for you," Jake insisted. "Don't make me drag you there alone."

Scott hesitated, but gave in to avoid Jake's persistent whining. "Alright, fine," he conceded reluctantly.

Jake grinned and turned back to the girls. "We go to USO show - you and Suzi should join us," Jake suggested with a grin.

"No Vietnamese allowed at USO," Mai said with a slightly angry tone.

"You come. I get you in. No problem."

Mai turned to Suzi and conversed in Vietnamese. They argued back and forth. Then turned back to Jake. "Okay. We go," said Mai thrilled at the chance to attend the American-only event.

Suzi clung to Scott's arm as they walked to the show. "You fly helicopters, yes? Very dangerous?" she asked in simple English. But Scott was still distracted and only nodded.

Frustrated, Suzi turned to Mai, "He not talk much."

"It's okay. He's strong silent type. Very good in bed," said Mai with a knowing nod.

Outside the makeshift performance area, a barricade was manned by military police checking IDs. Jake approached with Scott, Mai, and Suzi. The MP held up his hand. "Sorry, folks. Closed event.

Americans only."

Jake discreetly flashed his CIA credentials. "They're our interpreters for an important mission tonight," he lied. "Got approval from command to bring them in."

The MP peered at the credentials dubiously. He frowned at the girls, but then reluctantly nodded and lifted the barricade. "Alright, go on in."

Jake gave him a mock salute and led Scott, Mai, and Suzi inside before the MP changed his mind.

The makeshift performance stage was set up near the airbase tarmac. Rows of benches faced a small plywood platform framed by palm trees strung with lights. Airmen and soldiers were already packed into the seats, eager for the show to start.

In the trees just outside the secured area, Vietnamese civilians perched trying to get a glimpse. Others stood on car roofs and anything elevated they could find, hoping to see the famous American entertainer despite being banned from the event.

MPs patrolled the perimeter, shooing away anyone who got too close. Inside, Jake led Scott, Mai, and Suzi toward empty seats near the front. The girls chattered excitedly, thrilled to be inside something deemed off-limits to locals.

When the show started, the girls gossiped in Vietnamese about the dancers as Scott brooded, the day's trauma still haunting him. They admired the dancers' long legs and white skin. Very sexy.

As Redd Fox came on and greeted the crowd with a string of curse words, Scott laughed and started to relax. Suzi pulled his arm close to her breasts. She like this Scott better than the brooding Scott. Jake and Mai bantered and flirted through the show. For a couple hours, the war couldn't touch them. Scott was grateful

Suzi had pulled him out of his dark reverie.

Later that night, Scott awoke on the woven mat floor of Suzi's small, sparse hut. Moonlight filtered through the open window, casting a soft glow over Suzi's naked body as she slept soundly beside him.

Scott propped himself up on one elbow, allowing his eyes to trace slowly along Suzi's silhouette. The luminous light caressed her smooth skin and delicate curves. She looked so peaceful and beautiful lying there, dark hair fanned out around her head.

For a moment the war faded away and there was only this ethereal young woman next to him. Scott felt an unexpected tightness in his chest. He reached out a hand tentatively to brush a strand of hair from Suzi's cheek. She sighed in her sleep but didn't stir.

The crying of Suzi's infant son broke the spell. Scott quietly grabbed his pants and stepped over to the crib, not wanting the noise to wake Suzi from her slumber. He fished out a five dollar bill from his pocket and gently rubbed the baby's tummy with it. The crinkling paper soothed the infant back to sleep.

Scott carefully placed the five dollar bill in the crib next to the baby, hoping it would help Suzi care for her child.

Pulling on his clothes, Scott slipped outside.

Suzi's grandmother eyed him accusingly from where she slept in the front of the hut. Scott placed a one dollar bill by the grandmother before disappearing into the shadows, pleasure mixed with guilt.

The sun was just rising as Scott made his way back onto the airbase after his night with Suzi. He was exhausted, having gotten little sleep.

Scott headed straight for the showers, wanting to wash away the smell of cheap perfume. As he scrubbed, his mind kept replaying images of the young VC prisoner from yesterday. The distraction of the USO show and his night with Suzi had worn off and the war had come rushing back as it always did.

Clean but still weary, Scott went to the mess hall for some coffee. Jake was already there, looking bright-eyed. "So, you and that waitress Suzi really hit it off last night," Jake said with a knowing grin.

Scott just nodded, not wanting to encourage Jake's prying. His night with Suzi, while pleasurable physically, had left him with a nagging sense of shame. She was so young, dependent on meager tips from GIs just to feed her child.

"I've got to get prepped for today's mission," Scott mumbled before Jake could ask more questions. His friend meant well, but couldn't understand the darkness Scott felt creeping into his soul more each day in Vietnam...

After a long week of flying one mission after another, Scott headed to the base cantina just needing a beer. The small room was dimly lit, a few pilots and soldiers hanging out listening to scratchy Vietnamese pop music on the radio.

Scott sat at the worn bar. The bartender, an older Vietnamese woman, brought him a Tiger beer without him even asking. She knew her customers.

As he sipped his beer, the music shifted to an upbeat American hit song. A woman's laughter drew his attention to the small makeshift band stand in the back.

A blond woman in a crop top and fatigues was

dancing freely, her movements graceful and carefree. Scott was mesmerized by her energy.

When the song ended, the woman bounded up to the bar glowing with sweat. "One water please!" she said to the bartender cheerfully.

Up close, Scott was struck by her stunning beauty - sparkling blue eyes, full lips, flawless skin. She noticed him staring. "Enjoying the show?" she asked with a playful smile.

Scott blushed, caught off guard. "Sorry, didn't mean to stare," he apologized. "You're an amazing dancer."

"Well aren't you sweet," she replied and offered her hand. "I'm Allison."

"Scott." They shook hands. When their skin touched, Scott felt a spark of electricity. He was beyond intrigued.

"Are you one of the USO dancers?" Scott asked.

"Me? No, I'm a little too old for that," Allison replied with a laugh.

"No way. You can't be over twenty-two or twenty-three," Scott insisted.

Allison smiled. "Yes, I can. My legs can't keep up with those young girls."

"Baloney. I've seen you dance."

She stretched one leg gracefully. "I still have some moves, but I leave the official dancing to the pros."

"So what are you doing here?" Scott asked curiously.

"I'm the choreographer - I put together the USO show routines."

"A choreographer? That's really impressive."

Allison's eyes lit up. "It's been a lot of hard work, but I love it. Dance just speaks to my soul."

"Not everyone gets to pursue their true passion in

life like that," Scott replied.

"It's been my dream to open my own studio someday," Allison confided. "I want to inspire others through dance, like my teachers inspired me."

As they continued talking, Scott was captivated by her spirit and sense of purpose. It was clear dance meant everything to her. Too soon, last call was announced. "I'm headed to Hoi An in the morning," Allison said sadly.

Not ready for the night to end, an idea struck Scott. "Then let's make the most of our remaining hours," he suggested boldly.

"What about sleep?"

"Sleep is overrated."

She laughed, "Alright. But you will excuse me if I yawn. It's not you."

"You are excused in advance."

Allison's eyes sparkled with delight. Together they escaped into the tropical night, leaving war and responsibilities behind for a few stolen moments of joy.

They danced under the stars by the river's edge. Shared secrets and stories until the eastern horizon glowed with the coming dawn.

Scott escorted her to her tent to pack, then took her to the airfield where a C-47 was waiting. The rest of the entertainers and tour crew already on board.

They exchanged a bittersweet kiss before Allison reluctantly boarded the transport plane. "This can't be the end?" said Scott as she stood in the doorway.

"I guess that's up to you," she said then disappeared inside as the aircraft's engines started.

Scott wondered if they'd meet again, then decided to make damned sure they did.

The next day, Scott requested to use some of his saved-up leave. He hitched a ride on a supply plane to Hoi An air base, landing just as the USO show was starting.

The show was underway, but he caught Allison's eye backstage. She broke into a huge grin and discreetly blew him a kiss.

Afterwards, she rushed over and threw her arms around him. "You found me!" she exclaimed happily.

"Couldn't let you get away that easily," Scott teased.

Laughing, they strolled hand-in-hand down the cobblestone streets of Hoi An's old town, a wonderfully preserved window into Vietnam's past. Elegant yellow painted buildings with tiled roofs lined the narrow streets. Many still functioned as cafes, workshops, and stores as they had for centuries.

Intricate carvings decorated the wooden doorways and window shutters. Wrought iron balconies overlooked the bustling sidewalks below. Strings of colorful lanterns hung above, bathing the aged facades in a festive glow.

On the Tuple River, ancient cottages perched on stilts beside wooden boats. Across the water, the iconic Japanese Covered Bridge arched gracefully, its pagoda-style roof rising over the traffic passing under its eaves.

It was all so hauntingly beautiful, like stepping back through time. Scott and Allison wandered the streets hand-in-hand, pausing to peek into fragrant bakeries and workshops. The aura of history was palpable, and made their time together feel all the more meaningful. "Isn't this town amazing?" Allison said.

"It's something alright."

At the Japanese bridge, Allison insisted they take

cheesy couples photos. She made funny poses until Scott cracked up.

She's so full of life and unafraid, Scott thought.

In a lantern shop, they attempted to fold paper lanterns. Scott's collapsed immediately. "And that is a perfect demonstration of my artistic side," he said.

"It just takes practice," Allison encouraged. "Here, I'll help you." Together they reconstructed a lantern, playfully bickering and laughing.

After exploring Hoi An, they went to an open-air restaurant along the river. Strings of lanterns crisscrossed overhead, flickering in the breeze. The savory aroma of grilled meat and spices hung in the air.

They sat at a small candlelit table. Scott ordered in broken Vietnamese, making Allison laugh. The waiter brought pork and shrimp skewers with fresh rice noodles, spring rolls, and aromatic teas.

Between bites, Allison asked about Scott's family and childhood. He opened up about growing up in New England.

"It must have been idyllic surrounded by all that natural beauty," Allison mused. She told him about her passion for dance blooming in California.

When she mentioned visiting the ruins at My Son, Scott took her hand gently. "I'd love to see it with you," he said, mesmerized by her smile in the candlelight. "Tomorrow, I'll see if the motor pool can loan us a jeep."

In the morning, they drove through the lush countryside together in the open-air jeep. The wind ruffled Allison's golden hair as she pointed out rice paddies and water buffalo.

Arriving at the ancient ruins, they wandered hand-in-hand along stone pathways, past weathered temples and inscriptions in silence, taking in the historic beauty. Allison paused thoughtfully at a worn statue. "Can you believe this has stood here for over a thousand years? It's almost incomprehensible," she marveled.

Surrounded by heritage and nature, Scott felt peace - a world away from the war raging elsewhere. Time itself seemed to stand still in Allison's presence.

Back in town at dusk, they watched fishing sampans on the river returning to their homes. "I've never met someone like you," Scott said, kissing her.

Exhausted after the emotional day, they curled up on a bench by the river. Scott held Allison close as she drifted to sleep in his arms beneath the twinkling lanterns. Despite the hard bench, it was the most peaceful rest he could remember.

After a week, Scott again surprised Allison at her USO show at Phan Rang Air Base originally built by the Japanese during World War II. Wrapping her arms around him after the show, she said, "I missed you so much."

"The feeling is mutual," Scott said, then kissed her deeply.

Scott took Allison to an exclusive French restaurant overlooking a long beach where they sipped cocktails as the sun dipped into the sea. Allison starred out at the golden sky on the horizon and said, "God, this is all so…"

"Romantic?" said Scott.

"I was going to say perfect. But yeah, romantic overload."

"Too much?"

"No, not at all. What girl doesn't like romance? It's

just…"

"Just what?"

"The tour is ending soon."

"Yeah, I've been trying to forget that part."

"Me too."

There was a long silence. Allison could tell Scott was about to say something she wasn't ready to hear. She blurted out, "There's a waterfall near Thac Bao Dai. It's supposed to be beautiful… and secluded."

"Really?"

"Yeah. Maybe you could borrow another jeep from the motor pool and we could drive up their tomorrow."

"What about the show?"

"The girls know the routine now. I doubt I'll be missed. What do you think? Can you get a jeep?"

"I can do better than that. I'll get us a helicopter. The scenery must be amazing from the air."

Allison looked surprised. "Really? Can you just take a helicopter for the day like that?"

Scott leaned in close. "They don't ask many questions when they find out you work for intelligence."

"Intelligence? I thought you were a pilot for the Army?"

Scott considered for a moment, unsure how much to tell her, then said quietly, "Allison, I fly for the CIA."

It took Allison a moment to comprehend what Scott had said, then said a little too loudly, "You work for the CIA?!"

Scott looked around to ensure that nobody was listening. They were alone. "I wanted to sooner, but we're not supposed to tell anyone outside the agency."

"Not even me?"

"Well, yeah. Nobody. Some guys don't even tell

their wives."

"Well, that's a pretty damned big secret. I can't believe this. I thought I knew you."

"You do. I haven't changed. I'm still Scott." "No. No. Now, you're Scott the spy," said Allison pushing her chair back and rising.

"Wait, what are doing?" said Scott panicking.

"I need to think about this… this… bombshell."

"It's not a bombshell."

"For you it may not be. But for me… I gotta go."

"I'll go with you," said Scott pulling his wallet out to pay the bill.

"No. You stay here. I need to be alone."

Allison walked off leaving Scott looking like he just just got hit upside the head with a baseball bat.

Scott sat on the beach next to a carton of empty beer bottles. He stared out at the waves gentle crashing against the shore. A crescent moon hanging over the ocean. Scott heard footsteps in the sand behind him, but he didn't turn. Allison, her sandals in hand, sat down beside him and said, "I'm sorry I freaked out like that. I should be proud of you… serving your country like that. It was just such a shock. You guys are really good at keeping secrets."

"Yeah, kinda goes with the job," said Scott. "Do you still want to see me?"

Allison turned his face to hers and kissed him intensely, then said, "Hell, yeah."

"Good."

"Is that helicopter ride still in the cards?"

"Sure. We can do that."

"Okay, Mr. Secret Agent man. Make it happen."

The next morning, Scott and Allison boarded the small helicopter. Scott began starting up the turbine engine. The blades slowly began rotating, creating a deafening whine. Faster and faster they spun until becoming nearly invisible. Allison couldn't help but grin at the raw power of the machine as the blades disappeared in a blur.

Scott checked the gauges, gripped the controls, and increased the blade pitch. "Here we go!" he called to Allison over the roar. She gave him an excited thumbs up.

Scott gently lifted off, fine-tuning the pedals for stability as they rose over the airfield. With a smile at Allison, he banked left into the open sky ahead. As they flew over the lush tropical landscape, Allison gripped Scott's arm excitedly. "This is incredible!" she exclaimed over the roar of the engine and rotors. Scott smiled, happy to see her joy.

They flew low, weaving between jungle-covered mountains. Allison took in the stunning vistas of countless waterfalls plunging over sheer cliffsides and winding rivers below.

As Scott piloted them deeper inland, the increasing turbulence began to take a toll on Allison. Her stomach flipped and she started looking pale. Noticing her discomfort, Scott shouted over the engine noise, "Try picking a fixed point on the horizon and keep your eyes locked on it no matter how we turn!"

Allison scanned the distant jungle until she spotted a lone tree with a distinctive crooked top. She focused intently on it as the chopper banked and swayed. Though the aircraft continued bucking, keeping her eyes on that reference point helped relieve the building nausea.

Before long, they swept low over the secluded waterfall. Now feeling better, Allison sighed with relief as Scott landed in a clearing next to the pool below the waterfall.

Allison shakily climbed out, relieved to be back on solid ground. The fresh, misty air revived her. They hiked to the pool's edge, marveling at the raw natural beauty.

Pulling her coverup over her head and removing the silk wrap from her waist, Allison revealed a floral bikini. Pulling off his shirt and trousers, Scott had on green swim trunks. Allison stole a glance at his muscular body, then bit her lip and rolled her eyes in pleasant disbelief.

Caught up in the moment, Allison suddenly peeled off her top and shimmied out of her bikini bottoms. "Come on, live a little!" she called, diving into the cool pool naked.

Scott laughed and quickly stripped down to join her. "When in Rome!" he shouted, plunging in.

They swam playfully for a while, then Scott pulled Allison close for a passionate kiss beneath the thundering falls. They made love, wrapped in each other's arms amidst the swirling waters.

Drying off on the sunny bank, Allison turned to Scott. "This has been perfect, but it can't last. We're from different worlds," she said sadly.

Scott took her hand. "Let's not talk about that now," he replied.

"You're just one to live in denial?" Allison asked with a hint of a smile.

"Yep, works for me," Scott said lightly, pulling her

in for another kiss.

For now, the future faded away as they got lost in each other's arms once more, the waterfall thundering timelessly beside them.

As Scott flew them back from the waterfall, he and Allison could barely converse over the thump-thump of the helicopter blades. Allison gazed pensively out the window. "Are you okay?" said Scott seeing her tear up.

"I guess. I just don't know what's gonna happen when I leave in a week. I mean this has been great, but I want more," she said.

"I do too. So, we gotta work it out somehow."

"How? We're gonna be halfway around the world from each other."

"I know. And it's not gonna be easy, but if we both want it—"

Allison cried out and pointed past Scott's shoulder. He whipped his head around to see tracer rounds arcing up from the jungle canopy behind them. "Oh, shit!" said Scott as he banked the helicopter sharply right to evade the attack.

More bullets peppered the tail boom, metal fragments flying. Scott banked sharply, the helicopter's frame groaning with the strain. He zig-zagged evasively, the jungle canopy blurring past. An RPG rocket shot upwards and exploded against the underside of the aircraft, bucking like bronco. The helicopter pitched violently, warning klaxons ringing out as the damaged engine began to seize. A secondary explosion – the gas tank.

A piece of hot shrapnel ripped through Scott's back in a burst of blood and pain. Biting back agony, he struggled to maintain control as smoke filled the cabin. Flames crawled hungrily along the fuselage. Scott fought the aircraft controls, searching desperately for somewhere to land. "Brace yourself!" he cried through gritted teeth.

"Oh, God!" said Allison panicked.

"When we hit, you jump out as fast as you can and find cover."

The helicopter clipped trees, the ground rushing up. Branches smashed the helicopter's canopy, shattering the plexiglass. Scott pulled up desperately on the controls.

It slammed into the earth, skidding and rolling with an earsplitting metallic screech until tottering precariously on the edge of a ravine.

Adrenaline surging, Allison jumped out of the mangled wreck and ran for cover. She turned to see Scott still inside as the flaming wreckage teetered at the ravine's edge.

"Scott!" Allison rushed back and dragged him from the cockpit seconds before it tipped over the precipice and plunged downward in a fireball.

They collapsed, shocked. Smoke billowed up from the ravine. Scott's back wound oozed blood. "Oh, Jesus. You're hurt," said Allison pulling off her silk wrap as a bandage.

"We've got to get out of here."

"Okay but let me—"

"No, now."

"Alright. Where do we go?"

"The jungle. Hide."

Allison put Scott's arm around her shoulder and helped him walk. They stumbled into the foliage, pushing into the jungle. Scott groaned in pain. "It's okay. We're in the jungle. They can't see us."

"Blood trail."

Allison looked down. Scott was right. There was a trail of blood leading from the crash site. "Shit! What do we do?"

"Stop the bleeding. Keep moving."

Allison wrapped the wound as best she could with her silk wrap, then helped Scott to his feet. They moved deeper into the jungle. Allison look behind them – no blood trail but footprints in the mud. "Just keep moving," groaned Scott.

"Okay, we will. But you need a doctor."

"Yeah. Back at the base."

"Which way is the base?"

"Northwest."

"Which way is Northwest?"

"Sun sets in the West. North is on its right."

It took a moment to think it through, but Allison got her bearings. They continued toward the base. "How far is it?" Allison whispered.

"I don't know. Maybe five or six miles."

"Through this?!"

"We can do it. Just keep going."

"What if they catch us?"

"Just keep going."

"You're gonna bleed to death and I'm gonna be alone," said Allison starting to cry again.

"I'm not leaving you. I promise."

"Really?"

"Really. Just keep moving. Find a stream. We are gonna need water."

"Okay. A stream. There are lots of streams in the jungle. This is Vietnam. It's always raining."

"Right. You can do it."

Allison helped Scott hobble through the humid jungle, one arm holding him up, the other grasping a branch to slash through the foliage blocking their path.

Scott fought through the fiery pain in his back, focusing on putting one foot in front of the other. Allison's silk wrap was soaked with blood, but she dared not change it yet.

The light faded under the dense canopy. Strange cries echoed around them - monkeys, birds, who knows what else was lurking in the growing darkness.

"We need to rest soon," Allison whispered. "You've lost a lot of blood."

"No, keep going," Scott insisted between pained breaths. They struggled up a steep ridge, then Allison halted abruptly.

"Do you hear that?" She pointed to a narrow gulch where a trickle of water tumbled over mossy rocks. "The stream you wanted!"

Reaching it, she eased Scott down, rinsed his wound gingerly and washed the blood from her silk wrap. He gritted his teeth, but the cool water revived him slightly.

As Allison rewrapped the injury, the shriek of a leopard pierced the night. "What the hell was that?" said Allison.

"Leopard. Probably smells the blood."

"Is it dangerous?"

"We don't want to stick around to find out. Let's keep moving."

She peered around anxiously. "We'll be safe if we stay near water?" she asked Scott, helping to his feet.

"No. Leopards drink water too."

"Right, of course. Let's move away from the stream then."

She spotted an elevated ridge and half-dragged Scott up the steep rocky slope, scrambling on all fours at points.

Reaching the flat overlook, she propped Scott against a boulder. His face was pale and clammy. He looked at her and said, "Mud will hide our smell."

Allison rubbed mud on them both to disguise their scent from jungle predators. Settling close together, they kept alert for any rustling in the dark brush below.

"We rest for ten minutes, then keep going."

"It's dark. We can't see."

"Our eyes will adjust. We have to put distance between us and the Viet Cong."

"Can we do that?"

"Sure. If they're lazy."

They both laughed painfully.

"We're gonna make it, right?"

"Yep. One foot in front of the other."

"Okay. I believe you."

"Smart move," said Scott with a weak grin.

"Don't," said Allison give him a light punch in the arm.

Scott groaned. "Serves you right," said Allison.
"I need to close my eyes for a few minutes. Wake me in ten minutes if I fall asleep," Scott mumbled, closing his eyes from sheer exhaustion.

Allison knew he needed rest. She let him sleep, keeping vigil as the night sounds surrounded them. An hour passed. Finally, she gently shook Scott's good shoulder. "I'm sorry, I let you sleep longer," she whispered.

Scott blinked groggily as Allison pointed wordlessly down the ridge. A Viet Cong patrol moved through the jungle below toward the stream, sweeping flashlights over the underbrush.

Crouching low as possible, Scott and Allison froze. The Viet Cong patrol was at the ridge's base, sweeping flashlights methodically along the ground.

Scott could make out their muffled voices speaking Vietnamese as they examined the jungle floor. He locked eyes with Allison, signaling silently to remain still. If they ran, they would be heard, shot or captured.

One of the soldiers found their footprints in the mud leading up the ridge. The soldiers began ascending the rocky slope, following Scott and Allison's muddy footprints up toward their hiding spot. Each snap of a twig made Allison flinch.

Twenty yards below, the patrol paused, shining lights on the trail. Scott's heart hammered, as he readied himself to make a hopeless last stand.

Just then the shrill cry of a leopard pierced the jungle. The soldiers shouted and abruptly retreated down the ridge to give the big cat a wide berth.

The patrol moved off into the night. Scott and Allison finally exhaled, their lives spared by chance. On Scott's signal, Allison helped him up and they pressed onward through the darkness.

Leaning on Allison, Scott pushed forward through the suffocating jungle night. Each step shot pain through his back, but he focused on the terrain ahead lit by moonlight peeking through the canopy.

They moved as quickly as Scott could manage, ears straining for any sound of pursuit. The Viet Cong patrol could return at any moment.

After covering a painful mile, the incline gradually leveled out. The brush thinned and they stumbled into a clearing - the outskirts of a deserted hamlet.

Scott scanned the dirt roads and dark huts. No sign

of villagers or soldiers.

"What do you think?" whispered Allison.

"We can rest briefly," he whispered back.

Helping Scott sit against a tree, Allison tended to his wound, wiping caked mud away with trembling hands. The bleeding had slowed.

Searching the empty huts, Allison found a small pot with leftover rice covered in dried fish sauce and a gourd holding water. It wasn't much, but could help sustain them.

She brought it to Scott. They drank and ate ravenously with their hands, the salty rice giving them energy. After eating, Scott used a bandana from his pocket to gently wipe camouflage mud from Allison's face. "How much further?" Allison asked anxiously, glancing toward the dark jungle beyond the village.

"If we reach the river, we're halfway there," Scott assured her.

Resting for a precious few minutes, they left the ghostly village and oriented north. Keeping to the shadows, they moved toward the distant river, knowing it was their only hope.

The monsoon raged on, showing no signs of abating. Trudging through deepening mud, Scott and Allison pressed toward higher elevation through moonlit jungle. Scott and Allison tensed as lightning split the darkness and a distant rumble shook the ground beneath their feet.

"Monsoon's coming," Scott guessed grimly. "We need shelter, fast."

Leaning on each other, they staggered toward a sheer rock face ahead. Finding a shallow cave, they crawled inside just as rain lashed down in torrents.

Huddled together in the cramped space, they

listened to the monsoon rage outside. But soon water began seeping into their refuge. It was obvious, the tiny cave would flood.

"We have to keep moving!" Scott urged over the cacophony. They pushed back out into the storm, instantly drenched by warm rains.

Without warning, a wall of water crashed through the jungle, flash floodwaters swallowing the path, muddy torrents churning with tree limbs and debris. It slammed into them with crushing force, pulling them under the murky water.

Tossed violently, Scott managed to grab hold of a thick tree branch, nearly wrenching his shoulder from its socket. He gritted through searing pain, desperately clinging to the bobbing branch.

He glimpsed Allison's terrified face silhouetted in the muddy froth. As she neared, he shot out his other hand and seized her slender wrist with all his might. Scott heaved upwards with a bellow of pain through clenched teeth. Hauling Allison from the grips of the flood onto the muddy bank beside him. They crawled just out of reach of the deadly currents.

Gasping with effort, Scott met Allison's eyes. They shared a silent look of gratitude and resolve. Once more, he had saved her life as she had saved his.

She again helped him to his feet. They barely crawled beyond the flood's reach when Vietnamese voices rang out. The Viet Cong patrol. Taking cover behind a tree, they glimpsed soldiers approaching through the rain.

The VC leader took aim at the tree shielding them. Splinters exploded as submachine gun bullets shredded the trunk.

Scott and Allison tried to keep behind the tree trunk

that was quickly its girth. "What do we do?" said Allison with panic in her voice.

"When he runs out of ammunition and changes his magazine, we make a break for it," said Scott.

"What about the other soldiers?"

"I didn't say it was a perfect plan. But it's all we got."

Just as the tree cracked under the barrage of bullets, booming artillery fire erupted, decimating the VC patrol. Through the smoke charged fourteen American soldiers, firing them M16s.

Outnumbered and outgunned, the surviving VC made a break for it deeper into the jungle.

Scott and Allison limped from cover, waving desperately. The patrol hurried over and pulled them to safety. Their harrowing journey was finally over.

Scott woke to antiseptic hospital smells, his back heavily bandaged. He was lying on his stomach, face down in the padded hole of a recovery bed. The events in the jungle felt surreal and far away now.

As his eyes adjusted to wakefulness, he noticed a familiar face peering up at him from the floor. Allison lay under his bed so her smiling face would be the first thing Scott saw. "Welcome back," she said softly. "How are you feeling?"

Scott managed a weak smile. "Like I fought a tiger and lost. But better now seeing your face."

Allison's tour ended soon. Their conversation about the future of their relationship could no longer be avoided. She broached the subject hesitantly. "Come back to the US with me. We can build a life together there."

Scott smile at her thoughtfully. "I want that. Really I do, but I have to finish what I started here. This war won't last forever."

"I'm afraid, neither will we," she said tears welling up in her eyes.

"I suppose I know that's a possibility. But we've faced some pretty big challenges together. If we really love each other, waiting a couple of years should be a piece of cake."

"Maybe. A lot can happen in a couple of years. That's what scares me."

"Me too."

There was a long silence. Allison's eyes glistened with tears. "I'll wait for you. However long it takes. And I'll write every day."

"No promises," Scott replied sadly. "We're both smarter than that."

"Yeah. Still… we can hope."

"Okay. You write every day. I'll write once a week."

Allison kicked the bottom of the bed. Scott groaned.

They talked for hours, reminiscing happily, and sharing their heartache over parting. Finally, Allison rose up to Scott's face in the hole and gave him a goodbye kiss he would remember. With no more words to say, she disappeared from under the bed. She was gone.

Kate

October 25, 1970 - South Vietnam

The colossal storm churned northwest across the South China Sea, fed by warm tropical waters. Kate had quickly intensified into a Category 4 typhoon packing 140 mph winds and twenty-foot swells. Satellite images revealed a menacing cyclone wider than the entire state of Florida. Kate had South Vietnam dead in its sights.

In Da Nang, civilians scrambled to shutter windows and tie down any loose debris as Kate's outer bands lashed the coastline. Floodwaters swelled in the streets, lifting cars and swamping homes up to rooftops in low-lying areas.

Families took shelter wherever they could - in offices, hotels, churches. But many had nowhere to escape the tempest. Refugee shantytowns on the outskirts bore the brunt of the storm as flimsy structures of tin and thatch were ripped apart by the roaring wind.

Along the exposed coastal flats, towering waves eroded beaches, smashed piers, and surged inland, swallowing entire villages in white water fury. Police boats desperately tried to evacuate trapped fishing communities but could not reach all in time.

Inland, relentless sheets of rain flooded rice paddies and roads, turning dirt to mud, carrying away precious topsoil. Landslides rumbled down deforested mountainsides, consuming anything in their path. Entire hill tribes found themselves marooned.

For troops hunkered down on bases across the country, the storm forced operations to a standstill as it wreaked havoc. Flight crews worked feverishly to shelter aircraft, knowing Kate's winds could toss planes like toys.

The US Navy ordered ships out to sea to ride out the typhoon safely away from the coast. But dozens of swift patrol boats and amphibious transports were still battered in port.

Likewise, VC and NVA units took shelter underground or retreated from the battered coast. Mobile supply lines and troop movements bogged down in the endless quagmire left by the deluge.

For three days, Kate lingered over Vietnam, dumping triple the normal rainfall and unleashing 115 mph winds. When the last bands finally passed, over 300 civilians had perished, two division's worth of military material was destroyed, and tens of thousands were left homeless.

But as bad as the damage was, it could have been worse had Kate made landfall farther south. Instead, the storm veered back out to sea, finally dissipating over the Philippines.

In the wake of the disaster, Hueys dropped emergency supplies to evacuees in areas cut off by washed-out roads and bridges. Navy Seabees labored round the clock to reopen airports and repair swamped military bases. Nobody slept, only brief catnaps to give them more energy.

For troops who had endured Kate's violent passage, it was just another hardship in the grinding war. Both sides took the small mercy that the storm had crippled opposing operations equally.

Within weeks, the damage was largely repaired, the dead mourned, and missions resumed as if Kate had never unleashed her fury on Vietnam's flood-prone terrain. But for those who survived, the typhoon's scars would linger long after the last rains ceased.

Central Highlands, Laos

As the Vietnam War dragged on, domestic opposition and war weariness grew in the United States. Seeking to de-escalate and negotiate an end to the conflict, President Nixon instituted the policy of "Vietnamization" - gradually withdrawing US troops while transferring responsibilities to the South Vietnamese. This policy extended to the covert operations in Laos conducted by the Military Assistance Command Studies and Observations Group (SOG).

Though SOG's reconnaissance missions and tribal guerilla warfare had been successful in interdicting the Ho Chi Minh Trail supply network, they had come at a high cost in lives and resources. With popular support for the war waning, policymakers could no longer justify these operations.

In 1970, the first SOG personnel and facilities were pulled out of Laos and Thailand. SOG was disbanded piece by piece despite protests from field commanders who felt the tribal allies they recruited, trained, and fought alongside were being abandoned.

The SOG withdrawal meant Laos was now fully open to North Vietnamese Army forces and communist Pathet Lao insurgents. No longer disrupted by SOG and Montagnard raids, supplies flowed freely down the Ho Chi Minh Trail to support operations in South Vietnam. With their CIA backers also gone, the Hmong tribesmen who had formed the backbone of the guerilla army were left isolated and persecuted. Many fled their ancestral highlands, seeking refuge across the border in Thailand and Cambodia.

SOG's withdrawal marked America's relinquishing control in Laos. As the Laotian civil war tipped irrevocably in the communists' favor, SOG's former allies paid the price, hunted and displaced from their homelands.

Thunder rumbled as the final Hueys touched down at the SOG base. The teams hastily loaded gear, faces sullen.

Sergeant Tran approached his pregnant Montagnard girlfriend, Mai. He squeezed her hands, searching for words. "I have duty to my country, but I'll come back for you and our child," he said finally. "I promise."

Mai nodded, tears filling her eyes. "I will wait for you."

Nearby, Major Bridges said goodbye to the Montagnard chief Yehen. "I don't agree with this decision by my superiors. You have been loyal allies and you deserve better." Bridges unslung his CAR-15 submachine gun and held it out to Yehen. "Here, my friend. Keep fighting."

Yehen accepted the weapon grimly. "We will fight to the end... as you taught us."

The chief's comment stung with hypocrisy, but the SOG leader had his orders. As always, he would carry them out. He saluted the chief, then turned and walked toward the waiting Hueys. A sergeant moved beside him and said, "The yards deserve better than this."

Bridges stopped and turned to look the sergeant in the eye. "You don't think I know that? We have our orders and we will carry them out as we always do."

"What about them? We can't just leave them. The Pathet Lao will slaughter them."

"Stop your belly-aching and get on board your chopper, Sergeant," Bridges said firmly.

He didn't like it, but the sergeant obeyed as did all the SOG operatives.

The choppers lifted off, transporting the SOG teams from the mountain valley that had become their second home. They questioned if they would ever return or see their Montagnard allies again.

Below, the Montagnard gazed up at the fading helicopters, then exchanged uncertain looks. The tribes prepared for the attacks they knew were coming. Yehen called the Elders together to fortify defenses without their American allies. It was a hopeless situation, but they had no choice. Fight or die, those were the only options available.

It didn't take long before the NVA and Pathet Lao launched assaults on the abandoned SOG bases and the villages aligned with SOG. Red tracers lit the night as troops burst into homes, executing men and older boys. Women, children, and the elderly ran into the jungle for refuge. Thatched huts burned, livestock slaughtered. Even after years of fighting, the Montagnard were shocked by the Pathet Lao's violence as they took revenge against their enemy. Their NVA leaders stood by and watched, knowing that the example set in blood would warn any civilians from fighting against the communists.

When the enemy came to Muong Houn village, the Montagnard were waiting. Armed men appeared from hiding and raked the attackers with gunfire while women, children, and the elderly fled. Yehen led the defense, wielding the CAR-15 gifted by Bridges against those who had long persecuted his people. Without air support, the tribesmen were soon overwhelmed by the invaders' numbers and artillery. Their vengeance complete, the troops withdrew leaving only smoke and bodies.

After the communists had left, the surviving warriors and their families returned to the remains of their village and buried their dead. They gathered leftover belongings and livestock then disappeared silently into deep jungle.

Two hundred thousand displaced tribesmen and their families stole south into deep jungle, evading tracker teams. Entire Sedang, Nhung and Koho tribes embarked on the long march toward Cambodia. Some went to Thailand.

The grueling journey took its toll. Many perished from exhaustion, starvation, disease, or Pathet Lao ambushes. After weeks of hardship, the tattered refugees reached the border where Khmer Rouge troops waited in a series of ambushes. The Cambodian communists were determined not to allow the Laotian tribesmen a foothold in their country. Realizing the border was a cage not freedom, the Montagnard fled in panic into the trees as gunners cut them down. The slaughter went on for days until the grass was slicked red with blood, ending the tribes' long journey from their ancestral highlands. Those that survived, and there weren't many, broke into small groups and entered Thailand and South Vietnam where they lived out their days dreaming of the land they loved.

October 7, 1970 – White House, Washington DC, USA

Nixon sat at his desk, shuffling papers as technicians adjusted lights and cameras. In a few minutes, he would address the American people about Vietnam. An aide powdered Nixon's face and clipped a mic to his tie. "Thirty seconds to air, Mr. President," he said.

Nixon took a deep breath and collected his thoughts. He had announced the withdrawal of 150,000 more troops in the last six months. But the anti-war movement kept growing. He needed a bold stroke to regain momentum and faith in his leadership.

The TV camera light blinked on and the director pointed at him. Nixon looked directly into the lens. "Good evening. Tonight I want to discuss the prospects for peace in Vietnam and the next steps we must take. Our withdrawals have proceeded on schedule, yet the war continues. So I propose a five-point peace plan:

One - an immediate ceasefire throughout North and

South Vietnam.

Two - An end to all acts of force throughout Indochina.

Three - An Indochina peace conference including all parties.

Four - A supervised withdrawal of remaining US forces within six months.

And five - An end to US sanctions once our POWs are released and a truce concludes honorably."

Nixon stared into the camera intently. "With goodwill on all sides, we can reach a lasting peace. The sacrifices of our brave soldiers will not have been in vain. By transparency and bold action for peace, we can heal the wounds dividing our nation. The peace process begins tonight. God bless America and God bless each and every one of you. Good night."

The light blinked off. Nixon let out a breath and awaited the response from an American public weary of war but desiring stability and unity. He hoped this bold gambit would deliver the truce they craved.

Hanoi, North Vietnam

In response to Nixon's ceasefire proposal, the North Vietnamese denounced the proposal the next day as "a maneuver to deceive world opinion," but stopped short of rejecting it entirely. It was progress... sort of...

Sons of Ivory Coast

White House, Washington DC, USA

General Earle Wheeler walked briskly through the West Wing hallways, his polished dress shoes clicking on the marble floors. As Chairman of the Joint Chiefs, he did not require an escort, but still he felt each stare from the buzzing staff as he passed.

Arriving at the receptionist's desk outside the Oval Office, Wheeler straightened his uniform jacket and cleared his throat. "I have a meeting with the president."

The young receptionist nodded efficiently as she rose from her chair, "Yes, sir, he's expecting you."

She stepped swiftly to the large wooden door and knocked twice before opening it. "Mr. President, General Wheeler is here to see you," she called through the opening.

The gruff voice of Nixon answered for the receptionist to show the general inside. She motioned for Wheeler to enter holding the heavy door open for him.

Stepping into the Oval Office, Wheeler was greeted by the sight of Nixon rigidly poised behind the Resolute Desk, shoulders squared as if having his portrait painted. His intense gaze focused on Wheeler as he approached.

"Mr. President, thank you for seeing me on such short notice," Wheeler began, his voice faltering slightly.

"Of course, of course, Earle, please have a seat," Nixon replied briskly, though his body language remained closed off. He did not rise to greet Wheeler.

The general lowered himself cautiously into one of the wingback chairs facing the president. The White House decor shimmered with a sense of history and importance, contrasting Nixon's clear unease at idle small talk. Floor to ceiling drapes framed windows looking out over the National Mall.

"Mr. President, as you know we have over 500 American servicemen languishing in brutal POW camps across North Vietnam. After five years of captivity for many, their condition is deteriorating. We owe them more than standing by idly."

Nixon nodded somberly. "A tragic situation, no doubt. But North Vietnam remains off limits to ground operations per my orders. The political ramifications are too unpredictable."

"I understand your hesitation, Mr. President. But allowing the North to continue mistreating our men damages American prestige and lowers morale. I request authorization for a small surgical strike on a prison camp outside Hanoi. A demonstration that we can penetrate their defenses at will."

Nixon raised an eyebrow, intrigued by the bold

proposal. "Wouldn't such a raid carry risks of escalation?" said Nixon.

Wheeler clasped his hands. "It's possible, but the payoff outweighs those concerns. We're not seeking casualties or sustaining operations. This is about boosting morale for our captured troops, showing them their country has not abandoned them to their fate."

Nixon leaned back in his chair, steepling his fingers as he mulled over Wheeler's proposal. "You know Kissinger has been making progress at the Paris peace talks. This operation could upset the delicate balance just as we are nearing an agreement."

Wheeler nodded thoughtfully. "I understand your hesitation, Mr. President. But perhaps there is an argument to be made for rattling their cage a bit. Remind them no option is off the table."

Nixon raised an eyebrow. "Go on..."

"If we strike swiftly and sharply, the North may return to the negotiating table more pliable, eager to finalize a deal. The situation in Vietnam is still to our advantage. Press it."

The president swiveled in his chair, contemplating the idea. Risky, but not without potential upside. "Intriguing thinking, Earle. Those Ivy League academics at the State Department tend to be too cautious. Sometimes you have to crack a few eggshells."

Wheeler suppressed a smile. The president was taking the bait. "Precisely, Mr. President. Remind them who still holds the initiative. I assure you, this mission will send a powerful message."

Nixon pointed at the general. "I always say it's best when your opponent is back on their heels. Alright

Earle, you've convinced me. Proceed with your plan."

Wheeler allowed himself a tight smile. "Thank you, Mr. President. I know the perfect unit for the mission - our best Green Berets. I assure you they will succeed."

Nixon stood, signaling the meeting was over. "I expect nothing less, Earle. See that it's done swiftly and correctly."

Wheeler rose, shaking Nixon's hand firmly before exiting the Oval Office. As he walked back through the West Wing, the general began planning the operation that would send shockwaves through North Vietnam - codename Ivory Coast.

Covert Military Base, Eastern Thailand

Colonel Arthur "Bull" Simons stepped out of the jeep and into the oppressive jungle heat that hung over the covert military base in Thailand. Cicadas droned in the dense foliage surrounding the compound. As Bull walked past the guard station, he pulled at his sweat-soaked Green Beret uniform, wondering why he had been summoned on such short notice.

The base itself was an unimpressive cluster of faded green buildings joined by covered walkways. It lacked the amenities of stateside facilities, but offered seclusion deep in the wilderness, far from prying eyes. Even in Thailand there were spies.

Bull strode past the base's small admin building and medical clinic, circumventing the noisy mess hall. The operators here valued their privacy and space. Most chose to take meals alone.

Approaching the squat operations center, Bull entered through a creaky wooden door. Inside, the windows were shuttered and dim fluorescent bulbs provided the only light. The cool air smelled stale, with an undercurrent of coffee. Ceiling fans whirling overhead did little to keep the heat down.

Maps of Laos and Vietnam covered the walls, alongside grainy recon photos held up by pins and tape. Filing cabinets overflowed with intelligence reports stuffed haphazardly inside. It all seemed unprofessional. A tangle. Not his problem.

Bull waved off the saluting sergeant manning the duty desk and headed straight for the secure briefing room in back. A mission was clearly brewing, to require his urgent presence.

As Bull walked down the hall, his mind cycled through the possibilities. A high-value target needed eliminating? Or maybe the brass had finally green-lit operations in Haiphong Harbor to cut off supply lines from Russia and China.

Reaching the reinforced steel door of the briefing room, Bull straightened his beret and entered. Inside, he found two generals and three colonels sitting around a scarred oak table, their grim expressions suggesting an operation of the utmost importance. Bull came to attention, ready to receive his orders.

Bull recognized General Hamilton, a decorated veteran of Korea and one of the Army's most seasoned commanders. No paper pusher. The real deal.

"Have a seat, Colonel," Hamilton said, shaking his hand firmly. "Thank you for coming on such short notice. This mission requires the utmost secrecy."

Bull settled into a creaking leather chair, his gaze drawn to the grainy black and white photos on the table. "Of course, sir."

Hamilton's expression remained grave. "I'll get right to it then. As you know, we have over 500 Americans being held prisoner under brutal conditions across Vietnam. We've tolerated it for too long. These men deserve better from their country."

The general slid a photo across the table. "This is Son Tay prison, just twenty-three miles from Hanoi. We have credible reports of sixty-seven American POWs there, many in poor health. You and your Green Berets are going to break them out."

Bull gave a slight grin. He liked this assignment already. He scrutinized the aerial image. Guard towers. Wire fencing. Open courtyards. His pulse quickened. A raid deep in North Vietnam would be unprecedented.

"A mission like this could trigger a strong reaction from the NVA," said Bull.

"If successful, yes. That is our hope," said Hamilton.

"The biggest risk is leaked intelligence. If even the slightest hint of the prison being a potential target and the prisoners could be moved or used as bait against us."

Hamilton held up a hand. "Which is exactly why secrecy is paramount. The North Vietnamese cannot know we have Son Tay in our sights until it's too late. We need to move swiftly. Get your best men, analyze the target, and have an actionable plan ready within two weeks. Consider all contingencies."

"Understood, sir. We'll get it done."

Over the next fourteen days, Bull became consumed with plotting the perfect raid. He pored over maps and recon photos late into each night, searching for weaknesses and bottlenecks.

When reviewing the team roster, he knew that

Sergeant Shaw, his most experienced assaulter, would lead the breach. Sergeant Barnes and his team would handle recon. Doc Nelson was critical, as malnourished prisoners might not be ambulatory.

He made note of the 12,000 NVA soldiers just four miles away from the prison. If they reached the prison before his forces had rescued the prisoners, it could be a game changer. He would need a plan to stall them.

Most importantly, they needed to get in and out fast. Bull scribbled a note - "ten minute maximum on target." Surprise would be their most potent weapon.

Bull decided to insert the rescue team with helicopters by way of Laos, the closest point to the prison. It would be a long and dangerous journey.

After finalizing the assault plans, Bull gathered Shaw, Barnes, Nelson and a dozen more of his top operators. He briefed them on the bold operation. The rescue team would be made up of fifty-six Special Forces operators, ninety-two airmen, and twenty-eight aircraft. In addition, he brought on board a Navy SEAL demolitions expert and two Montagnard scouts. Everyone was excited about rescuing American POWs. There by the grace of God go I, was the thought.

Shaw crossed his arms. "No disrespect intended, sir, but this plan has more holes than my grandma's bloomers. We'd be dangling some mighty big balls over North Vietnam."

Nelson nodded. "Have to agree with Shaw here. Lot of risk fighting that deep in country. I know our capabilities, but still..."

Bull held up a hand. "I hear you both. But this is the best chance we'll get to rescue these men. Train hard the next seven days and we'll go over every detail until the plan is airtight. We aren't gonna let fear hold us back. That's not who we are."

Everyone nodded in agreement. It was exhilarating to be part of such a daring mission and worthy cause, even if it was risky.

Pentagon – Arlington, Virginia

General Wheeler reviewed the latest recon photos laid out on his desk, pausing on one of a small jungle camp.

"What am I looking at here?" he asked the intelligence officer.

"A newly identified POW camp in the Mekong Delta. It appears to be holding fifty South Vietnamese ARVN prisoners."

Wheeler leaned back in his chair, thinking. He had just assigned Bull the Ivory Coast mission to hit Son Tay prison. Perhaps this new target could be put to use as well.

"Pass these photos to Coronado right away. Have SEAL Team One draw up plans to hit this ARVN camp twenty-four hours after Ivory Coast goes down."

The officer raised an eyebrow. "A second mission so soon, sir?"

"Affirmative. Our South Vietnamese allies deserve the same effort as our own men. Hitting this target will strengthen our bond. Beside, the Viet Cong will never see it coming," Wheeler said.

"Yes, sir!" The officer hurried off to relay the orders.

Wheeler allowed himself a tight smile. Two swift, coordinated strikes would demonstrate unequivocally that neither the US or her allies would abandon their troops. The North about to learn that no prison camp was safe.

Covert Military Base, Eastern Thailand

The next week, the chosen rescue team tirelessly drilled the raid in a mock compound built to mirror Son Tay. Bull provided key guidance during exercises, pushing the men to shave seconds off their times and identify contingency plans.

"Faster, dammit!" he yelled as the team sprinted to breach the outer perimeter. "You've got ninety seconds max before the guards are all over you!"

The team reset and ran it again, blowing the charges and storming into the compound a few seconds quicker. But Bull was still not satisfied.

"Shaw, you missed a grenade throw into that machine gun nest, leaving Nelson exposed! Do it again, this time perfect!"

During the next rehearsal, Shaw lobbed his fake grenade flawlessly into the nest, while Nelson capped the surviving guard with a double tap from his silenced submachine gun.

"Better," nodded Bull. "But we need to shave off more time. Remember, you'll have disoriented prisoners in unknown conditions to deal with. Speed is life!"

After each drill, Bull gathered the men for a debrief, soliciting their feedback.

"The breach point is too narrow," said Sergeant Miller. "We're bottlenecking when we enter the main courtyard."

"Good catch," replied Bull, making a note. "We'll blow a second entry point through the east perimeter fence to split the enemy's formation."

He turned to Doc Nelson. "What problems do you see?"

Nelson gestured to the mock prisoners sprawled on the ground. "No telling what shape the POWs will be in after years of torture and malnutrition. We need two medics per team for triage and extraction."

"Agreed, I'll have Jones and Phillips join you in the courtyard," said Bull.

For seven intense days, the Green Berets honed every minute detail, shaving precious seconds off their extraction times. Bull drove them hard, but the rigorous preparation would prove essential in the unforgiving enemy territory.

By the final rehearsal, the team bristled with deadly focus and precision, ready to undertake the riskiest prisoner liberation ever conceived. There could be no room for error deep behind North Vietnamese lines.

Bull walked amongst the Green Berets doing final gear checks in the helicopter bay, assessing the handpicked volunteers for this mission. He saw only focus and determination in their eyes, willing to risk all to free their imprisoned brothers-in-arms.

These were the best America had to offer. Bull knew each man's reputation. He had studied their files for weeks, evaluating skills and mindsets. Only the elite had made the cut, coming together to form this precision strike force. Proud men who lived by a code - no one left behind.

Yet he also knew the brutal truth - not all would return safely from this mission. As their commander, Bull bore the weight of putting these men in harm's way.

He was proud of their determination and courage.

But also concerned for their lives soon to be endangered deep in enemy territory. Bull would do everything in his power to see them home again.

For the moment, he kept his doubts buried. His men needed to see only his confidence and resolve. The gravity of what they volunteered for could not be ignored, but their spirit could not waver.

They would soon strike a blow against cruelty. But the cost might be dear. Bull prayed these good men would endure what was to come.

He saw the Navy SEAL demolitions expert, the Air Force CCTs, the ex-Rangers serving with SF now. And his own Green Berets - the toughest warriors Bull had encountered in his long career.

Yes, Bull had crafted an instrument of war for this singular task. One with teeth and claws, able to reach far into the heart of darkness undetected.

These were his wolves now, straining against the leash for release. And before dawn, the enemy in their crosshairs would learn to fear the night again.

Skies Above North Vietnam

As the air armada passed the border between Laos and North Vietnam, Bull stood in the open door of the HH-53 Super Jolly Green Giant helicopter, squinting against the 120-mph winds blasting through the cabin. Far below, the inky jungle canopy of North Vietnam raced past in a blur.

Among the elite Green Berets preparing for the Son Tay rescue mission were two Montagnard tribesmen, recruited for their uncanny jungle skills. Loi and Nay each carried a handcrafted bow with a quiver of arrows.

Their people had fought alongside the Americans

for years, possessing unique wilderness abilities. Loi and Nay could track prey or foe for miles without being detected. A quick bow shot from the underbrush was their lethal calling card. Their long knives were their coup de grace.

The Montagnard sat silent and steady. While others checked rifles and explosives, their poison-tipped arrows required no maintenance. Bull had hand-picked them for this raid. Their stealth and tracking would prove invaluable on the approach march through unfamiliar terrain riddled with enemy patrols and traps.

Once near the camp, Loi's and Nay's silent arrows could eliminate any tower guards before they sounded the alarm. Surprise was the mission's main weapon - and these jungle hunters would help secure it.

The American armada was an airborne fortress, designed to protect the vulnerable helicopters carrying Bull and his Green Berets towards their target.

A trio of F-105G Wild Weasels streaked over the North Vietnamese countryside at 500 knots, hunting for SAM sites that could threaten the incoming rescue force. The early warning radars were easy for the Weasels to spot - flashing neon bullseyes in the darkness.

In the lead jet, Major Branson stared intently at his radar warning receiver. A high-pitched tone suddenly squealed over his headset - a Fan Song radar pinging from miles ahead - a SAM site powering up had just acquired them. "I've got a pop-up threat at 090, looks like an SA-2 battery," reported Branson. "Rolling in to engage."

The Weasels banked hard towards the enemy signals, arming their AGM-45 Shrike anti-radiation missiles. The Shrikes would home in on the radar emissions, like sharks to blood.

Approaching the SAM battery, Branson's backseater ID'd the target. As they closed in, tracer rounds arced up towards the jets from ground units. Nothing touched them. They were flying too fast. "Target acquired, firing Shrike!"

Branson couldn't see the target they were firing at. It didn't matter. The Weasel's homing radar knew where the SAMs were located. Branson jinked hard right as a single anti-radiation missile leapt from his wing, lighting its boosters, rocketing down toward the enemy radars painted with invisible energy.

Detonations ripped through the site, engulfing the equipment in flaming wreckage. Secondary explosions signaled the SAMs had been destroyed.

"Target destroyed!" Branson reported. "Threat eliminated, egressing the area."

The Wild Weasels climbed and accelerated away, ready for the next call to action. Their unique tactics and munitions would clear the skies so the choppers could strike deep into North Vietnam.

A lone Jolly Green HH-53 broke formation from the helicopter armada, charging ahead, flying fast and low over the North Vietnamese countryside. Inside were Sgt. Barnes and his recon team, tasked to land ahead and clear the area.

A Spectre AC-130 gunship was ready to rain down a hellstorm of cannon and mini-gun fire if called upon.

At the center, a small fleet of helicopters bore the precious human cargo - Green Berets, Air Force CCTs, and hand-picked special operators.

Staff Sergeant Mike Davis stood calmly inspecting his silenced MP5 submachine gun, bracing against the vibration of the HH-53's cabin. He glanced over at

Sergeant Vince Carter seated across from him. "So what do you think, Vince? Vegas odds on us making it back for breakfast tomorrow?" Davis shouted over the engine noise with a grin.

Carter checked his watch again before shouting back. "I got a nice gal waiting for me back at home! No way I'm dying tonight."

His buddy Corporal Bill Owens nudged him with an elbow. "Why not? You ain't got a snowball's chance with Betty-Sue anyway!"

The Green Berets around them erupted in laughter. Carter flipped Owens the bird before going back to staring out into the dark jungle speeding past below.

Up in the cockpit, the pilots exchanged an amused look. Transporting these elite operators always made for an interesting journey.

Back in the cabin, Bull stood gripping a handhold near the open door, face impassive as he watched the final minutes tick down.

The armada of helicopters and support aircraft raced through the night sky piercing deep into North Vietnam's airspace. Suddenly a warning blared across the radio - "Threat radar spiking, two MiG-21s inbound!"

Four F-4 Phantom II fighter escorts responded immediately. "Photon flight engaging bogies, defend the package." The Phantoms dropped back, locking their powerful radars on the approaching specks.

"Photon 1, visually acquired, MiGs at 2 o'clock high!" reported the lead F-4 pilot. The enemy aircraft were coming in fast, hoping to catch the armada by surprise.

"Photon flight, weapons hot! Brutus 1 you are cleared to engage." The American fighters arced up, ready to meet the threat head-on. Onboard computers tracked the streaking MiGs, waiting for missile lock.

"Brutus 1, Fox 1!" The lead Phantom loosed an AIM-7 Sparrow missile, its radar guidance system homing in on one the enemy planes. The MiG pilot jinked hard, popping flares, but the Sparrow lead the turns and detonated the enemy aircraft in a brilliant fireball.

"Splash one!"

The wingman MiG broke off, throttling away in full retreat as the F-4s circled back to the armada. The Phantoms had torn a hole in the North's defenses, ensuring safe passage in.

Onboard the helicopters, the Green Berets exchanged relieved looks. Their fighter escort crews had earned their pay - no enemy aircraft would threaten the mission again tonight.

The Green Berets fell silent, donning their gear and steeling themselves for the fight ahead. Jokes gave way to stone-faced professionalism.

It was time to get some of their own back from this awful war. And failure was never an option for the chosen sons of Ivory Coast.

Tracer fire arced up from the jungle as the helicopters approached the prison. Below, enemy troops with heavy machine guns were trying to shoot them down.

A flight of A-1 Skyraiders came screeching overhead to suppress the ground fire. "Rolling in hot!" reported the lead pilot.

The Skyraiders dove low over the jungle canopy, wings loaded with deadly napalm canisters. As the enemy muzzle flashes appeared, they pickled off the canisters.

The canisters tumbled down, erupting in great waves of flaming gel that coated the trees. Screams echoed from below as the enemy gunners were engulfed.

"Good hits, good hits!" called the wingmen as they pulled up from the strafing run. The jungle inferno raged, decisively silencing the ground threat.

Above, the Green Berets looked on approvingly. The prop-driven Skyraiders had brought the pain with a precise napalm strike, clearing the LZ for their insertion.

Approaching the remote jungle clearing designated as the insertion point, the pilot flared the Jolly Green that had sped ahead. The aircraft's wheels had barely kissed the grass before Barnes and his recon team spilled out, weapons up.

They quickly moved to the tree line, watching for any signs of ambush or NVA troops. The area appeared deserted, but they took no chances. Tense minutes passed as they scouted area around the landing zone searching for the enemy. Nothing.

Satisfied, Barnes clicked his radio twice - the all clear sign. The helicopter lifted off heading toward Laos to refuel.

The recon team had another perilous task - clearing a safe route between the LZ and Son Tay prison. They slipped into the jungle and melted into the darkness.

The four-man recon team flowed silently through the dense jungle, scanning ahead with night vision-mounted scopes. Their weapons swept back and forth, trailing burlap strips that mimicked the brush.

Sgt. Barnes halted, hearing faint sounds ahead. He held up a clenched fist, and the team instantly dissolved into concealment amidst the vegetation. Face paint and ghillie suits rendered them invisible.

An NVA patrol emerged on the trail, oblivious to the Green Berets hidden feet away. Barnes locked eyes with Chen, who touched the handle of his KA-BAR, then drew a finger across his throat, itching to engage the four enemy troops.

Barnes shook his head firmly. They were to remain ghosts. He waved two fingers forward - the patrol was not their mission tonight.

Chen nodded, disappointed but complying. The enemy wandered past unimpeded down the trail.

After the NVA had gone, Barnes gestured the team forward. Once again, they flowed through the jungle, weapons sweeping, focused on their objective.

The recon team moved silently over steep hills, circumventing enemy lookouts and villages on the perilous trek towards Son Tay.

Sergeant Barnes halted as his foot nudged against an almost invisible tripwire.

He traced it carefully to a stolen Claymore mine hidden in brush. Barnes disarmed the detonator while Corporal Chen marked the mine's location on their map.

Further along, they discovered punji pits dug along the approach, lined with sharpened bamboo stakes coated in excrement. Corporal Grover retrieved a long stick and carefully probed the ground ahead as they advanced.

Further along the route, the team spotted a small wooden box mounted on a tree with a mic cable running from it. Inside the box was a radio transmitting to the prison. Barnes drew his knife and silently cut the mic wire. The NVA would be blind to their incursion.

Finally, the prison camp emerged from the

vegetation. Barnes glanced at his watch. The armada would be arriving soon. There wasn't much time.

On Barnes's hand signal, the recon team slithered through the underbrush surrounding the prison, scanning for any security measures. The prison guards remained oblivious to the deadly threat lurking in the darkness mere yards away.

Through his night vision goggles, Barnes carefully scanned the compound and marked positions on an aerial recon photo of the prison. Guard towers stood at regular intervals along the exterior barrier, mounted with machine guns and searchlights. Inside, clusters of long, single-story prison barracks were visible.

Most critically, the recon team spotted two anti-aircraft gun emplacements situated on a small hill that gave them a commanding view of the camp and surrounding airspace. Barnes marked their position on the photo. Those weapons would need to be neutralized swiftly during the raid.

In the very center of Son Tay stood a sizable building. That was likely the solitary confinement and interrogation facility where POWs were tortured.

Approaching closer, the recon team could make out patrolling guards and spotlights sweeping across the interior courtyards. But Barnes was surprised. The number of troops seemed light for such important prisoners as American pilots and soldiers. It didn't feel right. It made him more cautious. Intelligence had reported 12,000 NVA soldiers stationed just four miles from the prison. It wouldn't take them long to get to the prison once it was under attack. He rechecked the position of the long-range radio antennae above the communications hut. It would need to be taken out first. Without direct communication to the prison, hopefully the NVA would send recon team before committing a larger force.

Once the prison was surveyed to Barnes's satisfaction and he had made his notes, he motioned for his team to take up positions around the camp. Alone, he returned back the way he and the team had come through the jungle to rendezvous with Bull and the main force. Once he reported his findings, he would lead them back through the jungle to the prison.

Riding in the Jolly Green as it approached the landing zone, Bull pulled the charging handle on his CAR-15, chambering the first round with a satisfying click. Everything came down to the next hour.

As soon as the helicopters touched down in the remote clearing, the Green Berets poured out and seamlessly established a security perimeter. The drills had been rehearsed to perfection. Men faced outward, weapons trained on the dark jungle. No orders were given; every operator knew their role.

The helicopters took off flying back toward Laos.

Bull watched with approval as his well-oiled machine assembled itself in the LZ. Complete silence. Their perimeter secured, they waited for recon to return.

After dropping off the rescue team, to the HH-53s transport helicopters were running low on fuel. They headed back toward Laos where refueling tankers were waiting. "Basketball 11, this is Eagle 1," the lead chopper radioed. "We are bingo fuel and require refueling, over."

"Copy that Eagle 1," replied the pilot of the trailing MC-130 tanker aircraft. "Bring your birds into the drogue, nice and easy."

The lead HH-53 slowed and eased back until the refueling probe extended from its nose slid smoothly into the tanker's trailing drogue. The chopper's frame shuddered as it locked in place.

"Contact!" called out the crew chief, flipping switches to transfer precious fuel into the helicopter's dry tanks.

One by one, the HH-53s slid into position behind the flying gas station, topping off for the final leg of their journey – the pick-up and return home. Radio chatter was minimal.

Within minutes, the hookups were complete. "Eagle flight refueled and ready for pick up," reported the lead pilot.

"Godspeed gentlemen," the tanker pilot replied. "Go get 'em."

The helicopters banked north, picking up speed as they headed back toward the prison.

Jungle Landing Zone, North Vietnam

Leaving his radio silent, Barnes approached the landing zone and spotted the scouts he knew were watching him. "Where's the colonel?' he said.

One of the scouts pointed behind toward the clearing.

Barnes entered the clearing. Bull approached and said, "What are we looking at?"

Barnes handed him the recon photo that he had marked up. "Everything is as we thought, except for two anti-aircraft emplacements up on this hill. They're new," he said pointing to his drawing. "They overlook the camp. We gotta take 'em out first before we enter the perimeter."

"Okay. Communication's hut?"

"Here. Long-range antenna."

"Do you think a sniper could take it out?"

"Maybe. Worth a try. Could delay reinforcements."

"Alright. Anything else?"

"Yeah. It felt light."

"What do you mean light?"

"The force guarding the camp is less than fifty. That seems light considering the prisoners."

"I agree. Do you think it could be a trap?"

"Possible."

"Did you see anything that would indicate a trap?"

"No. Just the low troop count... and a feeling."

Bull studied Barnes for a moment. He had known the man a long time. Nerves of steel, not prone to panic. Bull knew it would be unwise to discount Barnes's feeling. "Alright. We make sure our asses are covered... just in case."

"What about the 12,000 enemy troops stationed nearby? That's a pretty big 'just in case.'"

"We've got a Spectre gunship. It won't hold 'em off forever, but it sure as hell will slow 'em down."

Bull motioned to Sgt. Shaw to get ready to move the men. Barnes took the lead with the scouts flanking him on both sides as he moved back into the jungle.

Guided by Barnes, Bull led the assault force through the black jungle towards Son Tay prison. Taking more caution, the rescue force did not head straight for the prison. Instead, the column weaved back and forth like a snake. It took more precious time, but it was more secure. Everyone, not just the scouts, carefully scanning for traps or ambushes. They were taking no chances. All noise discipline was maintained. Hand signals only.

After a tense thirty minutes, Barnes raised a clenched fist to halt the column. Just ahead, through a screen of vegetation, the dark outline of the prison compound was barely visible.

Barnes moved forward alone. Three clicks of a tongue pierced the stillness - the recon team signaling from their concealed overwatch positions. Seconds later, two Green Berets emerged from bushes ahead, rifles ready.

Barnes greeted them with a nod. Chen hand signaled that everything was normal. No talking. Little movement. Silent and still.

Bull crouched forward to peer at the shadowy objective, still 500 meters out. Barnes pointed out the two anti-aircraft emplacements and the radio antenna. Bull nodded.

Using hand signals, Bull through Shaw maneuvered the Green Beret rescue team into position surrounding Son Tay prison. The Montagnard warriors Loi and Nay ghosted ahead, reaching the first guard tower flanking the northern perimeter.

Bull wasn't taking any chances. Two snipers would take out the radio antenna at the same time the guard towers and anti-aircraft guns were assaulted.

On the nearby hilltop overlooking the camp, Sergeant Shaw led a fire team to within fifty feet of the anti-aircraft emplacements. As the team kept watch and provided security, Shaw crawled forward and planted Claymore mines overlooking the twin ZPU-4 14.5mm guns. Covering the mines with foliage, he led the firing wires back to the fire team. Hooking up the triggers, he handed the devices off to the team and headed back down the hill to check on the rest of the rescue team.

The sky was beginning to lighten as dawn approached. Bull checked his watch - 0420 hours. They have moved with caution, but they were out of time. The assault needed to begin.

Having checked on the rescue team, Shaw reported back to Bull and used hand signals to indicate they were ready. Bull nodded. For the next five minutes, the jungle went deathly still, with only insects daring to break the silence. Bull took one last look at the compound making sure nothing had been overlooked. They were ready. He signaled Shaw - execute. In turn, Shaw signaled the Montagnard warriors who would begin the assault in silence.

In their hidden positions, Loi and Nay nocked their arrows. The faintest glow to the east offered enough light to aim. They shot in unison. The arrows pierced the throats of the two guards in the tower. Poison from the arrowheads entered their bodies causing immediate paralysis. Both died before they could signal their comrades. All was still quiet, Loi and Nay moved on to the next tower and repeated their actions. Two more guards fell.

With two guard towers out, the breaching team moved to the perimeter fence and cut the wire. More Green Berets moved up along with the Navy SEAL demolition specialist, ready to the enter the compound when signaled.

The two snipers set up their weapons nearby. They aimed at the same point on the radio antenna. They would fire together, hopefully shearing the antenna wires running up the bamboo pole.

Bull looked on. Everything was going to plan, but he knew that it was just a matter of time until

DAVID LEE CORLEY

something tipped off the enemy and all hell broke loose. His men were ready to react when that happened. There was no need for Bull to give a signal to his men. Enemy gunfire would be the signal to start the next phase of the operation – all out attack.

One of the guards hit with one of the Montagnard's poison arrows was still alive. Struggling to breath, he reached for his AK47 on the tower's wooden deck. Unable to lift it, he pushed it over the edge of the stairwell opening in the tower floor. It fell hitting the stairs on the way down and discharging a bullet with a crack that shattered the silence. Guards whipped around toward the tower.

Bull and his Green Berets wasted no time. The synchronized assault began without further instructions.

The two snipers fired. Both bullets hit home severing the antenna's wire, knocking out the radio. They gave each other a tight grin, neither knowing which bullet severed the wire, but each sure it was their own.

Green Berets used LAW rockets to takeout the other guard towers before their heavy machine guns could be fired. The explosions lit up the compound like roman candles.

On the hilltop, the Green Berets set off the Claymore mines with three sharp punches of the detonators. Seven hundred steel balls from each mine were launched into the NVA gun crews shredding them instantly. The Green Berets charged from their hidden position to finish off any survivors. It was a wasted effort. Everyone was dead. They placed demolition charges in the mechanics of the anti-aircraft guns and set them off once they were clear. The guns exploded followed by multiple secondary explosions as the ammunition cooked off from the heat. The anti-aircraft guns were destroyed... forever.

More breaching charges exploded, ripping gaping holes in the perimeter fences. Green Berets poured through the holes entering the compound and quickly spreading out to engage the enemy guards on the ground. Like vengeful spirits, the elite American soldiers moved as three-man fire teams spraying the compound with gunfire as they advanced. The element of surprise was total - the NVA guards reeled under the devastating wave of violence.

The Navy SEAL demolitions specialist pulled a string of explosive charges attached with detonation cord from his rucksack. He placed each charge at the bottom of the foundation columns for the prisoner kitchen and the mess hut for the guards. Two minutes later, he yelled "Fire in the hole" and detonated the charges. In thunderous succession the charges exploded with a terrible roar sending shards of wood in all directions, some pelting nearby Green Berets. When the smoke cleared, the buildings were gone leaving a new landing zone for two Jolly Green transport helicopters to carry the prisoners to safety.

As the assault continued, enemy survivors abandoned their posts and fled into the jungle only to be ambushed by hidden American teams waiting for the enemy's retreat. The Green Berets' planning and training had paid off.

While security teams cleared out the last of the resistance and set up defensive positions, search teams headed toward the prisoner barracks and interrogation facility.

Search Team One approached the solitary

confinement wing, expecting to find dozens of POWs being held in inhumane conditions. Breaching charges exploded, fracturing the steel door inward.

As the acrid smoke swirled, the Green Berets rushed in, training their rifle-mounted flashlights down the gloomy corridor. The cells stood silent as crypts.

Staff Sergeant Ruiz moved tactically from door to door, slicing off the padlocks with bolt cutters. He wrenched each cell open ready to confront the wretched conditions within.

But one after another, the cells were empty, holding only soiled floormats and buckets. Ruiz felt his stomach drop. Where were the prisoners?

"Medic!" came a sudden cry as an RPG exploded against a wall, spraying Staff Sergeant Miles with shrapnel. As Doc Ellison sprinted over, Miles waved him off - "I'm good! Keep clearing rooms!"

Across the compound, Search Team Two prepared to enter the main housing barracks. A breaching charge blasted the wooden entrance door to splinters.

The team leader charged through first, sweeping left then right with his submachine gun. Row after row of empty floormats awaited. No sign of occupants. Only strange silence.

As they cleared the last cells in the interrogation facility, Ruiz's search team discovered three emaciated Montagnard tribesmen locked in a holding cell.

Sergeant Tran, the team's translator, urgently questioned them.

"No Americans here," one warrior rasped. "We arrive one week ago. No food, little water since." The others nodded weakly in confirmation.

Sergeant Tran's expression fell as he turned to Ruiz, the team leader. "They've been here a week. They never saw any other prisoners. What the fuck in happening?"

The despondent search teams converged minutes later in the central courtyard, realization dawning that somehow the prisoners had vanished before they had arrived. They had struck only a shadow.

As the last team leader reported back, Bull slammed his fist against a wall in frustration breaking the bones in his hand. It hurt like hell, but he didn't care. The intel had been wrong. Fury turned to dejection. The risk and sacrifice had been for nothing.

Bull found his Green Berets gathered silently in the central courtyard of Son Tay prison, heads hung low after realizing no American POWs were here to rescue. He stepped up into the center of the courtyard to address the dejected men. "I know you're feeling the sting of failure right now," he began. "We came here on faulty intelligence that now leaves us empty-handed. That's not your fault."

The Green Berets looked up, bitterness and frustration in their eyes. All that risk and sacrifice for nothing.

"The brass and politicians will call this a failure, but they're not soldiers. They don't know a thing about courage and duty like you men do."

"But I'm telling you what they think is horseshit!" Bull bellowed. "You accomplished one hell of a feat today. There's not another unit on Earth capable of doing what you did."

He paced the courtyard, looking each man in the eye. "You plunged deep into enemy country, flawlessly executed the plan, and seized this prison in minutes flat overwhelming the enemy. I've never been more damned proud."

Bull pulled a lighter from his pocket. "Our mission was to rescue prisoners, but that ain't happening. So, let's burn this shithole to the ground and get the hell out of here!"

The Green Berets let loose a cheer and began gathering accelerants. Bull smiled watching his wolves' spirits restored. Together, they would raze the prison before exfiltrating back to home. The only thing they could be grateful for was that no Americans had lost their lives assaulting the camp and they had killed twenty-five NVA guards in the process.

The mission may have gone sideways, but the chosen sons of Ivory Coast had done their job with honor. And their bravery under fire would be remembered long after the politicians were forgotten.

November 22, 1970 - Mekong Delta, South Vietnam

The next night, three Navy helicopters hugged the dark jungle canopy, flying fast and low over the Mekong Delta. Inside were eight elite SEAL Team One operators and twelve ARVN Special Forces, united on a joint mission codenamed Operation Tailwind.

Their target - a remote POW camp hidden deep in the steaming Delta, believed to hold nineteen captured ARVN troops. Intelligence was sparse, but indicated lax defenses and patrols. Surprise would be key.

They had heard of the Green Berets' failure on the raid of Son Tay prison. The Green Berets were strong special operators. The SEAL and the ARVN were concerned that the same could happen to them. Missions like Tailwind depended on intelligence being accurate. But military intelligence often seemed like a good guess at best. It was a crap shoot every time.

"One mike out!" called the pilot over the thrum of the rotors. The SEALs and ARVN donned night vision goggles, chambered rounds in their silenced sub machineguns. Faces were painted black, Kit Carsons secured on their backs.

The lead bird flared and touched down in a small clearing near the objective. Before the skids sank into the mud, the door gunners readied themselves to lay down suppression fire into the jungle to secure a perimeter. But the jungle was still. No need to break silence.

The operators spilled out, immediately forming a 360-degree ring facing outward. Satisfied they hadn't been immediately engaged, SEAL Lieutenant Murphy nodded to his ARVN counterpart, Captain Tran.

Tran gestured two of his men forward into the vegetation to scout ahead. The rest of the unit tightened their circle, waiting and listening intently. Cicadas and bullfrogs were the only sounds that reached them.

Five tense minutes passed before a soft bird call carried through the humid air - the ARVN scouts signaling the all-clear. Murphy tapped Tran's shoulder and the joint force advanced toward the POW camp location.

They moved cautiously between mammoth mahogany and kapok trees, alert for any signs of activity. The camp was nestled deep in a draw only accessible by a narrow footpath. Foliage choked the way forward.

The point man's hand shot up in a clenched fist, halting the column's progress. He had spotted Punji spikes dug into the track, the pit's camouflaged cover nearly invisible.

With hand signals, the SEALs marked a bypass around the boobytrap. But their presence may have already been detected. Speed was now imperative before the guards could organize.

The force double-timed it down into the draw, through the vegetation they spotted the POW huts surrounded by bamboo fencing. A few sleepy sentries wandered the dirt compound.

Murphy pointed to the E&E team - they were up first. The two SEALs belly crawled ahead, det cord and satchel charges in hand. The main group hugged the jungle edge, weapons trained outward.

Reaching the fence line, the E&E specialists selected their breach points. Murphy watched for their signal, glancing repeatedly at his watch. Timing was everything on this high-stakes raid.

At precisely 00:15 local time, triple flashes from a shielded light marked the message - charges set. Murphy raised and dropped his fist - execute!

Thunderous explosions splintered the fencing in eruptions of dirt and smoke as the charges detonated. Before the debris had even landed, the SEALs and ARVN were rushing into the breached compound, weapons blazing.

Caught by utter surprise, the few guards present were quickly cut down. But the blasts had alerted a larger force who came swarming through the jungle toward the camp.

"We've got company! Perimeter positions!" yelled Lieutenant Murphy. The SEALs scattered to preset fields of fire, trading shots with the counter-attacking NVA boiling out of the jungle.

Trusting his men to keep the enemy at bay, Murphy led a fireteam to clear the POW huts, slicing the locks with bolt cutters. Inside they discovered nineteen disoriented but very alive ARVN troops.

"We're getting you out of here, just stay low!" Murphy told them through Tran's translation. The emaciated prisoners could hardly believe their rescue had come and did their best to keep up.

Under the cover of SEAL sniper fire, the newly freed ARVN troops were extracted one by one and escorted into the jungle away from the encroaching battle. The evacuation was systematic but tense.

As Murphy helped the final man cross the perimeter, he spotted NVA infantry flanking their western side, attempting to cut off the path to the LZ.

He rushed back, redirecting two SEALs to intercept the threat while calling in the SeaCobra gunships for immediate extract. They had accomplished their mission, but danger remained.

Within minutes the birds flared into the smoking POW compound, door gunners laying a suppressing stream of tracer fire from miniguns to hold back the NVA. The commandos piled in and the choppers lifted away just as RPGs streaked past in pursuit.

Inside the cabin, the ARVN prisoners stared wide-eyed at their grim-faced rescuers as the helicopters beat north to safety. For men long condemned to deprivation and torment, this night was nothing short of miraculous. The Intel had been right for once.

White House, Washington DC, USA

General Wheeler sat in the Oval Office as President Nixon processed the news of the previous night's raids. "Let me get this straight, Earle. Your men successfully rescued over a dozen South Vietnamese troops but failed to liberate any American POWs?" Nixon asked, his tone severe.

"That is correct, Mr. President," Wheeler confirmed. "The intelligence was flawed regarding prisoners held at Son Tay. A terrible mistake that I will personally investigate. Apparently, the prison's well had been contaminated during Typhoon Kate and the American prisoners were removed to another location. It was just bad luck on our part."

Nixon rose from his desk, shaking his head. "This failure will make America look weak on bringing our boys back home. The anti-war movement will have a field day."

Pacing the ornate rug, Nixon continued: "We cannot breathe a word of the bungled raid to the media. My reelection next year is already on shaky ground without this embarrassment added."

Wheeler's forehead creased. "But, sir, the brave actions of those Green Berets and SEALs deserve recognition. Their willingness to attempt the impossible against all odds—"

Nixon cut him off with a chop of his hand. "Don't be naive, Earle. The public doesn't care about sentiment or ARVN troops. They only care about American POWs. This will only hand ammunition to my political enemies."

Nixon looked Wheeler straight in the eye to ensure that what he was about to say was understood. "You will bury any mention of Operation Ivory Coast. As far as the record shows, it never happened. That's a direct order."

Wheeler stood and snapped to attention. "Yes, Mr. President. I will inform military press liaisons that any media questions should be stonewalled."

"See that you do," Nixon said, returning to his desk. "Now if you'll excuse me, I need to call Henry and smooth things over before word of this debacle reaches Paris."

"By your command, Mr. President," Wheeler replied crisply before exiting, bitterness on his tongue at the politics overriding honor. But his duty left no room for dissent.

Black Echo

Chu Chi District, South Vietnam

Just forty miles from Saigon, but a world away, the
American platoon moved silently through the dense
jungle, senses strained for any sign of the enemy.
Corporal Jackson took point, leading the men along a
narrow, winding trail. He paused as the trail opened up,
revealing a dark hole gaping in the earth - the entrance
to a tunnel.

Jackson held up a closed fist, signaling the patrol to
halt. The air was thick and humid, clinging to Jackson's
dark skin, glistening as he crouched near the tunnel
opening. The earth around him was damp from the
recent rains, and the smells of moist soil and vegetation
mingled with the lingering odor of gunpowder and
smoke. Somewhere in the dense jungle, a bird called
out, its cry sharp and lonely.

Jackson turned and caught Sergeant Miller's eye,
nodding his head slightly. They'd found VC tunnels
before, and Miller knew Jackson always volunteered to

search them. The men called him their "tunnel rat." But this time, Miller waved Jackson over. "I want Williams to check it out," Miller said in a low voice.

Jackson glanced back at Williams. The private was young, face still holding remnants of boyish roundness. He was only three weeks in country. "You sure about that, Sarge? Kid's greener than a Georgia pine."

Miller's face was set. "Only one way to fix that. He needs experience."

Jackson frowned, but knew better than to argue with Miller once he'd made a decision. With a resigned sigh, he turned to Williams. "Alright, Private, you heard the man. This one's yours."

Williams paled a bit but nodded, jaw set determinedly. Jackson walked him through the steps, keeping his voice low and steady. "No flashlight till you're sure you're alone. Use your senses - smell for cooking fires and fish sauce, listen for voices or movement. Go slow, but not too slow - don't want Charlie sneaking up behind you. Knife ready to strike before he knows you're there."

Williams took a shuddering breath as he stared into the dark maw before them. Jackson handed him a pistol and tucked a flashlight in his shirt pocket. Williams pulled out his KA-BAR. "You can do this, private," Jackson said firmly. "Just remember your training and watch your back. I'll be right here waiting when you come out."

After another moment of hesitation, Williams tightened his grip on his pistol and KA-BAR and lowered himself into the tunnel entrance. The darkness swallowed him as Jackson watched the space where he had disappeared, listening intently for any sign of trouble within.

He shook his head slightly - the kid was far too green for this. Jackson couldn't help thinking that if his skin was white instead of black, Miller might have listened. Would have at least heard him out instead of dismissing his concerns outright.

Jackson let out a quiet sigh. He was used to it by now - the wary looks from new recruits when they realized a black man outranked them, the whispered words behind his back. The assumptions that his promotions came from filling some quota, not from skill and experience.

He glanced over at Miller, but the sergeant studiously avoided meeting his gaze. Jackson wondered if this was a test for Williams as much as for himself - see if the green private would take orders from a black superior.

Jackson shook his head again. Whatever the reason, he couldn't afford to dwell on it now. Williams was still down there in the dark, alone. Jackson pushed the bitter thoughts away, listening for the young man's return. Rank and skin color didn't matter in the tunnel's suffocating blackness. And if Charlie found Williams before he found Charlie, none of it would matter anyway.

Inside the tunnel, Williams moved forward in a crouch, one hand against the damp earth to steady himself. His heart hammered in his chest as the darkness wrapped around him like a living thing. He paused, straining his ears, but heard nothing besides his own ragged breathing.

The faint light from the entrance soon disappeared as he crept deeper into the winding tunnel. He blinked rapidly, willing his eyes to adjust, but the blackness was absolute. He thought back to Jackson's instructions. No flashlight until he was sure he was alone.

But how could he know? The VC could be mere feet away, blended into the void, waiting for the right moment to strike. Williams tightened his grip on the knife, slick palm sweating against the handle.

He wondered why Sergeant Miller had chosen him for this. Because he was the FNG - the fucking new guy? He had heard the other men in the platoon talking. A new guy wasn't worth as much as a soldier with experience. They figured it was better for an FNG to get killed sooner rather than later so he didn't suffer as much.

A small voice in the back of his mind said it was his own fear talking. Jackson had more experience in these tunnels than anyone. If he said Williams could handle it, maybe he could.

Williams shook off the doubts and focused his senses. The dank air was tinged with the scent of smoke - cooking fires somewhere nearby. He thought he heard a faint rustling up ahead. Carefully, he eased forward, ears straining.

A sudden scuffling sound, almost behind him. Williams whirled, knife raised. Was that footsteps receding down a side passage? He held perfectly still, barely breathing. Had it just been some jungle creature? Or a VC, warned by Williams's own noisy approach?

His heart slammed against his ribs. Gripping his knife, Williams moved toward the sound. He had no choice but to keep going, and hope he found Charlie before Charlie found him.

Williams crept forward, cursing himself for making too much noise. The echoes of his movements had likely given away his position. He paused as the tunnel split into two smaller passages ahead. Which way had the sounds come from?

He hesitated, then chose the left passage. The earth sloped down at a gentle angle, leveling out into a wider chamber. Williams froze. The faintest hint of an odor reached his nose - fish sauce and rice. Close, so close.

His heart slammed against his ribs. Someone was mere feet away, hidden in the darkness. Williams tightened his grip on the knife, palms slick with sweat. He took a slow, shallow breath, willing his racing pulse to quiet.

There - a soft rustle of clothing, the intake of breath. The enemy was almost close enough to touch. Williams braced himself, focused on the sounds. As he heard the hint of movement, he struck. Williams stabbed blindly multiple time as fast as he could. He grabbed the man's uniform and pulled him closer within the reach of his knife. He felt the blade sink into soft flesh. A choked gurgle, then silence. He yanked the blade back, hot blood spilling over his hand. The body slumped heavily to the ground.

Williams stood paralyzed. He peered into the darkness but couldn't see the man he had killed. Only heard the final choked breaths fade into silence. Bile rose in Williams's throat. His first kill. Over before he even knew what had happened.

After a moment, he carefully moved deeper into the tunnel, wet knife leading the way. The passage twisted and turned, sloping gently downwards. He came to what felt like a larger chamber. This must be where the VC bunked down.

Slowly, he sheathed his knife and pulled out the flashlight, keeping it aimed at the ground. He held his pistol and steadied his breathing. Now came the moment of truth. If Charlie was down here, the light would draw them like moths.

With a prayer, Williams flipped on the flashlight. Three Vietnamese faces stared back at him, frozen for an instant. VC soldiers, rifles in hand but unused to the tunnel's tight space.

Muzzle flashes lit up the chamber like a strobe light, the bang-bang-bang of gunfire deafening.

Outside, Jackson heard the frantic shots. Cursing, he plunged into the tunnel, one hand tracing the earthen wall. That damned sergeant had gone too far this time. The kid was green as grass, no match for experienced VC fighters.

He came to the fork in the tunnel. He smelled spent gunpowder and took the left fork. Feeing the ground in front of him, Jackson's stomach twisted as his hand suddenly came away slick with blood. He felt a body, motionless. Was it Williams? He smelled fish sauce and relaxed. Charlie, dead. Grimly, Jackson moved on.

Rounding a corner, he saw a faint glow ahead. Approaching cautiously, knife drawn, he found Williams in the chamber, wild-eyed and shaking. Surrounded by the dead men he had managed to kill.

"Damn, kid," Jackson said in awe. He put a hand on Williams's shoulder, steadying him. "You done good. Let's get you back topside."

"What about the rest of the tunnel?" said Williams.

"I'll check it out once I get you out of here. You've killed enough for today."

Williams nodded jerkily. Jackson kept a grip on the private's arm as they made their way back up the passage, leaving the darkness and death behind.

Going Home

White House, Washington DC, USA

President Nixon paced across the Oval Office carpet with the Seal of the United States of America woven into the thick fibers. Soon to become the president's National Security Advisor, Henry Kissinger briefed him on the progress of troop withdrawals.

"Our policy of Vietnamization is proceeding well," Kissinger said. "Morale remains high amongst the South Vietnamese as they take on more responsibility defending their nation. More and more of our troops are moving into support roles rather than direct combat."

Nixon nodded. "I was elected to end this damned war honorably. The silent majority of Americans want our boys home and I plan on giving them what they want. Besides, the quicker we end this thing, the sooner the protestors will go back to their universities and quit hounding me. We need to move faster, Henry."

"Yes, Mr. President. Of course, there are risks if we accelerate the timeline," Kissinger cautioned. "The North is also determined."

"Perhaps, but I must answer to the American people," Nixon replied. "They are weary of war and calling for de-escalation. We cannot sustain this effort forever."

"There is one more consideration."

"What's that?"

"The peace talks. As we de-escalate, the North Vietnamese have less reason to negotiate."

"Yes. I've thought about that. It's a tricky situation. What do you suggest?"

"We need to occasionally bring out the big stick and remind them that we can still cause them a great deal of pain if we choose to."

"The big stick. I like that. Whack 'em over the head. Show 'em who's the big dog in this fight."

"Yes, Mr. President. Or perhaps just threaten to use the big stick without provoking them by using it."

"That's weak thinking, Henry. They're not gonna fall for that. We whack 'em. Put 'em on their heels. Then negotiate from a position of strength. That's the way to beat 'em."

"As you say, Mr. President."

Vietnam Jungle - December 1969

Sergeant Lake huddled with his platoon during a monsoon downpour. He had just heard that the 3rd Marine Division would begin withdrawing in weeks.

Private Cole shook his head angrily. "After all we sacrificed, now they just want to pack up and go home? We should be here until the job is done!"

"Yeah, who gives a damn what those protesters back home say!" Private Stern chimed in. "We're so close to winning, why quit now?"

Sergeant Lake remained silent, conflicted. Finally, he spoke. "I can't say I'm not ready to leave this hellhole. But it doesn't feel right abandoning the ARVN either. I hope Nixon knows what he's doing."

The debate back home over withdrawal continued, but out in the jungle, the war raged on. The Marines returned to their patrol, wondering if they were being asked to sacrifice in vain.

January 1970

The order came down just after the new year - the 9th Infantry Division would be one of the first to withdraw from Vietnam. After nearly five years of fighting the Vietcong and North Vietnamese Army throughout the Mekong Delta, the "Old Reliables" were heading home.

For many of the enlisted men, this was a moment they had dreamed of while slogging through steamy jungles and flooded paddies. Now that it was here, they had mixed emotions. "I can't wait to hug my son and sleep in my own bed again," said Corporal Bill Simpson as he helped load duffel bags onto a truck. "But seems like we're pulling out just when Charlie is getting stronger than ever."

His platoon sergeant, Greg Boyd, nodded. "That's the shit end of the stick. We never got close to winning this thing. Now we just have to hope the ARVN can hold the line on their own."

"You've seen 'em fight. Not much chance of that."

"I don't know. Some of 'em are good, some are real good. It all depends on their NCOs and unit commanders. God, help 'em."

Across the base, the division's commander General Julian Ewell assembled his officers one last time. "Our role is changing from combat to logistics," Ewell said. "We'll coordinate the ongoing withdrawal while continuing to support and train the South Vietnamese forces. I know many of you feel we're abandoning the job unfinished. That debate's above our heads now. Let's bring our boys back safe so this long war can end for all of us."

The remaining troops at the division's Dong Tam base tore down tents, packed equipment onto barges and convoys, and lowered the colors for the last time. As trucks rumbled toward waiting ships at Vung Tau, soldiers gazed back at the landscape that had dominated their lives for so long. Some wondered if they'd ever return to that beautiful country. Some never wanted to.

By August, the entire 9th Infantry was back on American soil. The returning veterans were greeted with parades and waving flags, but also anti-war protests shouting and carrying placards that read, "Welcome Home Baby Killers." Like much of the country, the division that had served so gallantly was divided on the war's legacy. But for the moment, they were just glad to be home.

June 1970

At the US base in Chu Lai, the flag of the Americal Division was furled for the final time. Nicknamed for the motto "Americans in the Americas," the division had seen some of the heaviest fighting of the Vietnam War. Now their strategic role was ending as well.

No one was happier than twenty-year-old private Sam Worth. He had arrived in-country only three months earlier. After surviving the horrors of Kham Duc and witnessing his sergeant vaporized by a landmine, he had feared he'd never make it home alive.

As Worth helped load the last ammo crates, his buddy Mike Phelps said, "A lot of good men didn't make it this far, Sam. We're the lucky ones. Let's promise to live our lives right to honor their memory."

Worth nodded, thinking of the fresh-faced draftees who arrived on the resupply chopper with him weeks earlier. Half were already dead or maimed. He silently pledged to make the most of his second chance.

On June 15, the division's commanding general Lloyd Ramsey gathered his staff one last time. "We were given a tough job and performed it well," Ramsey said. "Now let's bring our boys back to their families safe and sound."

The remaining Americal troops convoyed to waiting ships bound for Oakland. As they sailed under the Golden Gate Bridge, tears and cheers broke out at long last setting foot on American soil.

July 1971

At Bien Hoa Air Base outside Saigon, the 1st Cavalry Division was preparing for extraction. The "First Team" had been deployed since 1965, earning fame in the savage battle of Ia Drang valley. Six years and over 5000 deaths later, those who remained were ready to leave.

In the communications tent, Corporal Steve Taylor tightly rolled up the division flag. He had arrived as a wide-eyed nineteen-year-old. Now twenty-five, he was hardened, weary, and grateful to be getting out alive.

His friend Josiah Bell cleaned his rifle one last time. "Never thought this day would come," Bell said. "Feels like we're deserting our Vietnamese allies. But I've had enough of this shithole to last a lifetime."

Their commanding officer, Major General James Herbert, addressed the men one final time. "No group ever served with more courage," Herbert said, choking back emotion. "Now let's get back home to America!"

As the choppers lifted off the base for Bien Hoa Airport, pilots circled low over Saigon. The division that had backstopped South Vietnam's defense for so many years took one last look at the city they helped protect. Then the choppers turned east toward the port, beginning the long journey home.

January 1972

The fighting continued in Vietnam, but America's war was ending. President Nixon's Vietnamization policy brought home division after division, turning the ground war over to South Vietnam. Media coverage waned as American casualties tapered off, but the war remained deadly for Vietnamese troops.

No unit had seen more continuous combat than the 101st Airborne Division. Nicknamed "The Screaming Eagles," they had deployed in 1965 and distinguished themselves in fierce battles at Hamburger Hill and elsewhere. Eight years and over 4000 deaths later, the remaining "Screaming Eagles" were finally withdrawing.

The division's artillery units provided cover as the last air assault troops pulled out of firebases across the Central Highlands. At Bien Hoa Airbase, the last transport planes were already boarding troops for the flight home.

Master Sergeant Mike Davis took one last look around. "Lot of good men didn't make this day," he told the young paratroopers awaiting boarding. "You boys represent them now. Bring the division's legacy back with honor."

The C-130s taxied and took off in groups into the tropical night sky. As Vietnam receded below them, the paratroopers gazed down, saying silent goodbyes to those they left behind.

It would take years to withdraw, but America's direct ground involvement in Vietnam was ending after nearly a decade. South Vietnam would assume full responsibility for continuing the war. The returning veterans, their long ordeal was finally ending, were going home to try and rebuild their lives in a divided America which itself would need healing.

At the end of 1970, there were 335,800 American soldiers in Vietnam. 6,173 had been killed during the year. The South Vietnamese had 968,000 troops in their military, but many of those were on paper only. Many of the unit commanders accepted a soldier's pay as a bribe to mark them as present during roll call. The ghost soldiers would take up civilian jobs to earn a living while their commanders got wealthy off the money they collected. It seemed a fair trade... in South Vietnam. 23,346 South Vietnamese soldiers had been killed during the year. The North Vietnamese military stopping reporting their killed and wounded.

Letter to Reader

Dear Reader:

I hope you enjoyed *Chaos of War*. While there were many chapters that I was proud of writing, it was a book that left me a bit sad when I was finished. But then again, it's war, right? It should be sad. Anyway, I hope you liked it. The next novel in the Airmen Series is *Spectre of War* – Book 19. Here's a quick snapshot:

As the South Vietnamese grapple with the American military withdrawal, the Vietnam War continues to rage. Like a shark smelling blood in the water, the North Vietnamese push their growing advantage hoping to bring the war to a quick and reunite their country under a communist flag.

In Laos, Coyle and his aircrew continue to interdict enemy convoys on the Ho Chi Minh trail, disaster strikes. Heavily damaged, his gunship goes down in in the Laotian mountains. I can't tell you anything more or I will spoil it.

Oh, and there's lots of historical battles and suspense. I hope you like it.

Sharing my work with your friends and reviews are always welcome. Thank you for supporting The Airmen Series.

Regards,

David Lee Corley, Author

DAVID LEE CORLEY

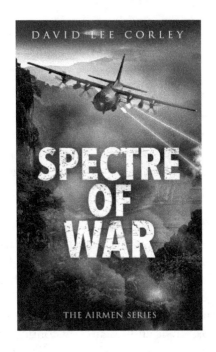

Author's Biography

Born in 1958, David grew up on a horse ranch in Northern California, breeding and training appaloosas. He has had all his toes broken at least once and survived numerous falls and kicks from ornery colts and fillies. David started writing professionally as a copywriter in his early 20's. At 32, he packed up his family and moved to Malibu, California, to live his dream of writing and directing motion pictures. He has four motion picture screenwriting credits and two directing credits. His movies have been viewed by over 50 million movie-goers worldwide and won a multitude of awards, including the Malibu, Palm Springs, and San Jose Film Festivals. In addition to his 24 screenplays, he has written fourteen novels. He developed his simplistic writing style after rereading his two favorite books, Ernest Hemingway's "The Old Man and The Sea" and Cormac McCarthy's "No Country For Old Men." An avid student of world culture, David lived as an expat in both Thailand and Mexico. At 56, he sold all his possessions and became a nomad for four years. He circumnavigated the globe three times and visited 56 countries. Known for his detailed descriptions, his stories often include actual experiences and characters from his journeys.

Printed in the USA
CPSIA information can be obtained
at www.ICGtesting.com
LVHW052010091123
763493LV00007B/271